# About

**Lynne Graham** lives in a keen romance read married, Lynne has five natural child. Her other dear to her heart, are adopted. The family has a variety of pets, and Lynne loves gardening, cooking, collecting allsorts and is crazy about every aspect of Christmas.

Mills & Boon novels were **Julia James'** first 'grown up' books she read as a teenager, and she's been reading them ever since. She adores the Mediterranean and the English countryside in all its seasons, and is fascinated by all things historical, from castles to cottages. In between writing she enjoys walking, gardening, needlework and baking 'extremely gooey chocolate cakes' and trying to stay fit! Julia lives in England with her family.

**Cathy Williams** is a great believer in the power of perseverance as she had never written anything before her writing career, and from the starting point of zero has now fulfilled her ambition to pursue this most enjoyable of careers. She would encourage any would-be writer to have faith and go for it! She derives inspiration from the tropical island of Trinidad and from the peaceful countryside of middle England. Cathy lives in Warwickshire her family.

# Tempted by the Tycoon

Tempted by the Tycoon
# Playing with Fire

LYNNE GRAHAM

JULIA JAMES

CATHY WILLIAMS

MILLS & BOON

First Published in Great Britain 2022
by Mills & Boon, an imprint of HarperCollins*Publishers* Ltd,
1 London Bridge Street, London, SE1 9GF

www.harpercollins.co.uk

HarperCollins*Publishers*
Macken House, 39/40 Mayor Street Upper,
Dublin 1, D01 C9W8

TEMPTED BY THE TYCOON: PLAYING WITH FIRE
© 2022 Harlequin Enterprises ULC.

*The Greek Tycoon's Blackmailed Mistress* © 2009 Lynne Graham
*A Tycoon to Be Reckoned With* © 2016 Julia James
*Secrets of a Ruthless Tycoon* © 2014 Cathy Williams

ISBN: 978-0-263-31821-0

This book is produced from independently certified FSC™ paper
to ensure responsible forest management.

For more information visit: www.harpercollins.co.uk/green

Printed and Bound in Spain using 100% Renewable electricity at
CPI Black Print, Barcelona

# THE GREEK TYCOON'S BLACKMAILED MISTRESS

## LYNNE GRAHAM

# PROLOGUE

'AN ENCHANTING child,' Drakon Xenakis remarked as he stood at a window, watching the little girl playing in the lush gardens of his grandson's villa. 'She reminds me of someone. I can't think who…'

Aristandros veiled his brilliant dark eyes, his lean, darkly handsome face unrevealing. He said nothing, although he had made a genetic connection at first glance. In his opinion it was impossible not to: that blonde hair, so pale that it was somewhere between white and silver, and those hyacinth-blue eyes and pouting pink mouth were like miniature identity-tags. Yes, fate had placed an immensely potent weapon in his hands and he would have no qualms about using it to get what he wanted. Aristandros always kept his conscience well under wraps. Neither failure nor consolation prizes were acceptable to him. Without a doubt he would triumph—and winning most often meant breaking the rules.

'But little girls need mothers,' Drakon continued, his proud carriage impressively upright in spite of his eighty-two years. 'And you specialise in—'

'Beautiful models,' Aristandros slotted in swiftly, conscious that the older man was likely to take a moralistic viewpoint and employ a more judgemental term for the women who entertained his grandson in the bedroom. 'Timon, however, left me his daughter to raise, and I have every intention of meeting that challenge.'

'Timon was a childhood playmate and a cousin, not your brother,' his grandfather countered in a troubled voice. 'Are you willing to give up the strings of gorgeous women and the endless parties for the sake of a child who isn't your own?'

'I have a large, well-trained and reliable staff. I don't think Calliope's impact on my life will be that catastrophic.' Aristandros had never sacrificed anything for anyone, nor could he imagine doing so. But, even if he did not agree with his grandfather's views, he respected him and he would allow the older man to have his say.

In any case, few men had more right to talk frankly on the score of family responsibility than Drakon Xenakis. The family name had long been synonymous with dysfunction and explosive scandals. Drakon blamed himself that all his children had messed up spectacularly as adults with their car-crash marriages, addictions and affairs. Aristandros's father had proved the worst offender of all, and his mother, the heiress daughter of another shipping family, had matched her husband in her appetite for self-indulgence and irresponsibility.

'If you think that, you're underestimating the responsibility you're taking on. A child who has already lost both parents will need a lot of your attention to feel secure. You're a workaholic, just as I was, Aristandros. We're brilliant at making money, but we're not good parents,' Drakon pronounced, his concern patent. 'You need to find a wife willing to be Callie's mother.'

'Marriage really isn't my style,' Aristandros countered coolly.

'The incident you are referring to took place when you were twenty-five years old,' Drakon dared to remark, watching the younger man's bronzed features shutter and chill at that less-than-tactful reminder.

Aristandros shrugged a broad shoulder. 'It was merely a brief infatuation from which I soon recovered.'

Aristandros was, however, pierced by a familiar tide of bitter anger. *Ella*. He only had to think her name to feel that anger. Seven years ago, he had put a price on the head of the one woman he'd wanted, and the one woman he still couldn't forget. He had sworn then that, one day, he would take revenge for what she had done to him. The engagement that never was—an unthinkable rejection. Yet, in some ways, hadn't Ella done him a favour? The early unanticipated disappointment and the sense of humiliation which she'd inflicted had ensured that Ari had never dropped his guard with a woman again. Instead he had concentrated on enjoying the fruits of his fabulous wealth while he'd steadily grown tougher, harder and more ambitious.

His meteoric success had made him a billionaire and the focus of much fear and envy in the business world. Drakon's plain speaking was a rare experience for Aristandros, whose aggressive instincts had brought him astonishing ascendancy and influence over others. Soon Ella too would have to make a bonfire of all her fine, noble principles and prejudices and dance to his chosen tune. He was looking forward to it. Indeed, he could hardly wait for the moment when she realised that he had what she most wanted. That first taste of revenge promised to be sweeter than heavenly ambrosia.

# CHAPTER ONE

ELLA sat as still as a statue in the smart waiting area.

Locked deep in her stressful thoughts, she didn't notice the admiring glances she received from the men walking past. In any case, she was accustomed to screening out the unwelcome notice that her physical beauty attracted. Her white-blonde hair, that rare shade most often seen only on children, turned heads as much as her bright blue eyes and slender, shapely figure. Her hands were tightly laced together on her lap, betraying her tension.

'Dr Smithson?' the receptionist said. 'Mr Barnes would like you to go in now.'

Ella got up. Beneath her outward show of calm, a burning sense of injustice was churning in her stomach. Her prayers had gone unanswered and common sense was still being ignored. She could only marvel that her own flesh and blood could have placed her in such a cruel position. When would enough be enough? When would her family decide that she had paid a steep enough price for the decision she had made seven years earlier? She was beginning to think that only her death would settle that outstanding account.

Mr Barnes, the lawyer she had first consulted two weeks earlier—a tall, thin man in his forties reputed to be at the very top of the tree when it came to complex child-custody issues—shook hands with her and invited her to take a seat.

'I've taken advice from the specialists in this area of the law, and I'm afraid I can't give you the answer that you want,' he told her with precision. 'When you donated eggs to your sister to enable her to have a child, you signed a contract in which you relinquished all claim to parental rights over any baby born subsequently—'

'Yes, I accept that, but as my sister and her husband are now dead surely the situation has changed?' Ella broke in with the urgency she was trying hard to keep under control.

'But not necessarily in your favour,' Simon Barnes responded wryly. 'As I mentioned before, the woman who carries the baby to birth is deemed to be its legal mother. So, although you are a biological parent, you cannot claim to be the child's mother. Furthermore, you have had no contact at all with the little girl since she was born, which doesn't help your case.'

'I know.' Ella was pale with strain and a curious feeling of shame, for she still found it hard to handle the fact that her sister, Susie, had pretty much cut her out of her life as soon as her infant daughter had entered the world. Ella had not even been allowed a photo, never mind a visit and a face-to-face encounter. 'But I'm still legally Callie's aunt.'

'Yes, but the fact that you were not named as a guardian in your sister and brother-in-law's wills does harm your case,' the lawyer reminded her tautly. 'Their solicitor will testify that the only party Callie's late parents were prepared to nominate was Aristandros Xenakis. Don't forget that he too has a blood tie with the child—'

'For goodness' sake, Aristandros was only her father's cousin, not an uncle or anything!' Ella proclaimed with helpless heat.

'A cousin and lifelong friend, who putatively accepted responsibility for the child in writing well before the accident that killed your sister and her husband. I need hardly add that you cannot reasonably hope to fight his claim to custody. He is an extremely wealthy and powerful man. The child is also a Greek citizen, as is he.'

'But he's also a single man with an appalling reputation as a hellraiser!' Ella protested fiercely. 'Scarcely an ideal father-figure for a little girl!'

'You are in dangerous territory with that argument, Dr Smithson. You too are single, and any court would question why your own family are not prepared to back you in your claim.'

Ella reddened at the humbling reminder that she stood alone and unsupported. 'I'm afraid that my relatives will not take a single step that might risk offending Aristandros Xenakis. My stepfather and my two half-brothers rely on his connections to do business.'

The lawyer released his breath in a slow hiss of finality. 'My advice is to accept that the law is unlikely to get you any closer to seeing the child, and that any attempt to challenge her current custodial arrangements will destroy any goodwill you might hope to create.'

Tears were burning like drops of fire behind Ella's

unflinching gaze as she fought to retain her self-discipline in the face of that bad news. 'You're telling me that there's *nothing* I can do?'

'I believe that the wisest move in your circumstances would be to make a personal approach to Aristandros Xenakis. Explain the situation and, on that basis, ask him if he will allow you to have contact with the child,' Simon Barnes advised ruefully.

Ella shivered at that piece of advice; it was like a sudden, bitingly cold wind blowing against her bare, shrinking flesh. Aristandros had Callie. Aristandros, who despised Ella. What possible hope did she have of gaining a sympathetic hearing from him?

'Some day you will pay for this,' Aristandros had sworn seven years earlier when she was only twenty-one and in the middle of her medical studies.

'Don't take it that way,' she had begged him painfully. 'Try to understand.'

'No. *You* understand what you have done to me,' Aristandros had urged, diamond-bright dark eyes hard as granite and cold as winter ice. 'I treated you with honour and respect. And in return you have insulted and embarrassed me and my family.'

Gooseflesh pebbling her skin beneath her clothes, Ella left the solicitor's office and headed home to the spacious loft apartment she had purchased jointly with her friend, Lily. The other woman, who was training as a surgeon, was still at work when she got back. Ella and Lily had met at medical school and had been friends ever since, initially pooling and sharing resources, like the apartment and a car, while offering each other support during stressful times.

In common with many young doctors, Ella worked long hours and had little energy left with which to stamp her own personality on her surroundings. She had still not got round to choosing a colour scheme for her bedroom. A pile of books by the bed and a piano in one corner of the airy living-area testified to how she liked to spend her free time.

Before she could lose her nerve, she rang the UK headquarters of Xenakis Shipping to request an appointment with Aristandros. A member of his staff promised to call her back, and she knew she would be checked out since she was not a business client. She wondered if he would even agree to see her. Maybe out of curiosity? Her tummy flipped at the prospect of seeing him again.

She could hardly remember the girl she had been seven years earlier when she'd broken her heart over Aristandros Xenakis. Young, inexperienced and naïve, she had been much more vulnerable than she had appreciated. Her strong sense of self-belief had ensured that she'd stood up for what she believed in, but living with that decision had proved much more difficult than she had expected. Moreover, she had not met another man, as she had dimly assumed she would back then. She had recently begun to believe that she would never meet anyone she wanted to marry.

Was that another reason why she had agreed to donate eggs to her infertile sister? Susie, two years her senior, had suffered a premature menopause in her twenties, and her only hope of motherhood had been through donated eggs. Susie had flown over from Greece to London where Ella had been working as a junior doctor in a busy A&E department to ask for her sibling's help.

Ella had been touched when Susie had approached her with her request. In truth, prior to that meeting, Susie had been as distant and critical of her outcast sister as the rest of the family. It had felt good to be needed, even better to be told that a baby born from her eggs would be much more precious to Susie than a baby born with the help of an anonymous donor. Of course, there had also been the greater likelihood of the child inheriting a closer physical resemblance to Susie through the use of her sibling's eggs.

Ella had not hesitated to agree to her sister's appeal. It would have been unimaginable for her to refuse. Susie had married Ari's cousin, Timon, and they'd had a good marriage. Ella had believed that a child born to the young couple would enjoy a happy, secure life. While Ella had undergone the screening tests and treatment for egg donation, she had also attended counselling and signed an agreement to make no future claim on any child born.

'You're not thinking this through,' Lily had argued at the time. 'This process is not as straightforward as you seem to think it is. What about the emotional reper-cussions? How will you feel when a child is actually born? You'll be the biological mother but you'll have no rights at all over the child. Will you envy your sister— feel that her child is more yours?'

Ella had refused to accept that there could be anything other than a positive outcome to the gift of her eggs. While she'd been undergoing the donation process, Susie had often talked about what a wonderful aunt Ella would be for her child. But, shockingly, Susie had rejected Ella from the day that Callie was born.

Indeed she had phoned Ella to ask her *not* to visit her in hospital, while also demanding that Ella leave her and her new family alone.

Ella had been horribly hurt, but she had tried to understand that Susie had felt threatened by her sibling's genetic input to her newborn baby. She had written to her sister in an effort to reassure her, but her letters had gone unacknowledged. In despair at the rift that had opened up, she had gone to see Timon when he was in London on business. Timon had admitted ruefully that his wife was eaten up with insecurity over Ella's role in the conception of their daughter. Ella had prayed that the passage of time would soothe Susie's concerns but, seventeen months after Callie's birth, Timon and Susie had died in a horrific car crash. And, as a final footnote, the young couple had been dead almost two weeks before anyone had thought to let Ella know, so that she hadn't even got to attend the funeral.

When Ella had finally found out that her only sister was dead, she'd felt terrifyingly alone—and not for the first time in recent years. Her father had died shortly after she was born, so she had never known him, and Jane, her mother, had married Theo Sardelos six years later. Ella had never got on with her stepfather, who was a Greek businessman. Theo liked women to be seen rather than heard, and he had turned his back on Ella in angry disgust when she'd refused to marry Aristandros Xenakis. The emotionally fragile Jane had never been known to oppose her dictatorial husband, so there had been no point appealing to her for support. Ella's twin half-brothers had sided with their father, and Susie had refused to get involved.

Ella sat down at the piano and lifted the lid. She often took refuge in music when she was at the mercy of her emotions, and had just embarked on playing an *étude* by Liszt when the phone rang. She got up to answer the call and froze in the middle of the room once she realised that she was talking to a member of Aristandros's personal staff. She made no attempt to protest when she was asked to travel to Southampton the following week to meet him on board his new yacht, *Hellenic Lady*; she was simply overwhelmingly relieved that he was actually willing to see her.

Yet Ella could not imagine seeing Aristandros Xenakis again, and when Lily returned from work her friend was quick to tackle her once she realised what she was planning to do.

'What is the point of you upsetting yourself like this?' Lily asked bluntly, her vivacious face unusually serious beneath her curly brown hair

'I would just like to see Callie,' Ella breathed tightly.

'Stop lying to yourself. You want much more than that. You want to be her parent, and what are your chances of Aristandros Xenakis agreeing to that?'

A stony expression stamped Ella's delicate features. 'Well, why not? How is he planning to continue partying with a baby of eighteen months?'

'He'll just pay people to look after her. He's as rich as that fabled king who touched things and turned them to solid gold,' Lily reminded her doggedly. 'And the first thing he's likely to ask you is what has *his* business to do with you?'

Ella paled; a streak of determined optimism had persuaded her to overlook certain realities, like Ari's hardline attitudes and probable hostility towards her. 'Someone needs to look out for Callie's interests.'

'Who had more right than her parents? But you're questioning their decision that the child should go to him. Sorry, I'm playing devil's advocate here,' Lily explained ruefully.

'Susie was hopelessly impressed by the Xenakis wealth,' Ella confided. 'But money shouldn't be the only bottom line when it comes to bringing up a child.'

'It's the size of a cruise ship!' Ella's taxi driver exclaimed while he leant out at his vehicle's window to scan the immense, sleek length and the towering decks of the white mega-yacht *Hellenic Lady*.

'Absolutely huge,' Ella agreed breathlessly, paying him and climbing out on to the quay. She smoothed damp palms down over the trousers of the elegant brown trouser-suit which she usually wore for interviews.

A young man in a smart suit advanced on her. 'Dr Smithson?' he queried, a good deal of curiosity in his measuring gaze. 'I'm Philip. I work for Mr Xenakis. Please, come this way.'

Philip was as informative as a travel rep escorting tourists. *Hellenic Lady*, he told her, was brand-new, built in Germany to Aristandros's exact specifications and about to make her maiden voyage to the Caribbean. As they boarded, various members of the crew greeted them. Philip ushered her into a lift while telling her about the on-board submarine and helicopters. Ella remained defiantly unimpressed until the doors slid back on the upstairs lounge, and her jaw almost dropped at the space, the opulence and the breathtaking panoramic views through the windows.

'Mr Xenakis will be with you in a few minutes,' Philip informed her, ushering her out onto a shaded upper deck furnished with beautifully upholstered seats.

At that announcement, Ella's rigid tension eased a little and she took a seat. A steward offered her refreshment and she asked for a cup of tea, because she thought that if she had something to occupy her hands she would be less likely to fidget. Her mind was rebellious, throwing up sudden memories of the most unwelcome kind. Just then, the last thing she wanted to recall was falling head over heels in love with Aristandros when she'd first met him. She had spent Christmas in Greece with her mother and stepfather, and in the space of one frantic month had lost her heart.

But was that so surprising? she asked herself now, striving to divest that event of any dangerous mystique. After all, Aristandros had it all: spectacular good looks, keen intelligence and all the trappings of wealth. And, in a nutshell, Ella had long been a swot, hunched over her books, while other girls had enjoyed a social life and experienced the highs and lows of consorting with the opposite sex. For the space of a month Ella had thrown her good sense out at the window and had just lived for the sound of Ari's voice, and every heart-stopping glimpse of him. Nothing else had mattered: not the warnings her family had given her about his ghastly reputation for loving and leaving women, nor even her studies or the career for which she had slaved and existed up until that point. And then, at the worst possible moment, her brain had finally kicked into gear again, and she had seen how crazy it was to envisage a fantasy future with a guy who expected her world to revolve entirely around him.

As her tea was served, she glanced up and saw Aristandros poised twenty feet away. Her throat closed over, her tummy executing a somersault. Her tea cup rattled its betrayal on the saucer as her hand shook. She couldn't swallow; she couldn't breathe. In a black designer-suit that was faultlessly tailored to his lean, powerful physique, ebony hair ruffling in the breeze and dark eyes glinting gold in the sun, Aristandros was an arrestingly handsome man. As he strode across the deck towards her—the epitome of lithe, masculine grace teamed with the high-voltage buzz of raw sexual energy—she was immediately conscious of a rather more shameful reaction. Heat pulsed low in her pelvis, and her face warmed.

'Ella…' Aristandros murmured as she got up to greet him, his attention welded to the delicate perfection of her features—the bluest of blue eyes, and the ripe, pink invitation of her mouth. Even wearing only a hint of make-up, and with her spectacular pale hair sternly clipped back, she looked utterly stunning, she was a naturally beautiful woman who walked past mirrors and reflections without a single glance. Her lack of vanity was the very first thing he had noticed about her and admired.

He caught her slim hand in his, long, brown fingers resting against the soft skin of her narrow wrist. Her hand felt hot, his felt cool. That sudden physical contact took Ella by surprise and she glanced up at him, bemused blue eyes connecting with the penetrating dark challenge of his. Suddenly her heart was beating very, very fast and interfering with her desire to show him a confident, composed exterior. She was close enough to catch the faint, musky scent of his skin overlaid with a spicy tang of cologne. That aroma was familiar enough to send a powerful and primitive message to her nerve endings and leave her senses spinning. Her breasts stirred inside her bra, her nipples lengthening as a dart of rampant responsiveness spread tingling needles of sensual awareness through her taut frame. Shame and dismay at her weakness clawed at her.

'I appreciate your agreeing to see me,' Ella told him hurriedly.

'Humility doesn't become you, Ella,' Aristandros drawled.

'I was only trying to be polite!' Ella snapped back at him before she could think better of it.

'You're very tense,' Aristandros husked, sibilant in tone as silk sliding on silk. His attention roamed from her normally glorious full mouth—currently compressed by the extent of her stress level—down to the full, sweet curve of her firm breasts screened by innocuous white cotton. He would dress her in the finest satin and lace; his groin tightened at the imagery roused by that thought.

Clashing with the perceptive glint in his brilliant dark-golden eyes, something trembled inside Ella. In a desperate attempt to distract him, she reclaimed her hand and said brightly, 'I like your yacht.'

Aristandros flung her a sardonic smile. 'No, you don't. You believe it's yet another example of my habits of conspicuous consumption, and you think I should have spent the money having wells dug somewhere in Africa.'

Colour washed as high as the roots of Ella's hair. 'I was a terrible prig at twenty-one, wasn't I? These days I'm not quite so narrow-minded.'

'The Xenakis Trust, which I set up, contributes a great deal to the most deserving charities,' Aristandros confirmed. 'You should find me worthy of approval now.'

Ella paled, because the meeting was not progressing in the way she had hoped. Every word he spoke seemed to allude in some way to the past she was keen to leave buried. 'We're neither of us the same people we were then.'

Aristandros inclined his arrogant dark head, neither agreeing nor disagreeing, and invited her to sit down again. Coffee was served for his benefit. 'I was surprised that you weren't at your sister's funeral,' he admitted.

Ella set down her tea with a sharp little snap. 'I'm afraid I didn't know about the accident until some time after it took place.'

His ebony brows pleated in surprise. 'Nobody in your family contacted you?'

'Not in the immediate family, no. It was my aunt, my mother's sister, who told me after the event. It was quite awkward, because she had assumed I already knew,' Ella explained reluctantly. 'Obviously the news came as a huge shock to me. Timon and Susie were so young. It's a devastating loss for their daughter.'

His lean, strong face was grave. 'And you're concerned about Calliope?'

'I'm sure that everyone in both families is equally concerned about her,' Ella countered.

Aristandros surveyed her with hard, dark eyes and bit out an appreciative laugh. 'Did dealing with patients finally teach you the art of tact?' he mocked. 'I doubt that anyone is quite as concerned as you appear to be—'

'There's something I need to explain about Callie...'

'You think I don't know that you're her biological mother?' The tall, powerful Greek's dark, deep drawl was laced with honeyed derision. '*Of course* I know that.'

Jolted by his assurance, Ella tilted her chin. 'I assume Timon told you?'

'Yes. Naturally, I was surprised. After all, you once told me that you didn't want children.'

'At twenty-one years old I didn't, and when my sole input to the process was donated eggs I didn't consider Callie to be *my* child when she was born. She was Susie and Timon's daughter.'

'How very selfless of you,' Aristandros murmured flatly. 'Yet in spite of that statement you are here.'

'Yes,' Ella acknowledged. 'I would very much like to see my niece.'

'Is that really what you came all this way to ask of me? One single visit with her, and then you walk away again never to look back?' Aristandros outlined with a look of disbelief.

Ella didn't know quite how to answer that. She was afraid to be too honest and reveal the depth of her longing to become a more important part of Callie's life. 'If that is all you're prepared to allow me. Something is better than nothing.'

Brilliant dark eyes rested on her. 'You want so little?'

Colour warmed her cheeks for dissemblance was not her style. She was entrapped by the power of his gaze, awesomely aware of the unyielding strength and shrewd intelligence of the man behind it. She did not dare lie to him, and knew that any form of evasion would be held against her. 'I think you know that I would like more.'

'But would more be in Callie's best interests? And

how badly do you want that access to the child?' Aristandros enquired huskily.

Ella snatched in a charged breath. '*Very* badly,' she admitted. 'I don't believe I've ever wanted anything so much.'

Aristandros loosed a sudden, grating laugh that took her aback. 'Yet she could have been *our* child. Instead, you made it possible for my cousin and best friend to become a father, and let your sister give birth to a little girl who was genetically half yours. Did it ever occur to you that I might find that particular arrangement offensive?'

The colour in Ella's cheeks slowly drained away, and her face took on the pinched quality of constraint. 'No, I'm afraid that possibility didn't occur to me, and I can only hope that you don't still feel that way now that you're Callie's guardian.'

'I got over it. I'm not the sentimental type, and I would *never* hold a child's parentage against her,' Aristandros fielded with a harsh edge of emphasis on that point. 'What I need to know now is how far are you prepared to go to get what you want? How much will you sacrifice?'

'Are you saying that it might be possible for me to establish an ongoing relationship with my niece?' Ella pressed, wondering why he was talking about sacrifices.

A slow, steady smile curved his handsome, chiselled mouth. 'If you please me, the sky's the limit, *glikia mou.*'

# CHAPTER TWO

ELLA was thoroughly chilled by the smile on Aristandros's lean, darkly handsome face and his casual term of endearment jarred on her. She had not forgotten what she was dealing with: a very rich and powerful male whose ego she had once dented. Quite accidentally dented, though, she affixed ruefully to that recollection. Their dialogue, however, had taken a sudden step into unknown territory and she genuinely didn't know what he was getting at.

'I'm not sure that I appreciate your meaning,' Ella said carefully, her hyacinth-blue eyes level and enquiring.

'You're far from being stupid,' Aristandros countered in his measured accented drawl. 'If you want to see Callie, you can only do so on *my* terms.'

Ella slid out of her comfortable seat and walked with quick harried steps over to the rails farthest away, eager for the breeze coming in off the sea to cool her anxious face. 'I know that—if I didn't accept that, I wouldn't be here.'

'My terms are tough,' Aristandros spelt out bluntly. 'You want Callie. I want you, and Callie needs a female carer. If we put those needs together we can come to an arrangement that suits all three of us.'

*I want you.* That was almost the only phrase she initially picked out of that speech. She was shocked. He still found her attractive—seven years on? Even in her sensible brown trouser-suit, when she was stressed out of her mind? In that first instant of astonishment, she almost turned round to tell him that he was the answer to an overworked doctor's prayers. That side of her life had not just taken a back seat while she'd studied and worked her steady path through all the medical hoops she had had to traverse to qualify, it had vanished.

She reminded herself that being wanted by Aristandros did not, by any stretch of the imagination, make her one of a select group. As a woman, she was clued up enough to go on a TV quiz show and answer virtually any question about Aristandros's highly volatile and energetic love-life. She knew that while his sexual skill and stamina in bed might be legendary according to the tabloid press, his staying power outside the bedroom was of exceptionally short duration. Since they had last met, a constant procession of gorgeous supermodels, starlets and socialites had briefly shared his fast-lane, champagne lifestyle before being ditched and replaced. He got bored *very* easily.

Indeed, Aristandros had gone on to fulfil every worst expectation that Ella had had of him seven years earlier. His relationships appeared to be short-lived, shallow, self-serving, and not infrequently featured infidelity. He had closely followed in the footsteps of his notorious father as a womaniser. Nothing Ella read about Aristandros had ever given her cause to regret refusing to marry him. He could no more have adapted to the restrictions of matrimony than a tiger could adjust to being a domestic pet. He would have broken her heart and destroyed her, just as her faithless stepfather had destroyed her mother with his extra-marital diversions. After twenty-odd years of marriage, Jane Sardelos had neither backbone nor self-esteem left.

'You're suggesting that, if I have sex with you, you'll let me see Callie?' Ella queried in a polite tone of incredulity.

'I'm not quite that crude, *glikia mou*,' Aristandros fielded. 'Nor so easily satisfied. I'm even prepared to offer you something I've never offered a woman before. I want you to move in with me—'

'To *live* with you?' Ella echoed in astonishment, a powerful wave of disbelief winging through her taut length.

'Live and travel with me as my mistress. How else could you look after your niece? Of course, there would be conditions,' Aristandros continued smoothly. 'You couldn't hope to work and still meet my expectations. Living with me and taking care of Callie would be a full-time occupation.'

'You haven't changed one little bit,' Ella framed shakily, even as her heart jumped in anticipation at the idea of having the freedom to take care of her niece. 'You still expect to take priority over everything else.'

Aristandros angled back his arrogant dark head, stubborn eyes hurling an unashamed challenge. 'Why not? I have known many women who would be delighted to make me and my interests their main priority in life. Why would I even consider accepting a lesser commitment from you?'

'But you can't make a child part of a deal like that!' Ella condemned fiercely. 'It would be immoral and horribly unscrupulous!'

'I don't suffer from moral scruples. I'm a practical guy who has no plans to get married to give Callie a mother. So, if you want to be her replacement mother, you have to play this as I want it played.'

He was offering her everything she longed for in return for surrendering everything she had worked so hard to achieve. It was blackmail and it was revenge in one cruelly potent weapon. 'After seven years, how can we go from having no relationship at all into living together? And me a *mistress*?' she questioned unevenly, the unfamiliar word thick and unwieldy on her tongue. 'It's crazy.'

Aristandros slowly unfolded his big powerful frame, from his seat and strolled towards her like a sleek panther on the prowl. His narrowed gaze blazed golden and welded to her, homing in on the soft pink of her mouth. 'It's not a problem for me. I find you amazingly attractive.'

'And that's *all* that it takes for you—lust?' Ella slung between gritted teeth with a look of distaste.

'Lust is all that we need concern ourselves with, *glikia mou*.' He lifted a hand and let confident finger-tips trace the proud curve of her cheekbone. Blue eyes spitting angry flame, she jerked her head away in a violent rejection of his touch. 'Let's keep it simple. I want you in my bed every night.'

'No *way*!' Ella launched back at him furiously.

'Of course, I can't force you into agreement,' Aristandros conceded, trapping her by the rails with his size and proximity, while staring down at her with burning resolve. 'But I'm a stubborn and tenacious man. I have waited a long time for this day. Many women would be flattered by my continuing interest.'

'Lust is not an interest!' Ella practically spat at him, her scorn unconcealed. 'This is all because I said no to you seven years ago, all because you never got me into bed!'

Towering over her slighter, smaller figure, Aristandros went very still at that charge. His dark eyes gleamed, diamond-bright and hard as granite. 'I let you say no because I was prepared to wait for you. This time around I'm not prepared to wait for anything.'

Butterflies danced in her tummy while rage preoccupied her thoughts and clenched her hands into fists. 'I can't believe you have the nerve to try this on me!'

He closed his hands over her fists to hold her entrapped. He bent his proud, dark head, his breath skimming her temples as he murmured thickly, 'But I always have the nerve in a fight, *koukla mou*. Fighting for what I want comes naturally to me and, if the stakes are high enough, I will risk *everything* to win. I wouldn't be a true Xenakis if I didn't occasionally sail too close to the sun.'

He was so close she couldn't breath, and she was trembling while her heart pounded as if she was running a marathon. He lowered his head to claim her lips and he kissed her slowly with an irresistible passion. Extraordinary, achingly familiar, that kiss was everything she had steeled herself to forget. For a timeless moment she was lost in the heat and pressure of his hungry urgency, shivering violently at the deeply erotic thrust and flick of his tongue into the tender interior of her mouth. Suddenly her body was flaring wildly out of her control, her nipples pinching into stiff, painful buds, moisture surging between her thighs. Memory took her back and she froze, shutting out and denying those shameful sensations while she shifted away from him in an abrupt, defensive movement that caught him by surprise.

'No,' she told him flatly, throwing her head back, little strands of silvery-pale hair breaking free of the clip to brush her cheekbones.

A wolfish smile slashed Aristandros's lean face. He made no attempt to hide his triumph. '"No" is very close to becoming a blatant invitation on your lips,' he derided softly.

'You can't buy me with Callie. I'm not up for sale, and I can't be tempted,' Ella swore, praying even as she spoke that she had the strength of character to make those statements true.

'Then we will all be losers, and perhaps the child most of all. I doubt if any other woman would be prepared to offer her the honest and genuine affection that you could give her,' Aristandros pronounced. 'Although many women will no doubt try to convince me otherwise.'

That final assurance was like a knife finding a gap in her armour to pierce her skin, penetrate deep and draw blood. The very thought of ambitious gold-diggers auditioning to be Callie's mother-substitute simply to impress her billionaire guardian hurt Ella immeasurably and threatened her composure.

'You're being so cruel,' she muttered tightly. 'I wouldn't have believed that you could be so cruel.'

Unmoved, Aristandros surveyed her with hard eyes. 'It's your choice—'

'There *isn't* a choice!' Ella gasped strickenly

'It's a choice you don't like. But be grateful there is a choice to make,' Aristandros urged harshly. 'I could have said no, you can't see Callie, and slammed the door shut in your face!'

Gooseflesh gave Ella's skin a clammy feel. It felt like the cold breath of reality making its presence felt, for of course what he said was true. In the circumstances, even a choice was a luxury, for he might have turned her request down flat. Furthermore, what happened next was entirely her decision. She glanced up at him from below her lashes. He was on some sort of power kick. With the options and offers that came his way every single day, how could he still be interested in her? Was it just the fact that she was one of the precious few to have turned him down? Wasn't that the real secret of her enduring attraction—her one-time refusal, her apparent unavailability? And wouldn't her pulling power wane fast once she was freely available?

'Just suppose I said yes,' Ella suggested in a driven undertone. 'Your interest in me wouldn't last longer than five minutes. What happens to Callie then? I'm there for about a week and then I vanish again?'

His lean, strong face had clenched hard. 'It won't be like that.'

Ella had to gnaw at the soft underside of her lower lip to prevent herself from screaming back at him in disagreement. It was always like that for him with women, wild, hot affairs that burnt out at supersonic speed. 'What would I know about being a mistress? I'm hardly the decorative type.'

Aristandros rested his attention on her, his golden-brown eyes smouldering below the luxuriant black fringe of his lashes, amusement curling his handsome mouth. 'Is there a type? I'm flexible and very open to new experiences.'

Unamused by this suggestive sally, Ella walked back to her seat and sank down as rigid-backed as if she had a fence post attached to her spine. 'If I did agree,' she said very stiffly, 'What would the ground rules be?'

'Your main objective would primarily be pleasing me,' Aristandros drawled, watching her grit her teeth as if he had said something unspeakably rude. 'Of course, there would be no other men in your life. You would always be available for me.'

'The any-time, any-place, anywhere girl? That's a male fantasy, Aristandros, not an achievable objective for a normal woman in today's world,' Ella countered drily.

'You're clever enough to live that fantasy for me. Focus all that career-orientated zeal on me, and you won't find me ungrateful. Give me what I want, and you will have everything that you want,' he traded in a powerful promise of intent.

'Callie.' She framed the name weakly because it encompassed so much and stirred such deep emotion in her. The child she had never seen but whom she longed to love as a daughter rather than a niece. Aristandros might enjoy almost unlimited power over them both, but Ella was quick to remind herself that she also had the power to make a huge difference in Callie's life. And she badly wanted the chance to be there to love and care for the little girl, who had already lost both mother and father at such a tragically young age.

Her rushing thoughts were so frantic and intense, she was beginning to develop a tension headache across her brow. She pressed the heel of her hand there and snatched in a steadying breath. 'How long have I got to decide?'

Aristandros flashed her a punitive appraisal. 'It's now or never. A today-only deal.'

'But that's outrageous! I mean, you're asking me to give up my career in medicine. Have you any idea what being a doctor means to me?'

'A very good idea. After all, you once chose your career over me,' Aristandros skimmed back, keen eyes dangerous.

'That wasn't the only reason I turned you down. I did that for the both of us—we would have made each other miserable!' Ella flung back at him a little wildly, her emotions finally outrunning her self-discipline. 'And let me warn you of one thing that isn't negotiable under any circumstances—if I agree, I will not tolerate infidelity in any guise.'

Strong emotion animated her features, brightening her eyes and flushing her cheeks with colour. It was a welcome glimpse of the passionate young woman he remembered, who had invested so much emotion in everything that mattered to her, but who had tellingly walked away from him without a backward glance.

'I'm not asking you to marry me this time. I won't be making any promises either,' Aristandros delivered in direct challenge. 'I should also warn you that, regardless of what happens between us, I will not give up custody of Callie. Timon trusted me to raise his daughter, and I hold that sacrosanct.'

A half-dozen fire-starting responses were ready to

tumble off Ella's tongue but she held them back, deeming the momentary pleasure of challenging him to be unwise at that point. She was willing to bet that he knew next to nothing about children or their needs, for he was an only child, raised as a mini-adult by parents who had had no time and even less interest in him. Even so, she could not believe that he would do anything that might harm the child in his charge. For her own peace of mind, she had to believe that if she succeeded in forging close ties with Callie he would recognise the damage that the sudden severance of those bonds would cause and make allowances.

'Ella…' Aristandros growled, impatience etched in every angular line of his lean, bronzed features. 'It's decision time, *glikia mou*.'

Ella pictured the imaginary child in her head and studied Aristandros with determined cool. Regardless of how she might feel about him and his methods, she still thought he was drop-dead gorgeous, and that was a plus, wasn't it? But how would it feel to engage in an unemotional sexual relationship with him, particularly when she was totally inexperienced in that line? She suppressed the critical part of her brain because she saw no point borrowing trouble in advance of the event. She forced herself to concentrate on Callie and shut out all the personal, selfish stuff like the injured pride, the fury and the sense of humiliation threatening her. If she gained the right to take care of Callie, couldn't she learn to cope with the rest?

'Okay.' Ella threw her head back and lifted her chin. 'But you'll have to give me time to work out my notice at work.'

\* \* \*

'Are you finished?' Dr Alister Marlow queried from the doorway of Ella's surgery as she lifted a cardboard box from the desk. The room looked bare.

'Yes. I took the bulk of my stuff yesterday.' As her colleague helpfully extended his arms, Ella relinquished the box and then took the opportunity to perform a last-minute check through the drawers. Finally she straightened. 'Will you ask the cleaning lady to keep her eyes peeled for a small photograph? It was of my father and I was attached to it,' she admitted ruefully ' I broke the photoframe last month and took out the photo, and now it seems to have vanished.'

'We'll keep an eye out for it.' The tall, broadly built blond man promised, concerned blue eyes resting on her. 'You look exhausted.'

'There's been so much to organise.' Ella said nothing about the considerable emotional fallout of having to resign from the job she loved. All her years of hard work had been nullified and all her goals had been wrenched from her. She would miss her work and her colleagues a great deal. She would not play any further part in what happened to her patients, nor would she see the benefits brought by the breast-care clinic she had helped to set up. Already she felt lost without the structure of her busy, demanding routine. It had all happened so fast, as by the time her unused holiday entitlement had been added in she'd had only had a couple of weeks' notice left to work.

'I can't say I approve of what you're doing, because you were too valuable a part of our team,' Alister remarked as they walked towards her car. 'But I do admire your commitment to your niece, and know that our loss will be her gain. Stay in touch, Ella.'

Ella drove home while reminding herself that the spacious loft would soon no longer be her home. Lily was buying Ella's share of the apartment. Ella would have preferred to retain her stake in the property, but had felt it would be unfair to impose that on Lily, who was reluctant to take a chance on a new flatmate. Of course she knew Lily would be quick to offer her a bed if she was in need, but it wouldn't be the same as owning her own place.

Just how long would it be before Aristandros tired of her? Her shadowed blue eyes gleamed with resentment, for she was convinced that their affair would be over within weeks. Her novelty value wouldn't last long. Then where would she be without a job and with no home to return to? The proceeds from her share of the apartment would not be enough to buy another property, and she would have to go back to renting again. But, when Aristandros did throw her out, her main concern would be Callie and whether or not she would be allowed to maintain a relationship with the little girl, Ella acknowledged worriedly. She had told nobody the truth about her impending intimate relationship with the Greek tycoon. She had simply said that she was going to help to take care of her orphaned niece whose life was currently based in Greece.

Lily, however, remained suspicious of that explanation. 'I'm trying so hard to understand all this. Do you really want Callie so much that you're happily giving up everything that matters to you?' She demanded that night over the restaurant meal they had organised for their last evening together. 'If it's just that you're getting broody, you could easily have a child of your own.'

'But I want to be with Callie—'

'*And* the oversexed billionaire?'

Reddening, Ella pushed her plate away. 'Aristandros happens to be Callie's guardian and a non-negotiable part of her life.'

'But you do have a thing for him, don't you?' the brunette said suddenly.

'I don't know where you got that idea,' Ella countered with a laugh that sounded more brittle than amused.

'Oh, maybe it was when I noticed you only bought tacky newspapers and magazines so that you could read about him and his exploits.'

'Why not? I was curious because I met him years ago and Susie was married to his cousin!' Ella protested.

Her friend was still watching her closely. 'That last Christmas you spent in Greece before your family started treating you like a pariah—that was when you met Aristandros Xenakis, wasn't it?'

More defensive than ever, for she preferred to hold on tight to her secrets, Ella shrugged a slim shoulder. 'My stepfather made sure we never missed a chance to rub shoulders with the super-rich Xenakis family. I suspect we first met as kids but I don't remember it. Aristandros is four years older than I am.'

'I just feel there's a history there that you're not telling me about,' Lily confessed. 'At the time, I thought you'd had your heart broken.'

Ella rolled her eyes while trying to suppress the memory of the nights she had cried herself to sleep and the days when only work had got her through the intense sense of loneliness and loss. But she had chosen and accepted those consequences when she'd realised that she couldn't marry the man she had fallen in love with. In any case, he had not made the smallest effort to change her mind on that score, had he? In truth her heart had got broken over a much longer term than most. A chip had been gouged out of her heart with every woman that had followed her in Ari's life. But all that was water under the bridge now, Ella reminded herself thankfully. She had lived to see her worst misgivings about Aristandros vindicated; she had made the right decision and had never doubted the fact.

Tomorrow morning, however, she would be picked up at nine, and she had no idea what happened next for Aristandros had not deigned to inform her. Would they be staying in London for long? Would she meet Callie tomorrow? Lying sleepless in bed that night, watching shadows fall on the bare walls, she recalled that Christmas vacation in Athens midway through her medical studies. Time rolled back and plunged her into the past...

Susie had collected her at the airport. Her sister had been single then, and in a very good mood as she'd chattered about the exclusive club she was taking Ella to that evening.

'I've just finished exams and I'm really tired, Susie,' Ella had confided 'I might just go to bed and give the socialising a miss.'

'You can't do that!' Susie had gasped. 'I wangled a special guest-pass for you, so you can't let me down. Ari Xenakis and his friends will be there.'

Susie, with her determination only to mix with the most fashionable crowd, and her strenuous efforts to ensure that her name appeared regularly in the gossip

columns, was the apple of their stepfather's eye. Theo
Sardelos expected women to be ornamental and frivolous. Ella's serious nature, her championship of her
mother and dislike of pretension were all traits that
made him feel uncomfortable.

For the sake of peace that evening, Ella accompanied
Susie. The club was noisy and very crowded. Surrounded by Susie and her pals, who had nothing more
on their minds but the hottest party or man on offer, Ella
was bored. She listened dutifully to tales of how outrageous Ari Xenakis was. He had dumped his last girl-
friend by text and her parents had had to pack her off
abroad to stop her stalking him. As the stories of his
wildness, fabled riches and volatility were traded round
the table, Ella registered in amazement that there still
wasn't a girl present who wouldn't give her right arm
to date him—in spite of his evident obnoxiousness.
When he was pointed out to her across the dance floor,
she registered another reason why he was so dispropor-
tionately popular: he was breathtakingly good-looking
with black hair, brooding golden-brown eyes and the fit
body of an athlete.

If one of their party hadn't collapsed, Ella was convinced that Aristandros would never have noticed her.
Lethia, the teenaged friend of one of Susie's mates,
suffered a seizure. Ella was shocked by the way everyone
abandoned the girl as she lay twitching and jerking at
the side of the dance floor. When Ella went to her assistance, Susie was furious. 'Don't get involved!' she
hissed, trying to drag her sibling back to their table. 'We
hardly know her!'

Ignoring Susie's frantic instructions that she keep her

distance, Ella placed Lethia in the recovery position
and made her as comfortable as possible while the
seizure ran its course. The other girls disclaimed any
knowledge of Lethia's health. Ella had to turn out the
girl's handbag to learn that Lethia appeared to be an epileptic and to be taking prescribed medication.

'Do you need some help with her?' someone asked
her in English. Turning her head, she found Aristandros
hunkered down by her side, his lean, handsome face surprisingly serious.

'She's an epileptic, and she needs to go to hospital
because she's been unconscious more than five minutes,' Ella told him.

Aristandros organised an ambulance, his cool in a
crisis welcome in the overexcited atmosphere surrounding them. He also contacted Lethia's family, who confirmed that she was a recently diagnosed epileptic.

'Why wouldn't anyone else help?' Ella sighed while
they waited for the ambulance.

'I suspect that most people assumed that her collapse
was drug-related and they didn't want to be associated
with her,' Aristandros explained.

'Nobody seemed to know that she suffers from
epilepsy. I suppose she didn't want people to find out,'
Ella guessed, her blue eyes compassionate. 'You spoke
to me in English. How did you know I was English?'

Dark eyes glinting with amusement, Aristandros
gave her a sardonic smile that made it extraordinarily
hard for her to breath. 'I had already asked who you
were before Lethia collapsed.'

Ella flushed, self-consciousness assailing her, because
she was convinced he could only have noticed her

because she didn't fit in. The other girls were like exotic birds in their skimpy designer outfits, while she was wearing a simple black skirt with a turquoise top. 'Why did you come over?'

'I couldn't take my eyes off you,' Aristandros confided. 'Lethia was just an excuse.'

'You dump women by text and then call them stalkers. I'm not interested,' Ella told him drily, switching to Greek, which she spoke fluently.

'There's nothing hotter than a challenge, *glikia mou*,' Aristandros husked, black lashes as long as fly-swats lowering on his dark, golden gaze...

# CHAPTER THREE

AT NINE the following morning, Ella slid into a silver limousine and watched her cases being loaded. Her hair
anchored in a knot at the nape of her neck, she was
dressed with care in a narrow grey skirt and a pinstripe
shirt. She was well aware that she didn't look like mistress material, but was proud of that fact. If Aristandros
wanted to waste his time trying to turn a level-headed un-
fashionable woman into a seductive bedroom hottie who
dressed to impress, then he'd one of those challenges that
he so professed to love on his hands.

Ella closed restive hands round the handbag on her
lap. Sex was just sex, and of course she could handle it.
Technically she knew a lot about men. Most probably
she wasn't the sexiest woman around—after all, she
had lived for years as if sex as an activity didn't exist.
Celibacy had only bothered her once, and that was while
she'd been seeing Aristandros. She could feel her cheeks
warming as she recalled that burning kiss on his yacht.
He was so slick, so practiced, that he knew all the right
moves to make. And she had always hated that sense of
being out of control. Aristandros, on the other hand,

would love getting her in that condition as it would crown his conviction that he was a hell of a guy both in and out of bed.

When the limo drew up by the kerb, Ella climbed out and surveyed the building before her in surprise. The sleek logo of a city lawyers' office greeted her frowning gaze. She walked into Reception, where she was immediately greeted and shown into a room. Aristandros swung round from the window to study her.

'What am I doing here?' Ella questioned before he could even part his chiselled lips. As always he looked amazing, the broodingly handsome image of bronzed good looks and highly expensive tailoring, a sophisticated business-tycoon to his fingertips. But even at first glance he was a great deal more than that, for he exuded a potent aura of power and self-assurance.

Dark-golden eyes narrowed and rested on her, roving from the full curve of her mouth to the swell of her breasts with a sensual appreciation that was as bold as it was blatantly male. Maddeningly aware of his appraisal, and conscious of the wanton awareness tingling between her thighs, Ella flushed a fierce pink.

'I have had a legal agreement drawn up by my lawyers here,' Aristandros informed her. 'I want you to sign it so that there are no misunderstandings between us in the future.'

As he gave her that explanation, Ella went very still and lost some of her colour. 'Why am I only being told about this now? For goodness' sake, I've already resigned from my job and agreed to sell my apartment!'

'Yes,' Aristandros agreed softly, not an ounce of apology in his reply.

Ella worked his agenda out for herself. 'You planned it that way? Now that I've burned my boats, I'm less likely to argue the terms?'

'What I love about you is your lack of illusion about me, *glikia mou*.' Aristandros drawled with sardonic amusement. 'You expect me to be a devious bastard and I am.'

Ella struggled to master her rocketing fury at the manner in which he had closed off any potential escape-hatches and destroyed any bargaining chips in advance. Aristandros was famed for his astute manipulative skills in business and his ability to spring a surprise on his opponents. No doubt it had been naïve of her not being better prepared for such tactics to be used against her. In fact it had not occurred to her that Aristandros might think it necessary to tie her up in some legal agreement, particularly as their arrangement was of an intimate nature.

'Did you actually discuss our future relationship with your lawyers?' Ella demanded, cringing at the idea, and incredulous that he could have gone to such insensitive lengths in his determination to bind her in legal knots.

'I always try to anticipate problems in advance. And a woman as strong-minded as you is likely to cause trouble if she can,' Aristandros forecast.

'But you discussed the fact that you want me to be your mistress!' Ella launched back at him in raw condemnation.

'It's scarcely going to be a secret when you live with me and are constantly seen by my side,' Aristandros responded in a direct challenge. 'I'm not going to pretend that you're just the nanny.'

Air scissored painfully through her dry throat as she dragged in a charged breath, for the level of his insolent indifference to her feelings infuriated her. 'You really don't give a damn about how all this makes me feel, do you?'

'*Should* I?' Aristandros raised an ebony brow. 'How much of a damn did you give when I had to tell all my friends and family that you were not, after all, about to become my wife?'

That controversial question flamed in the air between them like a physical blow. Ella paled, recalling the awful, squirming embarrassment and guilty discomfiture that she had suffered over the whole wretched mix-up that night seven years ago. 'I was *very* upset about it. But it wasn't my fault that you decided to simply assume that the fact I loved you meant I would give up medicine and marry you!' she replied accusingly. 'There was no malice on my part, either. Although I didn't want to marry you, I really did care about you, and the last thing I wanted to do was hurt you in any way.'

In receipt of that spirited speech of self-defence, his dark eyes turned almost black with derision, and his strong jawline clenched hard. 'You didn't hurt me. I'm not that sensitive, *glikia mou*.'

But his anger and desire for revenge seven years on were giving Ella a very different message. Aristandros had always enjoyed a glossy air of invulnerability over a core of indomitable strength that suggested he was too tough to be easily damaged. Yet it seemed to her now that her rejection had wounded him more than she had ever dreamt possible.

'Whatever,' Ella slashed back. 'It still doesn't excuse you for calling in lawyers to talk about the possible problems of an intimate relationship! Is nothing sacred?'

'Certainly not sex,' Aristandros parried drily. 'You need

to be aware that this is not a cohabitation agreement, and you will not be my partner in that sense, so you won't be able to claim anything from me at some future date.'

'Oh, I'm getting the message now!' Ella flung at him, temper racing up through her like flame reacting uncontrollably to a draught, her pride stung to the quick by his assurances. 'You're protecting your wealth, even though you know very well that I have no designs on your wretched money! My goodness, if money had been that important to me, I'd have married you when I got the chance!'

His dark eyes blazed burning gold with anger at that blunt exclamation. 'Here.' Without further ado, Aristandros scooped a document off the table beside him and extended it to her. 'Read it and sign it.'

Her slim legs feeling a tad wobbly in the support stakes, Ella sank down into the nearest armchair. It was a long and involved contract. As her angry resentment cooled, she digested the terms of the agreement. Soon horror at the extent of his ruthlessness was assailing her as heavily as a lump of concrete settling into her stomach. He had reduced their upcoming relationship to the coldest possible set of hard-hitting demands and embargos.

In return for the privilege of looking after Callie and having all her expenses met by him, Ella was to share his bed whenever he wanted while making every possible effort to meet his expectations of her in everything that she did. She was to live, dress and travel as and where he wished. In addition, she was to accept that what was referred to as his 'private life' was none of her business and that interference in that field would be considered a breach of their agreement. Her teeth ground together and she had to snatch in a breath to restrain another angry outburst

The conditions of what could only be called her proposed 'service' were unbelievably detailed and humiliating. How could any man have dared to discuss such confidential matters with his lawyers? Where had he got the nerve to dictate such unashamedly cruel and disparaging terms?

'This....this is outrageous!' Ella told him grittily. 'Why don't you just put a collar and a lead on me and refer to me as a pet?'

'I want the job description to be accurate before you take on the role,' Aristandros traded levelly. 'I am honest about what I want and expect from you. You won't be able to say that you weren't warned.'

As Ella read on, she grew ever more tense and rattled. He was even laying down advance restrictions on her contact with Callie—she would not have the right to take Callie out without his permission and accompanying security. At all times she was to respect Aristandros's position as her niece's sole legal guardian and take note of his instructions. Any attempt to remove Callie from his custody or to claim any rights over the little girl would result in her access to Callie being denied. Ella shivered at that brutal threat and glanced up at Aristandros, evaluating the intractable expression stamped in his lean dark features. No, he wasn't joking about any of it. He didn't want a mistress, and certainly not a partner of equal status; he wanted a slave on a round-the-clock mission to please him.

'Until this moment,' she muttered shakily. 'I didn't realise how much you hated me.'

'Don't be ridiculous.' Aristandros sent her a quelling glance.

'If I couldn't even *argue* with you, I couldn't breathe!' Ella hurled back in response.

'I expect occasional disagreements,' Aristandros countered with the air of a man making a generous allowance. 'But I will not accept continual hostility which might detract from my comfort.'

Ella was mute with dismay and disbelief at the iron rule he was trying to impose on her. The written agreement was a humiliating nightmare. She felt like her wings were being clipped and she would never fly free again. Aristandros was determined to own her body and soul, and control her every waking moment.

'We have wasted enough time discussing this. *Sign*,' Aristandros ordered flatly.

'Aren't I entitled to legal advice of my own before I sign anything? I haven't even finished reading it yet!'

'Of course you're entitled to seek legal advice, but that will hold matters up for at least another couple of weeks and extend the time you will have to wait to meet Callie,' Aristandros pointed out.

'I'm beginning to understand why you're so rich,' Ellie mumbled sickly. 'You know what buttons to push, how to put on the pressure.'

'Of course...' Aristandros spread shapely brown hands in a fluid movement '...I want you and I'm programmed to fight for you.'

'You fight very dirty,' Ella whispered, bending her head to read on, still shocked by the extent of the control he was determined to exert over her. She skimmed through the financial details of the ridiculously extravagant monthly allowance he was offering her, and the even more generous 'severance package' promised as consolation at the end of their relationship. How could she fight him? All that mattered to her at that moment was the promise of seeing Callie, being able to care for her and ensure that the child received the love and security she needed to blossom. She was not prepared to risk losing that opportunity.

'Will you sign?'

'If I sign right now, when will I see Callie?' Ella pressed.

'Tomorrow.'

Ella breathed in slow and deep and got up to put the document down on the table. 'I'll sign,' she said.

He summoned two lawyers and their signatures were duly witnessed. She couldn't look either man in the eye, for Aristandros had made her feel like a whore who was selling not only her body to him but also her self-will. She found it hard to credit that the same male had once treated her with pronounced respect and courtesy. She was convinced that rejection had made him hate her.

'What now?' she breathed when they were alone again.

'This…' His hands enclosed her firmly to pull her to him. Long fingers curved to her cheekbone, tipping up her mouth, and suddenly he was kissing her and instant explosions of reaction were fizzing through her bloodstream. His masculine urgency was incredibly exciting. A savage rush of sexual hunger engulfed her. With a helpless shiver she pressed herself to the hard muscular wall of his chest, impelled by the strain-

ing sensitivity of her breasts and the liquid heat
between her thighs to seek closer contact. She wanted,
needed, *craved* more than that connection. He closed
a hand to her hips, tilting her against him, and a low
sound of response broke low in her throat as she felt
the force of his erection even through their clothing,
and her own body leapt with instant answering need.

Aristandros lifted his handsome dark head and dealt
her a smile that was pure-bred predator. 'Frozen on the
outside, meltingly hot within, *koukla mou*. How many
other guys have there been?'

Ella hated him with so much passion at that instant
for daring to voice that insolent question that she could
barely vocalize, and her voice emerged with a husky
edge. 'A few,' she lied without hesitation, determined to
hide the fact that, to date, only he could extract that mad
inferno of response from her. 'I'm a passionate woman.'

A tiny muscle pulled tight at the corner of his expressive mouth. His eyes were as ice-cold as a mountain
stream. 'Evidently. But from here on in, all that passion
is mine. Is that understood?'

Not averse to taking on the guise of a *femme fatale*,
Ella looked up at him from beneath the long, silky lashes
that gave her blue eyes such definition against her fair
skin and pale hair. 'Of course.'

There was a moment's silence while Ella gathered
her wits and her courage. 'Will you tell me what Callie's
like?' she asked tautly.

Aristandros stilled in apparent surprise at the request.
'She's a baby. What can you say about a baby? She's
pretty—' He hesitated, as if recognising that more than

that superficial comment was required. 'She's, er, quiet, good; you would hardly know she was there.'

Ella lowered her lashes to conceal her dismay and concern at that description. A toddler of eighteen months should be lively, inquisitive and chattering, almost anything other than quiet and unobtrusive. Evidently her niece was still suffering the effects of losing her parents. 'Do you have a close relationship with her?' she queried, reluctant to say anything that he might translate as criticism of his guardianship of the little girl.

'Of course I do.' Aristandros frowned. 'Now, if that is all, the limo's waiting for you. You have appointments to keep.'

'Where?'

'I'm taking you to a gallery opening tonight. You'll need clothes.'

'I *have* clothes.'

'Not to suit my social life you don't,' he parried, drily enough to rouse colour to her cheeks. 'I'll see you later.'

Clutching her copy of the legal agreement, Ella got back into the car. She was deeply shaken by the encounter, which had imposed a challenging dose of hard reality on her. The chauffeur delivered her to a designer salon. Her arrival had clearly been pre-arranged. She was ushered from the door straight into a changing room, where detailed measurements of her figure were noted down. Within minutes a selection of garments was being brought for her to try on.

'And for the event this evening,' the senior sales-assistant murmured, fanning an elegant black cocktail-frock out in front of Ella like a bait to hook a fish, 'Mr Xenakis particularly liked this one.'

Ella breathed in deep to hold in an instant desire to state that the dress wasn't her style at all. In fact, she was stunned by the awareness that Aristandros had taken so personal an interest in what she was to wear. He had actually torn himself from the world of business to consider her appearance? Was that the true definition of a womanizer—a guy so tuned in to the female body that even choosing clothing could become a prelude to sex? She focused her anxious thoughts on Callie and achieved a state of grace equal to the task of donning the dress without comment. She was equally tolerant of every other piece of apparel presented to her, even the absurd collection of silky, frivolous lingerie. The new wardrobe was only a prop to enable her to play a part, she told herself soothingly. Unfortunately, the prospect of slipping into flimsy provocative underwear for Aristandros's benefit put Ella into a mood close to panic. Suddenly she was wishing she hadn't claimed a level of experience she didn't have.

The chauffeur took her to a beauty salon next. Ella had no objection to a little fine grooming. Indeed, it was a treat to have someone else do her hair and her nails, and the process of being made up by a professional beautician intrigued her. Colours and techniques were employed that she would never have dreamt of trying. Not for nothing had Aristandros called her '*koukla mou*'—my doll—she reasoned wryly. She was no longer required to be herself. Instead she was to be what Aristandros wanted her to be: a painted, pampered ultra-feminine remake of her former self programmed to behave like the mistress equivalent of a Stepford wife.

In an underground car-park, she got out of the limousine and was ushered into a lift. Aristandros lived in a tri-level penthouse apartment that overlooked Hyde Park. Luxurious acres of space seemed to run off in every direction from the imposing entrance-hall. She and her shopping were taken straight to the master bedroom. A swimming pool gleamed beyond the patio doors, alongside a sun terrace and the lush greenery of a rooftop garden. A maid, who addressed her in Greek, proudly demonstrated the lavish appointments of the dressing room where her clothes were to be stored, before showing her the opulent marble bathroom.

Ella discovered that she couldn't take her attention off the massive bed that occupied centre-stage in the bedroom. The divan was so big Aristandros would have to chase her round it to capture her, she thought crazily, her heart starting to beat very, very fast. Sex with Aristandros—something she had dreamt about seven years earlier and now cringed at the threat of, she acknowledged ruefully. Still, if practice made perfect, he ought to be better in bed than most.

The maid hung the black dress in readiness, while Ella selected a turquoise voile-and-lace bra and matching panties and then went for a shower. When she had put on these items, she posed in front of the bathroom mirror, noticing how the clinging fabric of the underwear clung to the fullness of her breasts and the swell of her hips, not to mention even more personal parts. Just then, the door opened without warning. A gasp was snatched from her parted lips, and she snatched up a towel to conceal her only partially clothed body. Her startled blue gaze was very wide.

Aristandros was in the doorway, seeming taller and

more powerfully built than ever. Having already discarded his jacket, his tie and his shoes, he was an aggressively masculine sight with his shirt hanging loose to frame a muscular brown slice of hair-roughened chest. 'You should have locked the door if you didn't want company,' he teased, eyeing the big white towel she was clutching to her chest with feverish hands. 'For a woman who has been with, and I quote *a few* men, you're very shy.'

Pride stiffened Ella's backbone and she flung her head high, blade-straight white-blonde hair feathering in a silken swathe across her flushed cheekbones. 'I don't have a shy bone in my body!'

'Drop the towel and prove it,' he advised lazily.

In a convulsive movement, her slim fingers released their grip and the towel tumbled to the marble floor. She knew it was silly, but she felt ten times more naked and self-conscious in the fancy lingerie than she would have felt in her own unadorned skin.

Aristandros looked, and made no attempt to hide the fact that he was looking and enjoying the view of her scantily clad curves. Her body tingled in all the private places as though a flame had passed too close to her skin. 'It pays to undress you, *glikia mou.*'

Ella dragged in a charged breath, the creamy swell of her breasts stirring, her swollen nipples visible below the lace. His brilliant eyes smouldered gold, and her mouth ran dry as he took a step forward and reached for her, sinking his hands below her hips to lift her up and settle her down on the marble vanity-unit as if she weighed no more than a child's toy.

'What are you doing?' she demanded.

'Appreciating you,' Aristandros husked, breathing in the soapy fresh scent of her skin as he bent over her, the hot blood pooling at his groin. *His* soap from *his* shower, *his* woman, right where she belonged. It was a moment of supreme sensual satisfaction for Ari. He pressed his warm mouth lightly to the tender skin at her collarbone, where a tiny pulse was beating out her tension. With the tip of his tongue he tasted her. His hands slid from her slim shoulders to brush the bra cups down and ease her pert breasts free of confinement. The sweetly curved mounds spilled forward, held high by the constraint of the bra, the stiff, pink crests drawing his attention.

'You're perfect.' He moulded the ripe swell of her brazenly exposed flesh and kneaded the tender tips. Taken by surprise, Ella was defenceless, mentally unprepared for a sexual challenge before nightfall. Her nipples were unbearably sensitive. Her head tipped back, and a moan broke from her throat as he stroked and pinched the distended buds. A warm, rich wave of sensational response was engulfing her even before he lowered his head to suck the rosy crests. Her control was sliding as inexorably as night followed day. Desire was sinking taloned claws of need into her treacherous body. He drove her lips apart with sudden mesmeric urgency, his tongue plundering the moist interior of her mouth while his skilled fingers traced the taut, damp stretch of material between her thighs and made her shiver violently.

At an unhurried pace, he eased below the triangle of fabric and circled the most sensitive point, teasing and toying with her delicate flesh. All lingering remnants of self-discipline were wrenched from her as he subjected her to his erotic mastery. Very soon she reached the stage where she could have wept with frustration and begged him on her knees for satisfaction. A husky sound of amusement broke from him as she dragged him closer with frantic hands, seeking the temporary consolation of physical contact that their position denied her.

'Take a deep breath, *khriso mou*,' Aristandros urged thickly. 'We have a gallery opening to attend, and I need a shower—'

'A gallery opening?' Only with the greatest difficulty did Ella extract herself from the all-encompassing sexual hunger that he had induced and return to reason again. It was like coming out of a coma to a brash new world. She was appalled to appreciate that Aristandros had virtually seduced her in his bathroom and was now trying to head for the shower while she still clung to him. She whipped her hands from him as though she had been burnt. 'Of course.'

'We have no time.' Aristandros lifted her down from the marble unit-top with strong hands. 'I don't want to treat you like a takeaway,' he murmured huskily. 'I want to enjoy you like a feast and appreciate every nuance.'

'A takeaway!' Ella repeated through gritted teeth of disdain.

Aristandros gazed down at her with shimmering golden-brown eyes fringed with spiky black lashes. 'You want me,' he countered with hard satisfaction. 'A time will come when you don't care *how* I take you…only that I do.'

That frightening forecast trickled down her taut spine like ice-water. 'Never,' she swore. 'I'd sooner die!'

A wolfish smile slashed his beautifully shaped mouth. 'I know women; I'm never wrong…'

'You were *once*,' Ella reminded him before she could think better of summoning up a recollection that could only alienate him.

His lean, dark face tensed, ruthless eyes cool on her face. 'Don't go there,' he warned her softly.

A deep chill formed inside her tummy. Regretting her incautious words, she turned her head away, shame and uncertainty clouding her blue eyes as she returned to the bedroom. For a split second she was recalling the short-lived joy of the moment when he had told her that he wanted her to marry him. Her happiness had turned to horror an instant later when he made a public announcement about their plans while spelling out the fact that she would be giving up medicine to concentrate on being a wife and a mother. Minutes later they had been engaged in a heated dispute in which it had swiftly become clear that Aristandros could be as inflexible in his expectations as a solid-granite rock and quite unapologetic about the fact too.

Rejection had swiftly followed her refusal to conform seven years back. Aristandros was very black and white. There was no going back with him, no halfway measures or compromises. The break-up had felt as swift, cruel and unjust as a sudden death. At least this time around, she reflected heavily, she knew what to expect if she crossed the line with Aristandros Xenakis. There would be no second chance to get it right...

# CHAPTER FOUR

'I ALMOST forgot,' Aristandros remarked, striding into a book-lined room off the imposing hall and leaving Ella to hover in the doorway.

Ella watched him lift a small shallow case from the desk. Her smooth brow pleated.

'Come here,' he urged with his usual impatience. 'You can't go out without jewels.'

'I don't have any,' she confided with an uneasy laugh.

'I'm starting off your collection, *glikia mou.*' Aristandros detached the glittering diamond necklace from its velvet bed as she approached him on stiff legs. 'Turn round.'

'I don't want it!' Ella told him sharply for, while she had tolerated the clothing, a dazzling river of diamonds felt too much like the biblical wages of sin. Her principles had already taken enough of a hit.

'But it is my wish that you wear it,' Aristandros spelt out, purposeful fingers curving to her shoulder to flip her round. The jewels felt very cold against her skin. She shivered as his fingertips brushed her nape. He spun her back round and, with a satisfaction undiminished by her bleak expression, surveyed the glittering tracery of jewels encircling her throat

Ella was surprised by the crush at the gallery opening. She had never dreamt that she would see so many well-dressed people and famous celebrity faces grouped in the same place. Nor had she ever received quite so much personal attention for, the moment she entered the room by Aristandros's side, every female head seemed to swivel in their direction. An audible buzz of conjecture accompanied their passage through the crowds. While Ari was engaged in discussing a sculpture with its creator, Ella strayed across the room. She was studying an enchanting painting of the seashore when she was accosted by a tall, leggy redhead whose perfect body was adorned by a tiny white satin dress.

'So, *you're* my replacement!' the woman snapped, settling her furious and accusing green gaze on Ella. 'Who the hell are you? Exactly *when* did Aristandros meet you?'

Ella knew exactly who the beautiful redhead was. Her name was Milly, she was a top model and probably Aristandros's most recent ex. Ella said nothing, for she had seen the tears in the other woman's eyes and recognised her distress.

'You won't get any warning that it's over. One day you're *in*, and the world's your oyster, and the next you're *out* and there's nothing you can do about it. He doesn't take your calls any more,' Milly recited chokily. 'Every door slams in your face!'

'There has to be many safer and more rewarding options for a woman as young and beautiful as you are,' Ella told her bracingly. 'Don't give him the satisfaction of knowing that you care.'

Milly studied her in wide-eyed bewilderment. 'You're being nice to me? Aren't you jealous?'

'No,' Ella declared with innate dignity. 'I'm not the jealous sort.'

Too late, she saw that the redhead's attention had shifted from her.

'Milly.' From behind Ella, Aristandros greeted the other woman politely.

'You're *not* jealous?' Aristandros queried in near disbelief as his ex-girlfriend vanished speedily back into the crush, unnerved by his ice-cold appraisal.

'Of course not,' Ella assured him, thinking of the seven years she had spent reading about his exploits with countless other women. Familiarity, she was convinced, had brought tolerance and common sense to her outlook. Everywhere Aristandros went, he was a target for ambitious women. That was a fact of life, and as long as he remained fabulously rich and gorgeous, the situation wasn't likely to change any time soon.

Dark eyes sardonic, Aristandros guided her back to the landscape of the seashore. 'It reminds me of Lykos…the beach below the house,' he remarked, inclining his imperious head to the gallery owner hovering a few feet away. 'We'll take it.'

Aristandros had inherited the Greek island of Lykos from his mother's side of the family. Once Ella had had a picnic there with him, and suddenly the years were rolling back inside her head and she was remembering how the breeze had whipped wildly at her hair while they ate. Wrapped up warm for the winter temperatures, she had listened with interest while Aristandros had outlined his plans to revitalise the island's failing economy and prevent the population from falling any further. His sense of responsibility for the small, isolated community living on Lykos had impressed her a great deal.

'Where will you hang the seascape?' Aristandros asked as they left the gallery.

'Where will *I* hang it?' she stressed in confusion. 'Are you saying that you are buying it for *me*?'

'Why not?'

'Because I don't want you buying stuff like that for me; the way you're splashing out cash on me is indecent!' Ella hissed frantically under her breath as they headed across the pavement to the silver limousine awaiting them. Crash barriers prevented the gathered members of the press from getting too close.

Her spine rigid, Ella blinked like an owl while cameras went off all around them, and questions and comments were hurled at Aristandros. Uppermost were the demands to know the identity of his new companion. But, in every way, Aristandros remained gloriously impervious to the media presence, settling into the limo beside her, 'Of course I'm going to buy you things; get used to it!'

'I'm only here with you because of Callie. Contact with her is the *only* reward I want,' Ella proclaimed, uneasy fingers brushing the diamond necklace in meaningful emphasis of the point.

The smooth planes of his lean features took on a cold, sardonic light, his brilliant gaze narrowing. 'No man wants to be told that his only attraction is an eighteen-month-old baby, *khriso mou*.'

Ella lifted her pale head high. 'Even if it's the truth?'

'But it's not the truth, it's an outright lie for which

you should hang your head in shame,' Aristandros traded without hesitation, his beautifully shaped mouth curling with derision. 'You want me as much now as you wanted me seven years ago. Don't make the child your excuse.'

Ella had lost colour. 'It's not an excuse. I may occasionally find you…attractive, but I wouldn't have done anything about it.'

'Too spineless?' Aristandros sent her a contemptuous glance. 'I didn't meet your narrow-minded requirements, so the fact that you wanted me and I wanted you meant nothing to you.'

'Don't be ridiculous…of course it meant something!' Ella flashed back. 'But you wanted me to be something I couldn't be.'

Aristandros closed a strong hand over hers to force her to turn and look at him. 'I only wanted you to be a *woman*, not a strident feminist—'

Ella sent him a flaming look of bone-deep resentment. 'I was never strident. I was sensible. We wanted totally different things out of life. It could never have worked.'

'No doubt time will tell,' Aristandros fielded very drily, releasing his hold on her hand.

The silence that laced their return to the penthouse gnawed at Ella's nerves. She was already wishing that she didn't speak first and think later. They were about to share the same bed, and she could barely believe that, never mind accept the idea in the mood she was in. 'If the painting's to be mine, I'll be hanging it here somewhere,' she told him abruptly, surrendering to a sudden need to bridge an atmosphere filled with tense, uneasy undertones. 'Because I don't have anywhere else to live at present.'

Aristandros sent her a sudden, satisfied smile, as if that bleak assurance was a heart warming plus on his terms. 'You live where I live now.'

An involuntary shiver ran down her taut spine as the level of dependency that that statement suggested continued to chill Ella and her independent soul to the marrow.

The tall, powerful Greek closed his hands over hers to turn her back to face him. Brilliant golden-brown eyes assailed hers. 'Don't fight the inevitable, *glikia mou*. Embrace these changes in your life. You might even find that you come to enjoy them.'

'*Never*,' Ella swore in a fierce undertone.

'I hear words on your lips that no other woman has ever dared to confront me with,' Aristandros confided, his deep drawl silky with indulgence. 'You are truly unique.'

Recognising his triumph at the position he had her in, Ella shut her eyes tight. So, when his mouth came down on hers without warning, her only weapon was her rage. But even as she braced her hands to his chest to push him angrily away she thought better of that move. She had made a devil's bargain, and now payment was due. While Aristandros kissed her, she stood like a statue, unresponsive as stone. But he played with her mouth, soft one moment, teasing the next, and then hot and male and hungry, until her thoughts were no longer clear and her resistance was breaking down, sensual response beginning to quiver through her treacherous body in an ever-swelling tide.

With a masculine growl of approval, Aristandros bent down and lifted her, swinging her up into his arms with easy strength to carry her into the master bedroom.

Her heart was racing so fast she couldn't catch her

breath. When he set her down, she kicked off her shoes. A soft glide of air brushed her backbone as her dress was unzipped. His sensual mouth was like a brand on hers. The slide of his tongue between her parted lips was an indescribable aphrodisiac that sent darts of heat and tingles of excitement quivering through her entire body. For an instant she was shattered by the awareness that she wanted him as fiercely as she wanted air to breathe. Guilty unease filtered through her, cooling her head for a moment as she tasted the bitter truth that she was weaker than she had thought she would be.

'Stop it,' Aristandros growled, scorching dark-golden eyes raking her troubled face.

'Stop what?'

'Thinking whatever you're thinking which is suddenly giving you all the animation of an Egyptian mummy.'

Discomfited colour bloomed across her cheekbones.

'In fact, don't think at all,' Aristandros urged force-fully. 'This is sex. You don't need to carve it up into little intellectual nuggets to be studied below a microscope. Be spontaneous…natural.'

'*Natural*?' Ella hissed at him tempestuously. 'This is the most unnatural thing I've ever done!'

His blue-shadowed jawline clenched. 'Only because you're fighting everything I make you feel.'

That he recognised her struggle, ineffective though it was, shook Ella, for it had not occurred to her that he might understand her that well. His impatience uncon-cealed, he dumped her down on the bed. 'This is sex', he had said with a detachment that ran contrary to her every instinct. But if their arrangement was to work, she reasoned, she had to stop judging him and wanting and expecting more than he was ever likely to give her. She had passed the last deadline: it was crunch time.

'How many guys did you say?' Aristandros enquired silkily, watching her shimmy beneath the sheet until only her shoulders could be seen.

Ella sat up, delicate facial bones tightening defensively. 'I *didn't* say!'

The silence stretched. A sardonic edge to his expressive mouth, Aristandros undressed, taking his time, every movement fluid with a grace that caught her eye no matter how hard she tried to avoid that side of the room. From the whipcord muscles of his shoulders to his beautifully defined torso, he was a vision of sculpted masculine perfection. He was also very well endowed and fully aroused, she could not help noticing. Her mouth ran dry and her heart began to pound.

'Less than fifty?' Aristandros asked casually.

Ella shot him an aghast glance.

'Definitely less than fifty,' he decided for himself.

'It's none of your damned business!' Ella launched back at him furiously. 'Stop making a production out of it!'

'Come out from below the sheet.'

In a series of violent movements, Ella kicked off the sheet and reclined back against the pillows in the exaggerated pose of a glamour model, with her spine arched to thrust out her chest. 'Satisfied?'

Aristandros raked his appreciative gaze over the voluptuous swell of her breasts in the turquoise bra. 'Not yet. Take it all off, *glikia mou*.'

Her blue-as-sapphire eyes rounded. '*Everything*?'

Aristandros inclined his handsome head in a confirmation that was a clear challenge. For a split second, Ella was rigid with rejection, and then she scrambled off the bed. Taking up a defiant stance, she peeled off her bra and discarded her knickers.

His attention nailed to her, dark eyes flaring hungrily over her pale, slender curves, Aristandros strode forward and snatched her up into his arms. 'I already feel like I waited a lifetime for you!' he growled, claiming her soft mouth with savage possessiveness even while his hands moulded to the pert mounds of her breasts and kneaded the swollen pink tips between his fingers.

Her body came alive with almost painful immediacy. Needles of bittersweet longing arrowed from her breasts to her pelvis, and awakened a hollow feeling that was swiftly followed by a sharp stab of desire that made her tummy muscles contract. His mouth on hers suddenly became a fierce necessity. The pressure of his hard, masculine lips and the erotic exploration of his tongue went some way towards satisfying the craving taking charge of her. The stimulating passage of his hands over her sensitised body made her push against the unyielding contours of his hard muscular torso. He backed her down on to the bed. Heat and restlessness had entered her bloodstream. All of a sudden she was alight with a need that she had known only once before. Then, as now, the power of that sexual hunger scared her with its unnerving strength. Of their own volition it seemed, however, that her hips lifted and her thighs eased apart, seeking ever more intimate contact with him.

Aristandros lifted his tousled head to look down at her, his smouldering gaze scanning her flushed cheeks and the swollen contours of her mouth. 'You'll enjoy yourself much more when you let go of that rigid self-control—'

'Don't taunt me,' Ella warned him grittily.

'I wasn't.' He frowned. 'I want this to be an unforgettable night.'

Her body a playground of tingling, energised responses, all of which seemed beyond her control, Ella shivered, so wound up with tension that it was an achievement just to think. She registered that this was Ari, the ultimate alpha male at his most driven, and seemingly sex was not quite as casual an event as he had made it sound. Even between the sheets he was set on scoring the highest possible results. At the same time, he was so beautiful that just looking at him turned her heart over. He shifted, the hair-roughened skin of his chest scratching against her jutting nipples and sending a scorching dart of extreme awareness down to the swollen heat and moisture at the very heart of her. In a movement that was utterly instinctive, she sank her fingers into his luxuriant black hair to drag him down to her and urge his mouth back onto hers again. He dealt her a frank look of surprise.

'You talk too much,' Ella told him baldly.

Laughter rumbled in his chest and then he kissed her. Complaint was the last thing on her mind, for in that department he had no equal. He kissed with an unholy passion. The all-encompassing hunger surged again and she clung to him, excitement taking over and overwhelming her final defences.

'*Se thelo*…I want you,' he bit out, studying her with dark-golden eyes that smouldered with appreciation. 'When you respond like this to me, it blows my mind, *khriso mou*.'

She writhed in whimpering reaction while he explored the slick, wet flesh between her thighs. She was so tender and he was so skilled that both stillness and silence were impossible for her. Sensation engulfed her with exquisite pleasure as he teased the tiny bud below the pale curls screening her feminine mound. All restraint was gone. Her entire being was centred on the throbbing need he had awakened and the wickedly tormenting expertise of his technique. The yearning hunger got stronger and stronger until it felt as though her whole body was primed on a knife-edge of intolerable tension and longing. When he finally tipped her off that edge into climax, it was as if an explosion began low in her pelvis and slowly, wonderfully, roared in wave after glorious wave through the rest of her.

She was still awash with wondering bliss and stunned by the intensity of the experience when Aristandros slid between her thighs and sunk his hands below her hips to raise her. His iron-hard shaft probed her lush opening, and she gasped at the strangeness of a sensation magnified by the incredible sensitivity of her tender flesh. He attempted to plunge deeper, but for an instant her body seemed to resist him. With a stifled exclamation he tipped back her knees to ease his entry. Her untried feminine sheath finally stretched to accommodate him, and she cried out at the sudden shockingly sensual pleasure of his penetration. Her heart was racing as he delved deeper into her, and she arched up, on fire with excitement and renewed hunger. Nothing had ever felt so amazing. She was spellbound by the heady exhilaration of his masculine dominance and the extraordinary pleasure that was building inside her again. Just moments later she surged feverishly to another sexual peak which shattered her like glass into a hundred glittering pieces and flung her into the sun. Stunned by the explosive intensity of the pleasure, she was better prepared when it happened yet again, before he achieved his own release.

In the aftermath of that wild rollercoaster experience, Ella was in shock and as physically weak as a newborn kitten, drained by her own extravagant response.

'My every dream comes true,' Aristandros purred as he stretched like a jungle cat in the heat of the sun. Rolling back to her, he dropped a kiss on her brow and studied her with unashamed satisfaction. 'A multi-orgasmic woman who sets my bed on fire, *khriso mou*.'

Ella was hugely embarrassed at having been so wildly responsive. She could not deny that sex with him had proved to be an extremely pleasurable activity. But, whether it was fair or otherwise, she pretty much hated him for the fact that he had made her enjoy herself. Her lovely flushed face bleak as a wintry day, she evaded his keen scrutiny because she felt she had let herself down. After all, she had planned just to tolerate his lovemaking, not leave him with the impression that he was an amazing lover.

'And so beautiful,' Aristandros remarked, trailing caressing brown fingers lazily through the silken tangle of white-blonde hair lying across her slim shoulder. 'But remarkably inventive with the truth.'

Her hackles rose instantly. Given the excuse, she pulled away from him and snapped, 'Meaning?'

'You said you'd had a lot of lovers. But I don't think there was even one.'

'Well, you'd be wrong!' she hissed furiously.

Aristandros captured her hand to imprison her when she began scrambling out of the other side of the bed. 'I've never shared a bed with a virgin before, but you felt as tight as one,' he imparted softly.

Affronted by the intimacy of that comment, Ella wrenched her hand out of his. 'Wishful thinking, eh?' she jibed, high spots of colour burning over her cheekbones. 'You're Greek to your backbone, aren't you? You've slept with scores of women but you don't want one who's enjoyed the same freedom. In fact, your ultimate hypocritical fantasy is a virgin!'

'Don't speak to me like that,' Aristandros intoned with an icy bite to his words.

'*Se miso*; I hate you!' Ella spat at him.

Stalking across the bedroom, Ella took refuge in the bathroom. She was trembling and her eyes were scratchy with the tears she was fighting back. He had become her first lover, but she would sooner have cut out her tongue than admit that fact to him. She didn't want to give him that satisfaction—the knowledge that she hadn't got really close to any man since he had walked out of her life seven years earlier, telling her that she would regret turning him down until her dying day. She had met other men, but sadly nobody who had had the same effect on her as Aristandros Xenakis. Having loved and lost him, she had been determined not to settle for anything less. And those high standards had ensured she'd stayed single and alone.

Recognising just how far she had now fallen from her own ideals hurt. Ari made her feel vulnerable and threatened. She already felt as though he had turned her inside out. She got into the shower to freshen up, still shaken that he should have noticed that she was something less than experienced. After years of athletic activity and the egg-donation process that had resulted in her sister conceiving, Ella had been confident that he would have no reason to ever guess the truth. Her pride utterly denied him any right to that truth.

She was wrapped in a towel when a knock sounded on the door. She flung it open. 'What now?'

'What's the matter with you?' Aristandros demanded rawly. 'We're good together. Tomorrow you meet Callie. What's wrong?'

The sound of her niece's name, the tacit reminder of their agreement, steadied Ella. 'Nothing's wrong. It's been a long day, and I suppose I'm tired,' she muttered, sidestepping him to leave the bathroom.

In the dressing room she selected a strappy nightdress and got back into bed, scolding herself for her loss of temper and control. She was being stupid. Antagonising Aristandros was pure insanity. Bitten, he would bite back, and she had the most to lose. She was not necessary to him and far from irreplaceable. Any number of women would be happy to assume the role of mistress, and none of them was likely to shout at him or insult him. He wasn't accustomed to that kind of treatment and he wouldn't tolerate it.

At dawn the following morning, she listened while Aristandros showered and dressed and left the room before she drifted off to sleep again. A maid wakened her a couple of hours later and told her that Aristandros would breakfast with her when she was ready. Aware that within a few hours at most she would be meeting Callie, Ella leapt out of bed with enthusiasm and rushed to get dressed. Breathless and unbelievably tense, she entered the elegant modern dining-room.

'Good morning,' she breathed stiltedly, every skin cell in her body jumping as Aristandros cast down his copy of the *Financial Times* and rose to his full, commanding height.

Having sex with him had increased her awareness by a factor of at least a hundred. Uneasily conscious of the intimate ache between her thighs and the still-swollen contours of her mouth, she felt the hot blood of embarrassment engulf her face with uncomfortable warmth even before she met his brilliant dark-golden eyes. He gave her a steady look that betrayed nothing beyond his rock-solid assurance and cool.

For some reason she remembered their first date seven years back, when he had wakened her whole family by arriving unannounced at an early hour to take her out sailing on his yacht. Her stepfather, had fawned on him to a mortifying degree while her twin half-brothers had hovered, unsure whether to approve or disapprove of a mega-rich Xenakis with a bad reputation taking an interest in one of their sisters. Only her mother had had reservations. Ella hadn't really appreciated just how rich, powerful and well-known Aristandros was until she saw the way other people treated him.

She was surprised by how much of an appetite she had, and she ate a good breakfast before asking tautly, 'Is Callie on her way here?'

'No. She'll be waiting for us on *Hellenic Lady* with her nurse. We're sailing home to Greece,' Aristandros informed her.

Like all of his family, Aristandros was never happier

than when he was on a boat. Susie had complained bitterly about Timon's love of the water, which she had not shared.

'I hope she likes me,' Ella muttered before she could think better of revealing that admission of insecurity.

'Of course she will.' Aristandros shot her a lingering look redolent of very male appreciation.

Her cheeks warming, Ella stirred her coffee.

'She's also very lucky I let you get out of bed this morning,' he husked.

Ella dealt him a startled glance from her vivid blue eyes.

Aristandros rested a lean-fingered brown hand on her slim thigh and urged her round to face him. 'I wanted to keep you awake all night. Moderation isn't my style, *koukla mou*.'

Wildly conscious of the unashamed hunger that had flared like liquid gold in his intense gaze, Ella found herself leaning forward to speed up the meeting of her mouth with his. She could not have explained what prompted her to make that encouraging move. But that spontaneous kiss was indescribably sweet and intoxicating, and it sent every nerve-ending jumping with vibrant energy and response. A quickening sensation thrummed low in her pelvis. A moment later, his hand was meshed in her hair, holding her to him, and a moment after that he had lifted her right out of the chair into his arms. Excitement blazed through her like solar flares as he carried her back to the bedroom…

# CHAPTER FIVE

ELLA was so taut with anticipation that her heart almost leapt out of her chest when she first saw Callie in the reception salon of the Xenakis yacht.

At a glance she recognised how much her biological child resembled her, with that silvery-blonde cap of hair and those almond-shaped blue eyes. She wondered with painful regret if ironically that pronounced similarity had unleashed Susie's insecurity over her role as Callie's mother. The little girl straightened up to turn away from the toy she was playing with and focused not on Ella but on Aristandros. But, instead of toddling forward to greet the tall Greek as Ella expected, Callie waved at him and smiled. Aristandros waved back.

'She always smiles when she sees me,' Aristandros commented, evidently content with the style of his greeting.

Ella went over to meet her niece and got down on her knees, her heart lurching as she studied the child, whose very blue eyes were curious. A shy little hand reached out to touch Ella's equally pale hair and then hastily withdrew again. Recognising Callie's fear of the unfamiliar, Ella began talking to introduce herself, and within minutes totally forgot the presence of Aristandros and the Greek nursemaid stationed on the other side of the vast salon. When she recalled their presence she looked back over there but Aristandros had gone.

She soon discovered that Callie lit up when she heard music and loved to dance. The little girl giggled in delight when Ella joined in, and the atmosphere became much more relaxed. When refreshments were served, Ella sat down to get acquainted with her niece's youthful nurse, Kasma, and find out about the child's routine. While the two women talked, Ella made a hat out of a napkin to amuse Callie, who was becoming fractious. Callie finally consented to sit on Ella's lap to enjoy a fruit snack. Momentarily the warm, solid baby weight of the toddler resting trustingly against her made happy tears wash the back of Ella's eyes; this was a moment that she had truly believed she would never know in reality. Just then, every sacrifice she had made seemed more than worthwhile.

Kasma had a good deal to tell her that was of interest. The young woman stood in too much awe of Aristandros even to imply criticism of her employer. Even so, what Ella learned from subtle questions soon convinced Ella that Aristandros had zero parenting skills and, quite possibly, no interest in rectifying that deficiency. By then Callie was fast asleep in her arms, and Ella followed Kasma down to the lower-deck cabin which was set up as a nursery and put her niece in her cot for a nap.

Keen to freshen up—something Ella hadn't had a chance to do earlier that day after their rushed late depar-

ture from the London penthouse—she returned to the
main cabin suite, where she took a shower in the superb
marble wet-room. She couldn't stop smiling as she relived
the afternoon that had just passed. The hours had just
melted away while she'd been with Callie. A stewardess
came to tell her that Aristandros was waiting for her in
the salon. Ella finished drying her hair, her body tingling
in outrageous tune with her thoughts, because she could
not forget the pure, erotic excitement of Aristandros's
love-making at the outset of the day, or the blissful release
she had once again experienced in his arms.

'A change of plan—we're flying to Paris in an hour,'
Aristandros announced when she joined him.

'Paris?' Her eyes homed in on him straight away and
involuntarily clung to his compellingly handsome
features. Even in the formal garb of a black pinstripe
business-suit and dark silk tie, he emanated a charge of
raw sexuality and animal energy that made her mouth
run dry as a bone. 'Why?'

'Some friends are having a party, and I'm looking
forward to showing you off.'

'But Callie's in bed and exhausted. She's just flown
in from Greece,' Ella reminded him uncomfortably.

'She can sleep during the flight.' Aristandros
shrugged, instantly dismissing her protest. 'Children
are very resilient. I must have travelled round the world
with my parents a score of times by her age. How did
you get on with her?'

'We got on great, but it'll take time for her to bond
with me.'

'You'll still be a better mother than Susie ever was,'
Aristandros forecast with a hint of derision.

Astonishment and annoyance at that criticism flared through Ella in defence of her late sister. 'What on earth makes you say that?'

Engaged in flicking through a business file, Aristandros raised a sleek ebony brow and glanced up again. 'I'm not afraid of the truth, and death doesn't purchase sainthood. You should never have agreed to your sister's request that you donate eggs to enable her to become pregnant. Susie couldn't handle it. An anonymous donor would have been a safer bet.'

'What are you talking about?' Ella demanded angrily.

Aristandros dealt her an impatient look. 'Don't tell me that you never realised that as far as Susie was concerned you were the kid sister from hell? You outshone her in looks and intelligence, and compounded your sins by attracting my interest.'

'That's complete nonsense!'

'It's not. Susie tried to lure me long before she ever looked at Timon, but I didn't bite.'

Ella was shattered by a piece of information that had never come her way before. Susie had been attracted to Aristandros? That possibility, that very private and dangerous little fact, had never once occurred to her. 'Is that honestly the truth?'

Aristandros frowned. 'Why would I lie about it? I wasn't pleased when Susie started dating Timon, but he fell hook, line and sinker for her.'

Ella had lost colour, the fine bones of her profile prominent below her creamy skin. All of a sudden things that she had not understood but which had given her an uneasy feeling were being explained—her sister's constant, tactless carping about Ari's inability to stay faithful throughout the period when Ella had been seeing him; her repeated angry accusations that Ella didn't appreciate just how lucky she was.

'No matter what your sister did, Timon forgave her because he loved her. But, when you made it possible for them to have a child together and Susie turned her back on that child, Timon couldn't accept it.'

Ella gave him a stricken appraisal. 'Susie turned her back on Callie? How?'

'She left their staff to take care of her. Having got the baby she insisted she could not live without, she rejected her. Timon was at his wit's end. He consulted doctors on her behalf. Susie refused to see them, and finally Timon began to talk about divorcing Susie and applying for sole custody of Callie. Their marriage was very much on the rocks when they died.'

Her consternation and sadness at that news palpable, Ella sank heavily down on a chair. 'I had no idea that the situation was so serious. If only I had known, if only Susie had been willing to see me and talk to me after Callie's birth, maybe *I* could have—'

'You were the last person who could have helped her. She was too jealous of you.'

'It's perfectly possible that Susie was suffering from severe post-natal depression. Didn't my family try to help her?' Ella prompted feverishly.

'I don't think they recognised the extent of the problem, or that they wanted to get involved once they realised that Susie's marriage was in grave trouble,' Aristandros said flatly.

Ella knew that in such circumstances her domineering stepfather would have urged her mother to mind her own business, and that her mother would not have had the backbone to stand up to him even if she'd disagreed. She felt unbearably sad. Had Susie been suffering from depression? Evidently, however, even Timon had been unable to persuade her sibling to seek professional help. Poor Callie had had a troubled and insecure life right from the moment of her birth. Ella thought that it was hardly surprising that the little girl was quiet and somewhat behind in her development.

'How much time have you spent with Callie?' Ella asked Aristandros.

His well-defined black brows pleated, as if he suspected a trick question. 'I see her every day that we're under the same roof.'

'But do you play with her? Talk to her? *Hold* her?'

Aristandros winced at those blunt questions. 'I'm not a touchy-feely guy. That's what you're here for.'

Ella breathed in deep and stood up. 'I don't want to offend you, but I have to be frank. At the moment, all you seem to do is wave at her from the doorway of her nursery once or twice a day.'

Aristandros frowned and threw up his hands in objection at her censorious tone. 'It's a little game we play. What harm does it do?'

Ella was hanging on to her temper only by a hair's breadth. He was not that obtuse. He could hardly believe that he was playing father of the year with a long-distance wave. 'Callie needs to be touched and talked to and played with. The reason she didn't rush to greet you today is because you've got her accustomed to only seeing you at a distance—and that's how you like it, isn't it? Hands-off parenting? But she needs real contact with you—'

'What am I supposed to do with a baby?' Lean, strong face hard with impatience and hauteur, Aristandros ground out that demand, clearly offended by her criticism. 'I'm a very busy man and I'm doing my best.'

'I know you are. You just need a little direction,' Ella murmured, suddenly wondering if the closest he had ever got to his own dysfunctional parents was a breezy, noncommittal wave from the nursery door. 'And then you'd be brilliant, because you always do well at anything you set out to do.'

His dark eyes gleamed at that assurance while a wicked slow-burning smile tilted his beautiful mouth. 'Flattery will get you nowhere, *glikia mou.*'

'Will you think again about flying to Paris—for Callie's sake?' Ella pressed softly.

'You don't do sweet and submissive well.'

Mortified by the derisive tone that let her know that he had seen straight through her attempt to talk him round to her way of thinking, Ella stood straight as a blade, colour burnishing her cheeks. 'I was trying to be tactful.'

'I don't like it. It doesn't suit you,' Aristandros spelt out without skipping a beat. 'On the very first day you meet Callie, do I need to remind you that I make all the decisions where she's concerned?'

Ella turned very pale at that blunt reminder. She met cold eyes, the warning look of a strong male who had no intention of allowing his authority to be challenged. Her tummy flipped. He made her appreciate all over again that he was the one in control, and that she was walking a dangerous path from which she could not afford to stray. It was clear that he intended to hold her to the very letter of the agreement he had made her sign. She had promised not to interfere in Callie's up-bringing. All of a sudden she was appreciating just how difficult it was likely to be to take care of Callie while following his rules.

'*We* come first in this instance, not the child. *Don't* let her come between us and cause discord,' Aristandros advised her with forbidding emphasis.

Ella wanted to tell him how selfish and unreasonable he was being, but he had just delineated her boundaries as a warning and she did not dare. Aristandros Xenakis had spent thirty-two years on the earth doing exactly what he liked at all times. She might try to guide, but he would never allow her to lead. Who was she to think she could change him? The chill in the atmosphere raised gooseflesh on her bare arms and she turned to leave.

'Where are you going?'

Her spine prickled with apprehension. 'I, er, need to work out what I'm going to wear this evening.'

'No need. As yet you don't have a proper wardrobe. My staff will organise a selection of dresses to be brought to my Paris home for you, and your maid will do your packing. There's very little that you need to do for yourself now.'

Ella flipped back round. 'Sometimes you scare me…' And the instant she voiced that admission she regretted it, but there it was: the complete unvarnished truth.

Aristandros cast aside the file and vaulted upright. His astute eyes were unreadable, his fabulous bone-structure taut. 'I don't want that.'

Ella pinned her tremulous lips closed. 'I can't help the way I feel.'

'You're one of the strongest women I've ever known,' Aristandros countered.

But he was making a coward of her because if she spoke her mind she stood to lose too much, Ella conceded bitterly. Aristandros closed a hand over hers and tugged her closer. With an imperious shift of his handsome head, he smoothed her fingers straight and linked their hands. 'If it's that important, I'll make more effort with Callie.' Unusually he hesitated, his wide, sensual mouth compressing. 'I don't know how to go about it, though. I didn't have a conventional childhood.'

Ella was well aware that even that minor admission of ignorance was a major step for him, and that any sort of change of heart on his part was to be warmly appreciated and encouraged, but she was still so tense and worked up that her hand trembled in his. 'I *know*,' she said feelingly, her heart lurching inside her, for his cruelly troubled childhood had been lived out in the full glare of the media spotlight thanks to his larger-than-life parents and was very well documented.

'My earliest memory is of my father shouting at my mother when I almost drowned in a swimming pool. They were either drunk or high…' A broad shoulder shifted, his strong face hardening. 'They were so busy fighting they left me out on the terrace and forgot about me again. I know what *not* to do if you have a child.'

'Yes, of course you do,' she agreed. 'When you're a kid it's so frightening when you see adults fighting and out of control. The first time I saw Theo hit my mother, I thought the world was going to end…' As Ella realised what she had inadvertently revealed, she was appalled by her carelessness, and she fell silent.

'Repeat that,' Aristandros urged, his narrowed gaze reflecting his stunned reaction. 'The first time you saw your stepfather *hit* your mother?'

Ella was aghast at what she had let drop. 'I don't want to talk about it. I really didn't mean to say that!'

Aristandros lifted a hand to tip up her chin so that her eyes were forced to meet his. 'But now that you have, there's no going back or denying it. Theo Sardelos is in the habit of hitting your mother?'

Ella was pale as death, and full of the shame she had never been able to shake over that sordid reality. 'I don't think the violence happens as much now as it once did…at least, I would hope not,' she confided jerkily. 'But it's been so long since I had any contact with them, I really have no idea.'

'Did he ever hit *you*?' Aristandros growled.

'No, only my mother. It's a pity he didn't have a legal agreement drawn up like you did before they got married, though I'm not sure she would have signed up if she'd known what she was in for!'

'What the hell are you saying?' Aristandros grated.

'Well, that's why he beat her up—she objected when he didn't come home at night. He was always with other women,' Ella explained grudgingly. 'I think he had affairs with every secretary he ever had, as well as with some of the friends Mum made over the years. Like you, he's very attractive to the opposite sex and an incorrigible womaniser.'

Brilliant dark eyes assailed hers with cold, hostile force. 'I've never hurt a woman in my life, nor would I.'

'I didn't insinuate that you would. That's not why you scare me,' Ella extended tightly. 'You scare me because you're so cold-blooded, so tough and determined to win every bout. It's your way or the highway, and trying not to fall foul of that is a constant challenge.'

'I don't want you to feel like that, but I can't change what I am.' Aristandros breathed, with a raw edge to his deep drawl. 'The fact you compared me to Theo Sardelos is revealing. You see us as similar personalities, a comparison which I absolutely reject. But I *am* shocked by what I have just learned. I can hardly credit that you never breathed a word to me about what was going on in your own home seven years ago.'

'It was a private matter. I grew up with a mother who swore me and my siblings to silence. We were brought up to be ashamed of it and keep it hidden. The violence was never, ever discussed. Everybody tried to pretend it didn't happen.'

'Even your brothers?' Aristandros prompted with growing incredulity. 'Susie never mentioned it to Timon either.'

'Susie just ignored it, and the twins were still quite young when I left home to go to university. I don't know how things stand now. I've always hoped it stopped, but I suspect that was rather foolish wishful thinking,' she muttered heavily. 'Look, can we please drop this subject?'

Unsympathetic to that plea, Aristandros settled his smouldering gaze on her. 'You thought I might be like your stepfather, didn't you? That's one of the reasons you wouldn't marry me.'

'I don't want to discuss this any more,' Ella told him quietly, and she turned on her heel and simply walked out of the salon. She was shaking like a leaf and cursing her unwary tongue. There was no way she could tell him the truth. Of course she had seen a similarity between him and her stepfather. But with Aristandros it had not been violence she feared, but the terrible pain, constant fear and suspicion of living with an unfaithful partner. She had loved him too much to face that prospect.

Ella was overseeing her packing when Aristandros strode into the state room. With a casual movement of one hand he dismissed the maid while wrenching off his tie with the other. 'You've kept too many secrets from me, *moli mou*,' he delivered harshly. 'I don't like that. I will tell you now—that *has* to change.'

Ella slanted a feathery brow. 'Just like that?'

Inflexible dark-golden eyes clashed with her defiant gaze. 'Just like that. Don't try to keep me out of the loop.'

'Ari…threats and warnings don't create the kind of atmosphere that encourages trust and the sharing of confidences,' Ella countered, the flush on her cheek-bones accentuating the sapphire brightness of her eyes.

Aristandros shrugged off his jacket. 'Exactly when were you planning to tell me that you have had no contact with your family for years?'

Ella stiffened. 'I already told you that when I admitted that nobody contacted me to tell me that Susie and Timon had died. There was a huge row the night I said I wouldn't marry you. I haven't seen my family since then.'

Aristandros frowned. 'The rift developed that far back?'

'Yes. As far as Theo was concerned, it was my duty to marry you for the good of the family. He was livid. My brothers thought I was insane to say no, as well. They took your side, not mine, because you're filthy rich and a profitable business connection and I'm not,' she advanced bitterly. 'If it had happened a couple of centuries ago, they would have cheerfully locked me up in a convent and left me there to rot for the rest of my life!'

'I didn't know your family had reacted that strongly. Timon did mention that you didn't come home any more, but I assumed that that was because you were too busy with your training,' Aristandros admitted. 'Now that you're with me and Callie, they can hardly continue to behave as if you don't exist.'

'Don't you believe it. I don't get on with Theo. I never did.'

'You don't need to get on with him or anyone else you dislike now,' Aristandros informed her lazily. 'My guest lists are extremely select.'

Ella tried not to think of her stepfather's rage if he found himself suddenly excluded from the Xenakis social circle, and stilled a shiver. She watched Ari peel off his shirt to reveal the rugged musculature of his powerful chest and flat, hard stomach. He really did have the most beautiful body, she acknowledged helplessly. Her nipples tightened into taut, swollen buds beneath her bra. A clenching tight sensation between her thighs made her tense. She was remembering the smooth, steely heat of his skin when she touched him, the tormentingly sexy slide of his strong, hard body against hers. The palms of her hands prickled. The tender flesh at the heart of her throbbed with awareness.

Aristandros surveyed her with a sardonic amusement that was shockingly aware. 'No,' he breathed. 'We haven't got the time. Pleasure is all the sweeter when deferred, *glikia mou.*'

When Ella registered that he had realised just how

she was feeling at that moment, she boiled alive with embarrassment and self-loathing. Did she really find him that irresistible? How could her body get so out of step with her pride that it betrayed her? Was she really such a sexual pushover that she could hardly wait for him to touch her again? Could the experience of physical pleasure change her so much, or make her feel so disgustingly *needy*? Ella stifled an inner shudder of distaste at that image. What was happening to her? All of a sudden she felt like a hormonal teenager suffering from an embarrassing crush that had got out of control.

Callie began crying at the airport. Over-tired and rudely awakened from her rest, the little girl was in no mood to find herself in strange places surrounded by unfamiliar faces and voices. By the time the Xenakis private jet took off, Callie was fully wound up and screaming at the top of her lusty lungs. Without a word, Ella went to assist Kasma, who was looking distinctly frazzled round the edges when Callie continued to sob in spite of all her efforts to the contrary.

'This is a nightmare. Mr Xenakis is being disturbed,' the young nursemaid said guiltily to Ella. 'That should never happen.'

Ella soon discovered that there was no magic solution capable of quickly settling an exhausted and very cross toddler who was merely expressing her distress at having her settled routine destroyed. Although Callie could be distracted for a few minutes, she would soon start grizzling again. Ella took her into the sleeping compartment, sat down on the bed and rocked and sang to the little girl. Miraculously that seemed to calm Callie down, but she then objected vociferously to Ella's every attempt to put her down again. Ella took charge of her for the flight.

'Give her back to her nurse,' Aristandros instructed when they were about to board the waiting pair of limousines in Paris.

Callie tried to cling and had to be prised off Ella, a process which caused sobs to break out again. Ella found it very hard to walk away.

'Well, I don't think we need to worry about the bonding process,' Aristandros remarked with an outstanding lack of tact and sympathy. 'You're clearly a whiz in the maternal stakes. It's only day one and Callie's already doing a great impression of a limpet.'

'She's upset,' Ella fielded tightly.

'One of life's lessons is that she can't always have you when she wants you,' Aristandros countered. 'For what is left of the afternoon you will be fully occupied.'

Indeed, Ella barely had time to catch her breath at his magnificent Paris townhouse before a parade of breathtaking evening gowns arrived for her perusal. A phalanx of beauticians followed to groom her for the party. This time Ella was less tolerant of the beauty regime imposed on her. Indeed, because she would have much preferred to spend time with Callie, she fretted through every step of having her nails, hair and make-up brought to a glossy standard of perfection that she could never have achieved for herself. A maid helped her into the rich blue dress she had picked to wear, and she surveyed her reflection. Her silvery-fair hair fell in a sleek curtain round her shoulders, the designer dress a wonderful frame for her tall, slender figure. Acknowledging that she had never looked so good in her life before, however, had no impact on her frustration at the prospect of having to go through the same prolonged beauty routine every time she went out in public.

Aristandros strode through the door. 'I want you to wear this set.'

Hugely conscious of his appraisal, Ella lifted the large jewel-case he had tossed down on the bed. As she lifted the lid on a magnificent sapphire-and-diamond necklace and earrings, she gasped. 'My goodness...I'm impressed.'

'So you should be. It's a family set.'

Ella tensed. 'Then I shouldn't be wearing it.'

'They've been mouldering in a safe for decades. Someone might as well wear them,' Aristandros decreed in a bored tone that strangled the further protest on her tongue.

Feeling more than ever like a doll being decked out in decorative trappings, Ella put on the jewels. 'I want to check on Callie before we leave,' she told him then, barely glancing in the mirror to see how the superb necklace and earrings became her.

'You have five minutes.'

Ella was dismayed to discover that her niece was still awake and crying intermittently. She had also pushed away the food that Kasma had tried to give her. Ella lifted the little girl out of her cot and examined her. She soon discovered that Callie was running a temperature and had swollen lymph-glands in her neck.

'What's wrong?' Aristandros demanded from behind her a few minutes later.

'I think Callie has tonsillitis. It's probably viral, so antibiotics won't do any good.'

Aristandros turned to the PA hovering at his elbow and instructed him to arrange for a doctor to call. Ella worried at her lower lip. Callie was miserable, and Ella didn't want to leave her. Aristandros flashed her a sardonic look, and her chin came up at what she recognised as a direct challenge. She sped over to Kasma and hastily wrote down her mobile-phone number so that the nurse could keep her in touch with developments. She squeezed Callie's hot little hand and walked away with guilty tears burning her own eyes.

'She's not seriously ill, is she?' Aristandros breathed.

'No, of course she isn't. She'll be fine.'

'So, remember that you're a doctor and stop over-reacting,' Aristandros urged. 'We're going to a party.'

'I'd rather stay here,' Ella admitted, wondering how he was contriving to make her feel guilty as well. Her desire to comfort Callie had nothing whatsoever to do with her being a doctor.

'But another doctor will be checking her out. She is in the best of hands. If there is further cause for concern, we will be informed,' Aristandros pointed out levelly.

Feeling that she was making an unnecessary fuss, Ella breathed in slow and deep, and caught her reflection in a giant mirror as they descended the sweeping staircase into the hall. She barely recognised herself with the spectacular jewels glittering at her throat and ears, and the glorious dress shimmering in the soft lights.

Aristandros closed a hand over hers. 'You look gorgeous, *moli mou*.'

# CHAPTER SIX

THE PARTY WAS BEING thrown by Thierry Ferrand, an international banker and one of Aristandros's closest friends. Thierry and his wife, Gabrielle, lived on the exclusive Avenue Montaigne near the Champs-Elysées, where a huge crowd of paparazzi was waiting on the street to catch photos of the guests arriving. This time round, Ella copied Aristandros, held her head high and acted as if the members of the press were invisible.

The Ferrand apartment had been transformed with jaw-dropping extravagance into a Moroccan backdrop for the party. The colourful tented walls, hanging lanterns and the hall fountain scattered with aromatic rose petals made Ella's eyes widen. Aristandros anchored her to his side and introduced her to their hosts. She took an immediate liking to Gabrielle, a lively brunette with a contagious smile.

'I believe you're a doctor?' Thierry Ferrand remarked.

'Yes, but I'm no longer practising,' Ella replied, a touch flatly.

Gabrielle studied her in surprise. 'But why not?'

'Ella plans to devote herself to my ward and her niece, Callie,' Aristandros advanced.

'It's not easy to settle into being a lady of leisure,' Gabrielle remarked. 'I'm a corporate lawyer, Ella, and by the time my maternity leave was over I was ready to *run* back to work!'

'You have a child?' Ella asked.

Gabrielle needed no further encouragement to part Ella from Aristandros and take her upstairs to show off her adorable ten-month-old daughter who was fast asleep in her cot. The two women chatted.

'You're so normal and natural, not Ari's usual style of companion,' Gabrielle commented, her curiosity unhidden. 'Several of his exes are here tonight, and the usual squad of man-hungry singles. I shouldn't have dragged you away from him. You can't afford to leave Ari alone for a moment. Women really do go mad for him.'

Ella shrugged, still bone-deep furious with Aristandros at his stony-hearted response to Callie's illness and his determination that Ella should leave her to attend the party. As far as Ella was concerned, at that moment any woman was welcome to him. 'Ari is very well able to look after himself,' she said lightly.

Her mobile phone rang before she rejoined Aristandros, and she stayed out in the hall where it was quieter to talk to Kasma. Callie was still miserable, thirsty, but refusing to drink because of her sore throat. Furthermore, her high temperature remained a source of concern. When Ella put her phone away she registered that Aristandros was watching her. He beckoned her with in an imperious gesture that brooked no refusal. Her full lips compressed; she felt like a disobedient dog having her choke-chain yanked.

Impervious to her mood, Aristandros ran an appreciative forefinger below the pouting line of her lower lip. 'You look like a queen tonight.'

Her bright-blue eyes gleamed. 'Worthy of your investment?'

'Only time will tell,' Aristandros traded in a typically oblique response. 'But you're definitely a trophy. Every man in the room has noticed you.'

'I'm thrilled,' Ella fenced in a bored monotone.

An appreciative glint lit his shrewd dark eyes, and smouldering sensuality curved his expressive mouth. 'Not now, but you will be later. I intend to make the most of the fact that you're mine to take home, *khriso mou*.'

With his security team acting as a protective filter, a constant flow of people tried to approach Aristandros. A few were friends, most were interested in talking business opportunities, but an equal number were chancers eager to take advantage of an opportunity to meet one of the richest men in the world. Ella, engaged in watching how other women reacted to him, was constantly amazed by how much blatant encouragement and flirtation came his way, even while she stood there right beside him. He introduced her to only a handful of people.

'Let's dance,' Aristandros urged, predictably getting bored with the social chitchat, and closing his hand over hers to extract her from the crush surrounding him at speed.

It was the first time in over an hour that he had even acknowledged her existence. They had barely reached the edge of the floor when Ella's mobile phone vibrated its call signal in her clutch bag. Extracting it in spite of Aristandros's exasperated scrutiny, she left him and returned to the hall to speak to Kasma.

She learned that the doctor had visited and confirmed Ella's diagnosis of tonsillitis and the treatment she had advised. The medication was finally kicking in to reduce Callie's fever and ease the pain of her sore throat. Lighter of heart, Ella went off in search of Aristandros, wondering whether he deserved to hear the good news or not.

Gabrielle intercepted her for a chat, and it was just after parting from her that Ella's phone rang yet again. Ella was astonished when she put the phone back to her ear and heard a voice she had truly believed she might never hear again.

'Ella…is that you?' Jane Sardelos was demanding. 'That friend of yours, Lily, gave me your number.'

'*Mum*?' Ella framed, dry-mouthed with shock, wandering restlessly over to a window and staring out sightlessly at the lights of Paris.

'Where are you?'

'I'm in Paris.'

'With *him*? I understand that there was a picture of you in a British newspaper with Aristandros Xenakis. I couldn't believe it was you, until it was confirmed. What are you doing with him?' her mother pressed feverishly.

'I'm living with him and helping to look after Callie,' Ella admitted with pronounced reluctance.

'Are you out of your mind? You wouldn't marry him when he asked you, but seven years on you're happy to be his whore?'

As that horrible word struck Ella like a physical blow, perspiration dampened her upper lip. 'It's not like that, Mum—'

'Of course it is. It couldn't be any other way with a Xenakis in a leading role. We're all disgusted and embarrassed by your behaviour. What do you think this does to our standing in the eyes of family and friends? How could you be so selfish? How could you shame us like this?'

'Morals have moved on for women since the Middle Ages,' Ella protested. 'I'm in a relationship with Aristandros. It doesn't mean I've become a whore.'

'Your stepfather says that, because of you, we won't be able to visit Callie now!' Jane Sardelos complained with a sob. 'He says that if we do it will look like we're condoning the situation.'

Ella was pale. 'That's untrue and unreasonable. You're Callie's grandmother, and your right to see her should not be influenced in any way by my relationship with Ari.'

'Every picture tells a story, Ella,' her mother interrupted bitterly. 'Only last month, Ari Xenakis was with another woman, one of a *very* long line of other women. Now, all of a sudden, you're wearing a designer dress and a fortune in diamonds round your throat that you could never have afforded to buy for yourself. So, tell me—if that doesn't make you a whore, what does?'

The phone went dead with wounding emphasis, denying Ella the chance to defend herself further. A little voice asked her wryly what more she could possibly have said when it was so clear that her parent wouldn't have been prepared to listen. Numb and sick inside, and with her mother's angry accusations still ringing in her ears, Ella replaced the phone in her clutch bag. A whore: it was not a word she had ever heard on her rather prim mother's lips before. But she knew who would have voiced that abusive word in the first instance: her stepfather. Theo would have stormed and

shouted until his wife was upset enough to call her
daughter and pass on the official family opinion personally. It would not have been the first time that Theo had
used her mother as his mouthpiece.

Gabrielle Ferrand approached and addressed Ella with
a strained look on her lovely face. 'I think you'd better
go and rescue Ari before a catfight breaks out over him.'

Frowning and totally distracted after her upsetting
phone call, Ella followed the brunette and saw
Aristandros seated in a lazy sprawl across a sofa. Three
gorgeous women literally had him surrounded. They
were all over him like a rash, laughing and chattering
and giving him looks, little touches and signals that
were blatant sexual invitations. Ella felt nauseous just
watching the scene, and she waited for Aristandros to
take back his own space. If ever a guy had been born to
look after himself without any help from anyone else,
it was Aristandros. But he made no move to rebut the
advances coming his way, and when one of the women
sprang up he accompanied her on to the dance floor.

'He's been on his own almost all evening,' Gabrielle
muttered frantically. 'He's not used to being neglected.'

'You're saying I've neglected him?' Ella queried
while she watched Aristandros and a sexy redhead salsa-
dancing with considerable dexterity and enjoyment. She
hadn't even known he could move like that. Seeing him
smile and allow his body to connect intimately with
another woman's hurt like a knife cutting through tender
skin. There was an enormous amount of flirtation going
on. She was glued to the spot, trapped by ghoulish curiosity and tormented by more pain than she could have
believed possible.

'I didn't mean to sound critical,' her companion retorted uncomfortably.

'Don't worry about it. Ari has more than his fair share of charisma. Women always make excuses for him when he behaves badly,' Ella commented, having met with that female reaction to Aristandros on many occasions seven years earlier. 'But I'm afraid I don't.'

Unfortunately, Aristandros was simply being himself—an unapologetic womaniser set on amusement. Ella, however, could not bear to have that fact paraded right under her nose, particularly when her mother's condemnation of their affair was stuck like a giant immoveable rock in the middle of her every thought and reaction. Surely only a woman worthy of the label 'whore' would stand by and just accept Ari's behaviour?

'I can't stay, Gabrielle. Will you tell Ari I've left? But don't rush to do it,' Ella advised, turning on her heel to move towards the front door.

'Don't do it, Ella. I really like you, and he'll be furious if you walk out on him,' the other woman protested. 'I'm sure you're right. He's only flirting…it means absolutely nothing to him. Women of that sort come onto him every day. But you're different, not least because you happen to be wearing the Xenakis sapphires and possess a brain.'

Ella glanced back at Aristandros and the redhead. She felt sick with rage and hurt, and the depth of her reaction terrified her. The hand she employed to push her hair off her hot, damp brow was trembling. She travelled down in the lift to the ground floor where the concierge called a taxi for her. Cameras flared as she departed alone and in considerably less state than she had arrived. By then she was willing to acknowledge that she was running away from her own feelings as much as she was turning her back on a scene of public humiliation. But she was horrified by her over-sensitivity and the powerful emotions churning around inside her. Why should it matter to her so much what Aristandros did? Wasn't she capable of switching off her emotional responses to him? Just then she didn't care about the agreement she had signed. She refused to act like some whore he owned and to do as he expected regardless of how he himself behaved. A dignified departure from the party was truly the only option she could live with.

Back at the townhouse she headed straight for the nursery. Callie was slumbering peacefully, while Kasma was also asleep in her bed in the next-door bedroom with the door ajar. Ella gazed down at the little girl with a volcanic mixture of relief, love and pain rocketing through her. She reminded herself that Callie had managed fine before she was around, and would scarcely miss her, and that while she stayed her mother would refuse to visit her granddaughter. How could she allow that to happen?

Her maid helped her remove the dress and the sapphires and brought her a case when she asked. Ella put on jeans and a T-shirt and packed the few personal items she had brought from London. Then the heavy thud of the front door reverberated through the whole house, and she went rigid.

'Ella!'

Ella gulped at the harsh sound of her name on Aristandros's lips. 'I'm up here…'

Aristandros filled the doorway, strong features taut, eyes blazing a challenge. 'What in hell are you playing at?'

Ella settled bright-blue eyes on him, her chin at a defiant angle. 'What were *you* playing at? If you think I'm going to stand around while you carry on with other women in front of me, you have another thought coming!'

'You don't walk out on me in a public place… *ever*!' Aristandros raked back at her in a tone of fierce condemnation.

'You can tear up the agreement. I'm leaving you, so all bets are off.'

'You're all grown-up now,' Aristandros lanced back with derision. 'You're not allowed to run away when things get too hot for you.'

'I've never run away from anything in my life!' Ella yelled back at him, her temper unleashing like a dam overflowing.

'You run from anything that upsets you.'

'I'm not upset!' Ella practically screamed at him.

'This is not the calm, sensible Ella that I know.'

'But you don't *know* me!'

A sleek ebony brow listed. 'Don't I?'

'No, you don't!' she repeated squarely.

Aristandros settled scornful dark eyes on her. 'I have to confess that I didn't expect quite such a hysterical reaction.'

'Who are you calling hysterical?' Ella threw the demand at him furiously. 'And why the use of that word, "expect"? Are you suggesting that you deliberately chose to flirt with other women to get a reaction out of me?'

His brooding gaze locked to her hectically flushed and lovely face, Aristandros spread brown hands in a graceful gesture that neither confirmed nor denied. 'Would I do something that calculating?'

'Yes!' Ella's seething gaze was glued to him, her accusing stance unabated. 'Yes, you would if it amused you, because you are the most naturally devious and manipulative man I have ever met.'

'I could simply have told you that you were behaving badly,' Aristandros sliced back. 'It's ill-mannered to keep on taking phone calls in company.'

Outraged by that censure of her own behaviour, Ella looked at him in raw disbelief. 'How *dare* you tell me that I was behaving badly?'

His sculpted jawline squared even more, and he settled his steady gaze on her with considerable cool. 'It's the truth. Your behaviour was atrocious this evening. You went out in a sulk and you never came out of it.'

'That's a ridiculous thing to say!'

'Is it? You didn't want to leave Callie.'

'So, I'm human and caring, which is more than anyone could say of your attitude tonight. You didn't give a damn that she was ill!' Ella condemned him hotly.

'Then why did I ensure that I spoke to the doctor who attended her? And why did I check back with Kasma after that?'

Ella ground her teeth together, while giving him a look that would have withered a lesser man. 'I didn't know you'd talked to the doctor…you didn't mention it.'

'In short, I was as informed as you were, with regard to your many phone conversations,' Aristandros skimmed back, smooth as glass.

An almost overwhelming desire to slap him threatened Ella's cracking composure. 'Maybe you did speak to the doctor.'

Aristandros dealt her a tough look. 'I'm not lying. I

may not get all emotional and dramatic like you do, but that doesn't mean that I wasn't also concerned about Callie tonight.'

In receipt of that cutting, hard-hitting reproof, Ella snatched in a deep, steadying breath. 'I apologise if I misjudged you on that score.'

'You did,' Aristandros drawled, rubbing salt in an already open wound.

'But I do not sulk…and I certainly wasn't sulking earlier!' Ella slung back at him angrily.

'Maybe you have another word for it, but you were definitely in a strop.'

'I was annoyed with you,' she admitted grudgingly.

'I'm not so thick-skinned that I didn't get the message, but it was juvenile to parade your mood in public.' Aristandros sent her a grim look. 'I'm a very private man and I value discretion, but tonight you made a scene for the gossip columns. Do it one more time and I'm sending you back to London.'

Ella sent him a fiery look of sheer loathing. 'You don't need to send me any place. I'm leaving. But, my word, you are good at turning the tables, You haven't said one word about your own inappropriate behaviour, except to imply that you were giving other women encouraging signals purely to rile me.'

Aristandros laughed out loud, the unexpected sound of his amusement shattering the tense atmosphere in the room. 'Not to rile you.'

'I don't give a damn what you do,' Ella hissed, slamming the case shut and closing it.

'Liar,' Aristandros framed silkily. 'For a woman who doesn't do jealousy, you were red-hot with it tonight.'

Ella went rigid, shot him a fuming appraisal and swung the case down. She was so mad she wanted to throw things at him. How dared he accuse her of being jealous? How dared he have the power to divine feelings she had not even admitted to herself? As she stalked across the room in a rage, he cut across her path and snatched the case off her. 'What the heck do you think you're doing?' she shouted at him.

'I'm preventing you from doing something very stupid, *moli mou*,' Aristandros growled, throwing open the door of the dressing room and slinging the case in there with a resounding crash.

'I'm not some whore who's going to take whatever you throw at her!' Ella flung at him wrathfully, adrenalin pumping like crazy through her veins and making it impossible for her to stay still or even think with any rationality. 'I'm not interested in your money or what you can buy me. I'm not impressed. Nothing you could give me would persuade me to tolerate the kind of treatment you gave me tonight!'

'Even if I admit that the only woman I want is you?' Aristandros chided, leaning elegantly back against the door to close it. 'Yes, I conducted an experiment tonight, I wanted a reaction.'

'An experiment?' Ella parrotted with raw incredulity.

'A harmless one. Only a very possessive woman would get so worked up at the sight of me dancing with another woman.'

Her slim hands clenched into fists. So much emotion was hurtling round inside her that she felt frighteningly violent, and yet terrifyingly vulnerable at the same time.

'But that's all that I did,' Aristandros continued steadily. 'Nothing else.'

The hard truth of that statement struck Ella like an avalanche powerful enough to knock her off her feet. So he had danced with another woman and smiled and laughed…big deal! Social interactions of that ilk were normal at parties. What had made her overreact to such an extent? Why did she feel like rage was ready to explode out of her because she couldn't contain it? He had wanted a reaction and she had given it to him. *Only a very possessive woman…* And in spite of all her denials she *was* possessive, wasn't she? Violently possessive, with feelings and responses born from years of sitting by on the sidelines looking at photos of Ari with other women and reading about his affairs. Lily had suggested it was an unhealthy obsession, and so it was, for it had fostered a bone-deep streak of jealousy that she had not even recognised for what it was.

'Maybe I overreacted.' Ella voiced those words as though they were composed in a foreign language she found hard to pronounce. It was an acknowledgement of folly which cost her pride dear. For a moment she was standing outside herself and wondering in horror at the raging mindless jealousy that had consumed her and almost persuaded her to burn every one of her boats. Had she truly been willing to sacrifice Callie in that conflagration as well? She was genuinely appalled.

The silence stretched, drawn tight by her strain.

Ella focused on Ari's lean, classic profile, her nervous tension at an incredible high. He had set her up to see how she would react to his flirtation, and he would have had to torture her to get an apology out of her. She hated him, not only for doing that to her, but also for appreciating that what he had made her feel scared her. Suddenly she did not want to probe the precise nature and cause of the madness that had overpowered her common sense. 'The last couple of days—all the changes in my life—have been an incredible strain,' she said instead, her low voice tight and stilted, because her pride was cringing at the excuse she was using.

'Of course,' Aristandros breathed with an almost instantaneous agreement of that explanation that took her aback.

She was standing beside a mirror, and she looked at herself. The illusion of perfection was gone now, replaced by tousled hair, smudged mascara, lipstick and a T-shirt bought at a rock concert.

'Sometimes I push too hard.' Aristandros murmured that concession without any expression at all. 'But don't ever walk out on me like that again.'

Ella jerked her head in agreement, her throat taut with self-restraint. He had pushed her so hard that he had almost broken her. She was scared that she was going to cry as her jangling emotions continued to surge without any hope of being vented. She was fighting to reinstate intelligence and control. He reached for her before she could seal shut the dangerous gaps in her mental armour. The intoxicating sensuality of his mouth met hers in a hot, melting collision.

She fell into that kiss like a drowning swimmer in search of air. Hunger exploded through her every nerve ending in a chain reaction. Her hands delved deep into his thick, black hair. She could feel the raw passion pent up in his powerful body, and even the clothing between them couldn't douse her awareness of the bold ridge of his erection. The sure knowledge of his desire made resisting her own need impossible. The taste of him went to her head, and she felt dizzy and breathless. He curved his hands to her hips and settled her on the side of the bed where he proceeded to dispense with the barrier of her jeans.

'I can't salsa dance like that,' Ella heard herself say abruptly. 'Like that redhead—'

'I can take care of that,' Aristandros declared, pushing up the T-shirt and burying his face in the scented valley between her high breasts, impatiently while he peeled her free of the expensive scraps of satin and lace that still separated him from her slender curves.

Her chest rose and fell rapidly with the short, straining breaths she drew. She was hyper-aware of his every move. The abrasive brush of his stubble against the smooth slope of her breasts sent a violent shiver through her. The scent of him that close left her liquid with longing. 'I want you,' she admitted in a driven undertone.

Lush black lashes lifted from scorching golden eyes. 'I have died and gone to heaven,' Aristandros breathed softly. 'I thought I was never going to hear those words from your lips.'

'We've only been together two days!' Ella protested.

'Since when have I had patience?' Aristandros traded, long fingers skating over the tormentingly tender flesh between her thighs with a provocative skill that caused a startled gasp to part the swollen contours of her lips.

Her head tipped back against the pillows and her spine incurved. A glorious, heavy lassitude was spreading through her limbs, closely followed by energising darts of erotic sensation. She strained up to him, moaning out loud when he used his sensual mouth to tease and taste her urgently sensitive nipples. There was a sweet, painful tightness gathering in her pelvis as her inner muscles tensed and her hips squirmed in a rhythmic pattern against the sheet. She wanted, *needed* him. He turned her over on to her stomach and raised her on to her knees.

For a split second Ella didn't know what he intended but, an instant later he plunged his fully engorged manhood into her yearning flesh. Shock and wild excitement gripped her in an overpowering wave. His every deep thrust sent a hot, primitive charge to electrify her. The erotic pleasure of his virile dominance ravished her sense, and she whimpered her delight, encouraging him with every yielding flex of her hips. The seething tension and disturbed emotions she had stored up were blown away by a spellbinding orgasm that flooded her body with ecstasy and drained her of energy.

'Better?' Aristandros muttered thickly, curving her into his arms in the dizzy, dreamy aftermath when she honestly felt that she would never move again.

'Still floating,' she whispered before she could think better of it.

He leant over her, keen dark eyes lustrous as polished jet beneath the fringe of his black lashes. 'So why do you fight me?'

Ella rested her head against a brown muscular shoulder, revelling in the intimate connection of their bodies and the gloriously familiar scent of his skin. 'I like a challenge?'

His incredibly handsome features taut, Aristandros closed his arms round her and studied her with sardonic force. 'Stop it now, *hara mou*. Making me angry is a bad idea.'

Ella let her fingers trail along the line of his ruthless but aesthetically beautiful mouth. 'It makes you more human, and no matter how hard I tried I couldn't ever be all giggly and flattering and submissive.'

'That's not what I want, either. Be natural, be yourself…the way you used to be without even trying,' Aristandros urged.

Ella lost colour and turned her head away, knowing there was no going back to the young woman he was remembering. Was that what he wanted from her—the impossible? The turning back of time? How could she be twenty-one years old again and in love for the first time in her life? Even thinking about being that vulnerable again turned her stone-cold with fear inside. Loving Ari again would be a one-way ticket to hell.

'If you stop looking for problems, you'll soon find that you can enjoy what we have,' Aristandros intoned with blistering conviction. 'We're sailing back to Greece tomorrow.'

But Ella was already recalling the crazy weeks when she had been twenty-one and madly in love with him. Everybody who was anybody had spent those weeks warning her that Ari Xenakis would quickly lose interest in her. That was his track record, and his appetite for beautiful women ensured that he had an intimidating reputation as a heartbreaker. Ella, however, remembered feeling ridiculously happy during that period. Cool reflection hadn't got a look-in. She had not continually rehashed their dates in her mind looking for hints that he might be considering a future with her, either, for that possibility had not even occurred to her. She had simply adored being with him and had lived for the moment.

He had taken her out sailing a lot, for long drives and lengthy meals, rarely inviting others to join them. They hadn't gone to many parties or clubs, and when they had they hadn't stayed long. They had talked constantly and she had been herself, for she had not known how to be anything else in those days. Hard as it was to credit now, she had believed she had met her soulmate in Ari. The second time she'd called a halt to their love-making he had just laughed and made no further attempt to persuade her into bed. When he'd invited her to his grandfather's seventy-fifth birthday celebrations, she'd been overjoyed, because she had known how close Drakon was to his grandson and had felt honoured to be invited to meet him.

Now, a good deal older and wiser, she lay in the darkness, dully, painfully, reliving that final evening.

'I love you,' Aristandros had told her squarely, and she had responded with the same words. And, although he had afterwards accused her of insincerity, she had really meant what she said.

'I want to be with you. Will you marry me?' he had asked.

And her heart had bounced as high as a rubber ball, since it had not occurred to her then that he might have made the offer with sacrificial restrictions attached, a sort of trick question which was likely to come back and haunt her and leave her heartbroken. She had dimly assumed that they would get engaged and that Ari would visit her in London and marry her once she had completed her training. When he had got up to make a speech in honour of his grandfather's birthday, he had announced their engagement—along with the news that she would be giving up medicine.

Reality had swiftly burst her bubble of happiness. After a ferocious argument he had dumped her, and minutes later retracted the announcement he had made. Her family had taken her home in disgrace, unable to believe or come to terms with the startling idea that she could possibly have refused to marry a Xenakis.

Aristandros catapulted her back into the present by hauling her up against his lithe, muscular frame. Blue eyes very wide, she clashed with his heavily lidded, smouldering, dark-golden gaze. This man, she acknowledged with a fast-beating heart, already had the power to make her feel bitterly jealous and act in an irrational way. He was dangerous, was a very dangerous threat in every way to her peace of mind.

'Once is not enough,' he growled sexily, half under his breath. 'I still want you, *moli mou*.'

And some very basic element in Ella exulted in her sexual hold over him. In that instant, her heart racing, her pulses quickening and her treacherous body quivering with anticipation, she was a slave to the promise of the pleasure he would give her and she had no time to spare for agonising over the label that other people might affix to her position in his life.

# CHAPTER SEVEN

TEN days later, Hellenic Lady arrived in Athens.

Ella was still in bed in the yacht's magnificent main state-room and she was devouring the British newspapers, several of which contained items about her. It was an extraordinary experience to suddenly see herself appear for the first time in print in the guise of a celebrity. In her case, however, her fame was purely borrowed from association with Aristandros. She was variously described as his 'new companion, Dr Dazzler', 'Calliope's sexy aunt' and 'the family black-sheep'. Her fascination only died when she came on a disturbing couple of paragraphs that suggested that her family had shut the door on her because she was a promiscuous wild-child.

Aristandros strode in, clad today in a dark pinstripe suit of faultless tailoring that made the most of his tall, well-built body. He was said to electrify a room when he walked into it, and Ella was certainly not immune to that effect. She tensed against the heaped-up pillows, sapphire-blue eyes very wide in the heart-shaped delicacy of her face.

'I've been working for four hours. One glimpse of you,' Aristandros husked, strolling over to the side of the bed, neatly sidestepping the sprinkle of discarded toys that betrayed Callie's visit earlier that morning, 'And I want to get straight back into bed.'

Her body tingled, nerve-endings uncurling in anticipation, heart rate speeding up. It was just sex, and she regularly told herself that fact. But she still had to acclimatise to the magnetic draw of wanting to rip his clothes off every time she saw him.

With an impatient sound he scooped up the heap of newspapers on her lap. 'Haven't you learned yet? You don't *ever* read your own publicity. I pay my lawyers to read it for me,' he confided, discarding the tumbled, crackling newspaper sheets in an untidy heap on the carpet. 'I did appreciate the Dr Dazzler line, but not the wild-child tag. Someone's confused you with your sister Susie, and an official apology will be appearing this week.'

Her full lower lip had parted from the upper. 'Are you saying you've complained?'

Aristandros shrugged and removed his jacket, pitching it on to the ottoman by the wall and removing his shoes. Smouldering dark-golden eyes assailed her as he straightened to his full six-foot-three-inches of height. 'I'm still convinced that you've only ever been a wild-child with me.'

'Well, you'd be wrong.'

'You're all talk and no action,' Aristandros quipped with a razor-edged challenge in his gaze. 'In bed you don't know how to do anything until I do it first!'

Cheeks as red as ripe strawberries, Ella slung him a

furious look. 'I suppose you think that that kind of crack is funny?'

'No, I find it highly entertaining that, while most women prefer to minimise the number of their past lovers, you want to claim more,' he drawled, smooth as silk.

'Why on earth are you getting undressed?' Ella demanded abruptly, finally taking notice of that fact.

'And, in spite of that scarlet past, she still has a mind as pure as driven snow. Haven't I corrupted you in any way?' Aristandros mocked, skimming off his boxers in a manoeuvre that soon made it blatantly obvious why he had stripped off.

'Oh…' A darting little frisson of sexual heat travelling through her slender length, Ella sank back into the pillows in a manner that might almost have been labelled inviting as he joined her in the bed.

'Oh…' Aristandros teased, reclining back and drawing her to him with clear intent. As her slim fingers found the bold, jutting length of his arousal, he emitted a roughened groan of appreciation. 'Oh *yes*,' he growled hungrily. 'You beat the hell out of a coffee break, *khriso mou*.'

For a split second, that quip made Ella hesitate, but in truth she found his sexual spontaneity and raw potency as irresistible as she found him. His sensual mouth on hers was like a brand that burned to create a flame that was never quite doused. No matter how much he kissed her, enough was never enough. His tongue thrust between her lips and released a flood of excitement that lit a feverish trail of response through her entire body. He wrenched her nightdress out of his path and closed his lips on a swollen pink nipple.

Sweet sensation gripped her while his knowing mouth

travelled between one taut peak and the other, laving and teasing her sensitised flesh until she moaned. With the impatient stroke of his forefinger, he probed the slick, wet welcome at the heart of her before pulling her under him with an unashamed urgency that thrilled her. He plunged into her hard and fast, and her eager body rose to meet his. Excitement was as intense and searing as a fire inside her. He pleasured her with long, forceful strokes, pushing back her knees to gain even deeper penetration. She felt like she had hitched a ride to the stars, and the spellbinding pleasure devoured her. She heard herself cry out and buck under him as breathtaking heat and the waves of ecstasy roared through her. In the sheer power of that sensual conflagration, she was helpless and mindless in her response. He slammed into her one last time with an uninhibited shout of satisfaction.

For a timeless moment she lay under him, rejoicing in his weight, the pound of his heart and the rasp of his breath. At that instant she felt as she often did, over-whelmed by the level of mind-blowing pleasure. But not so overwhelmed by physical sensation that she didn't enjoy the brush of his mouth against her brow in a salutation, and the tightening of his powerful arms around her in what might almost have been a hug. He didn't do hugs, but she lived in hope. She loved what he did to her in bed, but she loved the closeness in the aftermath even more, and never, ever stirred a muscle to break their connection before he did.

It was a shock when Aristandros tensed, voiced an unmistakeable Greek curse and pulled back from her in a violent movement that spoke more of rejection than of anything else.

Hard eyes struck her questioning gaze in a near-physical blow. He struck the wooden headboard with a powerful fist, and made her flinch back from him in consternation.

'What?' she gasped in bewilderment.

'I forgot to use a condom,' Aristandros bit out rawly.

'Oh…dear,' was all Ella could think to comment in that unbearably tense moment. The date when she was to start taking the contraceptive pill had not yet arrived, and she had warned him that other precautions would be necessary for the first couple of weeks they were together. Until now he had followed that rule with scrupulous care and had left no margin for error.

Aristandros sprang out of bed like a hungry tiger leaping on prey and swung round to glare at her. 'Is that all you've got to say?' he demanded icily. 'I don't want a child.'

A chill ran through Ella, and she wondered why that statement should feel like a slap in the face when she was equally as keen to avoid the trauma of an unplanned conception. She was frantically working out dates inside her head, which was difficult, as recent changes in her routine appeared to have unsettled her once-regular menstrual cycle. 'I'm afraid it probably wasn't the best time to overlook the precautions,' she admitted ruefully. 'I could be at my most fertile right now.'

'I can't believe I forgot!' Aristandros grated as if she hadn't spoken. 'I'm never careless.'

'Either of us could be infertile,' Ella remarked. 'You'd be surprised how common it is.'

Aristandros gave her a look of outrage and compressed his handsome mouth, as though the suggestion that he might not be able to father a child was a gross insult to his masculinity.

Ella stayed where she was until he had showered and departed. She was in shock, but she also felt that she had just received a much-needed wake-up call. For the past ten days she had been with Aristandros almost round the clock. He got up before six every morning to work with his personal staff. At eight, he joined Ella and Callie for breakfast. If he hadn't yet reached the stage of being able to totally relax and play with the little girl, he was at least unbending from his rigidity around her, and developing the ability to talk to her and get to know her.

Life on the vast luxury yacht was excessively comfortable and easy. The crew attended to their every need, and very often even before Ella realised that something was required or even available. She was waited on hand and foot and encouraged to be a lady of leisure, with nothing more important to consider than her next visit to the well-equipped beauty salon and its staff on the deck below. It was a lifestyle that could never have come naturally to her, but it gave her the opportunity to spend a great deal of time with Callie. The bond between Ella and her biological child already ran deep and strong. While she would never have chosen to frolic in a swimming pool for her own benefit, she was happy to do so when the purpose was to teach Callie to swim, and the occasions when Aristandros had joined them had proved by far the most entertaining.

'Sailing home to Greece' as Ari had termed it, had been more of a leisurely cruise than a straightforward trip between A and B. *Hellenic Lady* had called in at several islands. Aristandros had taken her out clubbing on Crete, and out to dinner on Corfu. Afterwards they had walked through the narrow streets of the old town hand-in-hand. And who had reached for his hand? Ella clamped cool palms to her agonised face. Hand holding? She felt ill. Just then her mortification was so intense that she honestly wanted to slap herself hard. How could she have been so stupid as to initiate such a foolish gesture? Romance had nothing to do with their relationship.

She was his mistress—the woman currently meeting the demands of his high-voltage sex drive—not his girl-friend, his fiancée or his wife. And, just as he had wanted, she was always sexually available, and not because she was afraid to be in breach of that outrageous contract that she had signed! No, indeed; the nagging hunger of desire that tormented her had nothing to do with contractual obligations or pride. She couldn't keep her hands off him, in or out of bed. The need to touch, to connect, was like a fever, a terrible temptation she fought day and night. She was appalled by how attached she had already become to being with Aristandros.

Yet nothing could have more clearly delineated the gulf between them than his reaction to the possibility of her falling pregnant. Somehow he had made her feel like a one-night stand he had picked up, a stranger he barely knew, a female body in which he had no interest once he had sated his most pressing sexual need. If she con-ceived, he would view it as a disastrous development, and she could only hope that the situation didn't arise.

Fresh from the shower and with a towel wrapped round her, she was walking back into the state room when Aristandros entered. 'Did I mention that I'm staging a social gathering at my Athens home this afternoon? No?' he queried lazily, when she gave him a look of frank dismay. 'I have some business to tie up with fellow investors and you'll be acting as my hostess.'

'Thanks for the last-minute warning!' Ella gasped.

'At least you don't need to worry about booking time in the beauty salon,' Aristandros quipped.

They flew from the yacht direct to the property. His villa on the Greek mainland was set in an unspoilt area of countryside. Surrounded by olive groves and vineyards, it enjoyed superb views of the mountains. Ella was surprised by the rural setting, for when she had last known Aristandros he and his grandfather had been very firmly rooted in the vast Xenakis townhouse in Athens.

'Drakon still prefers life in the city, but I like to escape the skyscrapers and the traffic at the end of the day, and here I'm still less than half an hour from the airport,' Aristandros advanced. 'I spend a lot of time on the island now. I can work from home, and it's very private.'

'It's beautiful here as well,' Ella commented, wondering just how many different properties he owned round the world, and even if he knew himself without having to think about it.

'The pearls look good on you.'

In receipt of that remark, Ella brushed the magnificent necklace at her throat with uneasy fingertips. It was matched by the pearl-drop earrings she wore, and most probably worth a fortune. A slender diamond-studded designer watch also encircled her wrist. She had no idea how much her growing collection of jewellery was worth, since nothing as vulgar as price was ever mentioned when Aristandros insisted on buying her a gift. The previous week an imposingly correct jeweller had flown out to the yacht with a magnificent selection of world-class gems for Ari's private examination. He had decided on the pearls, which were reputed once to have belonged to an Indian maharajah. Ella had already decided that when she and Aristandros parted she would leave all such unsolicited presents behind her.

Presumably Aristandros was accustomed to rewarding the women in his bed with gifts of extraordinary generosity. But the glorious jewels made her feel more like a trophy piece of arm-candy than ever, and frighteningly deserving of the offensive label her mother had fired at her: *Whore*. Was that how other people saw her as well—a costly parasite earning a rich reward for pleasing her tycoon lover in bed? She cringed inwardly at the suspicion that she had sunk so low. Ironically, at a moment when she was dressed from head to toe in designer clothing, and sporting fabulous gems, her once-healthy self-esteem was at a very low ebb. She was very much afraid that on Ari's terms she was just an expensive accoutrement, like a flash car—and, just as he only drove the world's most expensive cars, he wouldn't dream of showing off a woman without the spectacular looks, clothing and jewellery that paraded his wealth.

Catering staff already had the food and drinks for the reception organised. The house was immaculate, very contemporary in design, and perfect for large-scale entertainment. A svelte figure in a knee-length plum silk cocktail dress and stiletto heels, Ella joined Aristandros on the outside terrace where drinks were being served just as the first guests arrived. It was not very long before her cheeks were hot with self-consciousness. While everyone was scrupulously polite, it was brutally obvious that she was the focus of a great deal of curiosity. She tormented herself with worries of what stories might already have appeared in the local press about her. Ironically, it was the arrival of Ari's courteous grandfather, Drakon, which caused her the greatest embarrassment.

'Ella,' the dignified older man murmured, stooping to kiss her cheeks in a kindly salute of polished Xenakis charm. 'Is it rude to admit that, while I am delighted to renew our acquaintance, I very much regret meeting you in these circumstances?'

Lean, strong face broodingly dark and taut, Aristandros answered for her. 'Yes, it is rude, and quite unnecessary, Drakon. What circumstances?'

The elderly Greek's shrewd eyes withstood the challenge of his grandson's grim appraisal. 'Don't pretend to be obtuse, Ari,' he advised drily.

Rigid with mortification, and keen to escape the fallout and any further discussion, Ella was quick to move away to intercept Callie, who was toddling across the room to greet her. Helplessly smiling as the little girl came full tilt into her arms, Ella hugged her. Callie, adorable in a little blue-cotton dress, was as pretty as a picture, and already noticeably more confident and talkative than she had been when Ella had first met her. Callie expressed a desire for the toy rabbit that she took almost everywhere with her, and Ella was taking her back to Kasma to ask where it was when she heard the raised voices sounding from a room off the hall.

Behaving as if there was nothing untoward occurring,

the young nurse lifted Callie and took her back upstairs to look for the rabbit.

'If Callie is Ella's as you say,' Drakon Xenakis was thundering in Greek, 'Give her to Ella and let them both go!'

'I'm not prepared to let either of them go,' Aristandros drawled as quietly as if he was in church, his audible calm a striking contrast to his grandfather's anger. 'I had a very comprehensive agreement drawn up that suits Ella and I very well—'

'A *legal* agreement? Is this what I raised you to do— to corrupt a young woman who only wants access to her own child? Is this what it takes to appeal to your jaded appetites now, Ari? If you had a single streak of decency left, you would marry her, for you've destroyed her reputation!'

'The days when women needed to be whiter than white are long gone, Drakon. Thankfully I live in a world with far more enlightened sexual mores,' Aristandros retorted bitingly. 'Whether you believe it or otherwise, Ella is happy with me—'

'She's worth more than any of the gold-digging sluts you specialise in, and you're treating her worse than all of them! The only thing I see in this scenario is revenge, Ari…and it's ugly and unworthy of you.'

Nausea stirring in her stomach, and her blood running cold in her veins, Ella stumbled away from the partly open door before she could be caught in the act of eavesdropping. Drakon's opinion hit her as hard as a physical blow, because Ari's grandfather knew him well, indeed far better than she did. She had been quick to discard the idea of Aristandros acting in revenge—too quick? Certainly she had much preferred to believe that the secret of her ongoing attraction was more her being a *femme fatale* whom he had never forgotten. But how likely was that interpretation? Was it not more likely that Aristandros was taking revenge for her rejection all those years ago? He had made her walk away from her career, her home and even her principles. He had made her enjoy her captivity in the gilded cage of his life. No; he hadn't *made* her do anything, she acknowledged, trying to be honest with herself—she had made the choices she'd had to make to be with Callie, the daughter of her heart, and to be fair he had kept his promises.

Even so, revenge struck her as the more apt explanation for Ari's continuing interest in her. Why else would a man who could have the most beautiful women in the world settle for an inexperienced and unsophisticated doctor who was ill at ease with a party lifestyle? He would not have sacrificed his own desires and preferences for Callie's benefit. In fact, most probably Callie had merely been used as a weapon to put pressure on her biological mother. Having acquired the child, he had also acquired the perfect means to make Ella dance to his chosen tune, and that was exactly what he had done.

In the shaken-up state she was now in, it was the wrong moment for Ella to set eyes on her family for the first time in seven years. Her stepfather, a heavily built man with thick, grey hair, was standing on the terrace with a drink in his hand. Her mother, a slight, fair-haired woman in a pink dress, was by his side. Behind them stood two tall, dark young men—her half-brothers, grown to adulthood without her knowledge. Ella paled when Theo Sardelos looked right through her, and her mother, her face full of painful discomfiture, turned her head quite deliberately to avoid seeing her only surviving daughter. Her twin half-siblings, disdaining such pretences, stared stonily back at her, their scowling attitude one of pure belligerence.

Ella was very angry that Aristandros had put her family on the guest list without telling her. Conscious that she was not the only person present capable of noting that her family was giving her the cold shoulder, she forced herself to address her stepfather with a perfunctory greeting before turning to her mother to say, 'Would you like to come and see Callie?'

'No, she would not,' Theo Sardelos growled, slinging his stepdaughter a look of profound distaste as he answered for his wife, a controlling habit of his that Ella remembered with repulsion. 'Your presence here makes that impossible.'

Her olive branch broken and discarded unceremoniously at her feet, Ella did not respond. She knew the older man well enough to appreciate that he would relish any opportunity to embarrass her in front of an audience. Although it took considerable courage, she kept on smiling and moved on, beckoning a waiter to ensure a clutch of late arrivals were served at the buffet. Kasma brought Callie back down, and the little girl, her stuffed rabbit now tucked securely under her arm, sped back to Ella's side to clutch at her skirt in a possessive hold.

It took real effort for Ella to continue to play hostess and chat and smile as though nothing was wrong. Every so often she bent down to touch her hand gently on Callie's head and remind herself of what she had gained, and why she had forged her devil's bargain. Her thoughts were tumultuous. Aristandros had only told the truth to his grandfather: she *was* happy with him. Did that mean that at heart she was a slut? Sharing Ari's bed and being with him was more of a pleasure than a punishment. It shook her to admit that to herself. He had held her to ransom over an innocent child's head, and yet whenever he wanted her she was still his for the asking. What did that say about her? Shame and confusion engulfed her in a hot, creeping tide of remorse.

Lily had texted her only that day: *are you his Dr Dazzler by accident or design?*

Ella still didn't know how to answer that question. While the original design had been Ari's, it now sometimes seemed to her as though she had simply surrendered, and had used Callie as her excuse for doing so. When Aristandros touched her, she went up in flames. What had started out purporting to be a sacrifice had become a delight. If she was a victim, of revenge she was a willing victim and that reality made her cringe.

Lean, breathtakingly handsome face cool as ice-water, his carriage as always superb, Aristandros strode towards her. Nothing in his expression revealed any sign of annoyance over his recent dispute with his grandfather. Her heart lurched behind her breastbone, her mouth running dry as he rested a hand at the base of her spine and whispered, 'Why aren't you with your family?'

## CHAPTER EIGHT

ELLA shot him a darkling glance of disbelief. 'Why on earth did you invite my family when you knew there was a rift between us all?' she flung at him, half under her breath, furious that he had set her up for such a confrontation even after she had told him that her family was at odds with her and had been for years.

'I thought the invitation would help…I even thought you might be pleased to see them!' Aristandros responded, his strong face taut

'It was a serious mistake. You shouldn't have interfered. My family don't want to be around me when I'm with you,' Ella revealed in a bitter surge of confidence. 'In fact, Theo says they can't have anything to do with Callie while I'm here.'

Aristandros rested his stunned gaze on her, and swore below his breath. 'That's outrageous, *khriso mou*. He cannot insult you below my roof. Anyone who does so is an unwelcome guest.'

'There's not much you can do about it. He's a very stubborn man. Just ignore it, as I am, and hopefully in time he'll get over his pique. You shouldn't have asked them here.' Ella's teeth worried anxiously at her full lower lip as she absorbed the stormy flare of gold immediately lightening Ari's spectacular eyes. Assurances that he should *not have* done something went down like a brick with a guy who had based his entire life on doing what he wanted to do on every occasion. Callie vented a cross little sob and tugged at Ella's dress, while resting heavily up against her legs as tiredness took her over.

'Sardelos has upset you,' Aristandros growled. 'I will not tolerate that.'

'Stay out of this, it's not your business,' Ella hissed in a frantic undertone as she bent to comfort Callie, and lifted the child up into her arms. 'If you interfere any more it'll just cause endless trouble and resentment. I'm going to put Callie down for a nap. Promise me that you'll mind your own business.'

Aristandros dealt her a sardonic look of disbelief. 'You *are* my business. If they insult you, they insult me, for it is my wish that you be here and I will not tolerate any show of disrespect.'

Anchoring the little girl on her hip, and keeping her there with one straining arm—for Callie was no lightweight—Ella rested what she hoped was a soothing hand on his chest. 'Nobody is being disrespectful of you,' she hastened to assert in an effort to pour oil on troubled waters. 'Please don't get involved…*please*. Don't play with fire.'

With that final, urgent plea for forebearance, Ella headed off with Callie. Kasma offered to carry the little girl upstairs, but Ella demurred; in the mood she was in, the feel of Callie's clinging arms was comforting. The very last thing she needed was for Aristandros to wade

in to an already delicate situation. She was all too painfully aware that her mother invariably suffered when
Theo lost his temper

When she glanced down from the landing, she saw
the male guests were gathering in the hall, and then
moving on into Ari's office-suite, where a conference
room would house the investors' meeting he had mentioned. The sight of what had to be an excellent diver-
sion for unreliable masculine tempers and egos filled her
with a giant sense of relief. When business was at stake,
Aristandros would surely not waste his energy thinking
about anything else.

'Shoos,' Callie sounded importantly as Ella removed
her sandals. 'Socks.'

'Very good,' Ella applauded, turning up Callie's
earnest little face to drop a kiss on it.

'My goodness, she's talking now...'

Ella almost jumped out of her skin, and twisted her
head round to focus on the older woman in the
doorway. 'Mum?'

'Theo's gone into the meeting, and I asked a maid to
bring me up,' Jane Sardelos explained in a harried undertone. 'He would be furious if he knew I was here with you.'

'He gets furious far too easily. Why won't you leave
him?' Ella asked in a pained, heartfelt undertone that
betrayed her incomprehension on that score.

'He's my husband and he loves me. He's been a good
father and provider. You don't understand,' the older
woman proclaimed, just as she had throughout Ella's
teenaged years. 'Let me see my grandchild... She's the
very image of you, Ella.'

Ella noticed that the little girl showed no sign of recognising her grandmother. 'You haven't seen much of her, have you?'

'Susie was very difficult after the birth,' Jane murmured sadly as she stared down with softening eyes at the sleepy little girl and sat down beside the cot. 'She didn't want my advice, or anyone else's, and it was obvious that her marriage was breaking down and she didn't care. I saw Calliope a few times when she was very young, but Susie really didn't want to be bothered with visitors, and she was quite unpleasant on several occasions.'

'I think that Susie very probably had post-natal depression,' Ella contended gently.

'She wouldn't see a doctor, though.' Jane Sardelos shook her head heavily. 'I did what I could, but your sister was always very wilful and I'm afraid she paid the price for it. But I don't want you to pay a price as well.'

'Let's not talk about me,' Ella cut in hurriedly.

'Half the world is talking about you since you moved in with Ari Xenakis. He might want you today, Ella, but there are no guarantees for the next day, or the one after that. I shouldn't have called you what I did, but I was very upset when I found out that you were living with him.'

'I can't discuss Aristandros with you. I'm an adult and I've made my choice. I don't expect you to agree with it, but there's no point arguing about it, because it won't change anything. Mum, it's seven years since I even saw you,' Ella reminded the older woman painfully. 'Let's not waste this moment.'

'A moment is really all we have,' the older woman acknowledged tautly, scrambling up to wrap her arms round her taller daughter in a sudden jerky movement that betrayed the precarious state of her nerves. 'I've missed you so much, particularly after Susie passed away. But Theo is outraged by this situation. He says that because of your very public affair he's lost face.'

Ella hugged her mother back with warm affection. 'For goodness' sake, he always exaggerates—he is only my stepfather.'

'You've embarrassed the whole family,' another voice delivered in condemnation from the doorway.

Ella focused on her half-brother, Dmitri, as her mother backed away from her. 'Stop making excuses for your father,' Ella urged. 'He found fault with everything I ever did because I stood up to him. He doesn't like me and he never will.'

'Mum…in a few minutes Dad will be looking for you. You need to come back downstairs.' Having issued that warning, Dmitri turned away from Ella, who was livid with him for behaving like a pompous prat.

'Do you still live at home?' she asked her brother. Watching her mother turn pale with fear as she'd registered the risk of her husband discovering that she had defied his dictates took Ella back to all the years that she did not want to recall. Years blighted by sudden violence and discord, and Jane's increasingly pathetic attempts to make their warped family life seem normal.

'Not for years. Stavros and I have an apartment.'

'So, I can't ask you to look after Mum tonight,' Ella remarked stiffly.

Immediately grasping her meaning, Dmitri reddened, said nothing and concentrated on hurrying the older woman out of the room. He was as desperate to avoid conflict with his father as Ella had once been. She would never forget the tension of living in the Sardelos household, where everyone had worked hard in speech and action to avoid doing anything that might annoy Theo. While the initial conflict in the marriage had arisen over her stepfather's infidelity, he had soon found plenty of other issues to set his temper off.

'I'll try to phone you.' Jane flung the promise over a thin shoulder.

'Any time, and for any reason. I'll always be here for you.' Ella returned that assurance with a slight wobble in her strained voice. Until she had seen her mother again, she had not allowed herself to acknowledge how much she had missed the older woman's presence in her life.

Ella settled Callie for her nap, and left the nursery to return to the female guests milling round the terrace and the spacious drawing-room. She discovered that she was very much the centre of attention, and was reminded of how curious people always were about Aristandros—his lifestyle, his possessions, his women, his family and background, all of which had supplied years of gossip fodder for newspaper and magazine articles. Tactfully sidestepping the more intrusive questions, she moved from one knot of women to the next.

The men filtered back in little groups to their partners, and the guests began to go home. Drakon Xenakis made a point of bidding Ella goodbye before his departure. She was filled with consternation, however, when she saw her stepfather halt on the threshold of the room and simply jerk his head in her mother's direction in a peremptory signal that he wanted to leave. Even at a glance she could tell that the older man was incensed with anger, the colour high on his fleshy face, his mouth compressed into an aggressive whitened line. As she watched her stepfather, her brothers and her mother trooped out without a further word to anyone.

Ella tracked Aristandros down to the office that connected with the conference room.

'What the heck did you say to my stepfather?' she demanded curtly.

His personal assistants froze in incredulity, and she flushed, wishing she had exercised greater self-control, and waited until she could speak to him alone.

Face impassive, Aristandros lounged back against the edge of the desk behind him and viewed her with hard, dark eyes. 'Don't address me in that tone,' he told her with a chilling bite.

Ella was mortified when only then did he dismiss his staff with a meaningful shift of one authoritative hand. 'I'm sorry,' she muttered. 'I should have waited a moment.'

'All that I ask is that you remember your manners,' Aristandros responded grimly.

'I was concerned—I saw Theo stomping out in a complete rage. What happened?' she pressed, anxiously pacing the carpet in front of him.

'I informed Sardelos and your brothers that they are not welcome here if they cannot treat you with respect.'

Ella shot him an appalled look. 'I don't need you to fight my battles for me!'

'I invited them, and this is my house. Their behaviour was unacceptable. What I say goes, *khriso mou*.' Aristandros spelt out that reminder without a second of hesitation

'I've never seen my stepfather so angry, and no wonder! You humiliated him in front of his sons, and he'll blame me for that as well!' Ella lamented. 'I could kill you for interfering in something that has nothing to do with you.'

'I defended you and you're behaving as if *I* did something wrong?' Aristandros growled, his eyes smouldering dark gold with angry disbelief. 'You've let your stepfather bully you for so long that you can't see the wood for the trees. He needs to be shown his boundaries by someone he can't influence or control.'

Ella spun away from Aristandros, her thoughts heavily preoccupied with the likely fallout from the comeuppance which Theo had been given. Her stepfather set great store on his association with the Xenakis family; the sudden loss of that favourable social standing would not only humble him but also harm his business prospects. She wanted to yell and shout at Aristandros for acting with a heavy hand, but knew he had no comprehension of the likelihood that her mother would ultimately pay for her husband's sins.

'You interfered by inviting them here when you knew there was a serious rift between us,' she accused tautly. 'For goodness' sake, my mother phoned me in Paris to tell me that they thought I was acting like a whore with you!'

Aristandros went rigid. 'A *whore*?'

'Nobody suffers from the illusion that *I'm* the one paying for the designer dresses and the jewellery!' Ella slashed back bitterly. 'How do you expect people to view me?'

His brilliant gaze semi-screened by his lush, black lashes, Aristandros stared broodingly back at her, his eloquent mouth clenching hard. 'It's not a question I paused to consider—'

Ella raised a dubious brow. 'You didn't? Well, my goodness, you considered everything else that related to image. Why else was I repackaged as a dress-up doll?'

But Aristandros wasn't listening. He was frowning darkly. 'So that's why you walked out on me in Paris…'

Ella tossed her head, her pale hair fanning back across a flushed cheekbone and brushed away by an impatient hand. 'That phone call may have made me a little touchier than I should have been.'

He treated her to an austere appraisal. 'But once again it underlines how little you listen to what I tell you, *khriso mou.*'

The intimidating tension in the atmosphere was ringing alarm-bells in Ella's head. Aware of his renewed anger, but at a loss as to its cause, she blinked in bemusement. 'I'm not sure I know what you're getting at.'

'That you should have told me about that phone call that distressed you,' Aristandros grated impatiently. 'And don't you *dare* tell me that it was none of my business, because your behaviour that night spoke for you! I don't like the way you keep secrets from me. It's dishonest.'

Ella sucked in a startled breath at that hard-hitting denunciation. She could not credit what he was saying to her. 'You have some nerve to say that to me!' she slung back. 'Maybe there's a lot about you I don't like: a guy who uses lawyers to blackmail me into an indefensible agreement to let him do whatever he likes, while I do *only* as he likes. Is that what you call having a relationship? No wonder none of them last longer than five minutes! On what basis do you think I would give you my trust?'

'Stop there before this gets blown out of all proportion,' Aristandros advised harshly.

But Ella was trembling with pent-up emotion, and she could no more have held back what she was feeling inside than she could have contained a tornado. Her blue eyes were as bright a blue as the heart of a flame. 'Do you think I could trust a man who once told me he loved me and wanted to marry me, but who dumped me less than an hour later? And why—because I couldn't match the perfect blueprint of a wife that you had in your head? Because I had the audacity to want something more than love and your money to focus on? Would you have given up business and the art of making money to marry me?'

Aristandros had lost colour below his bronzed skin, and it lent a curious ashen quality to his usual healthy glow. He stared steadily back at her, however, predictably not yielding an inch of ground. 'We're not having this conversation,' he told her.

'I'm not asking for permission, and I'm not having a conversation. You may not have noticed yet but I'm *shouting* at you!' Ella yelled at him at full tilt, inflamed by his stony resistance to her verbal attack and his refusal to respond.

'*Stamates*…that is enough,' Aristandros bit out icily.

'I hate you…even your grandfather thinks you're treating me badly… Yes—not content with having lousy manners, I listen outside doors as well!' Ella threw wildly at him, tears burning her eyes, and rage swelling like a giant balloon inside her to restrict her breathing. 'I'm definitely not the perfect woman you think is your due. You'd better pray that I'm not fertile!'

And with that final parting shot, which was as low as she could think to sink, Ella fled out past the clutch of his staff in the hall who were trying to act like everything was normal and avoid looking at her. She took the stairs two at a time, with a huge sob locked halfway up her throat, and raced into the master bedroom—her fourth since she had moved in with him.

Ella very rarely cried. A sad film or a book could make the moisture well up, but it took a great deal to make her cry. Now she flung herself across the bed and sobbed her heart out. She was worried about her mother having to go home alone with an enraged and violent man who liked to use her as a punch bag. But, most of all, she was distraught over the row she had just had with Aristandros. It had started out a small argument and just grown and grown until it had torn apart the fragile fabric of the peace they had established, and destroyed the bonds they had somehow contrived to build. Now there could be no hiding from ugly but revealing truths, such as his fear that she might conceive a child he didn't want.

Why was she getting upset over being at odds with him? At least she had spoken her mind on the trust issue. She had trusted him once seven years back and look where that had got her—dumped, heartbroken and rejected by her family. Aristandros, however, had picked himself up in time-honoured Xenakis style from the debacle of the engagement that had only lasted five minutes with a widely reported cruise round the Mediterranean, where he had stopped off at various ports to booze and carouse non-stop with promiscuous women. Ella struck the mattress with a clenched fist. She was still so angry she wanted to scream. She hated him; she truly *hated* him!

But it was almost time for Callie to have her evening

meal, and Ella cherished her bedtime routine with the toddler. She hauled herself off the bed and groaned out loud when she saw her swollen eyes and ruined make-up. No longer having access to the beautician's tools, and in possession of very few cosmetics of her own, Ella did her best to conceal the ravages of her uncontrolled crying-jag.

Callie was a delight and a consolation that evening. Ella played with her in her bath, dried her little wriggling body and cuddled the little girl while she read her a story.

Callie was happily making quacking sounds when Aristandros appeared on the nursery threshold. 'I fancy eating out tonight,' he announced.

'I don't care if I never eat again,' Ella lied, for in truth she was starving, but could not have borne letting him get away with pretending that nothing had happened—even if she did suspect that that might be a wiser approach than running the risk of a post mortem about the row.

Callie slid off her knee and padded barefoot over to him, holding her arms up and demanding to be lifted. Possibly relieved that someone appeared to appreciate his presence, Aristandros crouched down and swept her up into his arms as if he'd been doing it for years. But in fact he had never done it before, and Ella watched slyly from beneath her lashes as Callie explored his hair, smothered him in wet kisses and yanked at his tie before settling down happily, trying to steal one of his shiny gold cuff-links.

'Quack,' Callie told him importantly, and then she stuck out a foot. 'Socks,' she added.

'You're not wearing any,' Aristandros pointed out.

Callie pouted. 'Shoos.'

'You're not wearing shoes either.'

'She's trying to dazzle you with her new words, not have a conversation,' Ella explained.

'It's more appealing than conversation,' Aristandros remarked, shrewd dark eyes skimming from Callie's smiling little face to Ella's frozen expression. 'You're sulking again.'

'I'm not sulking,' Ella pronounced through gritted teeth. 'I'm just can't think of anything to say to you.'

'Is there a difference?' Aristandros strolled across the room to lower Callie gently back down on to Ella's lap. As their eyes connected in an unexpected encounter, she was shockingly aware of the raw charge of his masculinity, and her mouth ran dry.

'I'm going out,' he said casually.

Ella almost called him back to say that she would go out after all. Watching him go out alone had no appeal whatsoever. Her contentment at her relaxing session with Callie ebbed fast. No woman in their right mind would encourage Aristandros to go out by himself—but no woman with any pride would accompany him after the day that had just passed and the words that had been exchanged, Ella reasoned with spirit. When Callie was safely asleep she went downstairs and ate a light meal without appetite, while she watched the clock and wondered how long he would stay out and who he was with. Athens was a lively, cosmopolitan city with many clubs.

Having decided on an early night, she went for a bath, then phoned Lily and finally told her friend everything she had previously withheld.

'He's a total bastard!' Lily hissed in disgust.

Ella winced, finding that opinion not as much to her taste as she might have hoped. 'Occasionally he's...very challenging.'

'I don't believe what I'm hearing. You're making excuses for him?'

'That wasn't an excuse,' Ella protested uncomfortably.

'Ella...in all the years of our friendship I have never understood your essential indifference to men. Now, finally, I do. You're insanely in love with Ari Xenakis— and I do mean *insane*, because by the sound of it he's already running rings round you!'

'Of course I'm not in love with him,' Ella retorted crisply. 'We have absolutely nothing in common. He's cold, selfish and arrogant, and I could never care about a man like that!'

'On the other hand,' Aristandros added lazily, striding into the bedroom without warning and startling her into dropping the phone, 'I'm very rich, very clever and very good in bed—a combination of traits which seems to keep you very well entertained, *khriso mou.*'

Ella fumbled clumsily for the phone again.

'It's okay...I heard,' Lily admitted. 'I think you've just met your match, Ella.'

Ella replaced the phone and stared at Aristandros. Her nipples stirred and peaked below her nightdress, becoming uncomfortably sensitive. His scrutiny burned like molten gold over her upturned face, and pink colour warmed her cheeks while her tummy performed a wicked little somersault of response. The atmosphere sizzled. She closed her eyes tight and snuggled down beneath the sheet, awesomely conscious of his presence, and tensing to the rigidity of an iron bar when the mattress gave under his weight

'*Se thelo*…I want you,' Aristandros breathed thickly as he eased her back into his arms.

'I thought you'd be out half the night,' she framed flatly, staying stiff and unresponsive against the hard, muscular heat of him.

'Not when you're in my bed waiting for me, *moli mou*.'

'I wasn't waiting for you!' she yelped.

Brushing back her tumbled silvery-blonde hair, he pressed his sensual mouth to the slender column of her neck, and she quivered beneath the erotic brush of his lips across her skin. 'Of course you were. Do you think I don't know when a woman wants me?'

'Quack,' Ella pronounced flatly.

Aristandros vented a husky laugh above her head. 'Meaning?'

'That normal dialogue is a waste of breath with a guy as vain and arrogant as you are.'

Aristandros extracted her from her nightdress without receiving or even appearing to need the smallest assistance from her. He proved that he was more than capable of rolling with the punches of that negative character-assessment. He nibbled at the tender skin below her ear, while his hands roved from the urgent jut of her swollen nipples to the slick, wet flesh between her thighs. She clenched her teeth and gasped, striving to resist temptation until he teased the tiny nub of arousal below her feminine mound, and suddenly resistance was more than she could bear. She twisted round in a violent movement and found his tormenting mouth for herself, burning for him and burning with shame simultaneously. He held her to him with strong hands and plundered her parted lips until she was breathless with desire. Then he lifted her over him and pushed up into her slick, tight depths with a long, guttural groan of pleasure.

'As long as you know that I still hate you,' Ella mumbled shakily, struggling not to lose herself entirely in the pleasure he had unleashed.

'I love the way you hate me,' Aristandros husked, long, brown fingers on her hips controlling her rhythm, and then rising to cup her swaying breasts and roll the sensitive crests.

She was dizzy with excitement and beyond thought. The waves of pulsating pleasure began low in her pelvis and slowly spread out in ever-increasing circles in a white-hot surge of shattering pleasure. She cried out, and her head fell back on her shoulders as the wild convulsions of ecstasy engulfed her.

Aristandros cradled her limp body and rolled over to a cooler spot in the big bed. 'Tomorrow we'll be on Lykos, and I don't think I'll let you out of bed for a week. You make me insatiable, *khriso mou.*'

Her brain kicked back into gear and she flinched, loathing herself for surrendering to the passion. 'I meant everything I said,' she told him doggedly.

'What a temper you have,' Aristandros mused lazily, his unconcern on that score palpable.

Her body still throbbing from the primal urgency of his possession, Ella pulled free of him and shifted over to the far side of the bed.

'No,' Aristandros said succinctly, and he reached for her with hands that brooked no argument and hauled her bodily back into contact with his long, powerful body. 'What you sow, you must reap, and I'm not finished yet.'

'I am!' But, as she spoke, the familiar signature tune she used on her mobile phone broke out in the tense silence.

'Ignore it,' Aristandros instructed. 'It's after midnight.'

Ella, by comparison, was accustomed to reacting with urgency to calls during the night, and she broke from his loosened hold and snatched up the flashing mobile-phone on the bedside table to answer it. An instant later, she threw her legs off the side of the bed and stood up to switch on the lamp. Although she couldn't yet understand what her mother was saying, she realised that the older woman was crying and that something was badly wrong.

'Calm down; I can't follow what you're saying. What happened? Did he hit you?'

Ella felt Aristandros pull himself up behind her. 'Are you still in the house?' she prompted her parent. 'Where is Theo? Look, whatever you do, don't go back in there,' Ella warned the weeping older woman. 'Stay where you are and I'll come and get you. No, of course it isn't a problem. Don't be silly, Mum. All I care about is you.' Putting her phone down, she turned to Aristandros. 'I need a car.'

Aristandros was already talking into the house phone and getting out of bed. He broke off to demand, 'Did Sardelos attack your mother? What happened?'

'What always happens,' Ella responded wearily. 'He has a few drinks, blames her for everything wrong in his life and hits her. He's in bed. She's in the park across the street. Why are you getting dressed?'

'I'm coming with you.'

Ella was already pulling on a pair of trousers. 'That's not a good idea.'

His handsome features were grim. 'I'm not leaving you to handle this alone. Your stepfather left my house in a rage this evening, and I was to blame for that.'

'You're not to blame for anything. Theo is the baddie here. I warn you: Mum won't report him to the police. I've tried a dozen times to persuade her to have him charged, but she won't, so he gets away with it every time. She's like an addict,' Ella muttered heavily. 'She won't give him up.'

'Are you planning to call your brothers?'

'I'll do what Mum wants me to do. I notice she phoned me rather than either of her sons.'

Twenty minutes later, Ella was approaching the park bench where her mother was huddled like an old discarded rug, her shoulders hunched, her head bent, so that even in the street light her face couldn't be seen. When Ella got her first proper look at her, she had to bite back an exclamation. Her face swollen and puffy with one eye almost sealed shut, Jane Sardelos was almost unrecognisable. Her lip was cut and distended, and she was cradling one arm as though it was hurting her.

'What's up with your arm?' Ella asked.

'Let's get her into the car first,' Aristandros urged.

'You brought him with you?' the older woman gasped in horror.

'I couldn't shake him off.' Ella helped her mother stand up and guided her towards the waiting limo. Once they were safe in the passenger seat, she bent to examine the arm and realised that the older woman's wrist was badly broken. 'We'll have to go to the hospital.'

'No hospital…I'll go to a hotel or something.'

'You don't have a choice,' Ella broke in. 'I think your wrist needs surgery, and the sooner it's done the better. Do you want me to call the boys?'

Jane shook her head in an urgent negative. 'No point in upsetting them as well.'

Aristandros raised a brow but made no comment. During the drive to the hospital and then their subsequent arrival, after he had called in advance, she was surprised by how gentle he was with her battered mother, who had never been one of his biggest fans. She was wryly amused when his natural charm began to draw the older woman out of her shell.

It was a very long night. After the x-rays had been carried out, Jane was given a thorough examination, and Ella was appalled by the bruising she saw on her parent's thin body. It was obvious to her that, if anything, her stepfather's attacks had become even more violent over the years. Surgery was immediately scheduled for her wrist. The police arrived beforehand, and Ella braced herself for her mother's usual evasive efforts to shield her husband from arrest and prosecution. Aristandros asked if he could speak to Jane privately for a moment and Ella stepped outside the room, curious as to his motive, but so sleepy that she was grateful for the chance to move around and wake up a bit.

She was shocked when she realised on her return that her mother was finally willing to give a true statement of events and press charges against Theo. She also seemed stronger, steadier and less afraid than she had been. While she was in the operating theatre, Aristandros made a series of phone calls.

'What did you talk about with Mum?' Ella asked.

'She wants a fresh start, and I pointed out that she can't have it without having Sardelos charged with assault, because only that will make him leave her alone. I also pointed out that she could well die during one of his assaults. I asked her to accompany us to Lykos to recuperate, but she wants to stay with your brothers until she's feeling better. I called them. They should be here soon.'

Ella was disappointed that Jane wouldn't be coming to the island, but she knew that her mother would very much enjoy fussing over her adult sons for a few weeks. She was amazed that Aristandros had triumphed where she had so often tried and failed. Her stepfather was finally going to be taken to court, and that was a source of tremendous relief to Ella. But perhaps it wasn't so strange, she conceded. Jane was always more easily impressed by a strong man than she was by a strong woman, and Ari's intervention and advice had been warmly appreciated and respected.

They remained at the hospital until Jane emerged from the operating theatre and had regained consciousness in the recovery room. The surgery had been long and complicated but successful. Ella fell asleep in the limousine, and wakened only when Aristandros settled her down on the bed.

'You were really great tonight with Mum,' she mumbled drowsily. 'I wasn't expecting that.'

'I'm not always the bastard you like to think I am,' Aristandros retorted with level cool.

Her heavy limbs sinking into the comfortable mattress,

Ella focused wryly on his lean, compellingly handsome face. 'I'm not stupid,' she told him. 'Leopards don't change their spots.'

# CHAPTER NINE

THE island of Lykos had undergone some changes since Ella's last visit seven years earlier. Aristandros had made the harbour much bigger and deeper to accommodate his yachts. The fishing boats looked like colourful children's toys beside *Hellenic Lady*. The island's little town, composed of lime-washed white houses adorned with traditional blue paintwork, stretched up the hill in neat tiers behind the harbour. The wedding-cake church with its ornamental bell tower sat in the shade of the plane trees edging the main square, and a windmill, long defunct but nonetheless charming, punctuated the winding road that led down to the far end of the island and the Xenakis house. Beyond the town stretched lush green hills studded with cypresses and olive groves and rather more buildings than she recalled.

'The last time we were here you told me that you wanted to get married in a church exactly like that,' Aristandros murmured.

'Did I…really?' Standing by the rail as the yacht docked, Ella was still suffering from the loss of the previous night's sleep. That reminder almost made her choke on the coffee she was drinking to wake herself up, and she secretly cringed over the knowledge that she could ever have been that gauche. 'I don't remember that.'

'I liked the fact that you didn't watch your every word around me. My parents got married here in the church of Ayia Sophia. My mother thought it was cute as well.'

'Lykos originally belonged to her family, didn't it?'

'Yes. She was an only child and a great disappointment to a shipping family, who longed for a son.'

'I just remember the portrait of her in the house. She was absolutely gorgeous.'

'She still holds the trophy for being the vainest woman I ever knew,' Aristandros remarked with a cynical shake of his proud dark head. 'In many ways she was lucky to die young. She could never have handled growing old.'

Ella thought it was sad that he could be so detached from the memory of his mother, a habit he had probably acquired for self-protection when he was a boy, cursed by not one but two wildly irresponsible parents who had refused to grow up and behave like adults. Too alike to stand each other for long, the warring pair had divorced by the time he was five years old.

Although Doria Xenakis had grown up with great beauty and wealth, both attributes had only been a means to an end for a young woman obsessed by her dream of becoming a famous actress. While his mother had chased endless drama-classes and roles, and thrown constant parties to entertain influential celebrities, Aristandros had been seriously neglected. He had twice been removed from her home by social workers for his own safety. Doria had finally died of a drug overdose at the age of thirty, and was only remembered in the film world for having starred in some of the worst movies ever made. Ari's father, Achilles Xenakis, an inveterate gambler, womaniser and drunk, had worked his way through multiple partners and repeated visits to rehabilitation centres after an unending succession of financial and sexual scandals. Achilles had died when he crashed his speedboat. Orphaned, Aristandros had moved in with Drakon at the age of fourteen.

Ella, Callie and Aristandros climbed into one of the cars waiting by the harbour while their luggage was stowed in another. Ella gazed out at the turquoise-blue sea washing the inviting white strand that circled more than half the island and, appreciating its emptiness, said, 'Are you still trying to keep the tourists out?'

'Why would I want to share paradise?'

'It would be the easiest way of revitalising the economy and persuading the younger people to stay on. A small, exclusive development near the town wouldn't interfere with your privacy.'

'Remind me to keep you well away from the town council. They'd elect you immediately,' Aristandros asserted. 'In recent years, I've brought in several businesses to provide employment, and the population is currently thriving—without the tourist trade and its attendant problems.'

Ella gave him a sunny smile. 'I'm sure you know what works best in your own personal little kingdom.'

'I do not regard the island as my kingdom,' Aristandros growled.

'I didn't mean to be controversial,' Ella declared unconvincingly.

Aristandros skated a long, reproving forefinger along one slender thigh clad in coffee-coloured linen trousers. 'Liar. You always liked getting under my skin, *moli mou*.'

'Constant agreement and admiration is bad for you. Too many people behave as if your every decision is an act of sheer brilliance.'

'It usually is,' Aristandros fielded. 'That's how I make so much money.'

Involuntarily, Ella grinned, for his self-assurance was immense and always bold as brass. She studied the big house perched like a land-locked ship on the cypress-studded hillside. The villa, designed by his late mother, overlooked a secluded cove where the clear waters reflected the sky.

'I have a project for you while you're here,' he said, greeting the staff assembled in the hall while Ella retrieved Callie from surging towards the stairs as fast as her little feet could carry her. 'Revamp the house and drag it out of the eighties. It always reminds me of a film set.'

The big screen was undoubtedly what had inspired his mother's opulent choice of décor, and the vast sunken living-area, marble floors and theatrical Greek columns. Ella was amazed that he had still not had the house renovated, and it made her wonder if he was more sentimental than he would ever be willing to admit. Doria's portrait still adorned one wall, along with many photographs of her taken with famous people.

Aristandros bore not the slightest resemblance to his blonde, brown-eyed mother. He did, however, look very like his handsome father. In terms of attractiveness, though, he easily outshone both his parents, Ella decided, shooting him a keen appraisal. While he had Achilles' looks, he had inherited his grandfather's sharp intelligence and business acumen. Daily exposure to Aristandros had simply made her more aware than ever that he was an extravagantly beautiful, intriguingly clever and challenging man. On paper he ticked all her boxes.

Turning pink as he intercepted her lingering scrutiny, Ella walked out hurriedly on to the sweeping terrace and wondered if Lily was right: was it possible that she had never got over loving Aristandros? Had she never moved on properly after that first disillusionment? The suspicion appalled her, for she liked to see herself as being sensible. The sort of woman who could continue to harbour a strong, secret preference for a notorious womaniser struck Ella as being silly, weak in resolution and certifiably insane.

'In three weeks' time we'll be attending a major charity performance at the opera in aid of the Xenakis Foundation. Dress formal,' Aristandros announced.

Ella suppressed a sigh. 'Where's it being held?'

'Athens.'

Ella saw Callie installed in the nursery, which the little girl clearly saw as home. Callie toddled over to a basket of toys and smiled as she dug out familiar favourites, her satisfaction at rediscovering them unhidden. Later, when Callie was in bed and Ella was dining out on the terrace with Aristandros, she breathed in deep. 'You know, I've barely been with you two weeks and this will be the sixth different bed I've slept in.'

Aristandros shifted a broad shoulder with nonchalant cool. 'Change is stimulating.'

'I know you don't want to hear this…'

Aristandros shifted a fluid brown hand in a silencing gesture. 'Then don't say it,' he advised drily.

'It's not fair to Callie. She needs a more settled home.'

'I don't normally trail her round the world with me as I have done recently,' Aristandros finally admitted. 'She's usually based here on the island.'

Guilt assailed Ella as she grasped the heart of the dilemma. 'She's travelling because I'm in the picture now and you know I want to be with her,' she guessed ruefully.

'While I want you to be with me. We're the perfect threesome,' he quipped. 'Be practical.'

Ella toyed with her delicious, light seafood starter, her appetite ebbing. *Be practical—remember the agreement you signed, remember who calls the shots around here, remember who says what goes as far as Callie's concerned.* But his lifestyle was unsustainable for a toddler, Ella reflected. More than anything Callie needed stability and routine to thrive, not to mention the same people around her.

Dark eyes reflective, Aristandros sipped his wine. 'I have a business trip next week. I'll leave you here.'

'Great.' Ella knew she was being thrown a consolation prize, but ironically she just as quickly found herself wondering whether his sudden willingness to leave her behind could relate to the fact that he was getting a little bored with her. Why not? she asked herself. Two weeks was a sizeable length of time for Aristandros to stay committed to one woman. And, if he was losing interest, how would she handle it?

Extinguishing that incendiary thought from her mind, for she saw no advantage in borrowing trouble in advance, she phoned her mother, who was still in hospital, after dinner. Jane was in reasonable spirits. Stavros and Dmitri were visiting her and had passed on the news that their father had been arrested and charged. Freed from the fear of her husband's violence, Jane had decided to go for counselling.

'Mum's dealing with this better than I thought she would,' Ella commented to Aristandros when he wandered out of the bathroom, only a towel linked round his lean hips and drops of water still sparkling on his hair-roughened chest. She would never have dreamt of adding that her mother thought she had misjudged him seven years earlier and had underestimated his potential for reliability. In her mother's eyes, Aristandros had suddenly become a knight in shining armour worthy of the highest praise.

'Hopefully it will give her a new lease of life. Sardelos had sucked all the energy out of her,' he pronounced grimly.

A slender figure in a shimmering emerald-green nightdress edged with lace, Ella shivered. 'I was only a child when they married, but I still remember how different she was before she met him—lively and outgoing. He turned her into a doormat.'

'Not something anyone could accuse you of.'

Her blood sang in her veins as she studied him. He made her feel like a teenager—a hopelessly infatuated teenager, who got a thrill every time he looked at her. 'Sometimes you make me very angry.'

A wicked grin slashed his handsome mouth, and her heart hammered as if he had pressed a switch. 'You make me hot in a very different way, *khriso mou.*'

For the first time Ella took the initiative, crossing the room to slide up against his hard, masculine body, revelling in every point of physical connection with an earthy streak she hadn't known she possessed until he'd brought it out in her. The very boldness of his arousal thrilled her. He parted her lips and let his tongue delve hungrily, deeply, and her bones seemed to melt beneath her skin while languorous heat and heaviness slowly uncoiled between her thighs. She detached the towel and looked up at him while she traced the impressive length of his erection.

'There's no hope for you in the wanton stakes,' Aristandros husked. 'You're still blushing.'

'Of course I'm going to blush if you're planning to offer a running commentary!'

'So, take my breath away, *moli mou.*'

And she did, kneeling down gracefully at his feet to deploy her slim hands and her full, sensual mouth to the task she had set herself. She used her knowledge of the male physique and her infinitely more intimate aware-ness of what he liked to pleasure him. Ella was always a high achiever at anything she set out to do. Ripples of helpless response began shuddering through his power-ful frame. He withstood her provocative attention for a very short time. His breathing audibly fractured, and then suddenly he was pulling her up and backing her down on the bed with scant ceremony.

'You excite the hell out of me!' he groaned, coming down on top of her and ravaging her luscious pink mouth until her senses swam.

He made love to her with mind-blowing power. Afterwards she lay shell-shocked with the intensity of the pleasure in his arms, her willowy body magically indolent and peaceful after her explosive release. He smoothed her hair gently back off her warm face. She kissed a smooth, muscular shoulder, catching the faint scent of cologne mingled with his own male scent, and drank in the smell of him like an addict. Right and wrong, she registered, no longer seemed so well-defined.

On some level she couldn't hold back what she was feeling any longer, and wasn't even sure that there was a point in such restraint while she lived with him and Callie. Sexually she found him irresistible, but his hold on her went much deeper than that. She was possessive of him and she cared about him as she had never yet cared for any other man. Yet he wasn't the young man she had fallen in love with any more. Those seven years apart had altered him. He was harder, more cynical and self-contained, and willing to go to any lengths to get what he wanted. Was it terribly wrong of her to feel special because he had gone to such extremes to get her back into his life again? And what was he doing to her once-firm moral compass?

In the early hours of the following morning she wakened and frowned at the familiar little cramping pains low in her stomach. A moment later she got out of bed and went into the bathroom to check out her suspicions. No, as she had thought, she wasn't pregnant, and it was time to start her contraceptive pill. The necessities taken care of, she returned to bed.

Aristandros was still fast asleep in a careless sprawl which took up more than his fair share of the bed, outsized though it was. With his jet-dark lashes almost long enough to hit his hard cheekbones, blue-black stubble outlining his angular jaw and sculpted mouth, and with his classic, aquiline profile relaxed, he looked gorgeous. Her insides chilled at the thought of how he might have reacted to an inconvenient pregnancy. He liked to control everything, and she couldn't have allowed him to exert control or influence in that field. She was grateful that the situation hadn't arisen.

'Hmm…' He shifted position and found her, a hand splaying across her stomach and then rising to cup a small, firm breast with a drowsy sound of masculine contentment. '*Ella*…'

'I'm not pregnant!' Ella just blurted it out, keen to get the news out, mortified by the idea that he was secretly dreading the possibility that she might have conceived.

Spiky black lashes lifted on startled dark-golden eyes. He was as instantly awake as if she had doused him with a bucket of cold water. 'Are you sure?'

'One hundred percent,' she declared.

His lean, strong face clenched. 'I would have taken care of you. You needn't have worried on that score.'

'We have enough problems without that particular one.'

'You still don't want children?'

'I didn't say that.'

'Just not children with me?' His expression sardonic, Aristandros released her and vaulted out of bed. 'I need a shower.'

Ella was bewildered by his behaviour. 'I assumed you would regard a pregnancy as a disaster and that you'd ask me to have a termination. You did tell me you didn't want a child.'

A bronzed vision of pagan masculinity, he surveyed her with brooding force from the bathroom doorway, and shrugged a broad shoulder. 'Then I thought about it and I reckoned I could live with it. Callie would probably enjoy having a playmate,' he murmured lazily.

'I wouldn't have suggested a termination. The main reason my father divorced my mother was that she tried to have me aborted—he stopped her on the way to the clinic. That kind of knowledge gives you a different take on an accidental pregnancy.'

Shocked by the content of that entire speech, Ella nodded slowly. 'I suppose it would.'

She tried to get her thoughts in order. Every time she thought she had Ari pigeon-holed, he confounded her expectations again. Think of him casually commenting that Callie would enjoy a playmate, admitting that, at the very least, he was uncomfortable with the idea of terminating a pregnancy that was merely inconvenient! *I reckoned I could live with it*—he could live with her having his baby. Well, she was still relieved that she wasn't about to face that challenge. He would have needed to be a good deal more enthusiastic and they would have had to have discussed the idea in advance before she could have allowed herself to regret the fact that she hadn't conceived.

Swallowing hard, she got back into bed. She had on several occasions in recent years gone through the experience of feeling broody, when the very sight of a baby or tiny clothes brought a lump to her throat and a powerful craving, but she would never have admitted anything so personal to him. Indeed her longing to see and hold her biological daughter had almost broken her heart for eighteen months. But, now fully aware of how incredibly lucky she was to have a loving healthy child like Callie in her life, she expected nothing more from Mother Nature.

Ella prowled round the modern building housing the doctor's surgery and emergency facilities which

Aristandros had funded on the outskirts of town. It was a rural doctor's dream, but apparently two doctors had already come and gone, bored with the lack of a social life on a small island and the inconvenience of having to step on a ferry to visit friends and family. Currently the position was vacant. Having checked out the patient numbers, Ella reckoned there was really only enough work for a part-time doctor, and she very much would have liked to put her name forward.

'We would be honoured to have you here,' the town mayor, Yannis Mitropoulos, assured her, having intercepted her and offered her a tour after she had been seen peering wistfully through a window.

'Unfortunately, I'm not looking for a job at present,' Ella advanced uncomfortably.

Had she been, she was convinced she would have been in harness within five minutes of accepting the job. Aristandros had devoted two days to showing her round the island, and had introduced her to many of the locals. But he had *not*, offered her an inspection of the unoccupied state-of-the-art medical building he had built, or admitted that Lykos lacked a doctor's services. Ella had only found out those facts for herself when she'd taken Callie into town. Whilst enjoying cold drinks at the taverna overlooking the picturesque harbour, she had found herself slowly and steadily being surrounded by hopeful people in search of off-the-cuff medical advice. Aristandros, however, appeared to have no conscience about keeping the only doctor on the island confined to home, hearth and bedroom.

In spite of that truth, over the past three weeks Ella had settled happily into life on Lykos. Aristandros had twice flown off on business trips without her, and she had been dismayed by the discovery that she missed him when he was out of reach. He was, however, surprisingly sexy and amazingly addictive during late-night phone conversations, she conceded with a covert smile.

She had come to terms with the fact that she loved him, and that she probably loved him a great deal more than she had seven years ago, which struck her as especially ironic when he had behaved so badly this time round. Back then she had expected perfection, a soulmate who shared her every thought and conviction and made no awkward demands of her. Now her expectations were rather more human-sized and, in any case, she knew that she and Aristandros were diametrically opposed by the simple fact that she was a modern female and he was very old-style macho male. Although she felt that Aristandros was being totally selfish and unreasonable in refusing to allow her to pursue her medical vocation, she was beginning to suspect that his being the centre of her world, the only other person she really had to think about besides Callie, was something he prized above everything else in their relationship. He was as possessive as she was, and seemingly unwilling to share her.

Ella had managed to adopt two homeless dogs since her arrival on Lykos. One, Whistler, a fluffy mongrel of indeterminate breed, had been injured by a fish hook and brought to her for attention for there was no vet on the island either. Ella had dealt with the little animal's lacerations and had offered to keep her while she healed. The second dog had arrived on the slender strength of the assurance that 'everybody knows the English are mad about dogs'. Bunny, inappropriately named by

Callie, was a boisterous Great Dane pup with paws the size of dinner plates, and he was accused of having sneaked off the ferry unattended. Both dogs were brilliant with Callie.

Aristandros had been taken aback by the sudden addition of two animals to the household, but had adapted wonderfully well after a lot of cool brow-raising over their antics, and had admitted that his mother had hated dogs and that he had never been allowed a pet. Ella thought his heart had been touched by Callie's enthusiasm for the dogs: the sight of the trio gambolling on the beach was quite something.

Of course Aristandros was learning to love Callie which was very entertaining to watch. For instance, he tried to teach Callie to say 'toes' and she continually came up with 'socks' or 'shoes'. She saw his pleasure when her daughter rushed to greet him and hug his knees. The child's innocent affection and playfulness drew him out of his cynical shell and made him patient and much less driven. When his mobile phone had been found in a vase of flowers, he'd insisted he had somehow dropped it in there, when everyone in the house knew that Callie was always trying to get her hands on his phone because the colours it flashed attracted her like a magnet.

It no longer mattered to Ella that Aristandros had fenced her in with an outrageous legal agreement. She had signed up for the long haul and was beginning to dare to hope that he might have as well. She was happier with him than she had ever dreamt she could be. The gift of a grand piano had been his most well-received present to date, and she was able to play her music every day on a superb instrument with wonderful tone, and she was already looking forward to teaching Callie. But the piano was only one of a number of fabulous presents with which he had surprised her. She had acquired designer handbags, perfume, sundry outfits and a fantastic sculpture of a sylph-like dancer that he had said reminded him of her. As she did not have endless legs and a large bosom quite out of proportion to the rest of her body, she had decided to be flattered by the unlikely comparison.

Aristandros was now accustomed to seeing her without make-up or a fancy hair-do, but dressed instead in casual beach-wear or jeans, and none of it had put a single dent in her apparent desirability. Her mother and her twin siblings had visited, and he had taken her brothers—who were not the world's most entertaining guys, out fishing and sailing without even being asked. She had been grateful, for her family now accepted their relationship, which made life a great deal smoother.

He had proved surprisingly understanding when she had been overjoyed after receiving a letter forwarded by Lily from Alister Marlow. As asked, Alister had notified the cleaner about the photo Ella had mislaid, and the small, faded snapshot of her late father had been found behind a piece of furniture. Ari had been sympathetic when he'd grasped that Ella had no memory of her father, who had died when she was only a baby. He, too, had been a doctor.

'Is that why you went in for medicine?' Aristandros had asked.

'No, I wanted to be a doctor from quite a young age, and as I got older it appealed more and more. I loved the idea of being able to fix people's bodies and solve their problems, but of course it's only occasionally that straightforward.'

But, when it came to the lack of commitment in relationships that Ella saw as Ari's most pressing problem, she convinced herself that she had the solution. If their sex life was good, Ari would surely have no reason to stray—but she despised herself for thinking that way and for being willing to accept those boundaries. Her pride told her she deserved more, but her brain told her that she already had as much as she could reasonably expect from Aristandros Xenakis in terms of attraction, attention and time. Even the newspapers were talking about what a quiet life he was leading of late.

In honour of the charity opera performance she was to attend that very evening, she had shopped for hours in Athens for a gorgeous dress and had promised to wear the sapphires with it. Aristandros had flown out the night before on a helicopter, and she was being picked up early evening. The beautician who worked on *Hellenic Lady* came to the house to do the honours, and Ella was admiring how well her hair looked when Ianthe, the housekeeper, came to her bedroom to tell her that Yannis Mitropoulos had phoned to ask if she would come and see his daughter who was pregnant and unwell.

Ella wasted no time in driving into the town to the surgery, with Ianthe in tow. Grigoria was a young first-time mother-to-be who was almost eight months' pregnant with twins. Her husband was in the army and away from home. Grigoria was very nearly hysterical, and clung so tightly to Ella that she had to prise herself free to examine her patient. What she learned was not good. Grigoria's blood pressure was sky high, and her hands and feet were swollen. Her condition was made more complex by the fact that she was a diabetic. Ella told Yannis that they needed the air ambulance, for she was convinced that his daughter was suffering from pre-eclampsia and needed urgent hospital treatment. It was a dangerous condition which would most likely only be cured by the delivery of the babies. She checked the records and rang the relevant hospital to forewarn them and get the advice of the gynaecologist on duty.

'You'll come with me?' Grigoria pleaded, clutching at Ella's arm frantically.

'I would be very grateful if you would,' Yannis added jerkily, tears in his eyes as he took her to one side and began to tell the very sad story of how his late wife had once gone on the same journey and, for possibly the same reason, and had died shortly after Grigoria's birth.

His daughter's state of mind was not helped by that inopportune recollection of her mother's demise. Ianthe ventured to remind Ella of the opera engagement, and the reminder cleared Ella's frown away; she was quick to work out how she could be in virtually two places at once, for both destinations were in the city. Determined to stay with Grigoria, Ella instructed the housekeeper to have her evening dress and jewellery delivered to Ari's house in Athens where she would be able to change for the evening, having left the hospital.

The flight in the air ambulance to Athens was fraught and tense; Grigoria was suffering increasing pain, and was seriously ill. It was a great relief to reach the hospital. Ella, preoccupied with her patient's condition, spared not a thought for her disrupted social arrangements until Grigoria's twins, two little girls, were safely delivered by Caesarean section. Her anxiety about Grigoria soothed by the knowledge that the young woman was receiving the best possible treatment, Ella only then registered that she had not even tried to contact Aristandros to tell him where she was. In a passion of dismay that she had been so thoughtless in relation to an engagement which he had made clear was an important event, she texted fervent humble apologies to him. She wasted no time trying to explain what had happened, but instead promised to join him by the time of the intermission.

More precious time was wasted while she found a taxi willing to take her out of the city. She contacted Ianthe to check that the dress had been delivered. Reassured on that score, Ella began worrying about how Aristandros would react to her appearance just before the end of the evening. Her heart sank. He hadn't responded to her text, which suggested to her that he was furious. Furthermore, she didn't feel she could blame him, since he had always been meticulous about contacting her well in advance in similar situations. Also, telling him that she had simply forgotten about him and the opera date because of a medical emergency was scarcely likely to prove a comfort to a male accustomed to the very best treatment when it came to the female sex.

By the time the taxi trundled up the long driveway to the imposing villa, Ella was very tense, because she was running against the clock and not doing very well. She rang the bell and, after a few moments, the house-keeper appeared, and her look of consternation was sufficient to warn Ella that her arrival was unexpected. Ella hastened past the older woman with a muttered explanation and apology. She sped upstairs, where she assumed her evening gown awaited her. There was no sign of it in the master bedroom, but she stilled in surprise on the threshold when she saw the scattered pieces of female clothing littering the floor. She frowned at the sight of the frilly black-and-turquoise bra and matching knickers, and wondered who on earth they could belong to. Unfortunately, she did not have to wonder for long.

The mystery was immediately solved when the bathroom door opened and a breathtakingly lovely blonde appeared, wearing only a towel. It was difficult to say which of them was the most discomposed by the unexpected meeting.

'Who are you? What are you doing in here?' Ella heard herself demand.

Aqua-green eyes challenged her. 'As I was here first, I could ask you the same thing.'

And, even as Ella parted her lips to speak again, a sick sensation took up residence in her tummy and perspiration beaded her brow. She wondered if she was the only woman in the world stupid enough to ask a beautiful half-naked woman what she was doing in her lover's bedroom. After all, the answer was so obvious the question didn't need asking. Striving to save a little dignity in a confrontation that had burst upon her with the abruptness of an earthquake, Ella retreated back to the doorway. She discovered that it was horrendously difficult for her to peel her stunned eyes from the blonde in the towel. A revolting, terrifying curiosity had her staring, and striving not to make bland comparisons. Her mind marched on regardless: she herself was older, less exciting in the curves department and, although her skin was good, she knew it wasn't quite as flawless. Rejecting those crazy, unsavoury evaluations, she spun on her heel and headed down the sweeping stairs at such a speed that she almost tripped over her own feet.

'Dr Smithson.' The housekeeper began speaking anxiously to Ella as she threw open the front door for herself, simply eager to be gone and leave the scene of her humiliation behind her. 'I'm sorry, but I didn't know you were coming.'

'It's okay. I'm fine,' Ella burbled, not wishing to deal with the woman's visible embarrassment. It was obvious that the housekeeper had a very good idea of what Ella had found upstairs. She just fled, hurrying down the drive as though a gale-force wind was powering her from behind. Her mind was a total blank. She didn't know what she was doing. She didn't know where she was going either. Shock had wiped her thoughts out, and fear of the pain of those thoughts was protecting her from them.

Aristandros had another woman. *Well, whoopee, Ella—what were you expecting? Did you think he had signed a one-woman-only pledge just because he had taken up with you?* It was not as if Aristandros had promised to be faithful. Indeed, he had gone to some trouble to declare that he was promising her no such thing in that wretched agreement. For all she knew he had a stable of other women stashed around the globe at his various properties or, indeed available to come at a call whenever he felt like a little variety.

Aristandros had gone into his Athens headquarters today, finished his day's work during the afternoon and had then come home with or to the very beautiful blonde and gone to bed with her. The bed had been made again. So the very beautiful blonde was tidy as well as clean! She pictured Ari's housekeeper telling him what had happened and flinched. Seeing a bus trundling along the road in the distance, she speeded up to reach the stop and flagged it down. It didn't matter where it was going, just as long as it got her safely away from the vicinity of the villa where she might be seen. Her phone vibrated in her bag and she dug it out and, refusing to even look at the message, she switched it off. She wasn't in any fit state to deal with Aristandros.

It was a warm, humid evening. Ella felt hot and her skin felt clammy, though her teeth kept on threatening to chatter in shock. She got on the bus and sat down at the back, her body lurching and swaying as the vehicle swung round corners. Why was she so shocked when Aristandros had only done what had always come naturally to him? Such a very beautiful girl, as well. If a man had always wanted the diversity and excitement of other sexual partners, he was unlikely to change. And no doubt, if she asked him, he would be honest with her about it.

Her mind went into free fall at the thought of him being *that* honest with her. Any admission of infidelity would cut like a knife and leave scars, haunting her for ever. But the images already tormenting her were no more comforting, she acknowledged wretchedly, for the idea of Ari in another woman's arms was her worst nightmare and always had been. Now it had finally happened, she was reeling from the pain she was experiencing.

But wasn't the extent of that pain her own fault, a self-induced punishment? What woman in her right mind would have fallen in love with Aristandros Xenakis and hoped for a happy ending? Countless women had tried and failed with him. Yet she was still crazy about him. She had held nothing back. In fact, a week ago, when she had watched Ari building a sand-castle with Callie—a real boy-toy skyscraper version of a sandcastle—she had wondered if she had made an appalling mistake when she'd turned his marriage proposal down seven years back. She had wondered if, against the odds, they might have found happiness together. She had known that although she loved her career and lived for its challenges it had never brought her the sheer, soaring happiness, excitement and contentment that he could just with his presence.

Her cheeks were wet with tears when she climbed off the bus at the terminal. What was she planning to do— run away and leave Callie behind? That option was absolutely out of the question. Hadn't Ari already accused her of running away when anything upset her? Ella bristled at that recollection. But exactly what was she doing now? She couldn't give up on Callie; she just *couldn't*! Whatever happened, whatever else she had to bear, there was no way she could give up on the little girl she loved. At the same time, however, she needed a few hours' grace to pull herself back together before she had to face Aristandros again. She decided that the wisest option was to find a hotel for the night.

She walked for ages before she came on a small establishment sited in a quiet street. Checking in, she was conscious of the receptionist's swiftly veiled curiosity,

and when she saw her reflection in the mirror in the *en
suite* bathroom of her hotel room she grimaced in horrified embarrassment at the state of her face. Her
mascara had run, and her eye shadow had smudged
where she'd wiped her eyes, and her hair was all messy.
She freshened up and then made herself switch her
phone back on. She couldn't stage a vanishing act for
very long. She had also left Aristandros standing at the
opera. Although that was the very least of what he
deserved, it would have gone down like a lead balloon.

Her phone rang within seconds of being switched on.

'Where the hell are you?' Aristandros growled.

'I'm sorry I didn't make it, but I need some space
tonight.'

'No!' It was thunderous. 'No space allowed. Where
are you?'

'In a hotel, a little place, not one you'd know. I really
do need to be alone for a while,' Ella breathed flatly,
wondering how she could possibly stand to be with him
ever again, how she could ever contrive to live with him
and the knowledge of his infidelity.

'You're not allowed to walk out on me under any circumstances,' Aristandros intoned in a fierce undertone.
'I will not tolerate it.'

'I'm not walking out on you.' Ella framed those
words with a sob trapped in her throat.

'Ella…' he breathed huskily.

Ella cut the call before she could let her turbulent
emotional mood betray her into revealing more than
she should. But he would soon find out through his staff
that she had met his trollop. No; where did she get off
calling another woman a trollop just because she had

slept with Ari? After all, she wasn't married to him. He was still a free agent in the eyes of the world.

Tears choking her, Ella, her slender body trembling, sank down on the end of the bed. As she always feared, her love for Aristandros was tearing her apart at the seams, destroying her strength and self-esteem, when really the only person she ought to be thinking about was Callie, who was safely asleep in her cot and blissfully ignorant of the messes adults could make of their relationships. But Ella recognised at that moment that she had to find a way to sort this mess out, because it was unlikely that she could trust Aristandros to make that effort.

More than an hour later, she jumped in surprise when a knock sounded at her door. Glancing out through the peephole, she could see nothing but a large probably male shape and she opened the door on the chain.

# CHAPTER TEN

'OPEN the door, Ella,' Aristandros instructed harshly.

Ella was shattered that he had found her so quickly. She shut the door, undid the chain and opened the door again. 'How on earth did you know where I was?'

His tension palpable, Aristandros was staring at her, his brilliant dark gaze roving from the crown of her head down to her feet and swiftly back up again. 'I have tracking devices in your mobile phone and your watch, so it was just a matter of switching on the surveillance equipment to locate you—'

Ella gaped at him aghast. '*Tracking devices*?' she parrotted.

'A precaution in case you were kidnapped, a standard security procedure,' Aristandros proclaimed matter-of-factly. 'I'm a very wealthy man, and it's possible that someone could try to target you because of your connection to me.'

'You fixed tracking devices on me?' Ella condemned him in angry disbelief, still back at that first admission. 'And you never said a word about it either.'

'I didn't want to make you nervous or scared. But

I'm not going to apologise for it, either,' Aristandros
added in an aggressive undertone. 'I needed to be sure
you were as safe as I could make you. It's my job to
protect you.'

'A tracking device,' Ella muttered shakily. 'Like I'm
a possession…a stolen car or something.'

'You are a hell of a sight more important to me. It was
no big deal until you went missing tonight and, let me
tell you, you've put me through complete hell in the
space of a few hours!'

Pale and drawn, Ella slowly breathed in. 'Have I
really?'

'Why didn't you phone me from the hospital? You
could have let me know what had happened, not cleared
off in an air ambulance as if I didn't exist!' Aristandros
launched at her, his strong bone-structure rigid beneath
his bronzed skin. 'Ianthe was out and I couldn't get
hold of her, so I had no idea an emergency had come
up. All the domestic staff knew was that you had gone
off somewhere with her. I was worried about you—'

'Why? What could possibly have happened to me on
the island?' Ella couldn't believe she was managing to
stay so calm.

Aristandros glowered at her as if that was a very
stupid question. 'You could have had an accident. I
knew something must have gone badly wrong when
you didn't show up at the opera house, because you're
usually very reliable.'

'Oh…'

'And then Yannis phoned after you had left the
hospital to rave about how wonderful you had been with
his daughter, and I began to understand what had

happened. But you never arrived at Drakon's house because he checked.'

'Drakon's house? Why would I have arrived there?' Ella questioned uncertainly.

'That's where you sent your dress.'

'Ianthe organised that.' Ella hesitated. 'I assumed it had been sent to the villa outside Athens.'

'Ianthe knew I had a bunch of guests staying there this week, so she wouldn't have sent it there.'

'Guests?' Ella echoed weakly.

'I understand that you may have met *one* of them,' Aristandros pointed out with laden emphasis.

Suddenly the atmosphere was so thick it could have been cut with a knife.

Ella was very still and she stood very straight. 'Is that what you call the young woman I met—a guest?'

'So you did rise—or should I say *sink*—to the worst possible conclusion,' Aristandros gathered, his sensual mouth compressed into a grim line of disapproval. 'Eda is my niece, the daughter of my father's youngest sister.'

Her stress level rising as his explanation gathered pace, Ella's brow had indented. 'Are you saying Eda was the girl I ran into? And that she's a relative of yours? If that's true, why was she in the master-bedroom *en suite*?'

'I have no idea. Her parents left her at the villa while they attended the opera because she refused to go. She's something of a handful, and fairly spoilt. Maybe she was trying out the facilities or just exploring while she had the house to herself. How should I know?'

Ella was mentally running through the explanation to see if it could fit what she had seen.

'You can ask her when you meet her tomorrow.'

'I'm going to meet her?' Ella framed uncertainly.

'I'm throwing a party on the island for my relatives tomorrow.'

As Ella began to hope that she had totally misinterpreted the girl's presence at the villa, her legs seemed to go hollow, and her head swam. That physical weakness was her body's response to the powerful rush of relief assailing her. 'Oh, my goodness,' she framed. 'I thought…'

Aristandros reached for her hands and pulled her closer. His dark-golden eyes were raw with reproach. 'Yes, you immediately assumed that I was *shagging* a sixteen-year-old behind your back!'

'She's only sixteen?' Ella mumbled, clinging to his hands to stay upright while she acknowledged that the girl had indeed looked very young.

'I prefer rather more mature specimens of womanhood, *khriso mou*,' Aristandros spelt out levelly. 'Although that does make me wonder why I'm with you, because sometimes you seem to react more like an impulsive airhead of a teenager than the intelligent adult I know you to be.'

A flood of hot moisture engulfed her eyes in a tide, and she blinked repeatedly while staring down at their still-linked hands. 'Her underwear was lying on the bedroom floor. She was only wearing a towel. I did think you must have been with her…'

'No.' His handsome jaw clenched. 'For that matter, I haven't been with anyone else since you came back into my life.'

Ella was so relieved by that admission that a sob escaped her. 'But that agreement said—'

'That was just me acting like a gorilla and beating my chest to ensure you had some healthy respect for me,' Aristandros admitted, gripping her hands so tightly in his that she was convinced they would go entirely numb. 'I'd like to go home now. I appreciate that it's late, but the helicopter is standing by at the airport, and I very much want to get back to the island tonight.'

'Okay.' Ella's voice was small and breathless, and she nodded in confirmation; the terrible, frightening tension and the fear of an unknown impossible future was leaving her piece by piece. There *was* no other woman in his life. He hadn't been with anyone but her since they'd got back together again. She had misunderstood, deemed him guilty when he was innocent. Her world had horizons and possibilities again, but she was almost afraid of accepting that fact.

'You're really shaken up,' Aristandros remarked, draping her bag over her shoulder and guiding her out of the room. 'I should be shouting at you for thinking the worst of me and putting me through a hellish evening of frustration and worry. I don't even like opera at the best of times, but tonight I felt trapped.'

'I'm sorry,' she muttered in the lift, and she wanted to lean up against him and cling but wouldn't let herself act that weak and feminine.

'You're never going to trust me, are you? Why do I get the feeling that I'm paying for your stepfather's sins?'

Ella ducked her head as he tucked her into the limo waiting outside. She had made a hash of things again. A sniff escaped her and then another. Aristandros wrapped both arms round her and almost squeezed the life's breath out of her. 'Don't be silly. You have nothing to cry about.'

'Maybe it was stupid, and I know I misunderstood, but I honestly thought you must have slept with her I was devastated!' Ella gasped out strickenly. 'And I didn't know what I was going to do because I couldn't give up Callie to walk away from you—I *couldn't*!'

Aristandros held her back from him. 'That's one worry you don't have to have ever again.'

'What do you mean?'

'I care too much about Callie to use her to control you. You were right. I shouldn't have involved her in our arrangement. That was inexcusable.' His darkly handsome features were taut and grim as he made that statement. 'Whatever happens between us, I will share custody of Callie with you. You love her and she loves you, and I have watched her blossom in your care. I will never try to separate you from her and you will both always enjoy my financial support.'

Ella was astonished by that far-reaching promise and the conviction with which he spoke. 'Why are you saying this now? Why have you changed your mind after forcing that iniquitous agreement on me?'

'I recognise that what I did was wrong from start to finish: using Callie as bait to trap you, forcing such an unscrupulous contract on you. Drakon was right in what he said, and he didn't know the half of what I imposed on you. Worst of all, I knew that what I was doing to you was wrong even as I did it. Yet I *still* went ahead with it,' Aristandros recounted heavily, his handsome head turned in profile to her, his mouth harshly compressed.

'Why, though? Was it all about revenge?' she pressed, desperate to understand what had motivated him

The silence lay like a blanket and the tension in his

big, powerful frame was so fierce she could feel it even though they were no longer touching. The limousine was already pulling in at the airport.

'Ari...?' she prompted. 'I need to know.'

'I told myself it was purely an act of revenge, but it wasn't. The truth is usually the most simple answer—and the simple answer is that I just wanted you, and that agreement bound you hand and foot to ensure you couldn't walk away again. I needed that protection before I could let myself get involved with you again,' he breathed in a driven undertone. 'But now I realise that I don't want to keep you only because I've got legal custody of your daughter.'

'So, if I want to leave and return to my life in London,' Ella whispered unevenly, 'You'll let me go and allow me to take Callie with me?'

'Letting you both go would kill me, but I won't go back on my word to you,' Aristandros declared with raw emphasis as the door beside her was whipped open by his driver.

Surrounded by his security team, they walked through the airport in silence. *I just wanted you.* Four little words that made a heck of a difference to Ella, and that kept on rhyming back and forth through her head, providing a much-needed mantra of hope. In spite of all the other options he must have had, he had returned to his past and blackmailed her back into a relationship with him. For the first time she registered that she had been and still evidently was much more important to Aristandros Xenakis than he had ever been willing to admit. He didn't want to lose either her or Callie, but he was willing to let them go free if that was what she decided she wanted.

As they waited in a VIP lounge, Ella was conscious of his scrutiny. She knew he was desperate to know what she intended to do next. He had removed the one threat that could have forced her to take whatever he threw at her. No longer did she need to stay with him purely for Callie's sake. His ferocious pride couldn't live with that concept. Blackmail, he had finally discovered, did have its drawbacks.

They were walking towards the helicopter with a neat, respectful space between them when Ella reached abruptly for a lean, brown hand across that divide. 'I want to stay with you,' she told him tautly.

Right there and then, Aristandros turned round and swept her straight into his arms, plunging his mouth down urgently on hers with a passion that blew her away. He had to practically carry her on board the helicopter after that. She was stunned by the level of his relief at her announcement, and could not have doubted his level of ongoing satisfaction over that news when he gave her a heart-stopping smile and retained a hold on her hand throughout the flight. The engine was so noisy that there was no chance of any further conversation until they arrived back on Lykos.

Ella kicked off her shoes just inside the front door when they arrived and padded off straight to the nursery to satisfy her desperate need to see Callie. When she looked up from the cot and the peacefully sleeping child, Aristandros was on the other side of it.

'I really screwed up tonight—the opera thing,' Ella said ruefully. 'I know it was important. I'm sorry I didn't make it.'

Aristandros gave her a wryly amused appraisal. 'You

left me standing. But then I'm used to you embarrassing me in front of my family.'

Ella blinked. 'Your…er…*family*?'

'Yes. Pretty much the whole tribe attended that benefit, and I was planning to show you off to them all.'

'My word; truthfully?' Ella prompted as she followed him out of the nursery. 'Why did you want to show me off?'

'Because I very much hope you're going to marry me, but I wasn't so stupid that I was going to make an announcement without thoroughly discussing terms with you in advance,' he explained smoothly.

Her bright-blue eyes grew very wide. 'You're proposing *again*?'

'A tactful woman would have left out that last word,' Aristandros told her, walking her out on to the terrace where a champagne bottle and glasses sat on the table. 'Are we celebrating or not?'

Ella winced. 'I'm totally, madly in love with you and just like the last time I really, really want to marry you and be with you for ever. But I also spent a large chunk of my life training to become a doctor.'

'And you can *still* be a doctor.' Aristandros frowned as she looked at him in shock. 'I was being very selfish, which I hate to admit comes naturally to me around you. My mother was so obsessed with the film world that she had no time or energy to spare even for me, never mind my father. I don't want a marriage like that. I once resented your medical career because you chose it over me.'

Her lovely face was pensive in the moonlight. 'No, I think I used it as my get-out clause because I'd suffered

Theo as a horrid example of a womaniser and I was so afraid of getting hurt. I should have had more faith in you.'

'We didn't have enough time together.' Aristandros lifted her hand and slid a ring on to her engagement finger. 'It's the same diamond I planned to give you seven years ago, but I've had it reset.'

'It's glorious.' Ella watched the glittering stone sparkle like starlight on her hand and a warm, deep sense of happiness began to fill her.

'We were too young then,' he admitted ruefully. 'If we'd been more mature we would have tried to find a compromise and a way of being together that we could both live with. Instead I lost my temper with you because you made me feel foolish, which was very superficial.'

'You really broke my heart,' Ella confided, ready to be totally frank now that she had his ring on her finger and a proper secure future to look forward to. 'I couldn't believe you'd ever loved me.'

'I loved you so much that I never found anyone else to replace you. With you I thought I could break the Xenakis tradition of bad marriages. I believed that settling down while I was still quite young into marriage would give me a much better prospect of happiness than, for instance, the life I've been leading since then.' His rich, golden eyes were full of regret. 'But I fell at the first challenge.'

Ella wrapped her arms round his neck, her fingers gently feathering through the silky, black hair at his nape. She wished she had understood him better seven years earlier and recognised that his troubled back-ground had made him crave a much more stable life with one woman rather than a succession. 'You were so all-or-nothing about everything, and then you just walked away from me and I never heard from you again.'

'You just walked away too,' he reminded her. 'I was too proud to chase after you, although I thought of looking you up when I was over in London at least fifty times.'

'There's never been anyone else for me. I never stopped loving you although I didn't realise that until recently.'

'I fell in love with you on our first date. You got drenched with sea spray and you laughed. Every other girl I knew would have thrown a fit.'

'I'm not vain, but I'm a jealous cat,' she warned him, cherishing the ease with which he could look back through those years and recall one tiny incident, in much the same way he had remembered her admiring comment about the church on Lykos. The idea that he loved her was becoming more and more real and credible with every passing second. She smiled, and soon discovered that she couldn't stop smiling.

'I've sown my wild oats, but I didn't enjoy myself so much that I want to do it again, *agapi mou*,' Aristandros confided with blunt sincerity. 'I wanted a second chance with you. I wanted to hear you say you'd misjudged me. But when I found out about your wife-beating stepfather I got a step closer to understanding why you were so unwilling to trust me. When you threw that jealous scene after the Ferrand party, I was overjoyed, because that proved that you still had feelings for me just as I did for you.'

'So, what do you want now?' Ella enquired tightly.

'All I really want now is more of what we already have. I'm very happy with you. To be frank, I was disappointed that you weren't pregnant. I want to have a baby with you.'

Ella released a happy sigh at the prospect and beamed at him. 'How soon can we start trying?'

Aristandros laughed with rich appreciation. 'Would tonight be too soon?'

Ella regarded him with eyes as starry as the night sky above. 'No; I'm available without appointment whenever you want.'

'I should warn you that I want you pretty much all the time, *latria mou*,' Aristandros admitted, bending down to press his mouth to hers and kissing her slowly and skilfully until the blood drummed through her veins in a passionate response. 'It's an effort to go away on business when I've got you in my bed.'

'I don't want you going anywhere right now,' Ella confessed, her hands curling into the lapels of his suit jacket at the mere mention of him needing to go away from her. 'I want you all to myself. Will we get married on the island?'

'Yes. And soon,' he urged. 'Speaking as a guy who was once engaged for about five minutes, I don't believe in long engagements.'

'Neither do I,' Ella agreed fervently, while she busily thought about wedding dresses and Callie as a little flower girl, not to mention the provision of a baby to keep Callie company. She was so happy at the prospect of those delights that her heart felt as though it was overflowing.


Fourteen months later, Ella watched Kasma tuck Ari's son and heir, Nikolos, into his cot.

At three months old, Nikolos was already revealing Xenakis traits of character. He was very impatient, and screamed the place down if he wasn't fed immediately if he felt hungry. He truly adored an audience of female admirers and basked in their attention. He was advanced for his age in size and development. He already looked as though he was likely to be as tall as his father, and he had definitely inherited his father's heartbreakingly charismatic smile.

These days Drakon Xenakis spent more time on Lykos than in Athens. He was enchanted by his grandson's perfectly ordinary family life with Ella, Callie and the new baby. It was what he himself had never managed to achieve with his own late wife and children, and he appreciated the commitment it took for such a busy couple to make it work.

The house had been virtually rebuilt during the extensive renovations Ella had organised and was now a much more comfortable family-orientated home. It had not been easy to live in the house while all the work had still been going on, particularly while Ella was pregnant, but with her mother's help, and that of the staff, Ella had managed.

Jane had got divorced. Theo was still in prison serving time for that final assault on his ex-wife, while Jane lived in a city apartment and enjoyed a healthy circle of friends with whom she shared interests. At least once a month the older woman visited her daughter and, if both Ella and Aristandros were abroad together, she came to stay and took charge of the household.

But actually Aristandros was travelling a great deal less than he once had and worked more from home, while Ella was putting in part-time hours as the island

doctor and taking an interest in the charitable endeav-
ours of the Xenakis Foundation. Just as Aristandros had
gone to a good deal of trouble to ensure that business
rarely parted them, Ella had been equally careful to
ensure that her job didn't steal too big a slice of her time
and energy, and after a year she reckoned that she had
got the balance exactly right. Plentiful help on the home
front had been invaluable, and Callie currently attended
a play group in town several mornings a week. That
winter the whole family would be moving to the Athens
villa to enable Ella to undertake a paediatrics course at
the hospital.

Ella was blissfully happy. She and Aristandros had
enjoyed a huge engagement party, and her wedding a
couple of months afterwards had been the fairy-tale
event that she had always secretly dreamt of having.
Although Ella had been just a little pregnant at the time,
she hadn't been showing. Lily had been her chief brides-
maid, and was currently applying for a surgical job at a
Greek hospital after meeting up with a Greek businessman of her own at the wedding.

Ella had been surprised when she'd fallen pregnant
so quickly, while Ari had merely had his unshakeable
faith in his own virility proven to his full satisfaction.
Callie was just at the age when a baby brother was a
source of fascination to her, and had had to be dissuaded
from treating Nikolos like a living, breathing doll. Ella
and Aristandros had formally adopted Callie, and although they were careful to tell the child only as much
as she could currently understand about her true beginnings and Timon, the little girl regarded them as her
mother and father.

When Ella heard the buzz of the helicopter passing overhead, she grinned and headed out to the terrace to watch it land. Lean, dark and stunningly handsome in his business suit, Aristandros strode towards her.

'How was New York?' she asked.

'I had a frantic schedule. I'm just glad to be home with my beautiful wife and children.' As Callie raced towards him chattering in excitement, Aristandros swung the little girl up and hugged her with an ease that would have been foreign to him a year earlier. He paused beside Ella and lowered his dark head to kiss her.

Tingles of sensual awareness ran up and down her spine and into more private places. 'I like the dress,' he growled.

'Daddy's talking like a bear,' Callie giggled, sliding down to the ground to run off again.

Ella twirled so that Aristandros got the full effect of the short, red strappy dress swirling round her slim legs. 'Happy anniversary,' she told him.

'What's on the agenda for tonight?'

'Dinner on the yacht, and we're spending the night on board so that we can have lots and lots of private time without being interrupted,' Ella told him cheerfully.

Her candour brought a deeply amused smile to his striking features. 'You know how to keep me happy.'

'I certainly hope so. I love you loads,' she confided, wrapping her arms round him.

'And I love the way you love me as much as I love you.' Aristandros gazed down at her with brilliant dark eyes. 'I want you to know that this has been the happiest year of my entire life, *agapi mou*.'

Ella knew that that was an admission to be truly treasured, and felt almost overwhelmed by emotion.

Over dinner on *Hellenic Lady*, they caught up after his three-day absence and he gave her a sapphire eternity-ring engraved with their son's name. Hand-in-hand they walked to their state room, which was adorned with fresh flowers, to share a wonderful night together, and an early morning disturbed neither by a baby's cries for attention nor a toddler's wistful demands for company.

But that rare silence felt a touch weird to both of them and, after a quick breakfast, they got in the speedboat to sail back to shore and they spent the rest of the day on the beach as a family…

# A TYCOON TO BE
# RECKONED WITH

## JULIA JAMES

For IHV, who gave me my love of opera.

# CHAPTER ONE

'You KNOW, IT'S you I blame.'

Bastiaan's aunt tried to laugh as she spoke, but it was shaky, Bastiaan could tell.

'It was you who suggested Philip go and stay in your villa at Cap Pierre!'

Bastiaan took the criticism on board. 'I thought it might help—moving him out of target range to finish his university vacation assignments in peace and quiet.'

His aunt sighed. 'Alas, it seems he has jumped out of the frying pan into the fire. He may have escaped Elena Constantis, but this female in France sounds infinitely worse.'

Bastiaan's dark eyes took on a mordant expression. 'Unfortunately, wherever in the world Philip is he will be a target.'

'If only he were less sweet-natured. If he had your... *toughness*,' Bastiaan's aunt replied, her gaze falling on her nephew.

'I'll take that as a compliment,' Bastiaan replied dryly. 'But Philip will toughen up, don't worry.' *He'll need to*, he thought caustically. Just as he himself had had to.

'He's so impressionable!' his aunt cried. 'And so handsome. No wonder these wretched girls make a beeline for him.'

*And, of course, so rich*, Bastiaan added cynically—
but silently. No point worrying his already anxious aunt
further. It was Philip's wealth—the wealth he would be
inheriting from his late father's estate once he turned
twenty-one in a couple of months—that would attract females far more dangerous than the merely irksome spoilt
teenage princess Elena Constantis. The real danger would
come from a very different type of female.

Call them what one liked—and Bastiaan had several
names not suitable for his aunt's ears—the most univer-
sal name was a familiar one: gold-diggers. Females who
took one look at his young, good-looking, impressionable and soon to be very rich cousin and licked their lips
in anticipation.

That was the problem right now. A woman who appeared to be licking her lips over Philip. And the danger
was, Bastiaan knew, very real. For Philip, so Paulette, his
housekeeper at Cap Pierre, had informed him, far from
diligently writing his essays, had taken to haunting the
nearby town of Pierre-les-Pins and a venue there that
was most undesirable for a twenty-year-old. Apparently
attracted by an even more undesirable female working
there.

'A singer in a nightclub!' his aunt wailed now. 'I cannot believe Philip would fall for a woman like that!'

'It *is* something of a cliché…' Bastiaan allowed.

His aunt bridled. 'A cliché? Bastiaan, is that all you
have to say about it?'

He shook his head. 'No. I could say a great deal
more—but to what purpose?' Bastiaan got to his feet.
He was of an imposing height, standing well over six
feet, and powerfully built. 'Don't worry…' he made his
voice reassuring now '… I'll deal with it. Philip will *not*
be sacrificed to a greedy woman's ambitions.'

His aunt stood up, clutching at his sleeve. *'Thank you,'* she said. 'I knew I could count on you.' Her eyes misted a little. 'Take care of my darling boy, Bastiaan. He has no father now to look out for him.'

Bastiaan pressed his aunt's hand sympathetically. His maternal uncle had succumbed to heart disease when Philip had just started at university, and he knew how hard her husband's death had hit his aunt. Knew, too, with a shadowing of his eyes, how losing a father too young—as he himself had when not much older than Philip—left a void.

'I'll keep Philip safe, I promise you,' he assured his aunt now, as she took her leave.

He saw her to her car, watched it head down the driveway of his property in the affluent outskirts of Athens. Then he went back indoors, his mouth tightening.

His aunt's fears were not groundless. Until Philip turned twenty-one Bastiaan was his trustee—overseeing all his finances, managing his investments—while Philip enjoyed a more than generous allowance to cover his personal spending. Usually Bastiaan did nothing more than cast a casual eye over the bank and credit card statements, but an unusually large amount—twenty thousand euros—had gone out in a single payment a week ago. The cheque had been paid into an unknown personal account at the Nice branch of a French bank. There was no reason—no *good* reason—that Bastiaan could come up with for such a transfer. There was, however, one very bad reason for it—and that he *could* come up with.

The gold-digger had already started taking gold from the mine....

Bastiaan's features darkened. The sooner he disposed of this nightclub singer who was making eyes at his cousin—and his cousin's fortune—the better. He headed purposefully to his study. If he was to leave for France in the morning, he had work to do tonight. Enterprises with portfolios the size of Karavalas did not run themselves. His cousin's fortune might be predominantly in the form of blue chip stocks, but Bastiaan preferred to diversify across a broad range of investment opportunities, from industry and property to entrepreneurial start-ups. But, for all their variety, they all shared one aspect in common—they all made him money. A *lot* of money.

The cynical curve was back at Bastiaan's mouth as he sat himself down behind his desk and flicked on his PC. He'd told his aunt that her son would toughen up in time—and he knew from his own experience that that was true. Memory glinted in his dark eyes.

When his own father had died, he'd assuaged his grief by partying hard and extravagantly, with no paternal guardian to moderate his excesses. The spree had ended abruptly. He'd been in a casino, putting away the champagne and generally flashing his cash lavishly, and it had promptly lured across a female—Leana—who had been all over him. At just twenty-three he'd been happy to enjoy all she'd offered him—the company of her luscious body in bed included. So much so that when she'd fed him some story of how she'd stupidly got herself into debt with the casino and was worried sick about it, he'd grandly handed her a more than handsome cheque, feeling munificent and generous towards the beautiful, sexy woman who'd seemed so keen on him…

She'd disappeared the day the cheque had cleared—heading off, so he'd heard, on a yacht belonging to a seventy-year-old Mexican millionaire, never to be seen again by Bastiaan. He'd been royally fleeced and proved to be a complete mug. It had stung, no doubt about it, but he'd learnt his lesson, all right—an expensive one. It wasn't one he wanted Philip to learn the same way. Apart from taking a large wedge of his money, Leana had damaged his self-esteem—an uncomfortably sobering experience for his younger self. Although it had made him wise up decisively.

But, unlike Bastiaan, Philip was of a romantic disposition, and a gold-digging seductress might wound him more deeply than just in his wallet and his self-esteem. That was not something Bastiaan would permit. After his experience with Leana he'd become wise to the wiles women threw out to him, and sceptical of their apparent devotion. Now, into his thirties, he knew they considered him a tough nut—ruthless, even...

His eyes hardened beneath dark brows. That was something this ambitious nightclub singer would soon discover for herself.

Sarah stood motionless on the low stage, the spotlight on her, while her audience beyond, sitting at their tables, mostly continued their conversations as they ate and drank.

*I'm just a divertimento*, she thought to herself, acidly. *Background music.* She nodded at Max on the piano, throat muscles ready, and he played the opening to her number. It was easy and low-pitched, making no demands on her upper register. It was just as well—the last thing she wanted to do was risk her voice singing in this smoky atmosphere.

As she sang the first bars her breasts lifted, making her all too aware of just how low-cut the bodice of her champagne satin gown was. Her long hair was swept over one bare shoulder. It was, she knew, a stereotypical 'vamp' image—the sultry nightclub singer with her slinky dress, low-pitched voice, over-made-up eyes and long blonde locks.

She tensed instinctively. Well, that was the idea, wasn't it? To stand in for the club's missing resident *chanteuse,* Sabine Sablon, who had abruptly vacated the role when she'd run off with a rich customer without warning.

It hadn't been Sarah's idea to take over as Sabine, but Max had been blunt about it. If she didn't agree to sing here in the evenings, then Raymond, the nightclub owner, lacking a *chanteuse*, would refuse to let Max have the run of the place during the day. And without that they couldn't rehearse…and without rehearsals they couldn't appear at the Provence en Voix music festival.

And if they didn't appear there her last chance would be gone.

*My last chance—my last chance to achieve my dream!*

Her dream of breaking through from being just one more of the scores upon scores of hopeful, aspiring sopranos who crowded the operatic world, all desperate to make their mark. If she could not succeed now, she would have to abandon the dream that had possessed her since her teenage years, and all the way through music college and the tough, ultra-competitive world beyond as she'd struggled to make herself heard by those who could lift her from the crowd and launch her career.

She'd tried so hard, for so long, and now she was on the wrong side of twenty-five, racing towards thirty, with time against her and younger singers coming up behind her. Everything rested on this final attempt—and if it failed… Well, then, she would accept defeat. Resign herself to teaching instead. It was the way she was currently earning her living, part-time at a school in her native Yorkshire, though she found it unfulfilling, craving the excitement and elation of performing live.

So not yet—*oh, not yet*—would she give up on her dreams. Not until she'd put everything into this music festival, singing the soprano lead in what she knew could only be a high-risk gamble: a newly written opera by an unknown composer, performed by unknown singers, all on a shoestring. A shoestring that Max, their fanatically driven director and conductor, was already stretching to the utmost. Everything, but *everything*, was being done on a tiny budget, with savings being made wherever they could. Including rehearsal space.

So every night bar Sundays, she had to become Sabine Sablon, husking away into the microphone, drawing male eyes all around. It was not a comfortable feeling—and it was a million miles away from her true self. Max could tell her all he liked that it would give her valuable insight into roles such as *La Traviata*'s courtesan Violetta, or the coquettish Manon, but on an operatic stage everyone would know she was simply playing a part. Here, everyone looking at her really thought she *was* Sabine Sablon.

A silent shudder went through her. Dear God, if anyone in the opera world found out she was singing here, like this, her credibility would be shot to pieces. No one would take her seriously for a moment.

And neither Violetta nor Manon was anything like her role in Anton's opera *War Bride*. Her character was a romantic young girl, falling in love with a dashing soldier. A whirlwind courtship, a return to the front—and then the dreaded news of her husband's fate. The heartbreak of loss and bereavement. And then a child born to take his father's place in yet another war...

The simple, brutal tale was told as a timeless fable of the sacrifice and futility of war, repeated down the ages, its score haunting and poignant. It had captivated Sarah the first moment she'd heard Max play it.

*What must it be like to love so swiftly, to hurt so badly?* she'd wondered as she'd started to explore her role. For herself, she had no knowledge—had never experienced the heady whirlwind of love nor the desolation of heart-break. Her only serious relationship had ended last year when Andrew, a cellist she had known since college, had been offered a place in a prestigious orchestra in Germany. It had been his breakthrough moment, and she had been so glad for him—had waved him off without a thought of holding him back.

Both of them had always known that their careers must come first in their lives, which meant that neither could afford to invest in a deeply emotional relationship which might jeopardise their diverging career paths. So neither had grieved when they'd parted, only wished each other well. Theirs had been a relationship based primarily on a shared passion for music, rather than for each other—friendship and affection had bound them, nothing more than that.

But this meant she knew that in order to portray her character now—the War Bride—as convincingly as she could, she would need to call on all her imagination. Just as she would need all her operatic abilities to do credit to the challenging vocal demands of the hauntingly beautiful but technically difficult music.

She reached the end of her song to a smattering of applause. Dipping her head in acknowledgement, she shifted her weight from one high-heeled foot to the other. As she straightened again, sending her gaze back out over the dining area, she felt a sudden flickering awareness go through her. She could hear Max start the introduction to her next number but ignored it, her senses suddenly on alert. She heard him repeat the phrase, caught him glancing at her with a frown, but her attention was not on him—not on the song she was supposed to have started four bars earlier. Her attention was on the audience beyond.

Someone was looking at her. Someone standing at the back of the room.

He had not been there a moment ago and must have just come in. She shook her head, trying to dismiss that involuntary sense of heightened awareness, of sudden exposure. Male eyes gazed at her all the time—and there was always movement beyond the stage…diners and waiters. They did not make her pause the way this had—as if there were something different about him. She wanted to see him more clearly, but the light was wrong and he was too far away for her to discern anything more than a tall, tuxedo-clad figure at the back of the room.

For the third time she heard Max repeat the intro—insistently this time. And she knew she had to start to sing. Not just because of Max's impatient prompt but because she suddenly, urgently, needed to do something other than simply stand there, pooled in the light that emphasised every slender curve of her tightly sheathed body. Exposed her to that invisible yet almost tangible scrutiny that was palpable in its impact on her.

As she started the number her voice was more husky than ever. Her long, artificial lashes swept down over her deeply kohled eyes, and the sweep of her hair dipped halfway across her jawline and cheekbone. She forced herself to keep singing, to try and suppress the frisson of disturbed awareness that was tensing through her—the sense of being the object of attention that was like a beam targeted at her.

Somehow she got through to the end of the number, pulling herself together to start the next one on time and not fluff it. It seemed easier now, and she realised that at some point that sense of being under scrutiny had faded and dissipated. As if a kind of pressure had been lifted off her. She reached the end of the last number, the end of her set, with a sense of relief. She made her way off-stage, hearing canned music starting up and Max closing down the piano.

One of the waiters intercepted her. 'There's a guy who wants to buy you a drink,' he said.

Sarah made a face. It wasn't unusual that this happened, but she never accepted.

The waiter held up a hundred-euro note. 'Looks like he's keen,' he informed her with a lift of his brow.

'Well, he's the only one who is,' she said. 'Better take it back to him,' she added. 'I don't want him thinking I pocketed it and then didn't show.'

Her refusal got Max's approval. 'No time for picking up men,' he said, flippantly but pointedly.

'As if I would…' She rolled her eyes.

For a moment, it crossed her mind that the invitation to buy her a drink might be connected to that shadowy figure at the back of the room and his disturbing perusal of her, but then she dismissed the thought. All she wanted to do now was get out of her costume and head for bed. Max started opera rehearsals promptly every morning, and she needed to sleep.

She'd just reached her dressing room, kicking off her high heels and flexing her feet in relief, when there was a brief knock at the door. She only had time to say, 'Who is it?' before the door opened.

She glanced up, assuming it would be Max, wanting to tell her something that couldn't wait. But instead it was a man she'd never seen before in her life.

And he stilled the breath in her lungs.

# CHAPTER TWO

BASTIAAN'S EYES ZEROED in on the figure seated at the brightly lit vanity unit with its trademark light-bulb-surrounded mirror. Backlit as she was by the high-wattage bulbs, her face was in shadow.

But the shadows did nothing to dim her impact. If anything it emphasised it, casting her features into relief. On stage, she'd been illuminated in a pool of light, her features softened by the distance at which he'd sat. He'd deliberately taken a table at the rear of the room, wanting at that point only to observe without being noticed in return.

It hadn't taken him more than two moments to realise that the female poised on the stage possessed a quality that signalled danger to his young, impressionable cousin.

Allure—it was an old-fashioned word, but that was the one that had come to his mind as his eyes had rested on the slender figure sensuously draped in low-cut clinging satin, standing in a pool of soft, smoky light, her fingers lightly curved around her microphone, the lustrous fall of her long blonde hair curled over her bare shoulder like a vamp from the forties.

Her mouth was painted a rich, luscious red, her eye make-up was pronounced, with long, artificial lashes framing luminous eyes. Seeing her now, close up, she was even more alluring.

*No wonder Philip is smitten!*

His eyes completed his swift scrutiny and he was interested to see a line of colour running along her cheekbones. *Curious…* he thought. Then the tightening of her mouth told him what had accounted for that reaction. It was not a blush—a woman like her probably hadn't blushed since puberty—it was annoyance.

Why? he found himself wondering. Women were not usually annoyed when he paid them attention. Quite the reverse. But this *chanteuse* was. It was doubly unusual because surely a woman in her profession was well used to male admirers courting her in her dressing room.

An unwelcome thought crossed his mind—was it his cousin's wont to hang out here? Did she invite him to her changing room?

*Just how far has she got with him?*

Well, however far it was, it was going to stop from now on. Whatever story she'd trotted out to Philip in order to get him to give her money, the gold mine was closing down…

She was looking at him still, that scarlet mouth of hers pressed tightly, and something sparking now in her eyes.

'*Oui?*' she said pointedly.

His eyelids dipped over his eyes briefly. 'Did the waiter not pass on my invitation?' he asked, speaking in French, which he spoke as well as English and a couple of other languages as well.

Her arched eyebrows rose. 'It was you?' she said. Then, without bothering to wait for a reply, she simply went on, 'I'm afraid I don't accept invitations to share a drink with any of the club's guests.'

Her tone was dismissive, and Bastiaan felt a flicker

of annoyance at it. Dismissive was not the kind of voice he was used to hearing in women he was speaking to. Or indeed from anyone he was speaking to. And in someone whose career relied on the attention and appreciation of others, it was out of place.

*Perhaps she thinks she does not need to court her audience any longer? Perhaps she thinks she already has a very comfortable exit from her profession lined up?*

The flicker of annoyance sparked to something sharper. But he did not let it show. Not now—not yet. At the moment, his aim was to disarm her. Defeating her would come afterwards.

'Then allow me to invite you to dinner instead,' he responded. Deliberately, he infused a subtly caressing note into his voice that he'd found successful at any other time he'd chosen to adopt it.

That line of colour ran out over her cheekbones again. But this time there was no accompanying tightening of her red mouth. Instead she gave a brief smile. It was civil only—nothing more than that, Bastiaan could see.

'Thank you, but no. And now...' the smile came again, and he could see that her intention was to terminate the exchange '...if you will excuse me, I must get changed.' She paused expectantly, waiting for him to withdraw.

He ignored the prompt. Instead one eyebrow tilted interrogatively. 'You have another dinner engagement?' he asked.

Something snapped in her eyes, changing their colour, he noticed. He'd assumed they were a shade of grey, but suddenly there was a flash of green in them.

'No,' she said precisely. 'And if I did, *m'sieu*—' the pointedness was back in her voice now '—I don't believe it would be any of your concern.' She smiled tightly, with less civility now.

*If it were with my cousin, mademoiselle, it would indeed be my concern...* That flicker of more than annoyance came again, but again Bastiaan concealed it.

'In which case, what can be your objection to dining with me?' Again, there was the same note in his voice that worked so well with women in general. Invitations to dine with him had never, in his living memory, been met with rejection.

She was staring at him with those eyes that had gone back to grey now, the flash of green quite absent. Eyes that were outlined in black kohl, their sockets dramatised outrageously with make-up, their lashes doubled in length by artificial means and copious mascara.

Staring at him in a way he'd never been stared at before.

As though she didn't quite believe what she was seeing. Or hearing.

For just a second their eyes met, and then, as if in recoil, her fake lashes dropped down over her eyes, veiling them.

She took a breath. '*M'sieu*, I am desolated to inform you that I also do not accept invitations to dine with the club's guests,' she said. She didn't make her tone dismissive now, but absolute.

He ignored it. 'I wasn't thinking of dining here,' he said. 'I would prefer to take you to Le Tombleur,' he murmured.

Her eyes widened just a fraction. Le Tombleur was currently the most fashionable restaurant on the Côte D'Azur, and Bastiaan was sure that the chance to dine at such a fabulous locale would surely stop her prevaricating in this fashion. It would also, he knew, set her mind instantly at rest as to whether he was someone possessed of sufficient financial means to be of interest to her. She would not wish to waste her time on someone who was not in the same league as his young cousin. Had she but known, Bastiaan thought cynically, his own fortune was considerably greater than Philip's.

But of course Philip's fortune was far more accessible to her. Or might be. If she were truly setting Philip in her sightline, she would be cautious about switching her attentions elsewhere—it would lose her Philip if he discovered it.

A thought flickered across Bastiaan's mind. She was alluring enough—even for himself... Should *that* be his method of detaching her? Then he dismissed it. Of course he would not be involving himself in any kind of liaison with a woman such as this one. However worthy the intention.

*Dommage...* He heard the French word in his head. *What a pity...*

'*M'sieu...*' She was speaking again, with razored precision. 'As I say, I must decline your very...*generous*... invitation'.

Had there been a twist in her phrasing of the word 'generous'? An ironic inflection indicating that she had formed an opinion of him that was not the one he'd intended her to form?

He felt a new emotion flicker within him like a low-voltage electric current.

Could there possibly be more to this woman sitting there, looking up at him through those absurdly fake eyelashes, with a strange expression in her grey-green eyes—more green now than grey, he realised. His awareness of that colour-change was of itself distracting, and it made his own eyes narrow assessingly.

For just a fraction of a second their eyes seemed to

meet, and Bastiaan felt the voltage of the electric current surging within him.

'Are you ready to go yet?'

A different voice interjected, coming from the door, which had been pushed wider by a man—a youngish one—clad in a dinner jacket, half leaning his slightly built body against the doorjamb. The man had clearly addressed Sabine, but now, registering that there was someone else in her dressing room, his eyes went to Bastiaan.

He frowned, about to say something, but Sabine Sablon interjected. 'The gentleman is just leaving,' she announced.

Her voice was cool, but Bastiaan was too experienced with women not to know that she was not, in fact, as composed as she wanted to appear. And he knew what was causing it...

Satisfaction soared through him. Oh, this sultry, sophisticated *chanteuse*, with her vampish allure, her skin-tight dress and over-made-up face, might be appearing as cool as the proverbial cucumber—but that flash in her eyes had told him that however resistant she appeared to be to his overtures, an appearance was all it was...

*I can reach her. She is vulnerable to me.*

That was the truth she'd so unguardedly—so unwisely—just revealed to him.

He changed his stance. Glanced at the man hovering in the doorway. A slight sense of familiarity assailed him, and a moment later he knew why. He was the accompanist for the *chanteuse*.

For a fleeting moment he found himself speculating on whether the casual familiarity he could sense between the two of them betokened a more intimate relationship. Then he rejected it. Every male instinct told him that whatever lover the accompanist took would not be female.

Bastiaan's sense of satisfaction increased, and his annoyance with the intruder decreased proportionately. He turned his attention back to his quarry.

'I shall take my leave, then, *mademoiselle*,' he said, and he did not trouble to hide his ironic inflection or his amusement. Dark, dangerous amusement. As though her rejection of him was clearly nothing more than a feminine ploy—one he was seeing through…but currently choosing to indulge. He gave the slightest nod of his head, the slightest sardonic smile.

'*A bientôt.*'

Then, paying not the slightest attention to the accompanist, who had to straighten to let him pass, he walked out.

As he left he heard the *chanteuse* exclaim, 'Thank goodness you rescued me!'

Bastiaan could hear the relief in her tone. His satisfaction went up yet another level. A tremor—a discernible tremor—had been audible in her voice. That was good.

*Yes, she is vulnerable to me.*

He walked on down the corridor, casually letting himself out through the rear entrance into the narrow roadway beyond, before walking around to the front of the club, where his car was parked on the forecourt. Lowering himself into its low-slung frame, he started the engine, its low, throaty growl echoing the silent growl inside his head.

'*Thank goodness you rescued me!*' she had said, this harpy who was trying to extract his cousin's fortune from him.

Bastiaan's mouth thinned to a tight, narrow line, his eyes hardening as he headed out on to the road, setting his route back towards Monaco, where he was staying tonight in the duplex apartment he kept there.

Well, in that she was mistaken—most decidedly.

*No one will rescue you from me.*

Of that he was certain.

He drove on into the night.

'Give me two minutes and I'll be ready to go,' Sarah said.

She strove for composure, but felt as if she'd just been released from a seizure of her senses that had crushed the breath from her lungs. How she'd managed to keep her cool she had no idea—she had only know that keeping her cool was absolutely essential.

What the hell had just happened to her? Out of no-where...the way it had?

*That* had been the man whose assessing gaze she'd picked up during her final number. She'd been able to feel it from right across the club—and when he'd walked into her dressing room it had been like...

*Like nothing I've ever known. Nothing I've ever felt—*

Never before had a man had such a raw, physical impact on her. Hitting her senses like a sledgehammer. She tried to analyse it now—needing to do so. His height, towering over her in the tiny dressing room, had dominated the encounter. The broad shoulders had been sleekly clad in a bespoke dinner jacket, and there had been an impression of power that she had derived not just from the clearly muscular physique he possessed but by an aura about him that had told her this man was used to getting his own way.

Especially with women.

Because it hadn't just been the clear impression that here was a wealthy man who could buy female favours—his mention of Le Tombleur had been adequate demonstration of *that*—it had been far, far more...

She felt herself swallow. *He doesn't need money to impress women.*

No, she acknowledged shakily, all it took was those piercing dark eyes, winged with darker brows, the strong blade of his nose, the wide, sensual curve of his mouth and the tough line of his jaw.

He was a man who knew perfectly well that his appeal to women was powerful—who knew perfectly well that women responded to him on that account.

She felt her hackles rise automatically.

*He thought I'd jump at the chance!*

A rush of weakness swept through her. Thank God she'd had the presence of mind—pulled urgently out of her reeling senses—to react the way she'd managed to do.

*What was it about him that he should have had such an effect on me?*

Just what had it been about that particular combination of physique, looks and sheer, raw personal impact that had made her react as if she were a sliver of steel in the sudden presence of a magnetic field so strong it had made the breath still in her body?

She had seen better-looking men in her time, but not a single one had ever had the raw, visceral, overpowering impact on her senses that this man had. Even in the space of a few charged minutes...

She shook her head again, trying to clear the image from her mind. Whoever he was, he'd gone.

As she got on with the task of turning herself back into Sarah, shedding the false eyelashes, heavy make-up and tight satin gown, she strove to dismiss him from her thoughts. *Put him out of your head*, she told herself brusquely. *It was Sabine Sablon he wanted to invite to dinner, not Sarah Fareham.*

That was the truth of it, she knew. Sabine was the

kind of woman a man like that would be interested in—
sophisticated, seductive, a woman of the world, a *femme
fatale*. And she wasn't Sabine—she most definitely was
not. So it was completely irrelevant that she'd reacted to
the man the way she had.

*I haven't got time to be bowled over by some arro-
gantly smouldering alpha male who thinks he's picking up a sultry woman like Sabine. However much he
knocked me sideways.*

She had one focus in her life right now—only one.
And it was *not* a man with night-dark eyes and devastating looks who sucked the breath from her body.

She headed out to where Max was waiting to walk her
back to her *pension*, some blocks away in this harbour-
side *ville* of Pierre-les-Pins, before carrying on to the
apartment he shared with Anton, the opera's composer.

As they set off he launched into speech without preamble. 'I've been thinking,' he said, 'in your first duet
with Alain—'

And he was off, instructing her in some troublesome
vocal technicalities he wanted to address at the next
day's rehearsal. Sarah was glad, for it helped to distance
her mind from that brief but disturbing encounter in her
dressing room with that devastating, dangerous man.

Dangerous? The word echoed in her head, taking her
aback. *Had* he been dangerous? Truly?

She gave herself a mental shake. She was being absurd. How could a complete stranger be dangerous to
her? Of course he couldn't.

It was absurd to think so.

# CHAPTER THREE

'BASTIAAN! FANTASTIC! I'd no idea you were here in France!' Philip's voice was warm and enthusiastic as he answered his mobile.

'Monaco, to be precise,' Bastiaan answered, strolling with his phone to the huge plate-glass window of his high-rise apartment in Monte Carlo, which afforded a panoramic view over the harbour, chock-full of luxury yachts glittering in the morning sunshine.

'But you'll come over to the villa, won't you?' his cousin asked eagerly.

'Seeking distraction from your essays…?' Bastiaan trailed off deliberately, knowing the boy had distraction already—a dangerous one.

As it had done ever since he'd left the nightclub last night, the seductive image of Sabine Sablon slid into his inner vision. Enough to distract anyone. Even himself…

He pulled his mind away. Time to discover just how deep Philip was with the alluring *chanteuse*. 'Well,' he continued, 'I can be with you within the hour if you like?'

He did not get an immediate reply. Then Philip was saying, 'Could you make it a bit later than that?'

'Studying so hard?' Bastiaan asked lightly.

'Well, not precisely. I mean, I *am*—I've got one essay

nearly finished—but actually, I'm a bit tied up till lunch-time…'

Philip's voice trailed off, and Bastiaan could hear the constraint in his cousin's voice. He was hiding something.

Deliberately, Bastiaan backed off. 'No problem,' he said. 'See you for lunch, then—around one… Is that OK?' He paused. 'Do you want me to tell Paulette to expect me, or will you?'

'Would *you*?' said Philip, from which Bastiaan drew his own conclusion. Philip wasn't at the villa right now.

'No problem,' he said again, making his voice easy still. Easier than his mind…

So, if Philip wasn't struggling with his history essays at the villa, where was he?

*Is he with her now?*

He could feel his hackles rising down his spine. Was that why she had turned down dining with him at Le Tombleur? Because she'd been about to rendezvous with his cousin? Had Philip spent the night with her?

A growl started in his throat. Philip might be legally free to have a relationship with anyone he wanted, but even if the *chanteuse* had been as pure as the driven snow, with the financial probity of a nun, she was utterly unsuitable for a first romance for a boy his age. She was nearer thirty than twenty…

'Great!' Philip was saying now. 'See you then, Bast—gotta go.'

The call was disconnected and Bastiaan dropped his phone back in his pocket slowly, staring out of the window. Multi-million-pound yachts crowded the marina, and the fairy tale royal palace looked increasingly besieged by the high-rise buildings that maximised the tiny footprint of the principality.

He turned away. His apartment here had been an excellent investment, and the rental income was exceptional during the Monaco Grand Prix, but Monte Carlo was not his favourite place. He far preferred his villa on Cap Pierre, where Philip was staying. Better still, his own private island off the Greek west coast. That was where he went when he truly wanted to be himself. One day he'd take the woman who would be his wife there—the woman he would spend the rest of his life with.

Although just who she would be he had no idea. His experience with women was wide, indeed, but so far not one of his many female acquaintances had come anywhere close to tempting him to make a relationship with her permanent. One thing he was sure of—when he met her, he'd know she was the one.

There'd be no mistaking that.

Meantime he'd settle himself down at the dining table, open his laptop and get some work done before heading off to meet Philip—and finding out just how bad his infatuation was…

'I could murder a coffee.' Sarah, dismissed by Max for now, while he focussed his attentions on the small chorus, plonked herself down at the table near the front of the stage where Philip was sitting.

He'd become a fixture at their rehearsals, and Sarah hadn't the heart to discourage him. He was a sweet guy, Philip Markiotis, and he had somehow attached himself to the little opera company in the role of unofficial runner—fetching coffee, refilling water jugs, copying scores, helping tidy up after rehearsals.

And all the time, Sarah thought with a softening of her expression, he was carrying a youthful torch for her that glowed in every yearning glance that came her way. He was only a few years older than her own sixth-formers, and his admiration for her must remain hopeless, but she would never dream of hurting his feelings. She knew how very real they seemed to him.

Memory sifted through Sarah's head. She knew what Philip was experiencing. OK, she could laugh at herself now, but as a music student she'd had *the* most lovestruck crush on the tenor who'd taken a summer master class she'd attended. She'd been totally smitten, unable to conceal it—but, looking back now, what struck her most was how tolerant the famous tenor had been of her openly besotted devotion. Oh, she probably hadn't been the only smitten female student, but she'd always remembered that he'd been kind, and tactful, and had never made her feel juvenile or idiotic.

She would do likewise now, with Philip. His crush, she knew perfectly well, would not outlast the summer. It was only the result of his isolation here, with nothing to do but write his vacation essays…and yearn after her hopelessly, gazing at her ardently with his dark eyes.

Out of nowhere a different image sprang into her head. The man who had walked into her dressing room, invaded her space, had rested his eyes on her—but not with youthful ardour in them. With something far more powerful, more primitive. Long-lashed, heavy-lidded, they had held her in their beam as if she were being targeted by a searchlight. She felt a sudden shimmer go through her—a shiver of sensual awareness—as if she could not escape that focussed regard. Did not want to…

She hauled her mind away.

*I don't want to think about it. I don't want to think about him. He asked me out, I said no—that's it. Over and done with.*

And it hadn't even been *her* he'd asked out, she reminded herself. The man had taken her for Sabine, sultry and seductive, sophisticated and sexy. She would have to be terminally stupid not to know how a man like that, who thought nothing of approaching a woman he didn't know and asking her to dinner, would have wanted the evening to end had 'Sabine' accepted his invitation. It had been in his eyes, in his gaze—in the way it had washed over her. Blatant in its message.

*Would I have wanted it to end that way? If I were Sabine…?*

The question was there before she could stop it. Forcibly she pushed it aside, refusing to answer. She was *not* Sabine—she was Sarah Fareham. And whatever the disturbing impact that man had had on her she had no time to dwell on it. She was only weeks away from the most critical performance of her life, and all her energies, all her focus and strength, had to go into that. Nothing else mattered—*nothing*.

'So,' she said, making her voice cheerful, accepting the coffee Philip had poured for her, 'you're our one-man audience, Philip—how's it going, do you think?'

His face lit. 'You were *wonderful*!' he said, his eyes warm upon her.

Damn, thought Sarah wryly, she'd walked into that one. 'Thank you, kind sir,' she said playfully, 'but what about everyone else?'

'I'm sure they're excellent,' said Philip, his lack of interest in the other performers a distinct contrast with his enthusiasm for the object of his devotion. Then he frowned. 'Max treats you very badly,' he said, 'criticising you the way he does.'

Sarah smiled, amused. 'Oh, Philip—that's his job. And it's not just me—he's got to make sure we all get it right and then pull it together. He hears *all* the voices—each of us is focussing only on our own.'

'But yours is *wonderful*,' Philip said, as though that clinched the argument.

She gave a laugh, not answering, and drank her coffee, chasing it down with a large glass of water to freshen her vocal cords.

She was determined to banish the last remnants from the previous night's unwanted encounter with a male who was the very antithesis of the one sitting gazing at her now. Philip's company eased some of the inevitable tension that came from the intensity of rehearsals, the pressure on them all and Max's exacting musical direction. Apart from making sure she did not inadvertently encourage Philip in his crush on her, sitting with him was very undemanding.

With his good-natured, sunny personality, as well as his eagerness and enthusiasm for what was, to him, the novelty of a bohemian, artistic enterprise, it wasn't surprising that she and the other cast members liked him. What had been more surprising to her was that Max had not objected to his presence. His explanation had not found favour with her.

'*Cherie*, anyone staying at their family villa on the *Cap* is loaded. The boy might not throw money around but, believe me, I've checked out the name—he's one rich kid!' Max's eyes had gone to Sarah. 'Cultivate him, *cherie*—we could do with a wealthy sponsor.'

Sarah's reply had been instant—and sharp. 'Don't even *think* of trying to get a donation from him, Max!' she'd warned.

It would be absolutely out of the question for her to take advantage of her young admirer's boyish infatuation, however much family money there might be in the background. She'd pondered whether to warn Philip that Max might be angling for some financial help for the cash-strapped ensemble, but then decided not to. Knowing Philip, it would probably only inspire him to offer it.

She gave a silent sigh. What with treading around Philip's sensibilities, putting her heart and soul into perfecting her performance under the scathing scrutiny of Max, and enduring her nightly ordeal as Sabine, there was a lot on her plate right now. The last thing she needed to be added to it was having her mind straining back with unwelcome insistence to that unnerving visitation to her dressing room the night before.

At her side, Philip was glancing at his watch. He made a face.

'Need to go back to your essays?' she asked sympathetically.

'No,' he answered, 'it's my cousin—the one who owns the villa on the *Cap*—he's turned up on the Riviera and is coming over for lunch.'

'Checking you aren't throwing wild all-night parties, is he?' Sarah teased gently, although Philip was the last type to do any such thing. 'Or holding one himself?'

Philip shook his head. 'Bastiaan's loads too old for that stuff—he's gone thirty,' he said ingenuously. 'He spends most of his time working. Oh, and having hordes of females trailing around after him.'

Well, thought Sarah privately, if Cousin Bastiaan was from the same uber-affluent background as Philip, that wouldn't be too surprising. Rich men, she supposed, never ran short of female attention.

Before she could stop it, her mind homed back to that incident in her dressing room the night before. Her eyes darkened. Now, *there* was a man who was not shy of flaunting his wealth. Dropping invitations to flash restaurants and assuming they'd be snapped up.

But immediately she refuted her own accusation.

*He didn't need money to have the impact he had on me. All he had to do was stand there and look at me...*

She dragged her mind away. She had to stop this—she *had* to. How many times did she have to tell herself that?

'Sarah!' Max's imperious call rescued her from her troubling thoughts.

She got to her feet, and Philip did too. 'Back to the grindstone,' she said. 'And you scoot, Philip. Have fun with your cousin.' She smiled, lifting a brief hand in farewell as she made her way back to the stage.

Within minutes she was utterly absorbed, her whole being focussed only on her work, and the rest of the world disappeared from sight.

'So,' said Bastiaan, keeping his voice studiedly casual, 'you want to start drawing on your fund, is that it?'

The two of them were sitting outside on the shaded terrace outside the villa's dining room. They'd eaten lunch out there and now Bastiaan was drinking coffee, relaxed back in his chair.

Or rather he appeared to be relaxed. Internally, however, he was on high alert. His young cousin had just raised the subject of his approaching birthday, and asked whether Bastiaan would start to relax the reins now. Warning bells were sounding.

Across the table from him, Philip shifted position. 'It's not going to be a problem, is it?' he said.

He spoke with insouciance, but Bastiaan wasn't fooled. His level of alertness increased. Philip was being evasive.

'It depends.' He kept his voice casual. 'What is it you want to spend the money on?'

Philip glanced away, out over the gardens towards the swimming pool. He fiddled with his coffee spoon some more, then looked back at Bastiaan. 'Is it such a big deal, knowing what I want the money for? I mean, it's *my* money...'

'Yes,' allowed Bastiaan. 'But until your birthday I... I *guard* it for you.'

Philip frowned. 'For me or *from* me?' he said.

There was a tightness in his voice that was new to Bastiaan. Almost a challenge. His level of alertness went up yet another notch.

'It might be the same thing,' he said. His voice was even drier now. Deliberately he took a mouthful of black coffee, replaced the cup with a click on its saucer and looked straight at Philip. 'A fool and his money...' He trailed off deliberately.

He saw his cousin's colour heighten. 'I'm not a fool!' he riposted.

'No,' agreed Bastiaan, 'you're not. But—' he held up his hand '—you could, all the same, be made a fool *of*.'

His dark eyes rested on his cousin. Into his head sprang the image of that *chanteuse* in the nightclub again—pooled in light, her dress clinging, outlining her body like a second skin, her tones low and husky...*alluring*...

He snapped his mind away, using more effort than he was happy about. Got his focus back on Philip—not on the siren who was endangering him. As for his tentative attempt to start accessing his trust fund—well, he'd made his point, and now it was time to lighten up.

'So just remember...' he let humour into his voice now '...when you turn twenty-one you're going to find yourself very, *very* popular—cash registers will start ringing all around you.'

He saw Philip swallow.

'I do know that...' he said.

He didn't say it defiantly, and Bastiaan was glad.

'I really won't be a total idiot, Bast—and…and I'm not ungrateful for your warning. I know—' Bastiaan could hear there was a crack in his voice. 'I know you're keeping an eye on me because…well, because…'

'Because it's what your father would have expected— and what your mother wants,' Bastiaan put in. The humour was gone now. He spoke with only sober sympathy for his grieving cousin and his aunt. He paused. 'She worries about you—you're her only son.'

Philip gave a sad smile. 'Yes, I know,' he said. 'But Bast, please—do reassure her that she truly doesn't need to worry so much.'

'I'll do that if I can,' Bastiaan said. Then, wanting to change the subject completely, he said, 'So, where do you fancy for dinner tonight?'

As he spoke he thought of Le Tombleur. Thought of the rejection he'd had the night before. Unconsciously, his face tightened. Then, as Philip answered, it tightened even more.

'Oh, Bast—I'm sorry—I can't. Not tonight.'

Bastiaan allowed himself a glance. Then, 'Hot date?' he enquired casually.

Colour ran along his cousin's cheekbones. 'Sort of…' he said.

'Sort of hot? Or sort of a date?' Bastiaan kept his probing light. But his mood was not light at all. He'd wondered last night at the club, when he'd checked out the *chanteuse* himself, whether he might see Philip there as well. But there'd been no sign of him and he'd been relieved. Maybe things weren't as bad as he feared. But now—

'A sort of date,' Philip confessed.

Bastiaan backed off. He was walking through landmines for the time being, and he did not want to set one off. He would have to tread carefully, he knew, or risk putting the boy's back up and alienating him.

In a burst, Philip spoke again. 'Bast—could I...? Could you...? Well, there's someone I want you to meet.'

Bastiaan stilled. 'The hot date?' he ventured.

Again the colour flared across his cousin's cheeks. 'Will you?' he asked.

'Of course,' Bastiaan replied easily. 'How would you like us to meet up? Would you like to invite her to dinner at the villa?'

It was a deliberate trail, and it got the answer he knew Philip had to give. 'Er...no. Um, there's a place in Les Pins—the food's not bad—though it's not up to your standards of course, but—'

'No problem,' said Bastiaan, wanting only to be accommodating. Philip, little did he realise it, was playing right into his hands. Seeing his cousin with his *inamorata* would give him a pretty good indication of just how deep he was sunk into the quicksand that she represented.

'Great!'

Philip beamed, and the happiness and relief in his voice showed Bastiaan that his impressionable, vulnerable cousin was already in way, way too deep...

# CHAPTER FOUR

BEYOND THE SPOTLIGHT trained on her, Sarah could see Philip, sitting at the table closest to the stage, gazing up at her while she warbled through her uninspiring medley. At the end of her first set Max went backstage to phone Anton, as he always did, and Sarah stepped carefully down to the dining area, taking the seat Philip was holding out for her.

She smiled across at him. 'I thought you'd be out with your cousin tonight, painting the Côte d'Azur red!' she exclaimed lightly.

'Oh, no,' said Philip dismissively. 'But speaking of my cousin…' He paused, then went on in a rush, 'Sarah, I hope you don't mind… I've asked him here to meet you! You *don't* mind, do you?' he asked entreatingly.

Dismay filled her. She didn't want to crush him, but at the same time the fewer people who knew she appeared here nightly as Sabine the better. Unless, of course, they didn't know her as Sarah the opera singer in the first place.

Philip was a nice lad—a student—but Cousin Bastiaan, for all Sarah knew, moved in the elite, elevated social circles of the very wealthy, and might well be acquainted with any number of people influential in all sorts of areas…including opera. She just could not afford to jeopardise what nascent reputation the festival might build for her—not with her entire future resting on it.

She thought rapidly. 'Look, Philip, I know this might sound confusing, but can we stick to me being Sabine, rather than mentioning my opera singing?' she ventured. 'Otherwise it gets…complicated.'

*Complicated* was one word for it—*risky* was another.

Philip was looking disconcerted. 'Must I?' he protested. 'I'd love Bastiaan to know how wonderful and talented you really are.' Admiration and ardent devotion shone in his eyes.

Sarah gave a wry laugh. 'Oh, Philip, that's very sweet of you, but—'

She got no further. Philip's gaze had suddenly flicked past her. 'That's him,' he announced. 'Just coming over now—'

Sarah craned her neck slightly—and froze.

The tall figure threading its way towards their table was familiar. Unmistakably so.

She just had time to ask a mental, *What on earth?* when he was upon them.

Philip had jumped to his feet.

'Bast! You made it! Great!' he cried happily, sticking to the French he spoke with Sarah. He hugged his cousin exuberantly, and went on in Greek, 'You've timed it perfectly—'

'Have I?' answered Bastiaan. He kept his voice studiedly neutral, but his eyes had gone to the woman seated at his cousin's table. Multiple thoughts crowded in his head, struggling for predominance. But the one that won out was the last one he wanted.

A jolt of insistent, unmistakable male response to the image she presented.

The twenty-four hours since he'd accosted her in her

dressing room had done nothing at all to lessen the impact she made on him. The same lush blond hair, deep eyes, rich mouth, and another gown that skimmed her shoulders and breasts, moulding the latter to perfection...

He felt his body growl with raw, masculine satisfaction. The next moment he'd crushed it down. So here she was, the sultry *chanteuse*, making herself at home with Philip, and Philip's eyes on her were like an adoring puppy's.

'Bastiaan, I want to introduce you to someone very special,' Philip was saying. A slight flush mounted in the young man's cheeks and his glance went from his cousin to Sarah and back again. 'This...' there was the slightest hesitation in his voice '...this is Sabine.' He paused more discernibly this time. 'Sabine,' he said self-consciously, 'this is my cousin Bastiaan—Bastiaan Karavalas.'

Through the mesh of consternation in Sarah's head one realisation was clear. It was time to call it, she knew. Make it clear to Philip—and to his cousin Bastiaan— that, actually, they were already 'acquainted.' She gave the word a deliberately biting sardonic inflection in her head.

Her long fake lashes dipped down over her eyes and she found herself surreptitiously glancing at the dark-eyed, powerfully built man who had just sat down, dominating the space.

Dominating her senses...

Just as he had the night before, when he'd appeared in her dressing room.

But it wasn't this that concerned her. It was the way he seemed to be suddenly the only person in the entire universe, drawing her eyes to him as irretrievably as if he were the iron to her magnetic compass. She couldn't look away—could only let her veiled glance fasten on him, feel again, as powerfully as she first had, the raw impact he had on her, that sense of power and attraction that she could not explain—did not want to explain.

*Call it.* She heard the imperative in her head. *Call it—say that you know him—that he has already sought you out...*

But she couldn't do anything other than sit there and try to conjure up some explanation for why she couldn't open her mouth.

Into her head tumbled the overriding question—*What the hell is going on here?*

Because something was—that was for sure. A man she'd never seen before in her life had turned up at the club, bribed a waiter to invite her to his table, then confronted her in her dressing room to ask her out... And then he reappeared as Philip's cousin, unexpectedly arrived in France...

But there was no time to think—no time for anything other than to realise that she had to cope with the situation as it was now and come up with answers later.

*'Mademoiselle...'*

The deep voice was as dark as she remembered it—accented in Greek, similar to Philip's. But that was the only similarity. Philip's voice was light, youthful, his tone usually admiring, often hesitant. But his cousin, in a single word, conveyed to Sarah a whole lot more.

Assessing—guarded—sardonic. Not quite mocking but...

She felt a shiver go down her spine. A shiver she should not be feeling. Should have no need of feeling. Was he *daring* her to admit they'd already encountered one another?

*'M'sieu...'* She kept her voice cool. Totally neutral.

A waiter glided up, seeing a new guest had arrived.

The business of Bastiaan Karavalas ordering a drink—
a dry martini, Sarah noted absently—gave her precious
time to try and grab some composure back.

She was in urgent need of it—whatever Bastiaan Karavalas was playing at, it was his physical presence that
was dominating her senses, overwhelming her with his
raw, physical impact just the way it had last night in her
dressing room. Dragging her gaze to him set her heart
quickening, her pulse surging. What *was* it about him?
That sense of presence, of power—of dark, magnetic attraction? The veiled eyes, the sensual mouth…?

Never had she been so aware of a man. Never had her
body reacted like this.

'For you, *mademoiselle*?' the deep, accented voice
was addressing her, clearly enquiring what she would
like to drink.

She gave a quick shake of her head. 'Thank you—no.
I stick to water between sets.'

He dismissed the waiter with an absent lift of his hand
and the man scurried off to do his bidding.

'Sets?' Bastiaan enquired.

His thoughts were busy. He'd wanted to see whether
she would disclose his approach to her the previous evening, and now he was assessing the implications of her
not doing so.

He was, he knew, assessing a great deal about her…
Predominantly her physical impact on him. Even though
that was the thing least relevant to the situation.

*Or was it?*

The thought was in his head before he could stop it.
So, too, was the one that followed hard upon its heels.

Her reaction to him blazed from her like a beacon.
Satisfaction—stabbing through him—seared in his veins.
That, oh, *that*, indeed, was something he could use…

He quelled the thought—this was not the time. She had taken the first trick at that first encounter, turning down the invitation he'd so expected her to take. *But the game, Mademoiselle Sabine, is only just begun...*

And he would be holding the winning hand!

'Sa...Sabine's a singer,' Philip was saying, his eyes alight and sweeping admiringly over the *chanteuse* who had him in her coils.

Bastiaan sat back, his eyes flickering over the slinkily dressed and highly made-up figure next to his cousin. 'Indeed?'

It was his turn to use the French language to his advantage—allowing the ironic inflection to work to her discomfiture...as though he doubted the veracity of his cousin's claim.

'Indeed, *m'sieu*,' echoed Sarah. The ironic inflection had not been lost on her and she repaid it herself, in a light, indifferent tone.

He didn't like that, she could see. There was something about the way his dark brows drew a fraction closer to each other, the way the sensual mouth tightened minutely.

'And what do you...sing?' he retaliated, and one dark brow lifted with slight interrogation.

'*Chansons d'amour,*' Sarah murmured. 'What else?' She gave a smile—just a little one. Light and mocking.

Philip spoke again. 'You've just missed Sabine's first set,' he told Bastiaan.

His glance went to her, as if for reassurance—or perhaps, thought Bastiaan, it was simply because the boy couldn't take his eyes from the woman.

*And nor can I—*

'But you'll catch her second set!' Philip exclaimed enthusiastically.

'I wouldn't miss it for the world,' he said dryly. Again, his gaze slid to the *chanteuse*.

A new reaction was visible, and it caught his attention. Was he mistaken, or was there, somewhere beneath the make-up, colour suffusing her cheekbones?

*Had she taken what he'd said as sarcasm?*

If she had, she repaid him in the same coin.

'You are too kind, *m'sieu*,' she said.

And Bastiaan could see, even in the dim light, how her deep-set eyes, so ludicrously enhanced by false eyelashes and heavy kohled lids, flashed fleetingly to green.

A little jolt of sexual electricity fired in him. He wanted to see more of that green flash…

*It would come if I kissed her—*

'Sa…Sabine's voice is wonderful.'

Philip cut across his heated thoughts. Absently, Bastiaan found himself wondering why his cousin seemed to stammer over the singer's name.

'Even when she's only singing *chan*—'

Sarah's voice cut across Philip's. 'So, M'sieu Karavalas, you have come to visit Philip? I believe the villa is yours, is it not?'

She couldn't care less what he was doing here, or whether he owned a villa on Cap Pierre or anywhere else. She'd only spoken to stop Philip saying something she could see he was dying to say, despite her earlier plea to him—

*Even when she's only singing* chansons *in a place like this.*

*I don't want him to mention anything about what I really sing—that I'm not really Sabine!*

Urgency filled her. And now it had nothing to do with not wanting Bastiaan Karavalas to know that Sarah Fareham moonlighted as Sabine Sablon. No, it was for a quite different reason—one that right now seemed far more crucial.

*I can't handle him as Sarah. I need to be Sabine. Sabine can cope with this—Sabine can cope with a man like him. Sabine is the kind of sophisticated, worldly-wise female who can deal with such a man.*

With the kind of man who coolly hit on a woman who'd taken his eye and aroused his sexual interest, arrogantly assuming she would comply without demur. The kind of man who rested assessing, heavy-lidded eyes on her, drawing no veil over what he saw in her, knowing exactly what impact his assessment of her was having.

*That* kind of man…

Philip's enthusiastic voice was a relief to her.

'You ought to spend some time at the villa, Bast! It really is a beautiful place. Paulette says you're hardly ever there.'

Bastiaan flicked his eyes to his cousin. 'Well, maybe I should move across from Monaco and stay awhile with you. Keep you on the straight and narrow.'

He smiled at Philip, and as he did so Sarah suddenly saw a revelation. Utterly unexpected. Gone—totally vanished—was the Bastiaan Karavalas she'd been exposed to, with his coolly assessing regard and his blatant appraisal, and the sense of leashed power that emanated from him. Now, as he looked across at Philip, his smile carved deep lines around his mouth and lightened his expression, made him suddenly seem…different.

She felt something change inside her—uncoil as if a knot had been loosened…

*If he ever smiled at me like that I would be putty in his hands.*

But she sheered her mind away. Bastiaan Karavalas

was unsettling enough, without throwing such a smile her way.

'Make me write all my wretched essays, you mean—don't you, Bast?' Philip answered, making a face.

But Sarah could see the communication running between them, the easy affection. It seemed to make Bastiaan far less formidable. But that, she knew with a clenching of her muscles, had a power of its own. A power she must not acknowledge. Not even as Sabine.

'It's what you came here for,' Bastiaan reminded him. 'And to escape, of course.'

His dark eyes flickered back to Sarah and the warmth she'd seen so fleetingly as he'd smiled at his young cousin drained out of them. It was replaced by something new. Something that made her eyes narrow minutely as she tried to work out what it was.

'I offered the villa to Philip as a refuge,' he informed Sarah in a casual voice. 'He was being plagued by a particularly persistent female. She made a real nuisance of herself, didn't she?' His glance went back to his cousin.

Philip made another face. 'Elena Constantis *was* a pain,' he said feelingly. 'Honestly, she's got boys buzzing all over her, but she still wanted to add *me* to her stupid collection. She's so immature,' he finished loftily.

A tiny smile hovered at Sarah's lips, dispelling her momentary unease. Immaturity was a relative term, after all. For a second—the briefest second—she caught a similar smile just tugging at Bastiaan Karavalas's well-shaped mouth, lifting it the way his smile at Philip had done a moment ago.

Almost, *almost* she felt herself starting to meet his eyes, ready to exchange glances with him—two people so much more mature than sweet, young Philip…

Then the intention was wiped from her consciousness.

Its tempting potency gone. Philip's gaze had gone to her. 'She couldn't be more different from *you*,' he said. The warmth in his voice could have lit a fire.

Sarah's long, fake eyelashes dipped again. Bastiaan Karavalas's dark gaze had switched to her, and she was conscious of it—burningly conscious of it. Conscious, too, of what must have accounted for the studiedly casual remark he'd made that had got them on to this subject.

*Surely he can't think I don't realise that Philip is smitten with me?*

Bastiaan was speaking again. 'Sabine is certainly much *older*,' he observed.

The dark eyes had flicked back to her face—watching, she could tell, for her reaction to his blunt remark. Had he intended to warn her? To show her how real his cousin's infatuation with her was?

How best to respond…? 'Oh, I'm ancient, indeed!' she riposted lightly. 'Positively creaking.'

'You're not old!' Philip objected immediately, aghast at the very idea. Adoration shone in his eyes. Then his gaze shifted to the dance floor in front of the stage, where couples had started to congregate. His face lit, 'Oh! Sabine—will you dance with me? Please say yes!'

Indecision filled her. She never danced with Philip or did anything to encourage him. But right now it would get her away from the disturbing, overpowering impact of Bastiaan Karavalas.

'If you like,' she replied, and got to her feet as he leapt eagerly to his and walked her happily out on to the dance floor.

Thankfully, the music was neither very fast—fast dancing would have been impossible in her tight gown—nor so slow that it would require any kind of smoochy embrace. But since most of the couples were in a traditional ballroom-style hold with each other, that was the hold she glided into.

Philip, bless him, clearly wasn't too *au fait* with so formal a dancing style, but he manfully did his best. 'I've got two left feet!' he exclaimed ruefully.

'You're doing fine,' she answered encouragingly, making sure she was holding him literally at arm's length.

It seemed an age until the number finally ended.

'Well done,' she said lightly.

'I won't be so clumsy next time,' he promised her.

She let her hand fall from his shoulder and indicated that he should let go of her too—which he did, with clear reluctance. But Philip's crush on her was not uppermost in her mind right now.

She was just about to murmur something about her next set, and this time make sure she headed off, when a deep voice sounded close by.

'Mademoiselle Sabine? I trust you will give me equal pleasure?'

She started, her head twisting. Bastiaan Karavalas was bearing down on them as the music moved on to another number. A distinctly slower number.

He gave her no chance to refuse. An amused nod of dismissal at his cousin and then, before she could take the slightest evasive action, Sarah's hand had been taken, her body was drawn towards his by the placing of his large, strong hand at her waist, and she was forced to lift her other hand and let it rest as lightly as she could on his shoulder. Then he was moving her into the dance—his thigh pressing blatantly against hers to impel her to move.

Instinctively Sarah tried to preserve her composure, though her heart was pounding in her ribcage. Her body was as stiff as a board, her muscles straining away from him as if she could increase the narrow gap between their bodies. His answer was to curve his fingers into her waist, and with effortless strength secure his hold on her again.

He smiled down at her.

It was a smile of pure possession.

Sarah could feel her blood surging in her body, quickening in every vein, heating her from within as she moved against his possessive clasp.

'So, *mademoiselle*, on what shall we converse?'

His smile had given way to a question in which both irony and amusement were mingled. And something else too—something she could not give a name to, but which seemed to send yet another quiver of excruciating physical awareness of his closeness to her.

Yet again she found herself clinging to the persona of Sabine. Sabine could cope with this—Sabine could let the potently powerful Bastiaan Karavalas sweep her off and yet keep her cool about it. Keep her composure. So what would Sabine do…say…?

'The choice is yours, *m'sieu*,' she answered, managing to keep her tone somewhere between insouciant and indifferent. Social…civil…just this side of courteous. She made herself meet his gaze, the way Sabine undoubtedly would—for what would Sabine be overset by in those dark, sensual eyes? And Sabine's ridiculously long fake lashes helped, Sarah thought with gratitude, because their length made it easier for her to look at him with a veiled expression—helped her feel protected from the impact those deep, dark eyes were having on her…

Abruptly, he spoke, yanking her back to full focus. 'Why did you not mention that you had already made my acquaintance?' he said.

Sarah felt her eyes widening. There was only one answer to give. 'Why didn't *you*?' she said. She sought to copy the dismissive inflection that Sabine would surely give.

Her answer was a sudden opacity in his gaze. 'You must know why—' he said.

From his dark, deep-set eyes a message blazed that was as clear as day...as old as time.

Sarah could feel her breath catch in her throat, her pulse leap—and suddenly Sabine, with all her worldly defences, felt a long, long way away.

'Why did you refuse to come to dinner with me?' Again, the question was blunt—challenging. Taking her by surprise.

'You were a complete stranger.' She sought for the only explanation that was relevant—whether or not it was one that Sabine would have made.

Thoughts flickered across her mind like random electric currents. Would Sabine have found that objectionable? Or would she have made her decision about whether to let a man take her to dinner—and what might follow—on quite different grounds?

*Such as if the man were the most devastating male she'd ever set eyes on—who'd had the most powerful impact on her she'd ever experienced—who'd stilled the breath in her lungs and sent her pulse into overdrive...*

But she was given no opportunity to think coherently about that, or about anything at all, because now his eyes had a glint in them that was setting her pulse racing even faster.

'Well, I am not a stranger now.'

*Not when I hold you in the intimacy of this embrace... your soft, satiny body in my arms, the warmth of your palm against mine, the brush of your thighs as we move to the music together...*

He felt the flush of heat beating in his veins. Telling him how susceptible he was to what she possessed.

The power to make him desire her…

His senses were overpowering him. There was a lingering perfume about her—not cloying, as he might have expected, but faintly floral. Her hair, curved around her shoulder as it was, was not sticky with spray but fine and silky. He wanted to feel it running through his fingers. Wanted to drink in the fine-boned beauty of her face, see again that flash of emeralds in her eyes…

A sudden impulse possessed him. To wipe her complexion free of the mask of make-up covering it and see her true beauty revealed.

'Why do you wear so much make-up?' His question came from nowhere—he hadn't meant to ask it.

She looked momentarily startled. 'It's stage make-up,' she answered. She spoke as if she found it hard to believe he'd asked.

He frowned. 'It does not flatter you,' he stated.

Now, *why* had he said that? he grilled himself. Why tell this woman such a thing?

*Because it is the truth—she masks her true beauty, her true self, behind such excess.*

Her expression changed. 'It's not designed to flatter—only to withstand the stage lighting. You don't imagine that I wear these spiders on my eyes for any other reason, do you?' Her voice was dry.

'Good,' he said, giving a brief nod.

Even as he did so he realised he was way off agenda. What on earth was he *doing*, talking about her stage make-up? Let alone expressing approval—relief?—that it *was* only make-up. He sought to resume the line of enquiry he'd started. That was the reason he was dancing with her—so that he could continue his assessment of her. Purely for the purposes for which he'd arrived in France, of course...

To free his cousin from her.

*Free her from Philip—*

The thought was there—indelible, inadmissible. He wiped it instantly. There was no question of freeing *her* from his cousin. It was Philip—only Philip—he was concerned about. That was what he had to remember.

Not the way her body was moving with his to the soft, seductive cadences of the music, drawing them closer and closer to each other...

Not the way her fragrance was coiling into his senses. Not the way his eyes were lingering on her face...her parted lips... The way he was feeling the soft breath coming from her...intoxicating him...

The melody ended. He stopped abruptly. Even more abruptly she disengaged herself from his grasp. But she did not move—simply stood there for a moment, continuing to gaze at him. As if she could not stop...

Her breasts, Bastiaan could see, were rising and falling as if her breathing were rapid—her pulse was more rapid still. Colour was in her cheeks, beneath the thick layer of foundation. He could just see it...sense it...

Her gaze was dragged from him, back across to where Philip was sitting, his expression a mixture of impatience at her absence, discontent that she had been dancing with his cousin, and his usual fixed regard of uncritical admiration.

She walked across to him—her dress felt tighter suddenly, and she was all too conscious of the swaying movement of her hips. She could almost *feel* Bastiaan Karavalas watching her...

She reached the table. Philip stood up immediately, his chair scraping.

'Phew!' she said, pointedly not resuming her seat. 'I'm worn out by dancing. Two dances and two partners—quite an evening for me!' She spoke with deliberate lightness, obvious humour. Reaching for her glass of water, she took a quick gulp, finding she needed it, then set it down. 'I must go backstage,' she said. 'Prep for my next set.'

Conscious that Philip's cousin was standing behind her, she could say very little else to Philip. She took a step away, encompassing Bastiaan Karavalas in her movement.

'I'll bid you goodnight,' she said, making her voice sound nothing more than effortlessly casual.

She had to get control back—the way Sabine would. Sabine would have been utterly unfazed by that slow, seductive dance with Bastiaan Karavalas. Sabine wouldn't have felt as if her whole body were trembling, her senses overwhelmed. No, Sabine would stay composed, unruffled—would be well used to men like Bastiaan Karavalas desiring her.

Philip was speaking and she made herself pay attention, drag her thoughts away from his cousin.

'I'll see you tomorrow at the…here…?' he asked.

Sarah was relieved that he'd just avoided saying *at the rehearsal.*

She smiled. A warm smile. Because she didn't want to hurt him, and his feelings were so transparent. 'Why not?' she said lightly. 'Unless…' And now her eyes found Bastiaan again. 'Unless you and your cousin have plans…? You must make the most of him while he's here.'

Dark lashes flickered over even darker eyes. She saw it—caught it. 'I may well be here some time,' Bastiaan Karavalas said. 'It all depends…'

She made no answer—could only give a vague, brief

smile and bestow a little wave on Philip, because she wanted to be nice to him, and he was so young, and felt so much...

And then she was gone, whisking away through a little door inset into the wall beside the low stage.

Slowly, Bastiaan sat down. Philip did too, but Bastiaan said nothing—his head was full. Far too full. Only one thought was predominant—he wanted to hear her sing... he wanted to feast his eyes on her again.

Feast so much more than his eyes...

# CHAPTER FIVE

As Sarah took her place on the stage she was burningly aware of those dark, heavy eyes upon her. It was the same sensation she'd had the previous night, when she hadn't known who was watching her—had only been able to feel it. As she felt it now, again, that same sense of exposure. But now there was so much more—now there was a frisson running through her body, her veins, that came from his heavy-lidded perusal.

*Why?* The question kept circling in her head. Why was she reacting like this? Why was this man—this dark, disturbing cousin of Philip—able to arouse such a response in her? Never, *never* before had she been so affected by a man.

By a man's desire for her.

*Because it is a desire that echoes in me too...*

That was the truth of it. Out of nowhere, like a bolt of lightning crashing into tinder-dry trees, he'd set her alight....

A sense almost of panic swept over her.

*I can't handle it. I'm not used to it. No man has ever made me feel this way—like I'm on fire, burning from the inside. I don't know what to do—how to react...*

Nothing with Andrew had prepared her for this. Nothing!

*I didn't know it was possible to feel this way. To feel this overwhelmed—this helpless.*

*This aroused...*

Standing there in the spotlight, knowing that the dark, heavy eyes of Bastiaan Karavalas were resting on her, that she was exposed to his view, her body had reacted as if her flesh were aflame.

She wanted to run, bolt from the stage, but that was impossible. Impossible to do anything but continue to stand there, the microphone between her fingers, her voice intimate.

While Bastiaan Karavalas looked his fill of her.

*No!* The cry came from within. *It isn't me he's gazing at—it's Sabine. Sabine is standing here, feeling like this.*

And Sabine—Sabine could handle it. Of course she could. Sabine was not helpless or overwhelmed by the blatant desire in those dark, heavy eyes.

Or by her own desire...

Sabine was who she must be to cope with what was happening to her, with the fire that was running in her veins, burning her senses. That was what she clung to as she worked her way through her numbers.

Never had her set seemed longer, and how she got through it she wasn't sure, but in the end she was heading off stage, filled with relief.

As she gained her dressing room she saw Philip waiting. He launched in as soon as he could.

'Sarah—this Sunday—will you...will you come over to the villa for lunch?' He got the words out in a rush, his eyes filled with eager hope. 'I've been wanting to ask you, but it was Bast who suggested it.'

She felt a quiver inside her, even though she strove to stanch it. *Why? Why had Bastiaan Karavalas suggested inviting her to his villa?*

And the only answer she could think of sent that quiver vibrating through her again, quickening her pulse.

*I don't have time for this. I don't have time to have Bastiaan Karavalas looking at me the way he does, have the impact on me he does. I just don't have time—not now. And I can't cope with it anyway—can't cope with him. I don't know how to respond or react. And, anyway, it isn't me he's inviting—it's Sabine! Sabine's the one he's drawn to—not me. He wants what Sabine would offer him...*

The hectic thoughts tumbled through her mind, incoherent and confused. She had to answer somehow—but what? And how?

'So, will you come? Please say yes,' Philip's eager voice pressed.

She pulled herself together forcibly. 'I'm…I'm not sure…' she got out.

'What's this you're plotting?'

Max's voice sounded behind her. It sounded amused, but with a pointedness in it that Sarah was not deaf to.

Philip turned. 'I was asking Sarah if she would come over to the villa for lunch on Sunday with my cousin and me,' he relayed.

'Cousin?' Max raised his eyebrows.

'My cousin—Bastiaan Karavalas,' supplied Philip. 'It's his villa I'm staying at. He's visiting me from Greece.'

'Karavalas…' murmured Max.

Sarah knew he was storing the information away and would check it out later—just as he'd checked out Philip's name. Any cousin of Philip's would be rich as well, and for that reason she knew she might be disheartened by what Max said next, but she could not be surprised.

Max smiled at Philip. 'Why wait till Sunday?' he said

blandly. 'Make it tomorrow—I'll rejig the schedule so Sarah can get away at noon. How would that be?'

Philip's face lit. 'Fantastic! I'll go and tell Bast now. Brilliant!'

He beamed at Sarah and Max, and then rushed off to front of house.

Sarah turned to Max. 'Max—' she began, about to remonstrate.

Max held up a hand. 'Say nothing. I know your opinion about asking Philip for money. But...' his voice changed 'But this Bastiaan Karavalas, the cousin—well, that's a different matter, isn't it? A grown man who owns a villa on Cap Pierre—and presumably a whole lot else—doesn't require kid-glove-handling, does he? So, *cherie*, off you go to lunch with these lovely rich people and make yourself agreeable to them.'

Sarah's expression hardened. 'Max, if you think—'

'*Cherie*, it's just lunch—nothing more than that. What did you *think* I was suggesting?'

He sounded amused, and it irritated Sarah. 'I don't know and I don't care,' she shot back, shutting her dressing room door in his face.

Consternation was flooding through her. She did not *want* to go over to Bastiaan Karvalas's villa and spend the afternoon there. She didn't want to spend a single moment more in his company. Didn't want another opportunity for him to work his dark, potent magic on her senses...

*I don't need this distraction. I have to focus on the festival—it's all that's important to me. Nothing else. I want Bastiaan Karavalas gone—out of my life!*

She stilled suddenly as she started to change out of her costume. Her mind raced.

Maybe going to the villa wasn't so bad an idea after

# CHAPTER FOUR

NESSA LOOKED UP at Luc Barbier, who was towering over her with a dark scowl on his face and stubble on his jaw. For a blessed foggy moment, just before the adrenalin kicked in, his words hung harmlessly in the air between them.

His hair was tousled, as if he'd been running a hand through it, and he was wearing a white shirt, open at the neck, revealing a glimpse of dark skin. Awareness sizzled to life, infusing her with an urgency she felt only around him.

And then his words registered. It was like an electric shock or a slap across the face. Nessa was wide awake, and she scrambled off the window seat to stand on wobbly legs.

Her hair was coming loose from where it had been piled messily on her head to keep it out of the way. She was thoroughly rumpled, she smelled of cleaning products and he really thought…? Bile rose in her throat.

'How dare you insinuate such a thing?' Her voice was scratchy from sleep and she was burningly aware—even as she said that—of how bad this looked. She cursed herself for allowing her weariness to get the better of her.

Luc's head reared back, arms folded across his chest.

'I walk into my bedroom and find a woman, pretending to be asleep, waiting for me...like I said, they're usually in my bed and wearing a lot less but the message is essentially the same. They're here for one thing.'

Nessa was speechless at his sheer arrogance. Eventually she managed to get out, through waves of indignation and far more disturbing physical reactions, 'Well, I hate to burst your ego bubble but that was the last thing on my mind. I was cleaning your room, then I sat down for a minute and I fell asleep. I apologise for that. But I did not come here to...to...'

He raised a brow. 'To seduce me?'

Before she could respond to that, he continued as if she hadn't spoken. 'I might as well tell you now that kinky role-play doesn't really do it for me. I'm a traditionalist that way. When I make love it's intense, thorough and without the need for embellishment.'

A flash of heat went up Nessa's spine to imagine just how intense his lovemaking would be. Little beads of sweat broke out between her breasts and in the small of her back. Anger rose too. Anger that it was him who was firing up all her nerve-endings.

'I am not here to *make love* with anyone. My only crime was to fall asleep on the job and if you'll excuse me now I'll leave you in peace.'

She went to step away and out of his orbit but he caught her arm after muttering something that sounded very French and rude under his breath. His hand encircled her whole upper arm and his fingers were brushing the side of her breast. Nessa's pulse rocketed, and in the dim lights of the room—*night had fallen outside...just how long had she been asleep?*—all she could see were the forbiddingly gorgeous lines of Luc's face.

'Peace?' He almost spat the word out. 'I've had precious little peace since your brother absconded with one million euros and then his temptress of a sister turns up to play sidekick. Just what is your agenda, Nessa? What game are you playing here? Because I warn you now that you will get burned if you think you can play with me and get away with it.'

His dark intensity was totally intimidating, but somehow Nessa managed to pull her arm free and step away. Shakily she said, 'I'm not playing any games. I wouldn't know how. I really didn't come here with some nefarious intention to seduce you.'

She bit her lip to stop a semi-hysterical giggle from emerging. She wouldn't know how to seduce her way out of a paper bag, never mind a man like Luc Barbier. The very notion was ridiculous.

His mouth thinned. 'You really expect me to believe that you fell asleep like Sleeping Beauty in the fairy tale, waiting for her prince?'

Heat rushed into her cheeks—she *had* been mooning about his suite like some lovelorn teenager earlier. It wasn't like her at all. 'I don't believe in fairy tales,' she said stiffly. 'And don't worry, I know you're no prince.'

He put two hands on her arms now, swinging her around to face him properly. His eyes had turned to cold steel. 'What's that supposed to mean?'

'I…' Words got stuck in Nessa's throat. She couldn't seem to concentrate on anything but Luc's face above hers. The sensual lines were mesmerising. 'I didn't mean anything.'

Except she had, she realised. She'd just articulated it badly. This man was no prince, he was a marauding sultan, or a king. Uncultivated and suave all at once. Infinitely hard but also soft, as when he'd put a hand to his horse.

His mouth twisted. 'I might never be a prince, but you're in no position to look down on me, the sister of a common thief who thought she could seduce her way to paying back her brother's debt. Like I said, you could have saved a lot of conversation if you'd been waiting in my bed naked instead of playing out this elaborate charade of innocence.'

Nessa's hand had lifted and connected with Luc's cheek before she even realised what she'd done. Shock coursed through her system as the sting registered on her hand and Luc's face turned from the blow. All her anger drained away instantly.

He turned back slowly, face even darker now, a livid handprint showing on his cheek. Horrified, Nessa used his name for the first time. 'Luc, I'm so sorry. But I didn't mean it like that, and Paddy's not a common thief. He's really not—'

'Stop talking, you little hellcat, I don't want to hear another word.' His voice was rough.

Before Nessa could even think of uttering another word, Luc had pulled her right into him, so that her body was welded to his. All she could feel was whipcord strength and heat.

All she could see were his eyes, fathomless and like molten steel. She realised he was livid and yet she felt no fear. She only felt an intense excitement. She opened her mouth but he said, 'Not another word.'

And then his mouth covered hers, and words were the last thing on Nessa's mind as heat fused with white light and poured into every vein in her body to create a scorching trail of fire.

Shock rendered her helpless to Luc's savage sensuality and her own immediately rampant response.

Luc's arm went around her back, arching her into

him even more, and his mouth began to move over hers. But this was no gentle exploration, and it left any other kisses she'd shared with boys in a far distant universe. This did not leave her cold, or unmoved. This was igniting her very soul.

It was mastery, pure and simple. And domination. And punishment. And yet despite all those things that should have had Nessa tensing and squirming to be free, she strained to be even closer, raising her arms to twine them about Luc's neck. If she could have climbed into his skin, she would have.

She opened her mouth under his, instinctively seeking a deeper kiss, wanting to taste him with every fibre of her being. His fingers threaded through her hair, catching her head, angling it so that he could give her exactly what she wanted, but on his terms.

He consumed her, demanding nothing less than total surrender, and Nessa knew only one thing: that she wanted to surrender, with no doubt or hesitation in her mind. It was as if every moment in her life had been building up to this conflagration.

She was drowning in liquid heat and could feel it, slippery, between her legs. Luc's mouth left hers and she heard a soft moan emanating from her mouth. He trailed kisses over her jaw and down her neck. Her head fell back, too heavy.

The only sounds in the room were harsh breathing and the *thump thump* of her heart. Luc's hand was on her shirt, deftly opening the buttons. Cool air hit her bare skin and her nipples drew into tight, hard points.

The world tipped on its axis and Nessa only realised moments later that Luc had sat down on the edge of the bed, bringing her with him so that now she sat on his lap. She was dizzy, and thought that this must be how it felt to be drunk: light-headed and euphoric.

He was pushing her shirt open, and she looked at him and saw an almost feral expression on his face. He cupped one of her lace-covered breasts. Breasts that had always felt very inadequate to Nessa. But now when she looked down she could see how she perfectly filled his palm. As if she'd been made for his hands alone.

He pulled down the lace cup, baring her flesh, and she bit her lip to stop from moaning, pleading. His thumb skated over one small hard nipple and it sent electric shocks through her whole body.

He looked at her and smiled and Nessa realised that he hadn't smiled at her once until now. And it was as devastating as she'd suspected it might be. Wicked, seductive, gorgeous and irresistible.

Lust and need cocooned them from reality, and for one wild second Nessa could almost convince herself that perhaps she was still asleep and this was all just a very vivid dream.

But she knew it wasn't a dream, and she knew that it was very important that she stand up and stop this.

Luc's head was dipping towards her breast and Nessa had never wanted anything more than to surrender completely to this moment, but something within her, some small sane voice, broke through. She put her hands on Luc's shoulders and levered herself off his lap, feeling like a foal trying to stand for the first time.

Luc just looked at her as if he couldn't quite believe she'd moved away, and Nessa realised she was half naked. She pulled at her shirt, scrambling to do up at least one or two buttons. The bare flesh of her breast chafed against the material, sensitised by his touch.

She forced out, through the clamour of her own desire, 'I didn't come here for this. I really didn't.'

Luc's body was hard and throbbed with a need to claim and possess, things he'd never felt for a woman before. Nessa was looking at him with wide eyes and flushed cheeks, and hair coming loose.

*I didn't come here for this.* Something slid into Luc's mind: the very rogue possibility that she *had* just fallen asleep while on the job. And then he dismissed it. She was playing with him and he would not be manipulated like this. He'd already exposed himself far too much. And the fact that she'd been the one to pull away, signalling she was more in control than he was, was even more exposing.

Luc forced his blood to cool, and stood up in a fluid motion. Nessa took a step back. The thought that she was stepping back from him in case he touched her again sent something dark into his gut. And something far more unwelcome: a feeling of vulnerability, something that Luc had rejected long ago. He was invulnerable.

'Sleeping with me isn't going to improve your, or your brother's, situation. I told you already that I don't play games, Nessa, so unless you're willing to admit that we both want each other with no strings attached then get out of here.'

His voice was so cold and remote it skated over Nessa's skin like ice. She hated his obvious cynicism, and wanted to deny his claim that she would manipulate him to gain favour for her brother, but self-preservation kicked in at the last moment. She fled, taking the basket of cleaning supplies with her.

When Nessa finally made it back to her room she closed the door behind her and rested against it. Her heart was still thumping out of time, and her whole body ached for a fulfilment she'd never needed before.

And she reeled with the knowledge that she'd almost lain back for Luc Barbier and handed him something she'd never handed anyone else. Her innocence. She'd almost tipped over the edge of allowing Luc to see her at her most vulnerable. A man who had shown her nothing but disdain and distrust.

Thank *God* she'd pulled back from the brink. She shivered now at the prospect of Luc looking at her when he'd discovered her virginity. She could already imagine the mocking look on his face, and how he would spurn her with disgust.

But then she thought of how he'd said, *Unless you're willing to admit we both want each other with no strings attached*, and she shivered again. But this time it wasn't with trepidation or humiliation. It was with an awful sense of illicit excitement.

Luc had turned the shower to cold, but that still hadn't cooled the lingering heat in his body. He couldn't believe how close he'd come to stripping Nessa O'Sullivan bare and taking her in a haze of lust.

She'd been the one to pull back. And even though Luc hadn't imagined the chemistry between them, it still got to him somewhere very vulnerable that she'd had more control than him.

He couldn't trust her, and yet he'd been about to sleep with her, complicating an already complicated situation even more. He shuddered to think of the hold she could have had over him after sleeping together. He hadn't yet known a woman who didn't try to capitalise on intimacies shared, even when they were only physical. And he had no doubt—in spite of her protestations otherwise—that she'd had an agenda.

He looked at himself in his bathroom mirror and scowled. If she thought that she could whet his appetite like this, and he would come running after her like a dog in heat, she was mistaken. Luc wouldn't be caught offguard again. She *was* resistable. Even if the pounding of his blood told him otherwise.

He pulled a towel around his waist and knotted it roughly, finding his mobile phone and picking it up. Within seconds he was issuing a terse instruction to the security firm he'd hired to seek out Paddy O'Sullivan, to step up their efforts.

Afterwards he threw the phone down and surmised grimly that the sooner they found Paddy and his money, the sooner he could get rid of the all too distracting Nessa O'Sullivan too.

Two nights later, Nessa was holding a tray full of champagne flutes filled to the brim, serving them at Luc's glitzy party. She was dressed in a white shirt and black skirt. The uniform of waiters everywhere. Hair up in a tight bun.

She could appreciate the breathtaking scene even as her arms felt as if they were about to drop out of the shoulder sockets. The unusually mild Irish spring day was melting into a lavender-hued dusk. Candles imbued the guests and room with a golden light.

She smiled in relief as some guests stopped and helped themselves to drinks on her tray, lightening her load marginally. And then her gaze tracked back inevitably to where one man stood out from the crowd—dark head and broad shoulders visible from every corner of the room.

Her main objective was to avoid coming face to face with Luc Barbier at all costs. The enormity of what had almost happened still sent shock waves through her body every time she thought of it. *So did the thought of a no-strings encounter,* added a wicked voice.

And even though she was trying to avoid him, she couldn't look away. Much like most of the women in the room, she'd noticed with a spurt of something suspiciously…possessive. He was dressed in a tuxedo and he was simply breathtaking. He was the epitome of virile beauty, but with that undeniable edge of something dark and dangerous.

As if reading her mind, two women stopped nearby and, in that way of seeing but not seeing Nessa, because she was staff, they were whispering loudly enough for Nessa to catch snippets.

*'Apparently he's an animal in bed…'*

*'They say he was found on the streets…'*

*'Petty crime…'*

*'Only got to where he has because he slept with Leo Fouret's wife and the husband bought him off to keep him quiet…'*

Nessa went still at that, something cold trickling down her spine. She hadn't heard that final, particular rumour before. Although, he *had* apparently left Leo Fouret's stables under less than amicable circumstances, before blazing a trail on his own.

The women moved away and then more guests approached Nessa, relieving her of her remaining drinks. She was only too happy to escape back to the kitchen to stock up. Just before she left, she cast one last glance in Luc's direction, but his head was bowed towards someone in conversation.

Lambasting herself for having listened to gossip, no

matter how inadvertently, Nessa forged a path through the crowd and away from Luc. She told herself that she wasn't remotely interested in what the women had been saying. And that she was truly pathetic to be feeling the tiniest bit sorry for him that he was surrounded by such fervent gossip in the first place.

There was no smoke without a fire, as her father loved to say on a regular basis. And from what she'd seen of Luc in action, she could almost forgive a married woman for falling under his spell.

'What on earth is Nessa O'Sullivan doing serving drinks at your party, Barbier? I'd hardly think she's short of a few bob!'

It took a second for Luc to register what the man beside him had said and when he did his wandering attention snapped into sharp focus. 'You know her?'

The man snorted. 'Of course I do—you forget Ireland is a small place. Her father is Paddy O'Sullivan, one of this country's best trainers—at one time. Before he hit the bottle and almost lost everything. Now of course they're back on top of the world, although I don't think Paddy will ever repair the damage to his reputation. Still, he doesn't need to now, not with the goldmine he's sitting on thanks to his son-in-law.'

Luc usually had an aversion to gossip but not this time. 'What are you talking about?'

Percy Mortimer, a well-known English racing pundit, turned to Luc. 'Nessa O'Sullivan is related to royalty—her older sister—who incidentally is also a very talented amateur trainer—is married to the supreme Sheikh Nadim Al-Saqr of Merkazad. He bought out their stud a few years back. Nessa's not a bad rider.

I've seen her in a couple of races over the years, but she doesn't seem to have made a proper impression yet.'

*What the hell?* Luc barely heard that last bit. Sheikh Nadim was a very serious contender in racing circles, and a billionaire. And Luc had had no idea that he owned a stables just down the road. *Nessa's family stud.* He reeled, although he didn't show it.

Percy was saying something else but Luc wasn't listening. His gaze was already scanning the crowd for a dark redhead. He'd seen her earlier—looking once again as if butter wouldn't melt, dressed in her white shirt and skirt. Even that small glimpse had been enough to cause a spike in his heart-rate.

*Damn.* Where was she, anyway?

Luc tried to move away but saw a group headed for him with Pascal leading the way. The look on Pascal's face told Luc that he had to stay exactly where he was.

Nessa would have to wait, for now. But he would track her down and this time there would be no games. Only answers to his questions. Like what the hell was she playing at, working for nothing to pay off her brother's debt when presumably she could ask for a handout from her billionaire brother-in-law?

Nessa's feet and arms were aching, and she knew she shouldn't be here, but after the party had finished and they'd been released, she found herself gravitating towards the stallions' stables. As if pulled by some magnetic force. As if that could help to ground her and fuse her scattered energies back together.

She'd been acutely conscious of Luc's every movement, all evening.

At one stage she'd caught his eye and it had seemed as if he was trying to communicate something telepathically. From the grim look on his face it hadn't been something particularly nice. And then, even though she'd skirted around the edges of the room, keeping far out of his orbit for the rest of the evening, she could have sworn she felt his dark gaze boring into her periodically.

She came to a stop in the middle of the stables when she realised that they were empty. She looked around and remembered belatedly that the stallions had been moved up to different paddocks and stables for a few days while these were being repainted and renovated.

There were white sheets piled high in a corner along with painting and cleaning paraphernalia. Nessa told herself it was just as well as she turned around to leave. The last thing she needed was to be caught again in the wrong place—

Her heart stopped when she saw the tall broad figure blocking the doorway, with only the moon behind him as a silhouette. Too late. *Luc.*

She could see that his bow-tie was undone and top button open, his jacket swinging loose and his hands in the pockets of his trousers.

He moved forward into the stables and she saw his stern expression revealed in the dim lighting. Immediately the space felt claustrophobic. Nessa's body tingled with awareness as he came close enough for her to see that there was also barely leashed anger in his expression.

She swallowed. 'I know I shouldn't be here—'

'That's not important. We need to have a little chat.'

Surprise robbed her voice for a moment and then she said, 'About what?'

Luc folded his arms. 'About why you've omitted to mention the not inconsequential fact that your sister is married to Sheikh Nadim Al-Saqr of Merkazad, *and* that he owns your stud farm.'

He continued, 'I'd imagine one million euro is short change to Sheikh Nadim Al-Saqr, so what the hell is Paddy doing jeopardising his career for a handout he could've begged off his brother-in-law, and why didn't *you* just pick up the phone to Nadim to sort this mess out?'

Nessa went hot and then cold as the significance of this sank in, and the realisation that someone must have recognised her at the party.

She said carefully, 'I didn't think it was relevant.'

Luc looked even more stern. 'Not good enough.'

Nessa swallowed. She knew she couldn't avoid an explanation. 'Nadim *did* buy our farm but he put it back into our name as a wedding gift for Iseult, my sister. It's ours again, he's just one of the shareholders. And I didn't want to involve him because this has nothing to do with Nadim or Iseult. My sister is due to have a baby in a couple of weeks and they don't need the stress.'

Luc stepped closer but Nessa was trapped, with a stable door at her back and nowhere to go. She was acutely aware of his tall, lean body and his scent.

'There's more to it than that,' he said. 'You and your brother avoiding asking for help just proves you're both involved in something that's gone beyond your control. I'm guessing Nadim wouldn't approve, and you don't want to bite the hand that feeds you.'

In a fierce low voice Nessa replied, '*No.* It's nothing like that. Why must you be so cynical and mistrustful?'

'Because,' he answered smoothly, 'I was born that way and nothing I've experienced has ever proved me wrong. Life favours the opportunistic. I should know.'

*I was born that way.* Nessa couldn't stop a rush of

curiosity and pity. The second time she'd pitied him this evening. But then she crushed it. Luc Barbier was the last man on the planet who needed anyone's pity.

He said, 'You could be free to walk away if you asked Nadim for help.'

Luc heard himself say the words even as something inside him rejected it immediately. Let her walk away? A hot surge of possessiveness rose up inside him. *He wanted her.*

She was looking at him, eyes huge, and for a second he could almost have imagined that she looked…*hurt*. A ridiculous notion.

Nessa shook her head and some long tendrils of red hair framed her face. 'No. I will not take the easy way out and cause my family distress. I promised Paddy that I wouldn't go to Nadim or Iseult.'

Luc was intrigued by this apparent loyalty. 'Give me one good reason why I shouldn't go to Nadim myself.'

An expression of panic crossed her face. 'I thought you didn't want this news to get out either!'

'I don't. But from what I know of the Sheikh, I think he would appreciate the need for discretion on his family's behalf. It would affect his name and reputation too.'

Nessa wrung her hands in front of her and it only drew Luc's attention to where the shirt strained slightly over her breasts. He dragged his gaze up.

'You have no right to involve them.'

Now he really wanted to know why she was being so stubborn on this. 'Give me one reason, Nessa, and make it a good one.'

She looked at him as if he was torturing her and then she answered with palpable reluctance. 'When our mother died Iseult was only twelve; I was eight. Our father couldn't cope with the grief. He went off the rails, and developed a drink problem. Iseult went to school, but she did the bare minimum so that she could take care of the farm, the horses and all of us.'

Nessa glanced away for a moment, her face pale. Luc felt at an uncharacteristic loss as to what to say but she looked back at him and continued. 'If it wasn't for Iseult shielding us from the worst of our father's excesses and the reality of the farm falling to pieces, we never would have made it through school. She shouldered far too much for someone her age…and then Nadim came along and bought the farm out and she felt as if she'd failed us all at the last hurdle.'

Nessa drew in a breath. 'But then they fell in love and got married, and for the first time in her life she's really secure and happy.'

'Married to a billionaire, conveniently enough.' The cynical comment was said before Luc had even properly thought about it, and it felt hollow on his lips.

Nessa's hands clenched to fists by her sides. 'Iseult is the least materialistic person I know. They love each other.'

Luc was a bit stunned by her vehemence. 'Go on.'

She bit her lip for a moment, and he had to stop himself from reaching out to tug it free of those small white teeth.

'My sister is truly happy for the first time in a long time. The only responsibility she now bears is to her own family. They had problems getting pregnant after Kamil so this pregnancy has been stressful. If she knew what was going on she'd be devastated and worried, and Nadim would do everything he could to help her. He might even insist on coming all the way over here, and she needs him with her now.'

She added impetuously, 'If you do talk to Nadim,

I'll leak it to the press about the money going astray. Maybe they'll be easier on Paddy than you've been.'

Luc just looked at Nessa for a long moment, and he had to admit with grudging reluctance that her apparent zeal to protect her family was very convincing. He'd never seen a mother bear with cubs, but he had an impression of it right now. And he didn't like how it had affected him when she'd mentioned her sister's happy family. For a second he'd actually felt something like envy.

It reminded him uncomfortably of when he'd been much younger and he and other kids from the flats would go into Paris to pick pockets or whatever petty crime they could get away with. Stupid kids with nothing to lose and no one at home to care what they got up to.

One day Luc had been mesmerised by a family playing in a park—a mother, father and two children. The kids had looked so happy and loved. An awful darkness had welled up inside him and he'd tasted jealousy for the first time. And something far more poignant— a desire to know what that would be like.

His friends had noticed and had teased Luc unmercifully, so he'd shoved that experience and those feelings deep down inside and had vowed never to envy anyone again. And he wasn't about to start now.

But eclipsing all of that now was the carnal hunger building inside him. He'd thought of little else but that incendiary kiss the other night. When he'd sought Nessa out after the party he'd told himself he could resist her. But the thick sexual tension in the air mocked him.

She called to him, even in those plain, unerotic clothes. She called to him, deep inside where a dark hunger raged and begged for satisfaction.

Suddenly it didn't matter who she was related to. Or if she was playing mind-games. She threw up too many questions, but there was only one question he was interested in knowing the answer to right now, and that was how she would feel when he sank deep inside her.

Luc closed the distance between them, and reached out to slide a hand around Nessa's neck, tugging her closer. Her eyes went wide and her cheeks bloomed with colour. She put a hand up to his and said, 'What are you doing?'

Luc's gaze was fixated on her mouth and he had to drag it away to look into those huge hazel eyes. 'Do you really expect me to believe that you're just an innocent who would do anything for her family? And that the other night was pure chance and chemistry?'

For a taut moment, Luc held his breath because he realised that some small kernel of the little boy he'd once been, yearning for something totally out of his orbit, was still alive inside him. He waited for Nessa to gaze up at him with those huge eyes and move closer, to tell him in a husky voice, *Yes, I'm really that innocent.* The worst of it was, he wasn't entirely sure that he wouldn't believe her.

But she didn't. She tensed and pulled back, jerking free of Luc's hand. Glaring up at him. 'I don't *expect* you to believe anything, Luc Barbier. You've got eyes in your head and if you choose to view the world through a fog of cynicism and mistrust then that's your prerogative.

'As for the other night—it was madness and a mistake. You won't have to worry why it happened because it won't happen again.'

Nessa had almost moved past Luc when his shocked brain kicked into gear and he caught her hand, stopping her. Every cell in his body rejected what she'd just said. She was walking away again. A savage part of himself rose up, needing to prove that she wasn't as in control as she appeared.

He pulled her back in front of him. 'You want me.'

She bit her lip and looked down. She shook her head. Luc tipped her chin up feeling even more savage. 'Say it, Nessa.'

She looked at him, eyes huge and swirling with emotion but Luc couldn't draw back now. Eventually she said with a touch of defiance, 'I might want you but I don't want to.'

Something immediately eased inside him. She glanced down again as if by not looking at him she could avoid the issue.

'Look at me, Nessa.'

For a long moment she refused but then she looked up, eyes spitting golden sparks, and it ignited the fire inside him to a burning inferno of need. He pulled her closer again. She put her hands up to his chest. 'No, Luc. I don't want—'

But he stopped her words with his mouth and used every ounce of his expertise to show her how futile her resistance was. Whatever else was happening around them, whatever she was saying, he could trust that this was true at least.

# CHAPTER FIVE

NESSA WANTED TO resist Luc—she really did. She hated that he still patently believed she'd orchestrated the other night. And that he most likely didn't believe what she'd told him about her family.

But it was hard to think of all of that when his mouth was on hers and he was sliding his tongue between her lips and possessing her with such devastating ease. Big hands moved down her back to her buttocks, cupping them and bringing her in close to where she could feel the bold thrust of his arousal. For her. Not for one of the stunningly beautiful women at the party. *Her.* Nessa O'Sullivan.

He drew back then and Nessa realised she was welded to him. Arms and breasts crushed against his chest. One arm kept her clamped to him, not letting her escape for a moment. He undid her hair so that it fell around her shoulders. He looked at it for a moment as if mesmerised and something inside Nessa melted.

He wrapped some hair around his hand and gently tugged so that her head came back. And then he kissed her again, dragging her deeper and deeper into the pit of a fire that she knew she couldn't walk away from again. She'd barely been able to the last time.

He pulled her skirt up until she felt cool air skate over

her heated skin. He palmed the flesh of her buttocks and the place between her legs burned with damp heat.

She broke away from the kiss, breathing rapidly, and looked at him. Her heart was racing. She couldn't look away from his eyes. They held her to account and she couldn't lie.

'What do you want, Nessa?' His fingers moved tantalisingly close to the edge of her panties. Her breathing quickened. One finger slid under the material, stroking. Her legs were weak.

'Do you want me to stop?'

*No!* shouted every fibre of her being. Nessa couldn't explain it and wasn't sure if she even wanted to investigate it, but she realised at that moment that she trusted him. She wasn't sure *what* she trusted exactly. Maybe it was that he wouldn't lie to her or spout platitudes. And so she convinced herself that if she said yes to this… whatever it was…she'd be under no illusions that emotions were involved.

He drew back marginally. 'Nessa?' And there it was—a glimmer of concern, showing a side to this darkly complex man that she suspected not many people ever got to see. She knew he would let her go if she insisted, even if his pride demanded her capitulation. Even as they both knew she would capitulate all too easily. But, she wanted this man with every cell in her body. She'd never wanted anything as much.

'Don't stop,' she whispered, reaching up to wind her arms around his neck again, pressing her mouth to his. Luc didn't hesitate. He gathered her even closer and backed her into the stall behind them, where she'd seen all the white sheets piled up in readiness for the work.

Nessa felt a soft surface at the backs of her legs that swiftly gave way, and she fell into the pile of sheets.

Luc looked down at Nessa, sprawled before him. Her skirt was up around her smooth thighs, and her untucked shirt strained across her chest. Her red hair spilled across the white fabric. It was probably one of the least romantic settings for lovemaking, but it was one of the most erotic sights Luc had ever seen. He was no longer aware of anything but the pounding in his blood and the need he felt in every cell of his body.

A small voice tried to get through to him, to remind him that he was no longer this uncivilised man, but it fell on deaf ears as he started to take off his clothes with the singular intention of joining their naked bodies as soon as possible.

Nessa stared up at Luc. The intense expression on his face might have scared her if she didn't feel as though she might have a similar expression on her face. He pulled off his jacket, dropping it to the ground, and then his bow tie. He started to open his shirt and Nessa's eyes grew wide as his magnificent chest was revealed bit by glorious bit until he was naked from the waist up. She could hardly breathe.

He came down over her, arms bracketing around her body, and his head dipped to hers, mouths fusing again in a series of long, drugging kisses that made Nessa want more, much more.

By the time he was opening her shirt, she was arching her back towards him in silent supplication. He pushed apart the material and pulled down the lace cups of her bra, exposing her breasts to his dark gaze as he rested on one arm beside her.

'*Si belle…*' he murmured before dipping his head and surrounding one tight peak in wet heat. Nessa might have screamed, she wasn't sure. She just knew that Luc's mouth on her bare flesh was almost more than she could bear. And he was remorseless, ignoring her pleas for mercy.

His mouth moved down over her belly, and he pulled up her skirt so that it was ruched around her waist. He stopped for a moment and looked at her in the dim light, watching her expression as his hand explored under the waist of her panties before gently pushing them down her legs.

Nessa sucked in a breath. This was more exposed than she'd ever been in her life, and yet it didn't scare her. She felt exhilarated.

Luc's gaze moved down her body and his hand rested between her legs, cupping her. Slowly, he started to move his hand against her and Nessa gripped his arms like an anchor.

He watched her again as one finger explored in a circle, through her secret folds of flesh and then right into the heart of her. Nessa's back arched and she squeezed her eyes shut. It was sensory overload. Her legs were splayed and Luc's hand was a wicked instrument of torture, as one finger became two, stretching her.

She lifted her head. 'I can't…' Was that her voice? So needy and husky?

'Can't what, *chérie*?'

'Can't cope…what you're doing, it's too much…'

He smiled and it was the smile of the devil. 'It's not nearly enough. *Yet.* Come fly with me, *minou*. Come on…'

She didn't understand what he was asking, but then he flicked his finger against the very heart of her. She tumbled blindly over an edge she had no chance of saving herself from.

If Luc had ever wanted to assert his dominance, he just had. With pathetic ease.

It took a long moment for Nessa to come back to her senses. She felt undone but deliciously sated. And yet there was something deeper, throbbing with need inside her, an instinctive knowledge of something even greater to come.

'*Ca va?*'

Nessa opened her eyes to see Luc looking at her. If he'd looked smug or remotely triumphant she might have wakened from this craziness but he didn't. He looked slightly…fascinated.

She nodded. She didn't know what she was but it was better than *okay*.

Luc's hand moved up to cup her breast, fingers finding and pinching her nipple lightly. Immediately her body was humming again, as if she hadn't just orgasmed.

She realised that Luc's chest was within touching distance and reached out shyly to touch him. Tentative, but growing more adventurous when she felt how warm he was, and the latent steel of his body underneath.

'You really don't have to pretend, *minou*.'

He sounded slightly amused. Nessa's hand stopped and she looked at him. 'Pretend…what are you talking about?'

'Pretend to be some kind of innocent. I told you I don't get off on games. It's really not necessary. I want you, more than I've ever wanted anyone else.'

She wasn't pretending; she *was* innocent! His face suddenly looked stark, as if he hadn't meant to say those words, and treacherously it robbed her of any words of defence. Somehow she knew that if she said anything, this would all stop and she wasn't ready for it to be over.

So she did the most selfish thing she'd ever done

in her life and said nothing. She touched him again, placing her mouth over his blunt nipples and exploring with her tongue, feeling ridiculously powerful when she heard him hiss between his teeth and felt him catch her hair again, winding it around his hand as if he needed to restrain her.

It was an incredible aphrodisiac to know she had any kind of effect on Luc Barbier.

She explored further, down his body, tracing her fingers over abs so tight that her own quivered in response. And then she reached his belt. There was a moment, and then he said gruffly, 'Keep going.'

So she undid the belt, sliding it through the loops, then his button and the zip. She could feel the potent thrusting bulge under the material and her hand started to shake as she drew the zip down.

Luc muttered something in French and then he was standing up and pushing his trousers down and off, taking his underwear with them. And now he was naked and fully aroused and Nessa couldn't speak, taking in his virile majesty.

'Touch me.'

Nessa sat up and reached out, curling her hand tentatively around Luc's rigid erection. She found it fascinating—the silky skin pulled taut over all that potent strength. There was a bead of moisture at the top, and, acting completely on instinct, she leant over and touched it with her tongue, tasting the tart saltiness. Her mouth watered and she wanted to wrap her whole mouth around him but he was pulling her away saying, 'Stop…or I won't last.'

Luc's brain was so fused with lust and heat and need that it was all he could do not to thrust between the tempting lushness of Nessa's lips. All rational thought had gone. He couldn't wait. He needed to feel her whole body around him, not just her mouth.

He moved over her, between her spread legs, and for a second the way she was looking up at him, with some expression he'd never seen on a woman's face before, almost made him stop, and take a breath. This was too crazy. Too rushed. He needed to get his wits back...

But then he felt her hands on his hips as if guiding him into her and he was lost again, drowning in need.

Nessa was filled with a raw sense of earthy urgency so sharp and intense she found herself reaching for Luc, wanting to bring him closer. He knelt between her legs, spreading them wider with his hands.

Nessa was vaguely aware that her shirt was open, her breasts bared and her skirt ruched around her waist. But any selfconsciousness fled when the head of his erection nudged against where she was so hot and wet. She instinctively circled her hips up to meet him.

Nothing could have prepared her though for that first cataclysmic penetration. She felt impaled. Luc was too big. He looked at her for a moment with a line between his brows and her heart stopped. *Did he know?* But then he slid in a little further. The discomfort faded as he filled her more, all the way until she couldn't breathe.

As he started to move in and out he lifted her leg and wrapped it around his hip, making him move even deeper inside her. Nessa was clasping his shoulders, needing something to hold onto as tension wound into a tight ball deep inside her.

She'd never felt anything like the glorious glide of his body in and out of hers. She was utterly consumed with the moment and what this man was doing to her.

She wrapped both legs around him now, digging her heels into his buttocks, wanting, needing more. Sweat made their skin glisten and their breathing was harsh as they both raced to the pinnacle of the climb.

Luc's movements became faster and Nessa could only cling on for dear life as the oncoming storm hurtled towards her. He arched her up towards him and found a nipple with his hot mouth, sucking it deep, and at that moment Nessa was flung into the eye of the storm and she cried out a release that went on, and on, and on.

Luc went taut above her and she felt the warm rush of his release inside her but at that point her brain was too burnt out to think of anything else but the oblivion that extreme pleasure brought in its wake.

After a long moment, with Luc's body embedded in hers, Nessa felt as if she were claiming him. Immediately she rejected it as a ridiculous notion. Luc Barbier was not a man who would ever be claimed. That much was obvious.

She unlocked her arms from around his neck. His breath was warm against her neck. He moved then and she winced as tender muscles protested. He didn't look at her as he pulled away and stood up.

Nessa felt self-conscious and realised how wanton she must look, spreadeagled and with her clothes in total disarray. She started to pull her shirt back over her chest, and her skirt down, feeling cold. She had no idea how to behave in this unorthodox and totally new situation to her—post-sex etiquette. In a stables. On sheets.

Luc was just standing there, half turned away, like a statue. Nessa's hands stilled and she came up on one elbow. Something caught her attention, a long angry scar that zigzagged down Luc's back. She remembered feeling it under her hand in the throes of passion. But it hadn't registered fully.

She sat up. 'What is that on your back?'

Finally, he looked at her and his face was expressionless. Little alarm bells went off.

'My scar?'

She nodded, horrified to imagine him suffering such violence.

'It's a reminder from a long time ago to not forget who I am or where I came from.'

Nessa didn't like how it almost sounded like a warning. 'That sounds serious.'

Luc looked at her. 'My scar isn't serious. What is serious is that we didn't use protection.'

Nessa insides seized with icy panic when she remembered feeling the warm rush of his release. How could she have let that happen?

And then she ordered her sluggish brain to kick into gear and breathed a sigh of relief, tinged with something much more disturbing, like regret. Which was crazy. After her experience losing her mother, Nessa had never relished the prospect of becoming a mother that could die and potentially devastate her family. No matter how cute her little nephew was, or how envious she felt when she saw his special bond with her sister.

She'd taken birth control in college but had stopped soon after leaving, not deeming it necessary when it had never been necessary there. Now she felt supremely naive and foolish.

She forced herself to look at Luc. 'I'm at a safe place in my cycle.'

Luc made a mirthless, almost bitter sound. 'I'm supposed to take your word for it?'

Anger surged at herself for being so lax and at his accusatory tone. She stood up, pulling her shirt together and her skirt down, hair wild and loose. She mustered up every atom of dignity she could given the circumstances and said coolly, 'Well, you'll have to just take my word for it. There were two of us involved, so why weren't *you* thinking of protection?'

Because for the first time in a long time he'd been a slave to his base desires, and protection had been the last thing on his mind.

The realisation sent shards of jagged panic into Luc's guts. How could he have forgotten one of his most stringent rules? He, who had vowed never to have children because he had no desire for a family. Family was anathema to him. And to forget that with this woman, of all women? She was the one most likely to turn around now and use this for her own gain. He might as well have just handed her a loaded gun.

Except even now, Luc was still acutely aware of Nessa's state of déshabillé and how much he wanted to tip her back onto the sheets and take her again. He reached for his trousers, pulling them on angrily, disgusted with his lack of self-control.

He was in the grip of a tumult inside him that he didn't know how to decipher or necessarily want to. All he knew was that what had just happened between him and this woman left anything else he'd ever experienced in the dust. It hadn't just been mind-blowing sex. It had been something else. Something that had affected him on another level.

More disgust ran through him—he'd just done what he expressly forbade his own employees from doing. And now he'd made things exponentially worse by not using protection.

Nessa was looking at him and he realised she was pale. He knew he was being a bastard—it had been his responsibility to protect them. Not hers. He ran a hand through his hair. 'Look, I'm sorry. I just… I don't ever forget about something as fundamental as protection.'

She still looked pale and his chest felt tight. 'What's wrong?' *Had he hurt her?* He was so much bigger than her and the last thing on his mind had been taking care, or being gentle.

*What's wrong? What's right?* Nessa glanced away for a moment feeling ridiculously vulnerable, and even more so after his apology. She hadn't expected cuddles and a heart-to-heart after sex with this man—no matter how much lust had clouded her brain. But she also hadn't expected him to be so obviously angry with himself.

*He hadn't even noticed that she was a virgin.* He'd thought she was acting innocent.

She forced herself to look at him and for a second could have almost imagined she'd dreamed up the last hour. He was dressed again, albeit without his tie and jacket. She still felt thoroughly dishevelled and at a disadvantage, and suddenly she wanted to pierce that cool disdain and self-recrimination.

'I don't know what this is between us but I'm not proud of myself,' she said.

Luc looked at her with no discernible change in his expression, but then she saw the merest flash of something almost like hurt cross his face. He stepped closer, and she could see his eyes burning and a muscle jumping in his jaw.

'You might be related to royalty but if you were seated at a banquet table right now and dressed head to toe in couture, you would still want me. Lust makes great levellers of all of us. As does crime,' he answered.

It took a second for Nessa to absorb what he'd said. She couldn't believe he'd misunderstood her. He turned away at that moment and, in spite of the turmoil she was feeling, she reached out, wrapping a hand around his arm. 'Stop.'

He turned around.

She swallowed. 'I didn't mean that I wasn't proud because it was *you*. I meant that I'm not proud because I feel like I'm betraying my family.'

His lip curled. 'It's just sex, Nessa. Don't overthink it.'

She immediately felt silly for opening her mouth. She let his arm go and stepped back. 'Forget I said anything.'

She was about to step around him and make her exit to lick her wounds and castigate herself for being so weak but this time he took her arm, stopping her and asking harshly, 'What is that?'

Nessa looked around and for a second couldn't see what he was looking at behind them. But then she noticed the unmistakable stain of red on the white sheets. Her blood. Her virginal blood.

She went icy cold, and then hot with humiliation. Quickly she stood in front of it. 'It's nothing.'

He moved her aside and looked closer. If the ground could have opened up and swallowed Nessa whole she would have jumped right in.

He looked at it for so long Nessa wished she'd taken the chance to escape. But then he moved back, and there was such a mix of expressions on his face that she was stunned into silence.

Luc couldn't believe what his eyes had just told him, and yet he couldn't stop thinking about all the moments when he'd thought she was putting on some act with the shy tentative kisses, the self-consciousness, and the way she'd run the other night.

But what beat at his brain most of all had been that

moment, when he'd felt her body clamping tight around him. It had made him stop, and look at her, but the question had barely formed in his mind before her muscles had been relaxing to let him go deeper, and he'd conveniently blocked the half-formed question out, too desperate to sate himself.

She'd been a *virgin*.

That knowledge filled him with too many things to untangle now. One of which was a fierce feeling of satisfaction that he'd been her first. It was something he'd never imagined feeling in a scenario like this.

'Why didn't you tell me?'

She opened her mouth and closed it again, and that only brought Luc's attention to those lush lips and how they'd felt on his body.

'Well?' he snapped. She flinched minutely and Luc bit back a curse at himself. He felt unmoored, boorish. Out of control.

A hint of defiance came into her eyes and it comforted him. This woman was no wilting lily.

'I didn't think it was relevant. Or that you'd notice.'

Luc burned inside at that. He had noticed but had dismissed it. 'I don't sleep with virgins.'

Nessa folded her arms and said tartly, 'Well, you just did.'

He felt the burn of more self-recrimination. 'If I'd known I wouldn't have been so…rough.'

Amazingly, Nessa blushed and glanced away. 'You weren't too rough.' She hesitated. 'It was okay.'

'Okay?'

She looked back at him. 'I mean, I don't know, do I? It was my first time.'

Her words propelled Luc forward and he caught her arms in his hands. She felt unbearably slender and deli-

She would keep this as brief as possible—it was the only sensible thing to do.

'M'sieu Karavalas,' she greeted him, with only the slightest smile at her mouth, a nod of her head.

An eyebrow lifted as he held a chair for her. 'Bastiaan, surely?' he murmured. 'Have we not advanced that far, *mademoiselle*?'

There was light mockery in his invitation to use his given name while reserving more formality for his own addressing of her. A mockery that played upon what he knew—*must* know—about her receptiveness to his masculine potency, his own appreciation of her charms...

She made no reply, merely gave a flickering social smile as she sat down while he resumed his seat.

'So, what have you done with Philip?' she asked. She kept her tone light, but this was, after all, the only reason that his cousin was here.

She saw a dark flickering cross his eyes. 'I've just returned from driving him to Paris,' he answered.

Sarah's eyes widened in surprise. *'Paris?'*

Bastiaan lifted his cognac glass. 'Yes,' he said smoothly. 'He's meeting his mother there, and visiting family friends.'

'So, how long will he be away?' she asked. She sought to keep her tone light, still, but it was hard—every nerve-ending was quivering with the overpowering impact this man had on her.

'Long enough.'

There was a hint of a drawl in his voice and it made her stare at him. She tried to quash the sudden flare in her veins as his veiled, unreadable gaze rested on her. A gaze that suddenly seared its message into her.

'And now, having disposed of the problem of my young cousin,' Bastiaan was saying, his voice dragging across her nerve-endings and making them flare with a kind of internal shiver that she felt in every cell of her body, 'we can move on to a far more interesting subject.'

Something in his face changed and he shifted slightly, relaxing back, it seemed to her, and lifting his cognac glass, his long, strong fingers curved around the bowl. His eyes rested on her with an open expression in them that was pinioning her where she sat.

She could not answer him. Could only sit, lips slightly parted, feeling her heart start to race. The rest of the room had disappeared. The rest of the *world* had disappeared. There was only her, sitting there, her body shimmering with a sensual awareness of what this man could do to her...

And then a smile flashed suddenly across his features. 'Which is, Mademoiselle Sabine, the subject of where we should dine tonight.' He paused, a light in his eyes. 'Last time you disdained my suggestion of Le Tombleur. But, tell me, does it meet with your approval tonight?'

'Tonight?' Her echo of his question was hollow, hiding the shock beneath. Hiding the sudden, overwhelming spike of adrenaline that had shot into her veins as she'd realised what he intended.

Amusement played about his well-shaped mouth. 'Do we need to wait any longer, Sabine?'

All pretence at formality was gone now. All pretence at denial of what had flared between them from the very first. There was only one reality now—coursing through her veins, pounding in her heart, sheering across her skin, quickening in her core.

This man—this man alone—who had walked into her life when she'd least expected it, least wanted it, could least afford to acknowledge it. This man who could set her pulse racing…in whose dark, disturbing presence her body seemed to come alive.

Temptation overwhelmed her. The temptation to say *Yes! Yes!* to everything he was offering. Simply to let his hand reach across the table to hers, to let him raise her to her feet, lead her from here and take her where he wanted…

To a physical intimacy, a sensual intensity, an embarkation into realms of sensuous possibility that she had never encountered before.

And why not? *Why not?* She was free, an adult and independent woman. Her emotional ties to Andrew, such as they'd been, were long gone. She was no ingénue— she knew what was being offered to her…knew it was something that would never come again in her life. For there could never be another man who would affect her the way this man could.

She could go with him as Sabine—the woman he took her to be—as assured as he in the world that this dark, powerful man moved in. A world of physical affairs that sated the body but left the heart untouched. As Sabine she could indulge in such an affair, could drink it to the full, like a glass of heady champagne that would intoxicate the blood but leave her clear-headed the following day.

The temptation was like an overpowering lure, dominating her senses, her consciousness. Then, like cold water douching down upon her, she surfaced from it.

*She was not Sabine.*

She was Sarah. Sarah Fareham. Who had striven all her life towards the moment that was so close now—the moment when she would walk out on stage and give the performance upon which her future life would depend.

*I can't go with him—I can't.*

She felt her head give a slow, heavy shake.

*'C'est impossible.'*

The words fell from her lips and her eyes were veiled beneath the ludicrously over-long false eyelashes.

His face stilled. 'Why?'

A single word. But she did not answer. Could not. Dared not. She was on a knife's edge—if she did not go now, right now, she would sever her resolve. Give in to the temptation that was lapping at her like water on a rising tide.

She shook her head again, drained her coffee cup with a hand that was almost shaking. She got to her feet. Cast one more look at him. One last look.

*The man is right—the time is wrong.*

'Goodnight, *m'sieu*,' she said, and dipped her head and walked away. Heading to the door beside the low stage, moving back towards her dressing room.

Behind her, Bastiaan watched her go. Then, slowly, he reached for his cognac. Emotion swelled within him but he did not know what it was. Anger? Was that it? Anger that she had defied his will for her?

Or anger that she had denied what burned between them like a hot, fierce flame?

*I want her—and she denies me my desire...*

Or was it incomprehension?

He did not know, could not tell—knew only that as his fingers clenched around the bowl of his cognac glass he needed the shot of brandy more than he needed air to breathe. In one mouthful he had drained it, and then, his expression changing, he pushed to his feet and left the club. Purpose was in every stride.

# CHAPTER SEVEN

SARAH'S FINGERS FUMBLED with the false eyelashes as she peeled them off her eyelids, then with shaky hands wiped the caking foundation off her face, not bothering to tackle her dark eye make-up. She felt as if she was shaking on the inside, her mind shot to pieces. She'd made herself walk away from him, but it hadn't seemed to help.

All she could see in her vision was Bastiaan Karavalas, saying in his low, deep voice, 'Do we need to wait any longer?'

Emotion speared in her—a mix of panic and longing, confusion and torment. An overwhelming urge to get away as swiftly as possible, to reach the safe haven of her room in the *pension*, surged through her. She wouldn't wait to change. She simply grabbed her day clothes, stuffing them into a plastic bag and seizing up her purse, then headed for the rear exit of the club. Max was long gone and she was glad.

She stepped out into the cool night air of the little road that ran behind the club—and stopped dead.

Bastiaan's Ferrari blocked the roadway and he was propped against it, arms folded. Wordlessly he opened the passenger door.

'Give me one reason,' he said to her, 'why you will not dine with me.'

His voice was low, intense. His eyes held hers in the dim light and would not release them. She felt her mouth open to speak—but no words came out. In her head was a tumult, a jumble of thoughts and emotions and confusion.

He spoke for her. 'You can't, can you? Because this has been waiting to happen since I first set eyes on you.'

The intensity was still in his voice, in his gaze that would not let her go.

She was still trying to find the words she had to find, marshal the thoughts she had to think, but it was impossible. Impossible to do anything but succumb. Succumb to the emotions that were coursing through her. Impelling her forward. She felt one last frail, hopeless thought fleeting through her tumbling mind.

*I tried—I tried to stop this happening. Tried to deny it, tried to prevent it. But I can't—I can't deny this any longer. I can't.*

It was all she could manage. Then, as she sank into the low, plush seat of the powerful, sleek car, she felt herself give in entirely, completely, to what was happening. Succumbing to the temptation that was the darkly devastating man closing the door on her, lowering himself in beside her, reaching to the ignition to fire the powerful engine and moving off into the night with her at his side.

Taking her where he wanted to take her.

Where she wanted to go.

She stole a sideways look at him. Their gazes clashed. She looked away again, out over the pavements and the buildings along the roadway. She knew what she was doing—and why. Knew with every pulse of blood in her veins and in the jittering of her nerves, which were humming as if electricity were pouring through her—a charge that was coming out of the very atmosphere itself.

Enclosed as she was, only a few inches away from the long, lean body of the man next to her, she felt the low, throaty vibration of the ultra-powerful engine of the car—was aware of the sleek, luxurious interior, of the whole seductive ambience of sitting beside him.

She knew that her body was outlined by her stage dress, that her image was that of a woman in the full glamour of her beauty. And that the man beside her, clad in his hand-made tuxedo, with the glint of gold of his watch, the cufflinks in his pristine cuffs, the heady, spiced scent of his aromatic aftershave, had contrived to make the situation headily seductive.

She gave herself to it. It was too late now for anything else. Far too late.

'Where are we going?' she asked. Her voice was low-pitched and she could not quite look at him. Could not quite believe that she was doing what she was doing.

He glanced at her, with half a smile curving his sensual lips. 'I attempted once before to take you to Le Tombleur—perhaps this time you will acquiesce?'

Had there been a huskiness discernible in his voice as he'd said the word 'acquiesce'? She couldn't be sure—could only be sure that there was some kind of voltage charging her body right now, one she had never experienced before. Somewhere inside her, disappearing fast, there was a voice of protest—but it was getting feebler with every moment she was here with Bastiaan, burningly conscious of his powerful masculine presence, of the effect he had on her that she could not subdue.

Beyond the confines of the car the world was passing by. But it was far, far away from her now. Everything was far, far away.

It did not take long to get to the restaurant, set in the foothills of the Alpes-Maritimes above the crowded coastline of the Riviera. She was helped from the car, ushered inside by the tall, commanding man at her side. The *maître d'* was hurrying forward, all attention, to show them to a table out on the terrace, looking down on where the lights of the Riviera glittered like a necklace of jewels.

She eased into her seat, ultra-aware of the tightness of her gown, the voluptuousness of her figure. Her eyes went yet again to the man sitting opposite her, studying his menu. What was it about him that he could affect her the way he did? Why was she so overwhelmed by him? Why had she been so fatally tempted to succumb to what she knew she should not be doing? To dine here with him *à deux*…

*And what would happen afterwards…?*

Her mind skittered away. She did not think—did not dare think. Dared only to go on sitting there, occupying herself by opening the menu, glancing blindly down at the complex listings. Was she hungry? She could not tell. Could tell only that her heart rate was raised, that her skin was flushed with heat…that her eyes wanted only to go on resting on the man opposite her.

'So, what would you like to eat?'

Bastiaan's voice interrupted her hopeless thoughts and she was glad. She made herself give a slight smile. 'Something light,' she said. 'In this dress anything else is impossible!'

It had been a mistake to make such a remark, however lightly it had been said. It drew a wash of scrutiny from the dark, long-lashed eyes. She felt her colour heighten and had to fight it down by studying the menu again. She found a dish that seemed to fit the bill—scallops in a saffron sauce—and relayed it to Bastiaan. He too chose fish, but a more robust grilled monkfish, and then there followed the business of selecting wine to go with it.

Choices made, he sat back, his eyes resting on her at his leisure. Satisfaction soared through him. Her yielding had not surprised him in the least, but it had gratified him. Now, at last, he had her to himself.

His sensation of satisfaction, of the rightness of it all, increased. Yes, seducing her would, as he had always planned, achieve his goal of quashing any ambitions she might have had concerning his cousin, but as they sat there on the secluded terrace, with the night all around them, somehow his young cousin seemed very…irrelevant.

'So,' he began, 'tell me about yourself, Sabine?' It was an innocuous question—and a predictable one—but he could see a veil flicker over her eyes.

'Myself?' she echoed. 'What is there to tell that is not evident? I am a singer—what else?' She sounded flippant, unconcerned. Studiedly so.

'What part of France do you come from?' Another innocuous polite enquiry—nothing more than that. Yet once again he saw that flicker.

'Normandy,' she answered. 'A little place not far from Rouen.' Her mother's birthplace, it was the part of France she knew best, and therefore it seemed the safest answer to give.

'And have you always wanted to be a singer?'

The lift of a shoulder came again. 'One uses the talents one is given,' she replied. It was as unrevealing an answer as she could think to give.

Bastiaan's eyes narrowed minutely.

Sarah saw the narrowing. Could he tell she was being as evasive as she could? She was glad that the sommelier arrived at that moment, diverting Bastiaan. But as the man departed, and Bastiaan lifted his wine glass, she felt his dark eyes upon her again.

'To our time together,' he said, and smiled.

She made herself lift her own glass and meet his eyes. It was like drowning in dark velvet. She felt her blood quicken, her breath catch. A sense of unreality over-whelmed her—and yet this was real...vividly, pulsingly real. She was sitting here, so close to the man who could set her senses on fire with a single glance.

Oh, this was ridiculous. To be so...so overcome by this man. She *had* to claw back her composure. If she were going to take refuge in being Sabine then she must be as poised and cool as that protection provided. With an inner breath she set down her glass and then let her glance sweep out across the glittering vista far below.

'If the food is as exceptional as the location, I can un-derstand why this place has such a reputation,' she mur-mured. It seemed a safe thing to say—and safe things were what she was clutching at.

'I hope both please you,' he replied.

His lashes dipped over his eyes. It was clear to him that she did not wish to talk about herself, but her very evasiveness told him what he wanted to know—that she was, indeed, a woman who presented to the world what she chose to present. For himself, he did not care. Sabine Sablon would not, after all, be staying long in his life.

'Does this have a Michelin star yet?' Sarah asked, bringing her gaze back to him. Another safe thing to ask.

'One. But a second is being targeted,' he answered.

'What makes the difference, I wonder?' Sarah asked. Safe again...

He lifted his wine glass. Talking about Michelin stars was perfectly acceptable as a topic. It lasted them until their food arrived, and then they moved on to the subject of the Côte d'Azur itself—how it had changed and developed, what its charms and attractions were.

It was Bastiaan who talked most, and he soon became aware that Sabine was adept at asking questions of him, keeping the conversation flowing.

And all the time, like a deep, powerful current in a river on whose surface aimless ripples were circling, another conversation was taking place. One that was wordless, silent, yet gaining strength with every politely interested smile, every nod, every lift of a fork, of a glass, every glance, every low laugh, every gesture of the hand, every shift in body position…every breath taken.

It was a conversation that could lead to only one end… take them to only one destination.

The place he had determined she should go. The place she could no longer resist him taking her to.

Sarah climbed back into the car and Bastiaan lowered his tall frame into the driving seat beside her. Immediately the space confining them shrank. Her mind was in a daze. Wine hummed in her veins—softening her body so that it seemed to mould to the contours of the leather seat. She heard the throaty growl of the engine and the powerful car moved forward, pressing her further into her seat. She could feel the low throb of her beating heart, the flush of heat in her skin.

But it was in *Sabine's* breast that her heart was beating. It was Sabine whose senses were dominated by the presence of this magnetic, compelling man beside her. Sabine who was free to do what she was doing now—ignoring everything in the world except this man, this night…

Sabine, alluring, sensual and sophisticated, could yield to the overpowering temptation that was Bastiaan Karavalas and all that he promised. Sabine had led her to this place, this time, this moment—a moment that Sabine would wish to come...would choose to be in...

*This is going to happen. It is going to happen and I am not going to stop it. I want it to happen.*

She did. It might be rash, it might be foolish, it might be the thing she had least expected would happen during this summer, but she *was* going to go with Bastiaan Karavalas.

This night.

And as for tomorrow...

She would deal with that then. Not now.

Now there was only her, and him, and being taken to where he was taking her. Wordless. Voiceless. Irreversible.

He took her to his apartment in Monte Carlo.

It was as unlike the villa on Cap Pierre as she could imagine. In a modern high-rise block, its decor sleek and contemporary. She stood by the huge-paned glass windows, gazing out over the marina far below, seeing the glittering lights of the city scintillating like diamonds, feeling the rich sensuality of her body, the tremor in her limbs.

Waiting...

Waiting for the man standing behind her, his presence, his scent overpowering her. Waiting for him to make his move...to take her into his arms...his embrace...his bed.

She heard him murmur something, felt the warmth of his breath on the nape of her neck, the drift of his hands around her shoulders, so light, feather-light, and yet with a silken power that made her breath catch, her lips part as the tremor in her limbs intensified. She felt the powerful touch of his palms glide down her bare arms, fasten on her wrists, and with a movement as subtle as it was irresistible, she felt him turn her towards him.

She lifted her face to him, lips parted, eyes deep and lustrous. She was so close she could feel the strength and heat of his body, feel the dark intensity of his gaze, of those eyes holding hers, conveying to her all that she knew was in her own eyes as well.

He smiled. A slow pull of his mouth. As if he knew what she was feeling, as if he were colluding with the strange, strong, heavy pulse of the blood in her veins. His eyes worked over her face leisurely, taking in every contour, every curve of her features.

'You are so beautiful…' It was a husky statement. 'So very beautiful…'

For one long, timeless moment his eyes poured into hers as they stood there, face to face, and then his hands closed around her slender, pliant waist and drew her to him slowly, very slowly, as if each increase in the pressure of his hands drawing her to him was almost against his will and yet as impossible for him to resist as it was for her to resist.

Nor did she want to—she wanted only to feel his mouth making its slow descent to hers, wanted him to fuse his lips to hers, to take her mouth, possess it, mould it to his, open it to his…

And when he did her eyes could only close, her throat could only sigh with a low sound of absolute pleasure, as with skill and sensual slowness his mouth found hers to take it and taste it. Somewhere inside her, very dimly, she could feel heat pooling. Her heart seemed to cease its beating as she felt the rich, sensual glide of his lips on hers, his mouth opening hers to him, his kiss deepening.

His hold on her waist tightened, strengthened, as the shift of his stance changed so that she was being cradled against him, and with a little shimmer of shocked response she felt how aroused he was.

His arousal fired hers so that her blood surged, her breath caught, the melding of her mouth to his quickened and deepened. Her hands lifted, closing around the strong breadth of his back, splaying against the smooth fabric of his dinner jacket. She felt her breasts crush against the wall of his chest. She heard his low growl, felt his palms pull her tighter against him.

Excitement flared through her. Every cell in her body was alive, sensitive, eager for more of what she was already experiencing. And then, as if on a jerking impulse, he swept her body into his arms, as if she were nothing more than a feather. He was striding away with her, his mouth still fastened upon hers, and the world beyond whirled as he deposited her heavily upon the cold satin surface of a wide, soft bed and came down beside her.

His mouth continued devouring hers, and one thigh was thrown over her as a kind of glory filled her. Desire, open and searing, flooded her. She felt her breasts tighten and tingle and threw back her head to lift them more. Another low growl broke from him, and then her arms were being lifted over her head and pinioned with one hand while his palm closed possessively over the sweet, straining mound of her breast. She gasped with pleasure, groaning, her head moving restlessly from side to side, her mouth, freed from his, abandoned and questing.

Was this her? Could it be her? Lying like this, flaming with a desire that was consuming her, possessing her, shameless and wanton?

His heavy thigh lay between hers and she felt her hips writhe against it, wanting more and yet more of the sensations that were being loosened within her. Did she speak? And if she did, what did she say? She did not know—knew only that she must implore him to bestow upon her what she was craving, yearning for, more and more and more...

Never had she felt like this, so deeply, wildly aroused. As if she were burning with a flame that she had never known.

He smiled down at her. 'I think it is time, *cherie*, that we discarded these unnecessary clothes...'

He jack-knifed to his feet, making good on his words. She could not move—could only gaze at him in the dim light as he swiftly, carelessly, disposed of what he was wearing. And then his hard, lean body was lowering down beside her, his weight indenting the mattress. She felt his nakedness like a brand, and suddenly, out of nowhere, her cheeks were flaring, her eyelids veiling him from her sight.

He gave a low, amused laugh. 'Shy?' he murmured. 'At *this* point?'

She couldn't answer him—could only let her eyes flutter open. And for an instant—just an instant—she thought she saw in the dim light a question suddenly forming in his...

But then it was gone. In its place a look of deep, sensual appreciation.

'You are beautiful indeed, *cherie*, as you are...but I want to see your beauty *au naturel*.'

A hand lifted to her shoulders, easing the straps away first on one side, then the other. With a kind of sensual delicacy he peeled her gown down her body to her waist, letting his gaze wander over her in that lazy, leisurely fashion that made the heat pool in her body. Then he tugged it further still, over her hips, taking with it her panties, easing the material down her thighs to free her legs. Now only her stockings remained, and with a sense of shock she realised what it was he was seeing of her...

'Shall I make love to you like this?' he asked, and there was still that lazy, sensual amusement in his voice.

She answered him. No, she would *not* be arrayed like that for him.

With swift decision she sat up, peeling her stockings from her body, tossing them aside with the belt that fastened them. Her hair was tumbling now, free and lush over her breasts, as she sat looking at him where he lay back on the coverlet, blatant in his own nakedness. She gazed down at him, pushing back her hair with one hand. He was waiting—assured, aroused, confident—conspiring with her to make the next move, and she was glad to do so.

Draping her long hair around one shoulder, she leant forward. Her breasts almost grazed his bared chest as she planted her hands either side of him.

'Where shall I start?' she heard herself murmur, with the same warm, aroused amusement in her voice as his had held.

An answering amusement glittered in his dark eyes. 'Take me,' he said, and the amusement was there in his deep voice too. 'I am yours.'

She gave a low, brief laugh, and then her mouth was gliding, skimming over the steel-hard contours of his chest. Lightly…arousingly.

For interminable moments he endured it, his arousal mounting unbearably, as she deliberately teased and tempted him. And then, with an explosive edge, he knew he could take it no longer. He hauled her down on him—fully on him—and the satisfaction he knew as he heard her gasp was all he needed to hear. He rolled her over beneath him, and with a thrust of his thigh parted her.

His mouth found hers—claiming and clinging, feasting and tasting. Urgency filled him. He wanted her *now*.

Almost he succumbed to the overwhelming urge to possess her as she was. But that would be madness—insanity. With a groan of self-control he freed himself, flung out an arm sideways and reached into the bedside drawer.

She was seeking to draw him back, folding her hands around him, murmuring, and he could hear the breathless moans in her throat as she sought him.

'Wait—a moment only...'

It was almost impossible for him to speak. His arousal was absolute...his body was in meltdown. He *had* to have her—he *had* to possess her. Had to complete what he had wanted to do from the very first moment of laying eyes upon her lush, alluring body, since he had first felt the response in those emerald eyes...

Oh, she might be as mercenary as he feared, as manipulative as he suspected, but none of that mattered. Only this moment mattered—this urgency, this absolute overriding desire for her that was possessing him.

A moment later he was ready, and triumph surged through him. At last he could take what he wanted—possess *her*, this woman who would belong to no one else but him...

She was drawing him down on her, her thighs enclosing his as her body opened to him, and with a relief that flooded through him he fused his body deep, deep within her own...

Immediately, like a firestorm, sensation exploded within him and he was swept away on burning flames that consumed him in a furnace of pleasure. For an instant so brief he was scarcely conscious of it, he felt dismay that he had not waited for her. But then, with a reeling sense of amazed wonder, he realised that she had come with him into the burning flames...that she was clinging to him and crying out even as he was, and that their bodies were wreathed in a mutual consummation that was going on and on and on...

Never before had he experienced such a consummation. Never in all his wide and varied experience had the intensity been like this. It was as if his whole mind and body and being had ignited into one incredible, endless sensation—as if their bodies were melding together, fusing like molten metal into each other.

When did it change? When it did it start to ebb, to take him back down to the plane of reality, of consciousness? He didn't know—couldn't say. Could only feel his body shaking as it returned slowly, throbbingly, to earth. His lungs were seizing and he could feel his heart still pounding, hear his voice shaking as he lifted himself slightly from her, aware that his full weight was crushing her.

He said something, but he did not know what.

She was looking at him—gazing up with an expression in her eyes that mirrored what he knew was in his own. A kind of shock. She was stunned by what had happened.

For one long moment they seemed just to stare at each other disbelievingly. Then, with a ragged intake of breath, Bastiaan managed to smile. Nothing more than that. And he saw her eyes flutter closed, as if he had released her. A huge lassitude swept over him, and with a kind of sigh he lowered himself again, settling her sideways against him, pulling her into his warm, exhausted body.

Holding her so close against him was wonderful, reassuring, and all that he wanted. His hands spread across her silken flanks, securing her against him, and he heard her give a little sigh of relaxation, felt one of her hands close over his, winding her fingers into his, and then, with a final settling of her body, she was still, her breathing quietening as she slipped into sleep.

In his final moment of remaining consciousness Bastiaan reached back to haul the coverlet over them both and then, when they were cocooned beneath, he wrapped his arm around her once more and gave himself to sleep, exhausted, replete, and in that moment possessing all that he wanted to possess on earth.


Something woke her—she wasn't sure what. Whatever it was, it had roused her from the deep slumber into which she'd fallen…a slumber deeper and sweeter than she had ever known.

'Good morning.'

Bastiaan, clad in a towelling robe, was looking down at her. His dark eyes were drinking her in. She did not answer. Could not. Could only hear in her head the words that had forced their way in.

*What have I done? Oh, God, what have I done?*

But she didn't need to ask—the evidence was in her naked body, in her lying in the bed of Bastiaan Karavalas.

Memory burned like a meteor, scorching through the sky. Awareness made her jack-knife. 'Oh, God—what time is it?' She stared at him, horror-struck.

His face pulled into a frown. 'Of what significance is that?' he demanded.

But she did not answer him—did not do anything except leap from the bed, not caring that she was naked. Not caring about anything except snatching, from wherever she could see them, her clothes from the previous night.

Dismay and horror convulsed her. She pushed into the bathroom, caught sight of herself in the huge mirror, and gave a gasping groan. Three minutes later she stumbled out—looking ludicrous, she knew, with her tangled hair tumbling over her shoulders, her evening dress from the night before crumpled and idiotic on her. But she didn't care—couldn't care. Couldn't afford to care.

She might be wearing Sabine's clothes, left over from the night before, but Sabine herself was gone. Sarah was back—and she was panicking as she had never panicked before.

'What the *hell*…?' Bastiaan was staring at her.

'I have to go.'

'*What?* Don't be absurd.'

She ignored him. Pushed right past him out into the reception room and stared desperately around, looking for her bag. Dimly she remembered that her day clothes were in a plastic bag that must, she thought urgently, still be in the footwell of Bastiaan's car. But there was no time for that now. No time for anything except to get out of here and find a bus stop…

*Oh, God, it will take for ever to get back. I'll be late—so late. Max will be furious!*

She felt her arm caught, her body swung round. 'Sabine—what is going on? Why are you running away?'

She stared, eyes blank with incomprehension. 'I have to go,' she said again.

For a second there was rejection in his eyes, and then, as if making a decision, he let her go.

'I'll call a cab—' he said.

'No!'

He ignored her, crossed to a phone set by the front door, spoke swiftly to someone she assumed was the concierge. Then he hung up, turned to look at her.

'I don't know what is going on, or why. But if you insist on leaving I cannot stop you. So—go.' His voice was harsh, uncomprehending. His expression blank.

For one timeless moment she was paralysed. Could

only stare at him. Could only feel as if an explosion was taking place inside her, detonating down every nerve, along every vein.

'Bastiaan, I—'

But she could not speak. There was nothing to say. She was not Sabine. She was Sarah. And she had no place here…no place at all…

He opened the front door for her and she stumbled through.

As she ran for the elevator she heard the door slam behind her. Reverberating through every stricken cell in her body.

# CHAPTER EIGHT

BASTIAAN WAS DRIVING. Driving as though he were being chased by the hounds of hell. The road snaked up, high into the Alpes-Maritimes, way beyond the last outpost of the Riviera and out into the hills, where bare rock warred with the azure skies. Further on and further up he drove, with the engine of the car roaring into the silence all around him.

At the top of the pass he skidded to the side, sending a scree of stones tumbling down into the crevasse below. He cut the engine but the silence brought no peace. His hands clenched over the steering wheel.

Why had she run from him? *Why?* What had put that look of absolute panic on her face?

Memory seared across his synapses. What had flamed between them had been as overwhelming for her as it had been for him—he knew that. Knew it with every male instinct he possessed. That conflagration of passion had set them both alight—*both* of them.

*It has never been like that for me before. Never.*

And she had gazed at him with shock in her eyes, with disbelief.

Had she fled because of what had happened between them? Had it shocked her as it had shocked him? So that she could not handle it, could not cope with it?

*Something is happening, Sabine, between us— something that is not in your game plan. Nor in mine.*

He stared out over the wide ravine, an empty space into which a single turn of the wheel would send his car— himself—hurtling. He tried to make himself think about Philip, about why he had come here to rescue him from Sabine Sablon, but he could not. It seemed...irrelevant. Unimportant.

There was only one imperative now.

He reached for the ignition, fired the engine. Nosed the car around and headed back down to the coast with only one thought in his head, driving him on.

Max lifted his hand to halt her. 'Take it again,' he said. His voice was controlled, but barely masking his exasperation.

Sarah felt her fingers clench. Her throat was tight, and her shoulders and her lungs. In fact every muscle in her body felt rigid. It was hopeless—totally, absolutely hopeless. All around her there was a tension that was palpable. Everyone present was generating it, feeling it. She most of all.

When she'd arrived at rehearsal, horrendously late, Max had turned his head to her and levelled her with a look that might have killed her, like a basilisk's. And then it had gone from bad to worse...to impossible.

Her voice had gone. It was as simple and as brutal as that. It didn't matter that Max wasn't even attempting to get her to sing the aria—she could sing nothing. Nothing at all.

But it was not the mortification of arriving so late to rehearsal, her breathless arrival and hectic heartbeat that were making it impossible for her to sing. It was because inside her head an explosion had taken place, wiping out everything that had once been in it.

Replacing it only with searing white-hot memory.

*Her night with Bastiaan.*

It filled her head, overwhelming her, consuming her consciousness, searing in her bloodstream—every touch, every caress, every kiss. Impossible to banish. Impossible for anything else to exist for her.

'*Sarah!*' Max's voice was sharp, edged with anger now.

She felt another explosion within her. 'I *can't*.' The cry broke from her. 'I just can't! It isn't there—I'm sorry... I'm *sorry*!'

'What the hell use is sorry?' he yelled, his control clearly snapping.

And suddenly it was all too much. Just too much. Her late arrival and the collapse of her voice were simply the final straw.

Alain, her tenor, stepped forward, put a protective arm around her shoulder. 'Lay off her, Max!' he snapped.

'And lay off the rest of us too!' called someone else.

'Max, we're exhausted. We *have* to have a break.'

The protests were mounting, the grumbling turning into revolt. For a dangerous moment Max looked as if he wanted to yell at them all, then abruptly he dropped his head.

'OK,' he said. 'Break, everyone. Half an hour. Get outside. Fresh air.'

The easing of the fractured tension was palpable and the company started to disperse, talking in low, relieved voices.

Alain's hand dropped from Sarah's shoulder. 'Deep breaths,' he said kindly, and wandered off to join the general exodus outdoors.

But Sarah couldn't move. She felt nailed to the floor. She shut her eyes in dumb, agonised misery.

Dear God, hadn't she said she must have no distractions. *None*. And then last night—!

*What have I done? Oh, what have I done!*

It was the same helpless, useless cry she'd given as she'd stood in Bastiaan's apartment naked, fresh from his bed.

Anguish filled her—and misery.

Then, suddenly, she felt her hands being taken.

'Sarah, look at me,' said Max.

His voice had changed—his whole demeanour had changed. Slowly, warily, she opened her eyes. His expression was sympathetic. Tired lines were etched around his eyes.

'I'm sorry,' he said. 'We're all burning out and I'm taking it out on you—and you don't deserve it.'

'I'm so sorry for arriving late,' she replied. 'And for being so useless today.'

But Max squeezed her hands. 'You need a break,' he said. 'And more than just half an hour.'

He seemed to pause, searching her strained expression, then he nodded and went on.

'Should I blame myself?' he asked. There was faint wry humour in his dry voice. 'Wasn't I the one who told you not to be late this morning? Knowing who'd turned up to see you? No, no, *cherie*—say nothing. Whatever has happened, it's still going on in your head. So...'

He took a breath, looking at her intently.

'What I want you to do is...go. Go. Whatever it takes—do it. I don't want to see you again this week. Take a complete break—whether that's to sob into your pillow or... Well, whatever! If this rich cousin of Philip is good for you, or bad, the point is that *he's* in your head and your work is not.' His voice changed. 'Even without last night you've hit the wall, and I can't force you through it. So you must rest, and then—well, we shall see what we shall see.'

He pressed her hands again, his gaze intent.

'Have faith, Sarah—have faith in yourself, in what you can accomplish. You are so nearly there! I would not waste my genius on you otherwise,' he finished, with his familiar waspish humour.

He stepped back, patting her hands before relinquishing them.

'So—go. Take off. Do anything but sing. Not even Sabine's dire ditties. I'll sort it with Raymond—somehow.'

He dropped a light kiss on her forehead.

'*Go!*' he said.

And Sarah went.


Bastiaan nosed the car carefully down the narrowing street towards the harbour. She was here somewhere—she had to be. He didn't know where her *pension* was, but there were a limited number, and if necessary he would check them all out. Then there was the nightclub as well—someone there at this time of day would know where she might be.

*I have to find her.*

That was the imperative driving him. Conscious thought was not operating strongly in him right now, but he didn't care. Didn't care that a voice inside his head was telling him that there was no reason to seek her out like this. One night with her had been enough to achieve his ends—so why was he searching for her?

He did not answer—refused to answer. Only continued driving, turning into the area that fronted the harbour, face set, eyes scanning around as if he might suddenly spot her.

And she was there.

He felt his blood leap, his breath catch.

She was by the water's edge, seated on a mooring bollard, staring out to sea. He felt emotions surge through him—triumph shot through with relief. He stopped the car, not caring whether it was in a parking zone or not. Got out. Strode up to her. Placed a hand on her shoulder.

'Sabine...' His voice was rich with satisfaction. With possession.

Beneath his hand he felt her whole body jump. Her head snaked around, eyes widening in shock.

'Oh, God...' she said faintly.

He smiled. 'You did not truly believe I would let you go, did you?' he said. He looked down at her. Frowned suddenly. 'You have been crying,' he said.

There was disbelief in his voice. Sabine? Weeping? He felt the thoughts in his head rearrange themselves. Felt a new one intrude.

'What has made you cry?' he demanded. It was not *him*—impossible that it should be him.

She shook her head. 'It's just...complicated,' she said.

Bastiaan found himself hunkering down beside her, hands resting loosely between his bunched thighs, face on a level with hers. His expression was strange. His emotions stranger. The Sabine who sat here, her face tear-stained, was someone new—someone he had never seen before.

The surge of possessiveness that had triumphed inside him a moment ago on finding her was changing into something he did not recognise. But it was moving within him. Slowly but powerfully. Making him face this new emotion evolving within him.

'No,' he contradicted, and there was something in his
voice that had not been there before. 'It is very simple.'
He looked at her, his eyes holding hers. 'After last night,
how could it be anything else?'

His gaze became a caress and his hand reached out
softly to brush away a tendril of tangled hair that had
escaped from its rough confines in a bunched pleat at
the back of her head. He wanted to undo the clasp, see
her glorious blond mane tumble around her shoulders.
Although what she was wearing displeased him, for it
seemed to be a shapeless tee shirt and a pair of equally
shapeless cotton trousers. And her face was blotchy, her
eyes strained.

Yet as he spoke, as his hand gently brushed the tendril from her face, he saw her expression change. Saw
the strain ebb from her eyes, her blotched skin re-colour.

'I don't know why you ran from me,' he heard himself
say, 'and I will not ask. But…' His hand now cupped her
chin, feeling the warmth of her skin beneath his fingertips. 'This I *will* ask.'

His eyes rested on hers—his eyes that had burned their
way into hers in the throes of exquisite passion. But now
they were simply filled with a single question. The only
one that filled his head, his consciousness.

'Will you come with me now? And whatever complications there are will you leave them aside?'

Something shifted in her eyes, in the very depths of
them. They were green—as green as emeralds. Memory
came to him. He remembered how he'd wanted to drape
her in emeralds. It seemed odd to him just then. Irrelevant. Unimportant. Only one thing was important now.

The answer she was giving him with her beautiful,
emerald-green eyes, which were softening even as he

held them. Softening and lightening and filling with an expression that told him all he needed to know.

He smiled again. Not in triumph this time, nor in possession. Just smiled warmly upon her.

'Good,' he said. Then he drew her to her feet. His smile deepened. 'Let's go.'

He led her to his car and helped her in.

*The rest of this week*, thought Sarah.

The wealth of time seemed like largesse of immense proportions. The panic that had been in her breast and the tension that had bound her lungs with iron, her throat with barbed wire, were gone. Just...*gone*. They had fallen from her as she had risen to her feet, had her hand taken by Bastiaan. Her feet felt like cushions of air.

*I've been set free!*

That was what it felt like. As if she had been set free from all the complications that had been tearing into her like claws and teeth ever since she'd surfaced that morning, realizing what she'd done. What *she*—Sarah, not Sabine—had done. And now... Oh, now, it didn't matter—didn't matter who she was.

Max understood—understood the entire impossibility of what had been tying her in knots for days now, ever since Bastiaan Karavalas had walked into her life.

*Right man—wrong time.*

But no more—not for a precious handful of glorious, wonderful, liberating days.

*I can do what I've been longing to do—what I succumbed to doing last night. This man alone is different from any I've ever known. What happened last night was a revelation, a transformation.*

She quivered with the memory of their passion as he

started the car, gunning the engine. She turned to look at him, her eyes as bright as stars.

'Where are we going?' she asked.

She had asked that last night and he had taken her to a new, glittering realm of enchantment and desire, passion and fulfilment.

'My villa,' he answered, his eyes warm upon her before he glanced back to steer the car out of the little town, along the road that curved towards the *Cap*.

Gladness filled her. The apartment in Monte Carlo was glitzy and glamorous, but it did nothing for her. It was his villa that charmed her.

'Wonderful…' she breathed. She felt as light as air, floating way, way up into the sky—the carefree, bright blue sky, where there were no complications to tether her down.

*I'm free from everything except seizing with both hands this time now! Right man—right time. Right now!*

Her spirits soared, and it seemed they were at the villa in minutes. For a brief interlude Sarah felt self-conscious about encountering Paulette again. If the woman had considered her a threat to Philip, what might she think of her cavorting with her employer? But Paulette, she discovered, had a day off.

'So we'll have to make our own lunch,' Bastiaan told her.

He didn't want to make lunch—he wanted to make love. But his stomach was growling. He was hungry. Hungry for food, hungry for her. He would sate both appetites and life would be good. *Very* good.

He had Sabine back with him, and right now that was all he wanted.

As he headed towards the kitchen he glanced out of the French windows to the terrace beyond. Only a few days ago they had lunched there, all three of them—he and Sabine and Philip.

It seemed a long time ago.

'So…' Bastiaan set down his empty coffee cup on the ironwork table on the villa's shady terrace and leant back in his chair, his eyes resting on Sabine. 'What shall we do now?'

The expression in his eyes made it totally clear what he would like to do—he'd sated his hunger for food, and now he wanted to sate a quite different hunger.

Across from him, Sarah felt her pulse give a kick—when Bastiaan looked at her like that it was hard to respond in any other way. Lunch had been idyllic. Simple *charcuterie* and *fromage*, with huge scarlet tomatoes and more of the luscious peaches they'd had the other day. It had felt a little odd to be here again, receiving such intimacy from Bastiaan.

*Has it really happened? Am I really here with Bastiaan, and are we lovers?*

But it was true—it really was—and for the rest of this glorious week it could go on being true.

A rich, sensuous languor swept through her as his gaze twined with hers. A wicked sparkle glinted in her own.

'The pool looks irresistible…' she murmured provocatively.

She almost heard him growl with frustration, but gallantly he nodded. 'It does indeed—especially with you in it.' His eyes glinted too. 'Do you want me to guide you back to the room you changed in last time? Or—' and now there was even more of a wickedly intimate glint in his eyes '—shall we dispense with swimsuits altogether?'

She laughed in answer, and disappeared off to change.

Maybe they could go skinny-dipping at night, under the stars…?

The water was wonderfully refreshing, and so was Bastiaan's company. There was a lot of playful frolicking, and from her more covert—and not so covert—appreciation of his strong, muscled physique. A thrill went through her. For now—for this brief, precious time—he was hers. How wonderful was that?

*Very* wonderful—and more than wonderful: incredible.

It was incredible when, on retiring to the bedroom in the villa to shower in the en-suite bathroom, she discovered Bastiaan could wait no longer.

He stepped inside the shower, hands slicking down her wet, tingling body. She gasped in shock and then in arousal as skilfully, urgently and devastatingly he took possession of her. As her legs wrapped around him and he lifted her up her head fell back in ecstasy, and it seemed to her that she had been transformed into a different person. A person who was neither the sultry Sabine nor the soprano Sarah, but someone whose only existence was to meld herself with this incredible, sensual male, to fuse her body with his, to burn with him in an explosion of physical pleasure and delight.

Afterwards, as they stood exhausted, with the cooling water streaming over them, her breath coming in hectic pants, he cut the shower, reached for huge fleecy towels and wrapped her up as if she were a precious parcel.

He let his hands rest over her damp shoulders, his eyes pouring down into hers. 'What do you do to me?' he asked. There was a strange quality in his voice, a strange expression in his dark eyes.

She let her forehead rest on his chest, the huge lassitude of the aftermath of passion consuming her now.

She could not answer him for it was a question that was in her own being too.

He swung her up into his arms, carried her through into the bedroom, lowering her down upon the cool cotton coverlet, coming down beside her. He drew her into his sheltering embrace, kissed her nape with soft, velvet kisses. And then exhausted, sated, complete, they slept.

When they awoke they made love again, slowly and softly, taking their time—all the time in the world—in the shuttered late-afternoon light of the cool room. And this time Bastiaan brought her to a different kind of ecstasy—a slow, blissful release that flowed through her body like sweet water after drought.

Afterwards they lay a little while in each other's loose embrace, and then Bastiaan lifted his head from the pillow.

'I know,' he told her, 'a great way to watch the sunset.'

It was indeed, Sarah discovered, a wonderful way to watch the sunset.

He took her out to sea in a fast, sleek motor launch that they boarded from the little quay at the rocky shore below the villa. Exhilaration filled her as Bastiaan carved a foaming wake in the darkening cobalt water, the sun low on the surface, turning the Mediterranean to gold as it kissed the swell.

He cut the engine, letting the silence settle around them, and she sat next to him, his arm casually around her shoulder, his body warm against hers. She could feel the gentle bob of the waves beneath the hull, feel the warmth of the sun on her face as she lifted it to its lingering rays. It was as if they were the only people in the world. Here out on the water, with Bastiaan's arm around her, she felt as if all that lay beyond had ceased to be.

Here there were no complications.

Here there was only Bastiaan.

*What is happening to me?*

The question wound in her mind between the circuits of her thoughts, seeking an answer she was not ready to find. It was far easier simply to go on sitting there, with the warm air like an embrace, the hugeness of the sea all around them, the rich gold of the setting sun illuminating them. This—now—was good. This was all she wanted. This was her contentment.

They headed back to shore in the gathering dusk.

'Would you like to eat out or at the villa?' Bastiaan asked.

'Oh, don't go out,' she said immediately. Then frowned. 'But I'm not very good at cooking, and I don't want you to have to…' she said uncertainly. Could a man like Bastiaan Karavalas really cook a meal?

He gave a laugh. 'We'll have something delivered,' he told her. 'What would you like?'

'Pizza?' she suggested.

He laughed again. 'Oh, I think we can do better than that,' he said.

And indeed they could.

On the Côte d'Azur, when money was no object, it seemed that gourmet meals could be conjured out of thin air.

As she took her place at the table on the terrace, in the warm evening air, it was to discover that a team of servers had arrived from a nearby Michelin-starred restaurant and were setting out their exquisite wares.

She and Bastiaan had already shared a glass of champagne before the meal arrived, and she felt its effervescence in her veins. Now, as the team from the restaurant departed, Bastiaan lifted a glass of rich, ruby Burgundy.

'To our time together,' he said. It was the same toast he'd given the night before, at Le Tombleur.

Sarah raised her own glass.

*Our time together...these few precious days...*

She felt emotion pluck at her.

From his seat, Bastiaan rested his eyes on her. She looked nothing like she had the night before when they had dined. And he was glad of it. She was wearing a pale blue kimono that he had found in a closet. In sheerest silk, it was knotted at the waist and had wide sleeves, a plunging neckline that gave the merest hint of the sweet swell of her breasts. Her glorious hair was loose, cascading down her back. She wore no make-up. Needed not a scrap of it.

*How beautiful she is. How much I desire her!*

He tried to remember why it was he had seduced her. Tried to remember his fears for Philip. Tried to remember how he had determined to foil her machinations. But his memory seemed dim. Flawed.

As he gazed on her they seemed unreal, those fears. Absurd...

*Did I misjudge her?*

That was the question that uncoiled itself in his mind. The question that pressed itself against his consciousness. The question which, with every passing moment he spent with her, seemed more and more...*unnecessary.*

Thoughts flitted through his mind. What evidence, after all, *was* there against her? Oh, Philip was lovestruck—that was undeniable. His every yearning gaze told Bastiaan that. But what of her? What of her behaviour towards Philip?

*I thought her nothing more than a blatant gold-digger—trying to exploit Philip's youth and vulnerability. But is she—was she?*

*I thought that she had blatantly switched her attentions to me—had manoeuvred me to get rid of Philip from the scene.*

But why, then, had she been so reluctant to go with him when he'd sought her out on his return from Paris? And why had she fled from him in his apartment that first morning? If she'd been no better than he'd thought her, wanting him for his wealth, she should have clung to him like glue. Not wept by the quayside while he'd searched so urgently for her.

Was that the behaviour of the woman he'd thought her to be? It couldn't be—it just *couldn't*.

*There is no evidence against her. From the very start she has confounded my suspicions of her—time after time. All I have to go on, other than my fears for Philip, is that payment that he made.*

That was the truth of it. Had he been conjecturing everything else about her? Feeding his suspicions simply because he'd wanted to protect his young cousin? He took a breath, fixed his eyes on her as she lifted her wine glass to answer his toast, looked across at him and smiled—her eyes like incandescent jewels, rich and glowing.

Emotion leapt in him, and in his head he heard his own voice, searing across his thoughts.

*There could be an explanation for why Philip paid out that money. All I have to do is ask him. There is no reason—none—to fear that it was to Sabine. She could be completely innocent of the suspicions I've had of her.*

As innocent as he wanted her to be. Wanted so much for her to be…

'To us,' he said, and let his eyes mingle and meld with hers—the eyes of this woman who could be everything he wanted her to be. And nothing he did not.

From this moment on he would not let his fears, his

suspicions, poison him. Would not let anything spoil his enjoyment of this moment, this time with her.

And nothing did—that was the bliss of it. Cocooned with her at the villa, he made love to her by day and by night— and *every* time it took him by storm. A storm not only of the senses but of something more.

*What is it you do to me?*

That was the question that came every time she lay cradled in his arms, her head on his chest, her arm like a silken bond around his waist, her body warm and flushed with passion spent.

The question had no answer—and soon he did not seek an answer. Soon he was content simply to let the hours pass with her. Time came and went, the sun rose and set, the stars wheeled in the clear sky each night as they lay out on the pool loungers, gazing upwards, hand in hand, the cool midnight breeze whispering over their bodies, the moon rising to cast its silver light upon them.

Who *was* this woman? Bastiaan asked of himself, thinking of all that he knew of her. It no longer seemed to matter. Not any more.

Sometimes he caught fragments of her life—a passing mention of the garden at a house in Normandy where, so he surmised, she must have grown up. The climate and the terrain so different from this sun-baked southern shore. Once he tried to draw her out about her singing, but she only shook her head and changed the subject with a smile, a kiss.

Nor did she talk to him about *his* life—only asked him about Greece. How it was to live there, with so much history, the history of millennia, pressing all around him. Of how he made his money, his wealth, she never spoke. She seemed quite oblivious to it. She did not ask to leave the villa—was content to spend each day within its confining beauty.

Meals were delivered, or concocted by them both—simple, hearty food, from salads and *charcuterie* to pasta and barbecues, prepared with much laughter and consumed with appetite. An appetite that afterwards turned to passion for each other.

*I didn't know it would be like this—having Sabine with me. I didn't think it would be this...this good.*

He tried to think back to a time when it had not been like this—when Sabine had not been with him, when all he'd had were his fears for Philip, his suspicions of her. But it seemed very far away—blurring in his head. Fading more and more with each hour. All that mattered to him now was being as they were now, lying side by side beneath the stars, hand in hand.

He felt her thumb move sensuously, lightly over his as their clasped hands hung loosely between them. He turned his head towards her, away from the moon above. She was gazing across at him, her face dim in the moonlight, her eyes resting on him. There was a softness in her face, in her eyes...

'Bastiaan...' Her voice was low, a sweet caress.

His eyes found hers. Desire reached into his veins. He drew her to her feet and wound his fingers into hers. Speared his hand into her hair, let his mouth find hers.

Passion, strong and sweet and true, flared at his touch. Drove them indoors to find each other, again, and yet again, in this perfect, blissful time they had together.

# CHAPTER NINE

'MY *PENSION* IS just there,' Sarah said, pointing to the corner of the street. 'I won't be five minutes.'

Bastiaan pulled the car over to the kerb and she dashed inside. She wanted to change into something pretty for the day. They were finally emerging from the villa, and Bastiaan was set on taking her to a place he was amazed she hadn't seen yet.

The picturesque little town of St Paul de Vence, up in the hills behind the coastline, was famous as a place frequented by artists. She was happy enough to go there—happy enough to be anywhere in the world right now, providing Bastiaan was with her and she with him.

*Bastiaan.* Oh, the name soared in her head, echoed deep inside her. She was seizing all that he was holding out to her so that there was nothing else except being with him, day after precious day, night after searing night.

*It's as if I were asleep and he has woken me. Woken my senses, set them alight.*

In her head, in her heart, emotion hovered like a fragile bubble, iridescent and glistening with light and colour. A bubble she longed to seize but dared not—not now, not yet. But it filled her being, made her breathless with delight, with joy. Joy that brought a smile to her face now, as she ran into the *pension*, eager to be as quick as possible so she could re-join Bastiaan without delay.

Five minutes later she was running down the stairs again, pausing only to snatch at the mail in her room's pigeonhole, dropping the envelopes into her handbag before emerging out onto the roadway. She jumped into the car and off they set.

Bastiaan's gaze was warm upon her before he focussed on the way ahead.

*She's changed her image yet again*, he found himself thinking. This one he liked particularly, he decided. Her hair was in a long plait, her make-up no more than a touch of mascara and lip gloss, and her skin had been warmed by the sun of the past few days to a golden honey. Her outfit was a pretty floral calf-length sundress in pale blue and yellow. She looked fresh and summery and beautiful.

And *his*. Oh, most definitely, definitely his!

Emotion surged within him. What it was, he didn't know—and didn't care. Knew only that it felt good— *so* good...

The route out of the *ville* took them past the nightclub where she sang. As they drove by he saw her throw it a sideways glance, almost looking at it askance, before turning swiftly away. He was glad to have passed it too— did not want to think about it. It jarred with everything that was filling him now.

He shook his head, as if to clear it of unwelcome thoughts. At the villa, safe in its cocoon, the outside world had seemed far, far away. All that belonged in it far, far away.

Well, he would not think of it. He would think only of the day ahead of them. A day to be spent in togetherness, on an excursion, with lunch in a beautiful place, a scenic drive through the hinterland behind the coast.

The traffic lights ahead turned red and he slowed down to a halt, using the opportunity to glance at Sabine beside him. She was busying herself looking at the contents of an envelope she'd taken out of the bag on her lap. It was, he could see, a bill from the *pension*. She gave it a cursory check, replaced it in her bag, then took out another envelope. Bastiaan could see it had a French stamp on it, but she was turning it over to open it, so he could not see the writing on the front.

As she ripped it open and glanced inside she gave a little crow of pleasure. 'Oh, how sweet of him!'

Then, with a sudden biting of her lip, she hurriedly stuffed the envelope back inside her handbag, shutting it with a snap.

Abruptly the traffic lights changed, the car behind him sounded its horn impatiently, and Bastiaan had to move off. But in the few seconds that it took a chill had gone down inside him.

Had he really seen what he'd thought he'd seen?

Had that been a cheque inside that envelope?

He threw a covert sideways glance at her, but she was placing her bag in the footwell, then getting out her phone and texting someone, a happy smile playing around her mouth.

Bastiaan found he was revving the engine, his hands clenching momentarily around the steering wheel. Then, forcibly, he put the sudden burst of cold anger out of his head. Why should Sabine *not* receive mail? And if that mail were from a man what business was it of his? She might know any number of men. Very likely did...

Another emotion stabbed at him. One he had not experienced before. One he never had cause to experience. Rigorously, he pushed it aside. Refused to allow his mind to dwell on the question that was trying to make itself heard. He would *not* speculate on just who might be sending her correspondence that she regarded as 'sweet.' He would not.

He risked another sideways glance at her as he steered through the traffic. She was still on her phone, scrolling through messages. As his gaze went back to the road he heard her give a soft chuckle, start to tap a reply immediately.

Bastiaan flicked his eyes towards her phone screen, hard though it was to see it from this angle and in the brightness of the sun. In the seconds his glance took a face on the screen impinged—or did it? It was gone as she touched the screen to send her message, but he could feel his hands clenching on the wheel again.

*Had that been Philip?*

The thought was in his head before he could stop it. He forced it out. It had been impossible to recognise the fleeting photo. It could have been anyone. *Anyone.* He would not let his imagination run riot. His fears run riot...

Instead he would focus only on the day ahead. A leisurely drive to St Paul de Vence...strolling hand in hand through its narrow pretty streets, thronged with tourists but charming all the same. Focus only on the easy companionable rightness of having Sabine at his side, looking so lovely as she was today, turning men's heads all around and making a glow of happy possession fill him.

It would be a simple, uncomplicated day together, just like the days they'd spent together at his villa. Nothing would intrude on his happiness.

Into his head flickered the image of her glancing at the contents of that envelope in her lap. He heard again her little crow of pleasure. Saw in his mind the telltale printing on the small piece of paper she'd been looking at...

*No!*

He would not think about that—*he would not.*

*Leave it be. It has nothing to do with you. Let your suspicions of her go—let go completely.*

Resolutely he pushed it from his mind, lifting his free hand to point towards the entrance to the famous hotel where they were going to have lunch. She was delighted by it—delighted by everything. Her face alight with pleasure and happiness.

Across the table from him Sarah gazed glowingly at him. She knew every contour of his face, every expression in his eyes, every touch of his mouth upon her...

Her gaze flickered. Shadowed. There was a catch in her throat. Emerging from the villa had been like waking from a dream. Seeing the outside world all around her. Being reminded of its existence. Even just driving past the nightclub had plucked at her.

The days—the nights—she'd spent with Bastiaan had blotted out everything completely. But now—even here, sitting with people all around them—the world was pressing in upon her again. Calling time on them.

Tomorrow she must leave him. Go back to Max. Go back to being Sarah again. Emotion twisted inside her. This time with Bastiaan had been beyond amazing—it had been like nothing she had ever known. *He* was like no man she had ever known.

*But what am I to him?*

That was the question that shaped itself as they set off after lunch, his powerful, expensive car snaking its way back towards Cap Pierre. The question that pierced her like an arrow. She thought of how she'd assumed that a man like him would be interested only in a sophisticated seductive affair—a passionately sensual encounter with a woman like Sabine.

Was that still what she thought?

The answer blazed in her head.

*I don't want it to be just that. I don't want to be just Sabine to him. I want to be the person I really am—I want to be Sarah.*

But did she dare? That was what it came down to. As Sabine she had the protection of her persona—that of a woman who could deal with transient affairs…the kind a man like Bastiaan would want.

*Would he still want me if I were Sarah?*

Or was this burning passion, this intensity of desire, the only thing he wanted? He had said nothing of anything other than enjoying each hour with her—had not spoken of how long he wanted this to last or what it meant to him, nor anything at all of that nature.

*Is this time all he wants of me?*

There seemed to be a heaviness inside her, weighing her down. She stole a sideways look at Bastiaan. He was focussed on the road, which was building up with traffic now as they neared Nice. She felt her insides give a little skip as her gaze eagerly drank in his strong, incisive profile—and then there was a tearing feeling in its place.

*I don't want to leave him. I don't want this to end. It's been way, way too short!*

But what could she do? Nothing—that was all. Her future was mapped out for her and it did not include any more time with Bastiaan.

Who might not want to spend it with her anyway. Who might only want what they were having now. And if that were so—if all he'd wanted all along was a kind of fleeting affair with Sabine—then she must accept it.

*Sabine would be able to handle a brief affair like this—so I must be Sabine still.*

As Sarah she was far too vulnerable…

She took a breath, steeling herself. Her time with Bastiaan was not yet up—not quite. There was still tonight—still one more precious night together.…

And perhaps she was fearing the worst—perhaps he wanted more than this brief time.

Her thoughts raced ahead, borne on a tide of emotion that swelled out of her on wings of hope. Perhaps he would rejoice to find out she was Sarah. Would stand by her all through her final preparations for the festival—share her rejoicing if they were successful or comfort her if she failed and had to accept that she would never become the professional singer she had set her sights on being.

Like an underground fire running through the root systems of a forest, she felt emotions flare within her. What they were she dared not say. Must not give name to.

*Right man—wrong time…for now…*

But after the festival Bastiaan might just become someone to her who would be so much more than this incandescent brief encounter.

'Shall we stop here in Nice for a while?'

Bastiaan's voice interrupted her troubled thoughts, bringing her back to the moment.

'They have some good shops,' he said invitingly.

The dress she was wearing was pretty, but it was not a designer number by any means. Nor were any of the clothes she wore—including that over-revealing evening gown she wore to sing in. He found himself wanting to know just how a dress suitable for her beauty would enhance her. Splashing out on a wardrobe for her would be a pleasure he would enjoy. And shopping with her would keep at bay any unnecessary temptation to worry about the cheque she had exclaimed over. He would not think about it—would not harbour any suspicions.

*I'm done with such suspicions. I will banish them—not let them poison me again.*

But she shook her head at his suggestion. 'No, there's nothing I need,' she answered. She did not want to waste time shopping—she wanted to get back to the villa. To be with Bastiaan alone in the last few dwindling hours before she had to go.

He smiled at her indulgently. 'But much, surely, that you *want*?'

She gave a laugh. She would not spoil this last day with him by being unhappy, by letting in the world she didn't want to think about. 'What woman doesn't?' was her rejoinder.

Then, suddenly, her tone changed. Something in that world she didn't want to let in yet demanded her attention. Attention she must give it—right now.

'Oh, actually…could we stop for five minutes? Just along here? There's something I've remembered.'

Bastiaan glanced at her. She was indicating a side street off the main thoroughfare. Maybe she needed toiletries. But as he turned the car towards where she indicated, a slight frown creased his forehead. There was something familiar about the street name. He wondered why—where he had seen it recently.

Then she was pointing again. 'Just there!' she cried.

He pulled across to the pavement, looked where she was pointing, and with an icy rush cold snaked down his spine.

'I won't be a moment,' she said as she got out of the car. Her expression was smiling, untroubled. Then, with a brief wave to him, she hurried into the building.

It was a bank. And Bastiaan knew, with ice congealing in his veins, exactly which bank it was—a branch of the bank that Philip's cheque for twenty thousand euros had been paid into...

And in his head, imprinted like a laser image, he saw again the telltale shape of the contents of that envelope she'd opened in the car that morning, which had caused her to give a crow of pleasure. Another cheque that he knew with deadly certainty she was now paying into the very same account...

A single word seared across his consciousness with all the force of a dagger striking into his very guts.

*Fool!*

He shut his eyes, feeling cold in every cell of his body.

'All done!' Sarah's voice was bright as she got back into the low-slung car. She was glad to have completed her task—glad she'd remembered in time. But what did *not* gladden her was having had to remember to do it at all. Letting reality impose itself upon her. The reality she would be facing tomorrow...

Conflict filled her. How could she want to stay here as Sabine—with Bastiaan—when Sarah awaited her in the morning? Yet how could she bear to leave Bastiaan—walk away from him and from the bliss she had found with him? Even though all the hopes and dreams of her life were waiting for her to fulfil them...

*I want them both!*

The cry came from within. Making her eyes anguished. Her heart clench.

She felt the car move off and turned to gaze at Bastiaan as he drove. He'd put on dark glasses while she'd been in the bank, and for a moment—just a moment—she felt that he was someone else. He seemed preoccupied, but the traffic in the middle of Nice was bad, so she did not speak until they were well clear and heading east towards Cap Pierre.

'I can't wait to take a dip in the pool,' she said lightly. She stole a glance at him. 'Fancy a skinny-dip this time?' She spoke teasingly. She wanted to see him smile, wanted the set expression on his face to ease. Wanted her own mood, which had become drawn and aching, to lighten.

He didn't answer—only gave a brief acknowledging smile, as fleeting as it was absent, and turned off the main coastal route to take the road heading towards Pierre-les-Pins.

She let him focus on the road, her own mood strained still, and getting more so with every passing moment. Going through Pierre-les-Pins was harder still, knowing that she must be there tomorrow—her time with Bastiaan over.

Her gaze went to him as he drove. She wanted, needed, to drink him in while she could. Desire filled her, quickening in her veins as she gazed at his face in profile, wanting to reach out and touch, even though he was driving and she must not. His expression was still set and there was no casual conversation, only this strained atmosphere. As if he were feeling what she was feeling...

But how could he be? He knew nothing of what she must do tomorrow—nothing of why she must leave him, the reality she must return to.

Urgency filled her suddenly. *I have to tell him—tell him I am Sarah, not Sabine. Have to explain why...*

And she must do it tonight—of course she must. When else? Tomorrow morning she would be heading back to the *ville*, ready to resume rehearsals. How could she hide that from him? Even if he still wanted her as Sarah she could spend no more time with him now—

not with the festival so close. Not with so much work for her yet to do.

A darker thought assailed her. Did he even *want* more time with her—whether as Sarah or Sabine? Was this, for him, the last day he wanted with her? Had he done with her? Was he even now planning on telling her that their time together was over—that he was leaving France, returning to his own life in Greece?

Her eyes flickered. His features were drawn, with deep lines around his mouth, his jaw tense.

*Is he getting ready to end this now?*

The ache inside her intensified.

As they walked back inside the villa he caught her hand, stayed her progress. She halted, turning to him. He tossed his sunglasses aside, dropping them on a console table in the hallway. His eyes blazed at her.

Her breath caught—the intensity in his gaze stopped the air in her lungs—and then, hauling her to him, he lowered his mouth to hers with hungry, devouring passion.

She went up like dry tinder. It was a conflagration to answer his, like petrol thrown on a bonfire. Desperation was in her desire. Exultation at his desire for her.

In moments they were in the bedroom, shedding clothes, entwining limbs, passions roused, stroked and heightened in an urgency of desire to be fulfilled, slaked.

In a storm of sensation she reached the pinnacle of her arousal, hips straining to maximise his possession of her. His body was slicked with the sheen of physical ardour as her nails dug into his muscled shoulders and time after time he brought her to yet more exquisite pleasure. She cried out, as if the sensation was veering on the unbearable, so intense was her body's climax. His own was as dramatic—a great shuddering of his straining body, the cords of his neck exposed as he lifted his head, eyes blind with passion. One last eruption of their bodies and then it was over, as though a thunderstorm had passed over a mountain peak.

She lay beneath him, panting, exhausted, her conscious mind dazed and incoherent. She gazed up at him, her eyes wide with a kind of wonder that she could not comprehend. The wildness of their union, the urgency of his possession, of the response he'd summoned from her, had been almost shocking to her. Physical bliss that she had never yet experienced.

And yet she needed now, in the aftermath, to have him hold her close, to cradle her in his arms, to transform their wildness to comfort and tenderness. But as she gazed upwards she saw that there was still that blindness in his eyes.

Was he still caught there, on that mountain peak they'd reached together, stranded in the physical storm of their union? She searched his features, trying to understand, trying to still the tumult in her own breast, where her heart was only slowly climbing down from its hectic beating.

Confusion filled her—more than confusion. That same darkening, disquieting unease that had started as they'd driven back from Nice. She wanted him to say something—anything. Wanted him to wrap his arms about her, hold her as he always did after the throes of passion.

But he did no such thing. Abruptly he was pulling away from her, rising up off the bed and heading into the en-suite bathroom.

As the door closed behind him an aching, anxious feeling of bereavement filled her. Unease mixed with her confusion, with her mounting disquiet. She got out of bed, swaying a moment, her body still feeling the aftermath of what it had experienced. Her hair was still in its plait, but it was dishevelled from their passion. Absently she smoothed it with her hands. She found that they were trembling. With the same shaky motion she groped for her clothes, scattered on the floor, tangled up with his.

From the bathroom came the sound of the shower, but nothing else.

Dressed, she made her way into the kitchen. Took a drink of water from the fridge. Tried to recover her calm.

But she could not. Whatever had happened between them it was not good. How could it be?

*He's ending it.*

Those were the words that tolled in her brain. The only words that could make sense of how he was being. He was ending it and looking to find a way of doing so. He would not wish to wound her, hurt her. He would find an…*acceptable* way to tell her. He would probably say something about having to go back to Athens. Maybe he had other commitments she knew nothing about. Maybe…

Her thoughts were jumping all over the place, as if on a hot plate. She tried to gather them together, to come to terms with them. Then a sound impinged—her phone, ringing from inside her bag, abandoned in the hallway when Bastiaan had swept her to him.

Absently she fished it out. Saw that it was Max. Saw it go to voicemail.

She stared blindly at the phone as she listened to his message. He sounded fraught, under pressure.

'Sarah—I'm really sorry. I need you to be Sabine tonight. I can't placate Raymond any longer. Can you make it? I'm really sorry—' He rang off.

She didn't phone back. Couldn't. All she could do was start to press the keys with nerveless fingers, texting her reply. Brief, but sufficient.

OK.

But it wasn't OK. It wasn't at all.

She glanced around the kitchen, spotted a pad of paper by the phone on the wall. She crossed to it, tore off a piece and numbly wrote on it, then tucked it by the coffee machine that was spluttering coffee into the jug. She picked up her bag and went out into the hallway, looked into the bedroom. The tangled bedclothes, Bastiaan's garments on the floor, were blatant testimony to what had happened there so short a while ago.

An eternity ago.

There was no sign of Bastiaan. The shower was still running.

She had to go. Right now. Because she could not bear to stay there and have Bastiaan tell her it was over.

Slowly, with a kind of pain netting around her, her mind numb, she turned and left the villa.

Bastiaan cut the shower, seizing a towel to wrap himself in. He had to go back into the bedroom. He could delay it no longer. He didn't want to. He didn't want to see her again.

Wanted to wipe her from existence.

*How could I have believed her to be innocent? How could I?*

He knew the answer—knew it with shuddering emotion.

*Because I wanted her to be innocent—I didn't want her to have taken Philip's money, didn't want it to be true!*

That was what was tearing through him, ripping at him with sharpest talons. Ripping his illusions from him.

*Fool!* Fool that he had been!

He closed his eyes in blind rage. In front of his very eyes she'd waltzed into that bank in Nice, paid in whatever it was she'd taken from Philip—or another man. It didn't matter which. The same branch of that bank—the very same. A coincidence? How could it be?

A snarl sounded in his throat.

Had that cheque she'd paid in this afternoon been from Philip too? Had that postmark been from Paris? Had it been his writing on the envelope? His expression changed. The envelope would still be in her bag, even if the cheque were not. That would be all the proof he needed.

*Is she hoping to take me for even more?*

The thought was in his head like a dagger before he could stop it. Was that what was behind her ardency, her passion?

*The passion that burns between us even now, even right to the bitter end...*

Self-hatred lashed at him. How could he have done what he'd just done? Swept her to bed as he had, knowing what she truly was? But he'd been driven by an urge so strong he hadn't been able to stop himself—an urge to possess her one final time...

One final time to recapture all that they'd had—all he'd thought they'd had.

It had never been there at all.

The dagger thrust again, into the core of his being.

He wrenched open the door.

She was not there. The rumpled bed was empty. Her clothes gone.

Emotion rushed into the sudden void in his head like

air into a vacuum. But quite what the emotion was he didn't know. All he knew was that he was striding out of the room, with nothing more than a towel snaked around his hips, wondering where the hell she'd got to.

For a numb, timeless moment he just stood in the hallway, registering that her handbag was gone too, so he would not be able to check the writing on the envelope. Then, from the kitchen, he heard the sound of the coffee machine spluttering.

He walked towards it, seeing that the room was empty. Seeing the note by the coffee jug. Reading it with preternatural calm.

> *Bastiaan—we've had the most unforgettable time. Thank you for every moment.*

It was simply signed 'S.'

That was all.

He dropped it numbly. Turned around, headed back to the bedroom. So she was walking out on him. Had the sum of money she'd extracted this time been sufficient for her to afford to be able to do so? That was what Leana had done. Cashed his cheque and headed off with her next mark, her geriatric protector, laughing at the idiot she'd fooled and left behind.

His mouth tightened. Well, things were different now. *Very* different. Sabine did not know that he was Philip's trustee, that he knew what she had taken and could learn if she'd taken yet more today. She had no reason not to think herself safe.

*Is she still hoping to take more from Philip?*

Memory played in his head—how Philip had asked him to loosen the purse strings of his main fund before his birthday—how evasive he'd been about what he wanted the money for. All the suspicions he'd so blindly set aside leapt again.

Grim-faced, he went to fetch his laptop.

And there it was—right in his email inbox. A communication today, direct from one of Philip's investment managers, requesting Bastiaan's approval—or not—for Philip's instruction to liquidate a particular fund. The liquidation would release over two hundred thousand euros...

*Two hundred thousand euros. Enough to free Sabine for ever from warbling in a second-rate nightclub.*

He slammed the laptop lid down. Fury was leaping in his throat.

Was that what Philip had texted her about? Bastiaan hadn't been mistaken in recognizing him as the sender—he could not have been. Was that why she'd given that soft, revealing chuckle? Was that why she'd bolted now, switching her allegiance back to Philip?

Rage boiled in Bastiaan's breast. Well, that would never happen—*never*! She would *never* go back to Philip.

*She can burn in hell before she gets that money from him!*

His lips stretched into a travesty of a smile. She thought herself safe—but Sabine Sablon was *not* safe. She was not safe at all...

And she would discover that very, very shortly.

# CHAPTER TEN

SARAH REACHED FOR the second false eyelash. Glued it, like the first, with shaky hands. She was going through the motions—nothing more. Hammers seemed to be in her brain, hammering her flat. Mashing everything inside her. Misery assailed her. She shouldn't be feeling it—but she was. Oh, she was.

It was over. Her time with Bastiaan was over. A few precious days—and now this.

Reality had awaited her. Max had greeted her with relief—and apology. And with some news that had pierced the misery in her.

'This is your last night here. Raymond insisted you show up just for tonight—because it's Friday and he can't be without a singer—but from tomorrow you're officially replaced. Not with the real Sabine—someone else he's finally found. And then, thank God, we can all decamp. We've been given an earlier rehearsal spot at the festival so we can head there straight away.'

He'd said nothing else, had asked no questions. Had only cast an assessing look at her, seeing the withdrawal in her face. She was glad of it, and of the news he'd given her. Relief, as much as she could feel anything through the fog of misery encompassing her, resonated in her. Now there was only tonight to get through. How she would do it, she didn't know—but it would have to happen.

As she finished putting on her lipstick with shaky hands she could feel hope lighting inside her. Refusing to be quenched. *Was* it over? Perhaps it wasn't. Oh, perhaps Bastiaan *hadn't* been intending to end it all. Perhaps she'd feared it quite unnecessarily. Perhaps, even now, he was missing her, coming after her…

*No!* She couldn't afford to agonise over whether Bastiaan had finished with her. Couldn't afford to hope and dream that he hadn't. Couldn't afford even to let her mind go where it so wanted to go—to relive, hour by hour, each moment she'd spent with him.

*I can't afford to want him—or miss him.*

She stared at her reflection. Sabine was more alien than ever now. And as she did so, the door of her dressing room was thrust open. Her head flew round, and as her gaze fell upon the tall, dark figure standing there, her face lit, joy and relief flaring in her eyes. Bastiaan! He had come after her—he was not ending it with her! He still wanted her! Her heart soared.

But as she looked up at him she froze. There was something wrong—something wrong with his face. His eyes. The way he was standing there, dominating the small space. His face was dark, his eyes like granite. He was like nothing she had seen before. This was not the Bastiaan she knew…not Bastiaan at all…

'I have something to say to you.'

Bastiaan's voice was harsh. Hostile. His eyes were dark and veiled, as if a screen had dropped down over them.

Her heart started to hammer. That dark, veiled gaze pressed down on her. Hostility radiated from him like a force field. It felt like a physical blow. What was happening? Why was he looking at her like this? She didn't know—didn't understand.

A moment later the answer came—an answer that was incomprehensible.

'From now on stay away from Philip. It's over. Do you understand me? *Over!*' His voice was harsh, accusing. Condemning.

She didn't understand. Could only go on sitting there, staring at him, emotion surging through her chaotically. Then, as his words sank in, a frown convulsed her face.

'Philip?' she said blankly.

A rasp of a laugh—without humour, soon cut short—broke from him. 'Forgotten him already, have you? Well, then…' and now his voice took on a different note—one that seemed to chill her deep inside '…it seems my efforts were not in vain. I have succeeded, it seems, in… *distracting* you, *mademoiselle*.' He paused heavily and his eyes were stabbing at her now. 'As I intended.'

His chest rose and fell, and then he was speaking again.

'But do not flatter yourself that my….*attentions* were for any purpose other than to convince you that my cousin is no longer yours to manipulate.'

She was staring at him as if he were insane. But he would not be halted. Not now, when fury was coursing through his veins—as it had done since the veils had been ripped from his eyes—since he'd understood just how much a fool she'd made of him. Not Philip—*him!*

*I so nearly fell for it—was so nearly convinced by her.*

Anger burned in him. Anger at her—for taking him for a fool, for exploiting his trusting, sensitive cousin and for not being the woman he'd come to believe, to hope, that she was.

*The woman I wanted her to be.*

The irony of it was exquisite. He'd seduced her because he'd believed her guilty—then had no longer been able to believe that she was. Then all that had been ripped and up-ended again—back to guilt.

A guilt he no longer wanted her to have, but from which there could be no escape now. *None.*

He cut across his own perilous thoughts with a snarl. 'Don't play the innocent. If you think you can still exploit his emotional vulnerability to you…well, think again.'

His voice became harsh and ugly, his mouth curling, eyes filled with venom.

'You see, I have only to tell him how you have warmed *my* bed these last days for his infatuation to be over in an instant. Your power over him extinguished.'

The air in her lungs was like lead. His words were like blows. Her features contorted.

'Are you saying…?' She could hardly force the words from her through the pain, through the shock that had exploded inside her, 'Are you saying that you seduced me in order to…to separate me from Philip?' There was disbelief in her voice. Disbelief on so many levels.

'You have it precisely,' he said heavily, with sardonic emphasis. 'Oh, surely you did not believe I would not take action to protect my cousin from women of your kind?'

She swallowed. It was like a razor in her throat. 'My kind…?'

'Look at yourself, Sabine. A woman of the world— isn't that the phrase? Using her *talents*—' deliberately he mocked the word she'd used herself when she'd first learnt who he was '—to make her way in the world. And if those *talents*—' the mockery intensified '—include catching men with your charms, then good luck to you.' His voice hardened like the blade of a knife. 'Unless you set your sights on a vulnerable stripling like my cousin—

then I will wish you only to perdition! And ensure you go there.'

His voice changed again.

'So, do you understand the situation now? From now on content yourself with the life you have—singing cheap, tawdry songs in a cheap, tawdry club.'

His eyes blazed like coals from the pit as he gave his final vicious condemnation of her.

'A two-cent *chanteuse* with more body than voice. That is all that you are good for. Nothing else!'

One last skewering of his contemptuous gaze, one last twist of his deriding mouth, and he was turning on his heel, walking out. She could hear his footsteps—heavy, damning—falling away.

Her mouth fell open, the rush of air into her lungs choking her. Emotion convulsed her. And then, as if fuse had been lit, she jerked to her feet. She charged out of the dressing room, but he was already stepping through the door that separated the front of house from backstage. She whirled about, driven forward on the emotion boiling up inside her. A moment later she was in the wings at the side of the stage, seizing Max by the arm, propelling him forward.

Anger such as she had never felt before in her life, erupted in her. She thrust Max towards the piano beside the centre spot where her microphone was. She hurled it into the wings, then turned back to Max.

'Play "Der Hölle Rache".'

Max stared at her as if she were mad. *'What?'*

*'Play it!* Or I am on the next plane to London!'

She could see Bastiaan, threading his way across the dining room, moving towards the exit. The room was busy, but there was only one person she was going to sing for. Only one—and he could burn in hell!

Max's gaze followed hers and his expression changed. She saw his hands shape themselves over the opening chord, and with a last snatch of sanity took the breath she needed for herself. And then, as Max's hands crashed down on the keyboard, she stepped forward into the pool of light. Centre stage.

And launched into furious, excoriating, maximum *tessitura*, her full-powered *coloratura* soprano voice exploding into the space in front of her to find its target.

Bastiaan could see the exit—a dozen tables or so away. He had to get out of here, get into his car and drive… drive far and fast. *Very* fast.

He'd done it. He'd done what he'd had to do—what he'd set out to do from that afternoon in Athens when his aunt had come to see him, to beg him to save her precious young son from the toils of a dangerous *femme fatale*. And save him he had.

Saved more than just his cousin.

*I have saved myself.*

*No!*

He would not think that—would not accept it. Would only make for the exit.

He reached the door. Made to push it open angrily with the flat of his hand.

And then, from behind him, came a crash of chords that stopped him.

He froze.

'Der Hölle Rache.' The most fiendishly difficult soprano aria by Mozart. Fiendish for its cripplingly punishing high notes, for the merciless fury of its delivery. An aria whose music and lyrics boiled with coruscating rage as *Die Zauberflöte*'s 'Queen of the Night' poured out seething venom against her bitter enemy.

*'Hell's vengeance boils in my heart!'*

Like a remotely operated robot, turning against his will, Bastiaan felt his body twist.

It was impossible. Impossible that this stabbing, biting, fury of a voice should be emanating from the figure on the stage. Absolutely, totally impossible.

Because the figure on the stage was *Sabine*. Sabine— with her tight sheath of a gown, her *femme fatale* blonde allure, her low-pitched voice singing huskily through sultry cabaret numbers.

It could not be Sabine singing this most punishing, demanding pinnacle of the operatic repertoire.

But it was.

Still like a robot he walked towards the stage, dimly aware that the diners present were staring open-mouthed at this extraordinary departure from their normal cabaret fare. Dimly aware that he was sinking down at an unoccupied table in front of the stage, his eyes pinned, incredulous, on the woman singing a few metres away from him.

The full force of her raging voice stormed over him. There was no microphone to amplify her voice, but she was drowning out everything except the crashing chords of the piano accompanying her. This close, he would see the incandescent fury in her face, her flashing eyes emerald and hard. He stared—transfixed. Incredulous. Disbelieving.

Then, as the aria *furioso* reached its climax, he saw her stride to the edge of the stage, step down off it and sweep towards him. Saw her snatch up a steak knife from a place setting and, with a final, killing flourish, as her scathing, scything denunciation of her enemy was hurled from her lips, she lifted the knife up and brought it down in a deadly, vicious stab into the tabletop in front of him.

The final chords sounded and she was whirling around, striding away, slamming through the door that led backstage. And in the tabletop in front of him the knife she'd stabbed into it stood quivering.

All around him was stunned silence.

Slowly, very slowly, he reached a hand forward and withdrew the knife from the table. It took a degree of effort to do so—it had been stabbed in with driving force.

The entire audience came out of their stupor and erupted into a tremendous round of applause.

He realised he was getting to his feet, intent on following her wherever she had disappeared to, and then was aware that the pianist was lightly sprinting off the stage towards him, blocking his route.

'I wouldn't, you know,' said the pianist, whom he dimly recognised as Sabine's accompanist.

Bastiaan stared at him. 'What the *hell* just happened?' he demanded. His ears were still ringing with the power of her voice, her incredible, unbelievable voice.

Sabine's accompanist made a face. 'Whatever you said to her, she didn't like it—' he answered.

'She's a *nightclub* singer!' Bastiaan exclaimed, not hearing what the other man had said.

The accompanist shook his head. 'Ah, no…actually, she's not. She's only standing in for one right now. Sarah's real musical forte is, as you have just heard, opera.'

Bastiaan stared blankly. 'Sarah?'

'Sarah Fareham. That's her name. She's British. Her mother is French. The real Sabine did a runner, so I cut a deal with the club owner to get free rehearsal space in exchange for Sarah filling in. But he's hired a new singer now—which is very convenient as we're off tomorrow to the festival venue.'

Bastiaan's blank stare turned blanker. 'Festival…?' He

seemed to be able to do nothing but echo the other man's words, and Bastiaan had the suspicion, deep down, that the man was finding all this highly amusing.

'Yes, the Provence en Voix Festival. We—as in our company—are appearing there with a newly composed opera that I am directing. Sarah,' he informed Bastiaan, 'is our lead soprano. It's a very demanding role.' Now the amusement was not in his voice any more. 'I only hope she hasn't gone and wrecked her voice with that ridiculous "Queen of the Night" tirade she insisted on.' His mouth twisted and the humour was back in his voice, waspish though it was. 'I can't think why—can you?'

Bastiaan's eyes narrowed. It was a jibe, and he didn't like it. But that was the absolute, utter least of his emotions right now.

'I have to speak to her—'

'Uh-uh.' The pianist shook his head again. 'I really wouldn't, you know.' He made a face again. 'I have *never* seen her that angry.'

Bastiaan hardly heard him. His mind was in meltdown. And then another question reared, hitting him in the face.

'Philip—my cousin—does *he* know?'

'About Sarah? Yes, of course he does. Your cousin's been haunting this place during rehearsals. Nice kid,' said Max kindly.

Bastiaan's brows snapped together uncomprehendingly. Philip *knew* that 'Sabine' was this girl Sarah? That she was in some kind of opera company? Why the hell hadn't he told him, then? He spoke that last question aloud.

'Not surprisingly, Sarah's being a bit cagey about having to appear as Sabine,' came the answer. 'It wouldn't do her operatic reputation any good at all if it got out.

This festival is make-or-break for her. For *all* of us,' he finished tightly.

Bastiaan didn't answer. Couldn't.

*She trusted Philip with the truth about herself—but she never trusted me with it!*

The realisation was like a stab wound.

'I have to see her.'

He thrust his way bodily past the pianist, storming down the narrow corridor, his head reeling, trying to make sense of it all. Memory slashed through him of how he'd sought her out that first evening he'd set eyes on her. His face tightened. Lies—all damn lies.

Her dressing room door was shut, but he pushed it open. At his entrance she turned, whipping round from where she was wrenching tissues from a box on her dressing table.

'Get out!' she yelled at him.

Bastiaan stopped short. Everything he had thought he'd known about her was gone. Totally gone.

She yelled at him again. 'You heard me! Get out! Take your foul accusations and *get out*!'

Her voice was strident, her eyes blazing with the same vitriolic fury that had turned them emerald as she'd hurled her rage at him in her performance.

'Why didn't you *tell* me you weren't Sabine?' Bastiaan cut across her.

'Why didn't *you* tell *me* that you thought me some sleazy slut who was trying it on with your precious cousin?' she countered, still yelling at him.

His expression darkened. 'Of course I wasn't going to tell you that, was I? Since I was trying to separate you from him.' A ragged breath scissored his lungs. 'Look, Sabine…'

'I am *not* Sabine!'

Sarah snatched up a hairbrush from her dressing table and hurled it at him. It bounced harmlessly off his broad chest. The chest she'd clung to in ecstasy—the chest she now wanted to hammer with her fists in pure, boiling rage for what he'd said to her, what he'd thought of her...

What he'd done to her...

*He took me to bed and made love to me, took me to paradise, and all along it was just a ghastly, horrible plot to blacken me in Philip's eyes.*

Misery and rage boiled together in the maelstrom of her mind.

'I didn't know you weren't Sabine. Do *not* blame me for that,' Bastiaan retaliated, slashing a hand through empty air. He tried again, attempting to use her real name now. 'Look... Sarah...'

'Don't you *dare* speak my name. You know *nothing* about me!'

His expression changed. Oh, but there *was* something he knew about her. From the shredded remnants of his mind, the brainstorm consuming him, he dragged it forth. Forced it across his synapses.

She might be Sabine, she might be Sarah—it didn't matter—

'Except, of course,' he said freezingly, each word ice as he spoke it, 'about the money. Philip's money.'

She stilled. 'Money?' She echoed the word as if it were in an alien tongue.

He gave a rough laugh. Opera singer or nightclub singer—why should it be different? His mouth twisted. Why should 'Sarah' be any more scrupulous than 'Sabine'?

'You took,' he said, letting each word cut like a knife, 'twenty thousand euros from my cousin's personal account. I know you did because this afternoon you paid another cheque into the very same bank account that the twenty thousand euros disappeared into.'

Her expression was changing even as he spoke, but he wouldn't let her say anything—anything at all.

'And this very evening, after you'd oh-so-conveniently cut and run from my villa, I got a request to release *two hundred thousand* euros from my cousin's investment funds.' His eyes glittered with accusation. 'Did you not realise that as Philip's trustee I see *everything* of his finances—that he needs my approval to cash that kind of money? Running back to him with whatever sob story you're concocting will be in vain. Is *that* why you left my bed this afternoon?'

'I left,' she said, and it was as if wire were garrotting her throat, 'because I had to appear as Sabine tonight.'

She was staring at him as if from very far away. *Because I thought you'd had all you wanted from Sabine.*

And he had, hadn't he? That was the killing blow that struck her now. He'd had exactly what he'd wanted from Sabine because all he'd wanted was to separate her from Philip and to keep his money safe.

Behind the stone mask that was her face she was fracturing into a thousand pieces…

Her impassivity made him angry—the anger like ice water in his veins. 'I'll tell you how it will be,' he said. 'Philip will go back to Athens, safely out of your reach. And you—Sabine, Sarah, whoever the hell you are— will repay the twenty thousand euros that he paid into your bank account.'

Her eyes were still on him. They were as green and as hard as emeralds.

'It wasn't my bank account,' she said.

Her voice was expressionless, but something had changed in her face.

A voice came from the doorway. 'No,' it said, 'it was mine.'

# CHAPTER ELEVEN

SARAH'S EYES WENT to Max, standing in the doorway.

'What the *hell* have you done?' she breathed.

He got no chance to answer. Bastiaan's eyes lasered him. 'Are you claiming the account is yours? *She* went into that bank this afternoon.'

'To pay in a cheque for three thousand euros my father had just sent me to help with the expenses of mounting the opera. I paid it directly into Max's account.'

She was looking at Bastiaan, but there was no expression in her face, none in her voice. Her gaze went back to Max.

'You took Philip for *twenty thousand euros*?' There was emotion in her voice now—disbelief and outrage.

Max lifted his hands. 'I did not ask for it, *cherie*. He offered.'

Bastiaan's eyes narrowed. Emotion was coursing through him, but right now he had only one focus. 'My cousin *offered* you twenty thousand euros?'

Max looked straight at him. 'He could see for himself how we're stretched for funding—he wanted to help.' There was no apology in his voice.

Bastiaan's eyes slashed back to Sarah. 'Did you know?'

The question bit at her like the jaws of a wolf. But it was Max who answered.

'Of course she didn't know. She'd already warned me not to approach him.'

'And yet,' said Bastiaan, with a dangerous silkiness in his voice, 'you still did.'

Max's eyes hardened. 'I told you—he offered it without prompting. Why should I have refused?' Something in his voice altered, became both defiant and accusing. 'Are we supposed to starve in the gutter to bring the world our art?'

He got no answer. The world, with or without opera in it, had just changed for Bastiaan.

His eyes went back to Sarah. Her face was like stone. Something moved within him—something that was like a lance piercing him inside—but he ignored it. He flicked his eyes back to Max, then to Sarah again.

'And the two hundred thousand euros my cousin now wishes to lavish on a fortunate recipient?' Silk over steel was in his voice.

'If he offered I would take it,' said Max bluntly. 'It would be well spent. Better than on the pointless toys that rich men squander their wealth on,' he said, and there was a dry bitterness in his words as he spoke.

'Except—' Sarah's voice cut in '—that is exactly what Philip is planning to do.'

She opened a drawer in the vanity unit, drew out her phone, called up a text, pointed the screen towards Bastiaan.

'This is the text he sent me today, while we were driving to St Paul de Vence.' Her voice was hollow.

His eyes went to it. Went to a photo of the latest supercar to have been launched—one of those he and Philip had discussed over dinner in Villeneuve.

The accompanying text was simple.

*Wouldn't this make a great twenty-first birthday present to myself? I can't wait!*

Underneath, he could read what she had replied.

*Very impressive! What does Bastiaan think? Check with him first!*

Sarah was speaking. 'I was as tactful as I could be—I always have been. I don't want him hurt, whatever he thinks he feels about me, but I never wanted to encourage him. And not about this, either,' she replied, in the same distant, hollow voice. 'I know you're not keen on him having such a powerful car so young.'

Harsh realisation washed through Bastiaan like a chilling douche. Philip had been so evasive about why he wanted money released from his funds...

*But it wasn't for her—none of the money was for her...*

And she was not, and never had been, the person he'd thought her...not in any respect whatsoever. Neither nightclub singer, nor gold-digger, nor any threat at all, in any way, to Philip.

*My every accusation has been false. And because of that...*

His mind stopped. It was as if he were standing at the edge of a high cliff. One more step forward and he would be over the edge. Falling to his doom.

Sarah was getting to her feet. It was hard, because she seemed to be made of marble. Nothing seemed to be working inside her at all. Not in her body, not in her head. She looked at Bastiaan, at the man she'd thought he was. But he wasn't. He was someone quite different.

'You'd better go,' she said. 'My set starts soon.' She

paused. Then, 'Stay away from me,' she said. 'Stay away—and go to hell.'

From the doorway, Max tried to speak. 'Sarah...'

There was uncertainty in his voice, but she just looked at him. He gave a slight shrug, then walked away. Her eyes went back to Bastiaan, but now there was hatred in them. Raw hatred.

'Go to hell,' she said again.

But there was no need to tell him that. He was there already.

He turned and went.

Sarah stood for one long motionless, agonising, endless moment, her whole body pulled by wires of agony and rage. Then tears started to choke her. Tears of fury. Tears of misery.

Aching, ravening misery.


His aunt was staring at him from across her drawing room in Athens. Bastiaan had just had lunch with her and Philip, and now, with Philip back at his studies, his aunt was cornering him about his mission to the Riviera.

'Bastiaan, are you telling me that this girl in France is actually some sort of opera singer and *isn't* trying to entrap Philip?'

He nodded tautly.

His aunt's expression cleared. 'But that's wonderful.' Then she looked worried. 'Do you think he's still... *enamoured*, though? Even if she isn't encouraging him?'

He shook his head. 'I don't think so. He's full of this invitation to go to the Caribbean with Jean-Paul and his family.' He cast his aunt a significant look. 'Plus, he seems to be very taken with Jean-Paul's sister, whose birthday party it is.'

Philip's mother's face lit. 'Oh, Christine is a sweet

girl. They'd be so well-suited.' She cast a grateful look at her nephew. 'Bastiaan—*thank you*. I cannot tell you how grateful I am for setting my mind at rest about that singer and my boy!'

His eyes were veiled for a moment, and there was a fleeting look that he hid swiftly. His expression changed. 'I made one mistake, though,' he said.

*More than one...*

His throat closed, but he forced himself to continue. 'I let Philip drive my car while we were there—now he's determined to get one of his own.'

His aunt's face was spiked with anxiety. 'Oh, Bastiaan—please, stop him. He'll kill himself!'

He heard the fear in her voice, but this time he shook his head. 'I can't stop him—and nor can you. He's growing up. He has to learn responsibility. But—' he held up a hand '—I *can* teach him to drive a car like that safely. That's the deal I've struck with him.'

'Well...' her acquiescence was uneasy, but resigned '...if you do your best to keep him safe...'

'I will,' he said.

He got to his feet. He needed to be out of there. Needed it badly. He was heading off to his island, craving solitude. Craving anything that might stop him thinking. Stop him feeling...

*No—don't go there. Just...don't.*

As he walked towards the front door Philip hailed him from his room. 'Bast! You will come, won't you? To Sarah's premiere? It would be so great if you do. You only ever saw her as Sabine—she'd love you to see what she can really do. I know she would.'

His eyes veiled. What Sarah would love was to see his head on a plate.

'I'll see,' he temporised.

'It's at the end of next week,' Philip reminded him.

It could be tomorrow or at the end of eternity for all the difference it would make, Bastiaan knew. Knew from her brutal, persistent refusal to acknowledge any of his texts, his emails, his letters. All of them asking… *begging* one thing and one thing only…

His mind sheered away—the way he was training it to. Day by gruelling day. But it kept coming back—like a falcon circling for prey. He could sail, he could swim, he could walk, he could get very, very drunk—but it would not stay out of his head.

Three simple words. Three words that were like knife-thrusts to his guts.

*I've lost her.*


'Sarah?'

Max's voice was cautious. It wasn't just because of the thorny issue of Philip's generosity and Max's ready acceptance. He was treating her with kid gloves. She wished he wouldn't. She wished he would go back to being the waspish, slave-driving Max she knew. Wished that everyone would stop tiptoeing around her.

It was as if she had a visible knife wound in her. But nothing was visible. Her bleeding was internal…

It was their first rehearsal day at the festival site, a small but beautiful theatre built in the grounds of a château in northern Provence. She was grateful—abjectly grateful—to be away from the Riviera…away from the nightclub. Away from anything, everything, that might remind her of what had happened there…

But it was with her day and night, asleep and awake, alone and with others, singing or not.

Pain. A simple word. Agonizing to endure.

Impossible to stop.

'Are you sure you want to start with that aria?' Max's enquiry was still cautious. 'Wouldn't you rather build up to it?'

'No,' she said.

Her tone was flat, inexpressive. She wanted to do this. Needed to do it. The aria that she had found impossible to sing was now the only one she wanted to sing.

She took her position, readied herself—her stance, her throat, her muscles, her breathing. Anton started to play. As she stood motionless, until her entry came, thoughts flowed through her head…ribbons of pain…

*How could I not understand this aria? How could I think it impossible to believe in it—believe in what she feels, what she endures?*

Her bar came. Max lifted his hand to guide her in as the music swelled on its pitiless tide. She gazed blindly outward, not seeing Max, not seeing the auditorium or the world. Seeing only her pain.

And out of her pain came the pain of the War Bride, her anguished voice reaching out over the world with the pain of hopes destroyed, happiness extinguished, the future gone. The futility, the loss, the courage, the sacrifice, the pity of war…all in a single voice. *Her* voice.

As her voice died away into silence…utter silence… Anton lifted his hands from the keyboard. Then he got to his feet, crossed to her. Took her hands. Kissed each of them.

'You have sung what I have written,' he told her, his voice full. It was all he said—all he needed to say.

She shut her eyes. Inside her head, words came. Fierce. Searing.

*This is all I have. And it will be enough. It will be enough!*

But in the deepest recesses of her consciousness she could hear a single word mocking her.

*Liar.*

Bastiaan took his seat. He was up in the gods. He'd never in his life sat so high above the stage, in so cheap a seat. But he needed to be somewhere where Philip, down in the stalls, could not see him.

Bastiaan had told him that, regrettably, he could not make it to the opening night of *War Bride*.

He had lied.

What he did not want—could not afford—was for Philip to let Sarah know he would be there.

But he could no more have stayed away than remained in a burning building.

Emotion roiled within him as he gazed down. Somewhere behind those heavy curtains she was there. Urgency burned in him. She had blocked him at every turn, denied him all access.

Even Max, when he'd asked for his intervention, had simply replied, 'Sarah needs to work now. Don't make any more difficulties for her.'

So he'd stayed away. Till now.

*Tonight—tonight I have to speak to her. I have to.*

As the house lights went down and the audience started to settle, conversation dimming, he felt his vision blur. Saw images shape themselves—tantalizing, tormenting.

Sabine, her eyes glowing with passion, gazing up at him as they made love.

Sabine, smiling, laughing, holding his hand.

Sabine—just being with her, hour by hour, day by day, as they ate, as they swam, as they sunbathed and stargazed.

Sabine—so beautiful, so wonderful.

*Until I threw her away.*

He had let fear and suspicion poison what they'd had. Ruin it.

*I did not know what I had—until I lost it.*

Could he win it back? Could he win *her* back?

He had to try—at least he had to try.

'OK, Sarah, this is it.' Max was pressing his hands on her shoulders, his eyes holding hers. 'You can do it—you know you can.'

She couldn't respond, could only wait while he spoke to the others, reassuring them, encouraging them. He looked impeccable in white tie and tails, but she could see the tension in him in every line of his slight body. She could hear the audience starting to applaud and the tuning up of the players in the orchestra die away as Max, their conductor for the evening, took the podium.

She tried to breathe, but couldn't. She wanted to die. Anything—anything at all to avoid having to do what she was going to have to do. What she had been preparing for all her life. What she had worked for in every waking second, allowing nothing else to lay claim to an instant of her time, a moment of her concentration.

Least of all the man who had done what he had to her. Least of all him. The man who was despicable beyond all men, thinking what he had of her, judging and condemning her as he had, while all the while…all the while…

*He made love to me and thought me nothing better than a cheap little gold-digger. Right from the start— from the very moment he laid eyes on me. Everything was a lie—everything! Every moment I spent with him was a lie. And he knew it the whole time!*

No, she had not allowed such vicious, agonizing thoughts into her head. Not one. She'd kept them all at bay—along with all those unbearable texts and voice-mails that she'd deleted without reading or listening to. Deleted and destroyed, telling him to go to hell and stay there. Never, ever to get in touch again.

Because all there was in her life now was her voice—her voice and her work. She had worked like a demon, like one possessed, and blocked out everything else in the universe. And now this moment, right now, had come. And she wanted to die.

*Dear God, please let me do OK. Please let me get it right—for me, for all of us. Please.*

Then the small chorus was filing out on to the stage, and a moment later she heard Max start the brief overture. She felt faint with nerves. As they took their places the familiar music, every note of which she knew in every cell of her body, started to wind its way through the synapses of her stricken brain. The curtain rose, revealing the cavern of the auditorium beyond, and now the chorus was starting their low, haunting chant—their invocation to vanishing peace as the storm clouds of war gathered.

She felt her legs tremble, turning to jelly. Her voice had gone. Completely gone. Vanished into the ether. There was nothing—nothing in her but silence...

She saw the glare of the stage lights, the dimness of the auditorium beyond, and on his podium Max, lifting his baton for her entrance cue. She fixed her eyes on him, took a breath.

And her voice came.

High and pure and true. And nothing else in the universe existed any more except her voice.

Unseen, high above in the gods, Bastiaan sat motionless and heard her sing.

The knife in his guts twisted with every note she sang.

For the whole duration of the opera, as it wound to its sombre conclusion, Bastiaan could not move a muscle, his whole being riveted on the slender figure on the stage. Only once did he stir, his expression changing. During the heartrending aria of grief for her young husband's death, with the agony of loss in every note. His eyes shadowed. The poignancy of the music, of her high, keening voice, struck deep within him.

Then the drama moved on to its final scene, to her song to the unborn child she carried, destined to be another soldier, in yet another war. And she, the War Bride, would become in her turn the Soldier's Mother, destined to bury her son, comfort his widow—the next War Bride, carrying the next unborn soldier…

As her voice faded the light on the stage faded too, until there was only a single narrow spot upon her. And then that, too, faded, leaving only the unseen chorus to close the timeless tragedy with a chorale of mourning for lives yet to be lost in future conflicts. Until silence and darkness fell completely.

For a palpable moment there was complete stillness in the house—and then the applause started. And it did not stop. Did not stop as the stage lights came up and the cast were there, Sarah, and the other soloists stepping forward. The applause intensified and the audience were rising to their feet as Max walked out on to the stage with Anton at his side, and then both of them were taking Sarah by the hand, leading her forward to a crescendo of applause.

Bastiaan's palms were stinging, but still the applause continued, and still his eyes were only for her— for Sarah—now dropping hands with Max, calling her tenor forward, and the other soloists too, to take their share of the ovation, breaking the line to let the chorus take theirs, and then all the cast joined in with applause for the orchestra taking their bows.

He could see her expression—beatific, transfigured.

He could stay still no longer. He rose from his seat, jolted down the staircase to the ground floor, out into the fresh night air. His heart was pounding, but not from exertion. Walking swiftly, purposefully, he pushed open the stage door, walked up to the concierge's booth.

'This is for Max Defarge. See that he gets it this evening.' He placed the long white envelope he'd taken from his inside jacket pocket into his hand, along with a hundred-euro note to ensure his instruction was fulfilled. Then he walked away.

He couldn't do this. What the hell had he been thinking? That he could just swan into her dressing room the way he had that first night he'd seen her sing?

*Seen Sabine sing—not Sarah!*

But the woman he'd heard tonight had not been Sabine—had been as distant from Sabine as he was from the stars in the sky. That knife twisted in his guts again, the irony like acid in his veins. That he should now crave only the woman he had thrown away....distrusted and destroyed.

His mobile phone vibrated. Absently he took it out—it was a text from Philip.

Bast, you missed a sensation! Sarah was brilliant and the audience is going wild! Gutted you aren't here. Am staying for the after-party soon as the audience clears. Can't wait to hug her!

He didn't answer, just slid the phone away. His heart as heavy as lead.

# CHAPTER TWELVE

SARAH WAS FLOATING at least six inches off the ground. The champagne that Max had splashed out on was contributing, she knew, but mostly it was just on wings of elation—the buoyancy of abject relief and gratitude that she had given the performance of her life.

Elation filled them all—hugs and kisses, tears and laughter and joy lifting them all above the exhaustion that their efforts had exacted from them. But no one cared about exhaustion now—only about triumph.

She could scarcely believe it, and yet it was true. All true. Finally all true.

'Am I dreaming this?' she cried to her parents as they swept her into their arms. Her mother's face was openly wet with tears, her father's glowing with pride.

Her mother's hand pressed hers. 'Whoever he is, my darling—the man you sang about—he's not worthy of you.' Her voice was rich with sympathy and concern.

Sarah would not meet her mother's eyes.

Her mother smiled sadly. 'I heard it in your voice. You were not singing of the loss of your soldier. It was real for you, my darling—*real.*'

Sarah tried to shake her head, but failed. Tried to stop the knife sliding into her heart, but failed. She could only be grateful that Max was now embracing her—for the millionth time—and drawing her off to one side. He found a quiet spot in the foyer area where the after-party was taking place and spoke.

'This has just been given to me,' he said.

His voice was neutral. Very neutral. Out of his pocket he took a folded piece of paper and opened it, handing it to Sarah. She took it with a slight frown of puzzlement. Then her expression changed.

'I'm glad for you,' she said tightly. It was all she could manage. She thrust the paper back at Max.

'And for yourself?' The question came with a lift of the brow, speculation in his eyes, concern in his voice.

She gave her head a sharp, negative shake. Turned away bleakly. Heading back into the throng, she seized up another glass of champagne, more hugs, more kisses. And suddenly, a huge bear hug enveloping her.

'Oh, Sarah… Sarah—you were brilliant. Just *brilliant*! You were *all* brilliant!'

It was Philip—sweet, lovely Philip—his face alight with pleasure for her. She hugged him back, glad to see him. But automatically, fearfully, she found her gaze going past him. And there was another emotion in her eyes—one she did not want to be there but which leapt all the same.

It died away as he spoke again. 'I just *wish* Bast could've been here. I told him I really, *really* wanted him to hear you do your real stuff—not all that inane Sabine garbage.' He released her from his hug.

She smiled fondly. 'Thank you for all your loyalty and support. It means a great deal to me,' she said sincerely, because his youthful faith in her had, she knew, been a balm to her. 'And Philip?' She pressed his hands, her voice serious now. 'Listen—don't *ever* let types like Max take money off you again. He was out of order.'

He coloured again. 'I wanted to help,' he said.

For a second, just a second, her eyes shadowed with pain. Philip's 'help' had exacted a price from her and she had paid heavily. Was still paying.

Would pay all her life…

'You did,' she said firmly. 'And we're all grateful—you helped make all this possible!' She gestured widely at the happy scene around them.

'Great!' He grinned, relieved and reassured.

She, too, was relieved and reassured. Philip's crush on her was clearly over, there was no light of longing in his eyes any more. Just open friendliness. 'We all liked you hanging around—with or without that hefty donation to us. Oh, and Philip?' Her face was expressive. 'That monster car you want to get for yourself—please, just do *not* smash yourself up in it!'

He grinned again. 'I won't. Bast's teaching me to drive it safely.' He blew her a kiss as he headed off. 'One day I'll deliver you to the artists' entrance at the Royal Opera House Covent Garden in it—see if I don't.'

'I'll hold you to that,' she said fondly.

She turned away. Covent Garden… Would she make it there? Was what had happened tonight the first step on her journey there?

Fierce emotion fired through her.

*I have to make it. I have to!*

Work and work alone must consume her now. No more distractions.

The words echoed in her head, mocking her. How often had she said them?

Even right from the start, when her eyes had set on the man who had invaded her dressing room that night, invaded her life…

*Invaded my heart…*

She felt a choke rising in her throat, constricting her breathing. She forced it back. She would not give in to it. Would not give in to the bleakness that was like a vacuum inside her, trying to suck all the joy out of this moment for her.

*My work will be enough—it will be!*

That was all she had to remember. All she had to believe.

Lie though it was...

An hour later she had had enough of celebration. The exhaustion she'd blanked out was seeping through her again.

Her parents had gone, yawning, back to their hotel in the nearby spa town. Philip was getting stuck into the champagne with the chorus, with a lot of laughter and bonhomie.

Helping herself to a large glass of water, Sarah found her feet going towards the French windows. Cool fresh air beckoned her, and she stepped out onto a paved area. There was an ornate stone-rimmed pond at the end of a pathway leading across the lawn, with soft underwater lights and a little fountain playing. She felt herself wandering towards it.

Her elation had gone. Subsumed not just by exhaustion but by another mood. Seeing Philip had not helped her. Nor had what Max had disclosed to her. Both had been painful reminders of the man she wanted now only to forget.

But could not.

She reached the pond, trailed her fingers in the cool water, her gaze inward. Back into memory.

*Sun sparkling off the swimming pool as Bastiaan dived into it, his torso glistening with diamond drops of water.*

*His arm tight around her as he steered the motorboat
towards the gold of the setting sun. His eyes burning
down at her with passion and desire. His mouth, lowering to hers...*

She gave a little cry of pain. It had meant nothing—
nothing to him at all. False—all false!

Bitter irony twisted inside her.

*I thought he wanted me to be Sabine—a woman of the
world, alluring and sensual, willing and eager for an instant romance. But all along Sabine was the woman he
wanted to destroy.*

And destroy her he had.

Too late she had discovered, after a few brief, fleeting
days of passion and desire, how much more she wanted.
Wanted as Sarah—not Sabine.

Pain shot through her again. And too late she had discovered what she was to Bastiaan...what she had been all
along, through every kiss, every caress, every moment
she'd spent with him.

Discovered that she had lost what she had never had
at all.

The choke rose in her throat again, but she forced it
back. She would not weep, would not shed tears. She
snatched her hand from the water, twisted around, away
from the stone pond.

And looked straight at Bastiaan.

He walked towards her. There was a numbness in him,
but he kept on walking. She stood poised, motionless,
looking so achingly beautiful, with her gold hair coiled
at her nape, her slender body wreathed in an evening
gown of pale green chiffon.

As he drew closer, memory flashed. The two of them
sitting behind the wheel of his boat, moving gently on

the low swell of the sea, her leaning into him, his arm around her waist, as he turned its nose into the path of the setting sun, whose golden rays had burnished them as if in blessing.

Another memory, like a strobe light, of them lying together, all passion spent, during the hours of the night, her slender body cradled in his. Another flash, and a memory of the fragrance of fresh coffee, warm croissants, the morning sun reaching its fingers into the vine-shaded terrace as they took their breakfast.

Each memory became more precious with every passing hour.

Each one was lost because of him. Because of what he'd done to her.

He could not take his eyes from her. Within him emotion swelled, wanting to overtake him, to impel him to do what he longed to do—sweep her into his arms. He could not—dared not. Everything rested on this moment—he had one chance…one only.

A chance he must take. Must not run from as he had thought to do, unable to confront her in the throng inside, at the moment of her triumph in her art. But now as she stood there, alone, he must brave the moment. Reclaim what he had thrown from him—what he had not known he had possessed.

*But I did know. I knew it with every kiss, every embrace, every smile. I knew it in my blood, my body—my heart.*

As he came up to her, her chin lifted. Her face was a mask. 'What are you doing here? Philip said you weren't here. Why did you come?'

Her words were staccato. Cold. Her eyes hard in the dim light.

'You must know why I am here,' he said. His voice was low. Intense.

'No. I don't.' Still staccato, still that mask on her face. 'Is it to see if I'm impressed by what you've done for Max? All that lavish sponsorship! Is it by way of apology for your foul accusations at me?'

He gave a brief, negating shake of his head and would have spoken, but she forged on, not letting him speak.

'Good. Because if you want to sponsor him—well, you've got enough money and to spare, haven't you? I want none of it—just like I never wanted Philip's.' She took a heaving breath, 'And just like I want nothing more to do with you either.'

He shut his eyes, receiving her words like a blow. Then his eyes flared open again. 'I ask only five minutes of your time, Sab—Sarah.'

He cursed himself. He had so nearly called her by the name she did not bear. Memory stabbed at him—how he had wondered why Philip stammered over her name.

*If I had known then the truth about her—if I had known it was not she who had taken money from Philip...*

But he hadn't known.

He dragged his focus back. What use were regrets about the past? None. Only the future counted now—the future he was staking this moment on.

She wasn't moving—not a muscle—and he must take that for consent.

'Please...please understand the reasons for my behaviour.'

He took a ragged breath, as if to get his thoughts in order. It was vital, crucial that he get this right. He had one chance...one chance only...

'When Philip's father died I promised his mother I would always look out for him. I knew only too well that he could be taken advantage of. How much he would become a target for unscrupulous people.'

He saw her face tighten, knew she was thinking of what Max had done, however noble a cause he'd considered it.

He ploughed on. 'Especially,' he said, looking at her without flinching, 'women.'

'Gold-diggers,' she said. There was no expression in her voice.

'Yes. A cliché, but true all the same.'

A frown creased between Bastiaan's eyes. He had to make her understand what the danger had been—how real it could have been.

*If she had truly been the woman I feared she was.*

'I know,' he said, and his mouth gave a caustic curl of self-derision, 'because when I was little older than Philip, and like him had no father to teach me better, a woman took me to the cleaners and made a complete fool of me.'

Did he see something change in her eyes? He didn't know—could only keep going.

'So when I saw that twenty thousand euros had gone from Philip's account to an unknown account in Nice… when I heard from Paulette that Philip had taken to hanging around a nightclub endlessly and was clearly besotted with someone, alarm bells rang. I *knew* the danger to him.'

'And so you did what you did. I know—I was on the receiving end.'

There was bitterness in her voice, and accusation. She'd had enough of this—*enough*. What was the point of him going on at her like this? There wasn't one. And it was hell—just hell on earth—to stand here with him so close, so incredibly close.

So unutterably distant… Because how could he be anything else?

She made herself say the words that proved it. 'I get the picture, Bastiaan. You seduced me to safeguard Philip. That was the only reason.' There was a vice around her throat, but she forced the words through.

She started to turn away. That vice around her throat was squeezing the air from her. She had to get out of here. Hadn't Bastiaan Karavalas done enough to her without jeopardizing everything she had worked to achieve?

'*No.*'

The single word, cutting through the air, silenced her.

'No,' he said again. He took a step towards her. 'It was not the only reason.'

There was a vehemence in the way he spoke that stilled her. His eyes were no longer veiled…they were burning—burning with an intensity she had never seen before.

'From the moment I first saw you I desired you. Could not resist you even though I thought you were Sabine, out to exploit my cousin. *Because* I thought that it gave me…' he took a breath '…a justification for doing what I wanted to do all along. Indulge my desire for you. A desire that you returned—I could see that in every glance you gave me. I knew you wanted me.'

'And you used that for your own ends.' The bitterness was back in her voice.

He seemed to flinch, but then he was reaching for her wrist to stay her, desperate for her to hear what he must say—*must* say.

'I regret everything I did, Sarah.' He said her name with difficulty, for it was hard—so hard—not to call her by the name he'd called her when she was in his arms. 'Everything. But not—not the time we had together.'

She strained away from him. 'It was fake, Bastiaan. Totally fake.' There was harshness in her voice.

'Fake?' Something changed in his voice. His eyes. His fingers around her wrist softened. 'Fake…?' he said again.

And now there was a timbre to his voice that she had heard before—heard a hundred times before…a thousand. She felt a susurration go through her as subtle as a breath of wind in her hair. As caressing as a summer breeze.

'Was *this* fake?' he said,

And now he was drawing her towards him and she could not hold back. The pulse in her veins was whispering, quickening. She felt her breath catch, dissolve.

'Was *this* fake?' he said again.

And now she was so close to him, so close that her head was dropping back. She could catch the scent of his body, the warmth of it. She felt her eyes flutter shut and then he was kissing her, the softness of his lips a homage, an invocation.

He held her close, and closer still, cupping her nape to deepen his kiss.

Bliss eased through her, melting and dissolving. Dissolving the hard, bitter knot of pain and anger deep inside her. He let her lips go, but his eyes were pouring into hers.

'Forgive me—I beg you to forgive me.' His voice was husky, imploring. 'I wronged you—treated you hideously. But when I made those accusations at you—oh, they were tearing me to pieces. To have spent those days with you, transforming everything in my life, and then that final day…' He shut his eyes, as if to shut out the memory, before forcing himself to open them again, to speak to her of what had haunted him. 'To think myself duped—

because how could you be that woman I'd feared you were when what we had was so…so wonderful.'

His voice dropped.

'I believed all my fears—and I believed the worst fear of all. That you were not the woman I had so wanted you to be…'

He gazed down at her now, his hand around her nape, cradling her head, his eyes eloquent with meaning. And from his lips came the words he had come here to say.

'The woman I love—Sabine or Sarah—*you* are the woman I love. Only you.'

She heard the words, heard them close, as close as her heart—the heart that was swelling in her breast as if it must surely become her very being, encompassing all that she was, all that she could be.

She pressed her hand against the strong wall of his chest, glorying in feeling her fingers splay out over the hard muscle beneath his shirt. Feeling the heat of his body, the beat of his heart beneath her palm.

Wonder filled her, and a whitening of the soul that bleached from her all that she had felt till now—all the anger and the hurt, the fury and the pain. Leaving nothing but whitest, purest bliss.

She gazed up at him, her face transformed. He felt his heart turn over in his breast, exultation in it.

'I thought it impossible…' she breathed. 'Impossible that in a few brief days I could fall in love. How could it be so swift? But it was true—and oh, Bastiaan, it hurt so *much* that you thought so ill of me after what we'd had together.'

*To love so swiftly—to hurt so badly…*

She saw him flinch, as if her words had made a wound, but he answered her.

'The moment I knew—that hellish moment when I knew everything I'd feared about you, all I'd accused you of was false…nothing but false… I knew that I had destroyed everything between us. You threw me out and I could do nothing but go. Accept that you wanted nothing to do with me. Let you get on with your preparations for tonight without my plaguing you.'

His voice changed. 'But tonight I could keep silent no longer. I determined to find you—face you.' A rueful look entered his dark eyes. 'I bottled it. I was too… too scared to face you.' His gaze changed again, becoming searching. 'What you've achieved tonight—what it will bring you now—will there be room for me? *Can* there be?'

She gave a little cry. 'Oh, Bastiaan, don't you see? It's *because* of what I feel—because now I know what love is—that I can achieve what I have tonight…what will be in me from now for ever.'

She drew back a little.

'That aria I sang, where the War Bride mourns her husband's death…' She swallowed, gazing up at him with all her heart in her eyes. 'She sings of love that is lost, love that burns so briefly and then was gone. I couldn't sing it. I didn't understand it until—'

He pulled her into his arms, wrapping them tight around her. 'Oh, my beloved, you will *never* feel that way again. Whatever lessons in love you learn from me will be happy ones from now. Only happy ones.'

She felt tears come then, prickling in her eyes, dusting her lashes with diamonds in the starlight. Bastiaan—*hers*. Her Bastiaan! After such torment, such bliss! After such fears, such trust. After such anger, such love…

She lifted her head to his, sought his mouth and found

it, and into her kiss she poured all that was in her heart, all that she was, all that she would be.

An eternal duet of love that they would sing together all their lives.

## EPILOGUE

SARAH LAY ON the little sandy beach, gazing up at the stars which shone like a glittering celestial tiara overhead. There was no sound but the lapping of water, the night song of the cicadas from the vegetation in the gardens behind. But her heart was singing—singing with a joy, a happiness so true, so profound, that she could still scarcely credit it.

'Do you remember,' the low, deep voice beside her asked, 'how we gazed up at the stars by the pool in my villa at Cap Pierre?'

She squeezed the hand that was holding hers as she and Bastiaan lay side by side, their eyes fixed on eternity, ablaze overnight in the Greek sky.

'Was it then?' she breathed. 'Then that I started to fall in love with you?'

'And I with you?'

Her fingers tightened on his. Love had come so swiftly she had not imagined it possible. And hurt had followed.

*But the pain I felt was proof of love—it showed me my own heart.*

Now all that pain was gone—vanished and banished, never to return! Now, here with Bastiaan, as they lay side by side on the first night of their married life together, they were sealing their love for ever. He had asked her where she wanted to spend her honeymoon but she had seen in his eyes that he already knew where he wanted them to be.

'I always said,' he told her, 'that I would bring my bride to my island—that she alone would be the one woman I would ever want here with me.'

She lifted his hand to her mouth, grazing his knuckles with a kiss.

'I also always said—' and his voice was different now, rueful and wry '—that I would know who that woman would be the moment I set eyes on her.'

She laughed. She could do that now—now that all the pain from the way he had mistrusted and misused her was gone.

'How blind I was! Blind to everything that you truly were! Except…' And now he hefted himself on to one elbow, rolled on to his hip to gaze down at her—his beloved Sarah, his beloved bride, his beloved wife for all the years to come. 'Except to my desire for you.'

His eyes blazed with ardour and she felt her blood quicken in its veins as it always did when he looked at her like that, felt her bones melting into the sand beneath her.

'That alone was true and real! I desired you then and I desire you now—it will never end, my beautiful, beloved Sarah!'

For an instant longer his gaze poured into hers, and then his mouth was tasting hers and she was drawing him down to her. Passion flared and burned.

Then, abruptly, Sarah held him off. 'Bastiaan Karavalas—if you think I am going to spend my wedding night and consummate my marriage on a beach, with pebbles digging into me and sand getting into places I don't even want to think about, then you are—'

'Entirely right?' he finished hopefully, humour curving his mouth.

'Don't tempt me,' she said huskily, feeling her resolve weaken even as she started to melt again.

*But you do tempt me...*

The words were in Bastiaan's head, echoing hers, taking him back—back to the time when he had been so, so wrong about her. And so, so right about how much he wanted her. He felt his breath catch with the wonder of it all. The happiness and joy that blazed in him now.

He got to his feet, crouched beside her, and with an effortless sweep scooped her up into his arms. She gave a little gasp and her arms went around his neck, clinging to him.

'No,' he said firmly, 'you're right. We need a bed. A large, comfortable bed. And, as it happens, I happen to have one nearby.'

He carried her across the garden into the house behind. It was much simpler than the villa in Cap Pierre, but its privacy was absolute.

The grand wedding in Athens a few hours ago, thronged with family and friends, with Sarah's parents, his aunt and his young cousin—Philip having been delighted at the news of their union—and even his own mother, flown in from LA, seemed a world away.

Max had delivered Sarah fresh from rehearsals for a production of *Cavalleria Rusticana*—with himself directing and Sarah singing 'Santuzza' at a prestigious provincial opera house in Germany—making it very clear to her that the only reason he was tolerating her absence was because she happened to be marrying an extremely wealthy and extremely generous patron of the opera, whose continued financial sponsorship he fully intended to retain.

'Keep the honeymoon short and sweet!' Max had ordered her. 'With your career taking off, it has to come first!'

She'd nodded, but had secretly disagreed. Her art and her love would always be co-equal. Her life now would be hectic, no doubt about that, and future engagements were already being booked up beyond her dreams, but they would never—*could* never—displace the one person who for all her life would stand centre stage to her existence.

She gazed up at him now, love blazing in her eyes, as he carried her into the bedroom and lowered her gently upon the bed, himself with her.

'How much…' he said huskily, this man she loved. 'How much I love you…'

She lifted her mouth to his and slowly, sweetly, passionately and possessively, they started together on their journey to the future.

\* \* \* \* \*

# SECRETS OF A
# RUTHLESS TYCOON

**CATHY WILLIAMS**

# CHAPTER ONE

IN THE DIMINISHING light, Leo Spencer was beginning to question his decision to make this trip. He looked up briefly from the report blinking at him on his laptop and frowned at the sprawling acres of countryside reaching out on either side to distant horizons which had now been swallowed up by the gathering dusk.

It was on the tip of his tongue to tell his driver to put his foot down, but what would be the point? How much speed would Harry be able to pick up on these winding, unlit country roads, still hazardous from the recent bout of snow which was only now beginning to melt? The last thing he needed was to end up in a ditch somewhere. The last car they had passed had been several miles back. God only knew where the nearest town was.

He concluded that February was, possibly, the very worst month in which to have undertaken this trip to the outer reaches of Ireland. He had failed to foresee the length of time it would take to get to his destination and he now cursed the contorted reasoning that had made him reject the option of flying there on the company plane.

The flight to Dublin had been straightforward enough but, the minute he had met his driver outside the airport, the trip had evolved into a nightmare of traffic, diversions and, as they'd appeared to leave all traces of civilisation behind, a network of bleak, perilous roads made all the more threatening by the constant threat of snow. It hung in the air like a death shroud, biding its time for just the right unsuspecting mug to come along.

Giving up on all hope of getting anything useful done, Leo snapped shut his laptop and stared at the gloomy scenery.

The rolling hills were dark contours rising ominously up from flat fields in which lurked a honeycomb network of lakes, meandering streams and rivers, none of which was visible at this time of the late afternoon. Leo was accustomed to the almost constant artificial light of London. He had never had much time for the joys of the countryside and his indifference to it was rapidly being cemented with each passing mile.

But this was a trip that had to be undertaken.

When he reflected on the narrative of his life, he knew that it was an essential journey. The death of his mother eight months previously—following so shortly after his father's own unexpected demise from a heart attack whilst, of all things, he had been playing golf with his friends— had left him with no excuses for avoidance. He had to find out where he really came from, who his real birth parents were. He would never have disrespected his adoptive parents when they were alive by searching out his birth family but the time had come.

He closed his eyes and the image of his own life flickered in front of him like an old-fashioned movie reel: adopted at birth by a successful and wealthy couple in their late thirties who had been unable to have children of their own; brought up with all the advantages a solid, middle-class background had to offer; private school and holidays abroad. A brilliant academic career followed by a stint at an investment bank which had been the springboard for a meteoric rise through the financial world until, at the ripe old age of thirty-two, he now had more money than he could ever hope to spend in a lifetime and the freedom to use it in the more creative arena of acquisitions.

He seemed to possess the golden touch. None of his acquisitions to date had failed. Additionally, he had been bequeathed a sizeable fortune by his parents. All told, the only grey area in a life that had been blessed with success was the murky blur of his true heritage. Like a pernicious weed, it had never been completely uprooted. Curiosity had always been there, hovering on the edges of his consciousness, and he knew that it would always be there unless he took active measures to put it to rest once and for all.

Not given to introspection of any sort, there were moments when he suspected that it had left a far-reaching legacy, despite all the advantages his wonderful adoptive parents had given him. His relationships with women had all been short-lived. He enjoyed a varied love life with some of the most beautiful and eligible women on the London scene, yet the thought of committing to any of them had always left him cold. He always used the excuse of being the kind of man whose commitment to work left little fertile ground on which a successful relationship could flourish. But there lurked the nagging suspicion that the notion of his own feckless parents dumping him on whatever passing strangers they could had fostered a deep-seated mistrust of any form of permanence, despite the sterling example his adoptive parents had set for him.

He had known for several years where he could locate his mother. He had no idea if his natural father was still on the scene—quite possibly not. The whereabouts of his mother was information that had sat, untouched, in his locked office drawer until now.

He had taken a week off work, informing his secretary

that he would be contactable at all times by email or on his mobile phone. He would find his mother, make his own judgements and he would leave, putting to rest the curiosity that had plagued him over the years. He had a good idea of what he would find but it would be useful having his suspicions confirmed. He wasn't looking for answers or touching reconciliations. He was looking for closure.

And, naturally, he had no intention of letting her know his identity. He was sinfully rich and there was nothing like money to engender all the wrong responses. There was no way he intended to have some irresponsible deadbeat who had given him up for adoption holding out a begging bowl and suddenly claiming parental love—not to mention whatever half-siblings he had who would feel free to board the gravy train.

His mouth curled derisively at the mere thought of it.

'Any chance we could actually get this car into fifth gear?' he asked Harry, who caught his eye in the rear-view mirror and raised his eyebrows.

'Aren't you appreciating the wonderful scenery, sir?'

'You've been with me for eight years, Harry. Have I ever given any indication that I like the countryside?' Harry, strangely, was the only one in whom Leo had confided. They shared an uncommonly strong bond. Leo would have trusted his driver with his life. He certainly trusted him with thoughts he never would have shared with another living soul.

'There's always a first, sir,' Harry suggested calmly. 'And, no, there is no way I can drive any faster. Not on these roads. And have you noticed the sky?'

'In passing.'

'Snow's on the way, sir.'

'And I'm hoping that it will delay its arrival until I'm through…doing what I have to do.' From where he was sitting, it was hard to see where the sky met the open land. It was all just a black, formless density around them. Aside from the sound of the powerful engine of the car, the silence was so complete that, with eyes closed, anyone could be forgiven for thinking that they were suffering sensory deprivation.

'The weather is seldom obedient, sir. Even for a man like yourself who is accustomed to having his orders obeyed.'

Leo grinned. 'You talk too much, Harry.'

'So my better half often tells me, sir. Are you certain you don't require my services when we reach Ballybay?'

'Quite certain. You can get a cab driver to deliver the car back to London and the company plane will return you to your better half. I've alerted my secretary to have it on standby; she'll text you where. Make sure you tell my people to have it ready and waiting for when I need to return to London. I have no intention of repeating this journey by car any time soon.'

'Of course, sir.'

Leo flipped back open the laptop and consigned all wayward thoughts of what he would find when he finally arrived to the furthermost outer reaches of his mind. Losing yourself in pointless speculation was a waste of time.

It was two hours by the time he was informed that they were in Ballybay. Either he had missed the main part of the town or else there was nothing much to it. He could just about make out the vast stillness of a lake and then a scattering of houses and shops nestling amidst the hills and dales.

'Is this it?' he asked Harry, who tut-tutted in response.

'Were you expecting Oxford Street, sir?'

'I was expecting a little more by way of life. Is there even a hotel?' He frowned and thought that allowing a week off work might have been over- estimating the time he would need. A couple of days at most should see him conclude his business.

'There's a pub, sir.'

Leo followed his driver's pointing finger and made out an ancient pub that optimistically boasted 'vacancies'. He wondered what the passing tourist trade could possibly be in a town that time appeared to have forgotten.

'Drop me off here, Harry, and you can head off.' He was travelling light: one holdall, suitably battered, into which he now stuffed his slim laptop.

Already, he was making comparisons between what appeared to be this tiny town of splendid isolation and the completely different backdrop to life with his adoptive parents. The busy Surrey village in which he had been brought up buzzed with a veritable treasure trove of trendy gastropubs and designer shops. The landscape was confined and neatly manicured. The commuter links to London were excellent and that was reflected in the high-end property market. Gated mansions were hidden from prying eyes by long drives. On Saturdays, the high street was bursting with expensive people who lived in the expensive houses and drove the expensive cars.

He stepped out of the Range Rover to a gusty wind and freezing cold.

The ancient pub looked decidedly more inviting given the temperatures outside and he strode towards it without hesitation.

Inside the pub, Brianna Sullivan was nursing an incipient headache. Even in the depths of winter, Friday nights brought in the crowds and, whilst she was grateful for their patronage, she yearned for peace and quiet. Both seemed about as elusive as finding gold dust in the kitchen sink. She had inherited this pub from her father nearly six years ago and there were no allowances made for time out. There was just her, and it was her livelihood. Choice didn't feature heavily on the menu.

'Tell Pat he can come and get his own drinks at the bar,' she hissed to Shannon. 'We're busy enough here without you carrying trays of drinks over to him because he broke his leg six months ago. He's perfectly capable of getting them himself, or else he can send that brother of his over to get them.' At one end of the bar, Aidan and two of his friends were beginning to sing a rousing love song to grab her attention.

'I'll have to chuck you out for unruly behaviour,' she snapped at Aidan as she slid refills for them along the counter.

'You know you love me, darling.'

Brianna shot him an exasperated look and told him that he either settled his tab in full, right here and right now, or else that was the last pint he was going to get.

She needed more people behind the bar but what on earth would she do with them on the week days, when the place was less rowdy and busy? How could she justify the expenditure? And yet, she barely had enough time to function properly. Between the bookkeeping, the stock taking, the ordering and the actual standing behind the bar every night, time—the one thing she didn't have—was galloping past. She was twenty-seven years old and in the blink of an eye she would be thirty, then forty, then fifty, and still doing the things she was doing now, still struggling to kick back. She was young but, hell, she felt old a lot of the time.

Aidan continued to try his banter on her but she blocked him out. Now that she had begun feeling sorry for herself, she was barely aware of what was going on around her.

Surely her years at university had not equipped her to spend the rest of her life running this pub? She loved her friends and the tight-knit community but surely she was entitled to just have some *fun*? Six months of fun was all she had had when she had finished university, then it had been back here to help look after her father who had managed to drink himself into a premature grave.

Not a day went by when she didn't miss him. For twelve years after her mother had died it had been just the two of them, and she missed his easy laughter, his support, his corny jokes. She wondered how he would feel if he knew that she was still here, at the pub. He had always wanted her to fly away and develop a career in art, but then little had he known that he would not be around to make that possible.

She only became aware that something was different when, still absorbed in her own thoughts, it dawned on her that the bar had grown silent.

In the act of pulling a pint, she raised her eyes and there, framed in the doorway, was one of the most startlingly beautiful men she had ever seen in her life. Tall, wind-swept dark hair raked back from a face that was shamefully good-looking. He didn't seem in the slightest taken aback by the fact that all eyes were on him as he looked around, his midnight-black eyes finally coming to rest on her.

Brianna felt her cheeks burn at the casual inspection, then she returned to what she was doing and so did everyone else. The noise levels once again rose and the jokes resumed; old Connor did his usual and began singing lustily and drunkenly until he was laughed down.

She ignored the stranger, yet was all too aware of his presence, and not at all surprised that when she next glanced up it was to find him standing right in front of her.

'The sign outside says that there are vacancies.' Leo practically had to shout to make himself heard above the noise. The entire town seemed to have congregated in this small pub. Most of the green leather stools assembled along the bar were filled, as were the tables. Behind the bar, two girls were trying hard to keep up with the demands—a small, busty brunette and the one in front of whom he was now standing. A tall, slender girl with copper-coloured hair which she had swept up into a rough pony tail and, as she looked at him, the clearest, greenest eyes he had ever seen.

'Why do you want to know?' Brianna asked.

His voice matched the rest of him. It was deep and lazy and induced an annoying, fluttery feeling in the pit of her stomach. 'Why do you think? I need to rent a room and I take it this is the only place in the village that rents rooms…?'

'Is it not good enough for you?'

'Where's the owner?'

'You're looking at her.'

He did, much more thoroughly this time. Bare of any make-up, her skin was satin-smooth and creamy white. There was not a freckle in sight, despite the vibrant colour of her hair. She was wearing a pair of faded jeans and a long-sleeved jumper but neither detracted from her looks.

'Right. I need a room.'

'I will show you up to one just as soon as I get a free moment. In the meantime, would you like something to drink?' What on earth was this man doing here? He certainly wasn't from around these parts, nor did he know anyone around here. She would know. It was a tiny community; they all knew each other in some way, shape or form.

'What I'd like is a hot shower and a good night's sleep.'

'Both will have to wait, Mr…?'

'My name is Leo and, if you give me a key and point me in the right direction, I'll make my own way upstairs. And, by the way, is there anywhere to eat around here?'

Not only was the man a stranger but he was an obnoxious one. Brianna could feel her hackles rising. Memories of another good-looking, well-spoken stranger rose unbidden to the foreground. As learning curves went, she had been taught well what sort of men to avoid.

'You'll have to go into Monaghan for that,' she informed him shortly. 'I can fix you a sandwich but—'

'Yes—but I'll have to wait because you're too busy behind the bar. Forget the food. If you need a deposit, tell me how much and then you can give me the key.'

Brianna shot him an impatient glance and called over to Aidan. 'Take the reins,' she told him. 'And no free drinks. I've got to show this man to a room. I'll be back down in five minutes, and if I find out that you've helped yourself to so much as a thimble of free beer I'll ban you for a week.'

'Love you too, Brianna.'

'How long would you be wanting the room for?' was the first thing she asked him as soon as they were out of the bar area and heading upstairs. She was very much aware of him following her and she could feel the hairs on the back of her neck rising. Had she lived so long in this place that the mere sight of a halfway decent guy was enough to bring her out in a cold sweat?

'A few days.' She was as graceful as a dancer and he was tempted to ask why a girl with her looks was running a pub in the middle of nowhere. Certainly not for the stress-free existence. She looked hassled and he could understand that if it was as busy every night of the week.

'And might I ask what brings you to this lovely part of Ireland?' She pushed open the door to one of the four rooms she rented out and stood back, allowing him to brush past her.

Leo took his time looking around him. It was small but clean. He would have to be sharp-witted when it came to avoiding the beams but it would do. He turned round to her and began removing his coat which he tossed onto the high-backed wooden chair by the dressing table.

Brianna took a step back. The room was small and he seemed to over-power it with his presence. She was treated to a full view of his muscular body now he was without his coat: black jeans, a black jumper and the sort of olive-brown complexion that told her that, somewhere along the line, there was a strain of exotic blood running through him.

'You can ask,' Leo agreed. Billionaire searching for his long-lost, feckless parent wasn't going to cut it. One hint of that and it would be round the grapevine faster than he could pay her the deposit on the room; of that he was convinced. Checking his mother out was going to be an incognito exercise and he certainly wasn't going to be ambushed by a pub owner with a loose tongue, however pretty she was.

'But you're not going to tell me. Fair enough.' She shrugged. 'If you want breakfast, it's served between seven and eight. I run this place single-handed so I don't have a great deal of time to wait on guests.'

'Such a warm welcome.'

Brianna flushed and belatedly remembered that he was a paying guest and not another of the lads downstairs to whom she was allowed to give as good as she got. 'I apologise if I seem rude, Mr...'

'Leo.'

'But I'm rushed off my feet at the moment and not in the best of moods. The bathroom is through there...' She pointed in the direction of a white-washed door. 'And there are tea- and coffee-making facilities.' She backed towards the door, although she was finding it hard to tear her eyes away from his face.

If he brought to mind unhappy memories of Daniel
Fluke, then it could be said that he was a decidedly more
threatening version: bigger, better looking and without the
readily charming patter, and that in itself somehow felt
more dangerous. And she still had no idea what he was
doing in this part of the world.

'If you could settle the deposit on the room...' She
cleared her throat and watched in silence as he extracted
a wad of notes from his wallet and handed her the required amount.

'And tell me, what is there to do here?' he asked, shoving his hands in his pockets and tilting his head to one
side. 'I guess you must know everything...and everyone?'

'You've picked a poor time of year for sightseeing, Mr...
eh...Leo. I'm afraid walking might be a little challenging,
especially as snow is predicted, and you can forget about
the fishing.'

'Perhaps I'll just explore the town,' he murmured. Truly
amazing eyes, he thought. Eyelashes long and dark and in
striking contrast to the paleness of her skin. 'I hope I'm
not making you nervous... Sorry, you didn't tell me your
name, although I gather it's Brianna...?'

'We don't get very many strangers in this part of town,
certainly not in the depths of winter.'

'And now you're renting a room to one and you don't
know what he does or why he's here in the first place.
Understandable if you feel a little edgy...' He shot her a
crooked smile and waited for it to take effect; waited to
see her loosen up, smile back in return, look him up and
down covertly; waited for the impact he knew he had on
women to register. Nothing. She frowned and looked at
him coolly, clearly assessing him.

'That's right.' Brianna folded her arms and leaned
against the doorframe.

'I…' He realised that he hadn't banked on this. He actually hadn't expected the place to be so small. Whilst he had acknowledged that he couldn't just show up on his mother's doorstep and do his character assessment on the spot, he was now realising that the other option of extracting information from random drinkers at some faceless, characterless bar close to where the woman lived was quite likely also out of the question.

'Yes?' Brianna continued to look at him. She might be grateful for the money—it wasn't as though people were falling over themselves to rent a room in the depths of winter—but on the other hand she *was* a single woman, here on her own, and what if he turned out to be a homicidal maniac?

Granted it was unlikely that a homicidal maniac would announce his intentions because she happened to ask, but if he seemed too shifty, just too untrustworthy, then she would send him on his way, money or not.

'I'm not proud of this.' Leo glanced around him. His gaze settled on an exquisite watercolour painting above the bed and moved to the row of books neatly stacked on the shelf just alongside it. 'But I jacked in a perfectly good job a fortnight ago.'

'A perfectly good job doing what?' Brianna knew that she was giving him the third degree; that he was under no obligation to explain himself to her; that she could lose trade should he choose to spread the word that the landlady at the Angler's Catch was the sort who gave her customers a hard time. She also knew that there was a fair to middling chance that Aidan had already had a couple of free whiskies at her expense, and that Shannon would be running around like a headless chicken trying to fill orders, but her feet refused to budge. She was riveted by the sight of his dark, handsome face, glued to the spot by that lazy, mesmerising drawl.

'Working at one of those big, soulless companies...' Which was not, strictly speaking, a complete lie, although it had to be said that his company was less soulless than most. 'Decided that I would try my luck at something else. I've always wanted to...write, so I'm in the process of taking a little time out to try my hand at it; see where that takes me...' He strolled towards the window and peered out. 'I thought a good place to start would be Ireland. It's noted for its inspiring scenery, isn't it? Thought I would get a flavour of the country...the bits most people don't see; thought I would set my book here...'

He glanced over his shoulder to her before resuming his thoughtful contemplation of the very little he could actually see in the almost complete, abysmal darkness outside. 'The weather has knocked my progress off a little, hence—' he raised his shoulders in a rueful, elegant shrug '—here I am.'

A budding author? Surely not. He certainly didn't *look* like one, yet why on earth would he lie? The fact that he had held down a conventional job no doubt accounted for that hint of *sophistication* she was getting; something intangible that emanated from him, an air of unspoken authority that she found difficult to quite define but...

Brianna felt herself thaw. 'It gets a little quieter towards the end of the evening,' she offered. 'If you haven't fallen asleep, I can make you something to eat.'

'That's very kind of you,' Leo murmured. The passing guilt he had felt at having to concoct a lie was rationalised, justified and consigned to oblivion. He had responded creatively to an unexpected development.

Getting her onside could also work in his favour. Publicans knew everything about everyone and were seldom averse to a bit of healthy gossip. Doubtless he would be able to extract some background information on his mother and, when he had that information, he would pay her a visit in the guise of someone doing business in the area—maybe interviewing her for the fictitious book he had supposedly jacked his job in for. He would add whatever he learnt to whatever he saw and would get a complete picture of the woman who had abandoned him at birth. He would get his closure. The unfinished mosaic of his life would finally have all the pieces welded together.

'Right, then…' Brianna dithered awkwardly. 'Is there anything you need to know about…the room? How the television works? How you can get an outside line?'

'I think I can figure both out,' Leo responded dryly. 'You can get back to your rowdy crew in the bar.'

'They are, aren't they?' She laughed softly and hooked her thumbs into the pockets of her jeans.

Without warning, Leo felt a jolt of unexpected arousal at the sight. She was very slender. Her figure was almost boyish, not at all like the women he was routinely at-tracted to, whose assets were always far more prominent and much more aggressively advertised; beautiful, overtly sexy women who had no time for downplaying what they possessed.

He frowned at his body's unexpected lapse in self-con-trol. 'You should employ more people to help you out,' he told her abruptly.

'Perhaps I should.' Just like that she felt the change in the atmosphere and she reminded herself that, writer or not, guys who were too sexy for their own good spelled trouble. She reminded herself of how easy it was to be taken in by what was on the outside, only to completely miss the ugly stuff that was buried underneath.

She coolly excused herself and returned to find that, just

as expected, Aidan was knocking back a glass of whisky
which he hurriedly banged on the counter the second he
spotted her approaching.

Shannon appeared to be on the verge of tears and, despite what Brianna had told her, was scuttling over with
a tray of drinks to the group of high-spirited men at the
corner table, most of whom they had gone to school with,
which Brianna thought was no reason for them to think
they could get waitress service. Old Connor, with several
more drinks inside him, was once again attempting to be
a crooner but could scarcely enunciate the words to the
song he was trying to belt out.

It was the same old same old, and she felt every day of
her twenty-seven years by the time they all began drifting off into an unwelcoming night. Twenty-seven years old
and she felt like forty-seven. The snow which had thankfully disappeared for the past week had returned to pay
them another visit, and outside the flakes were big and fat
under the street lights.

Shannon was the last to leave and Brianna had to chivvy
her along. For a young girl of nineteen, she had a highly developed mothering instinct and worried incessantly about
her friend living above the pub on her own.

'Although at least there's a strapping man there with
you tonight!' She laughed, wrapping her scarf around her
neck and winking.

'From my experience of the opposite sex…' Brianna
grinned back and shouted into the darkness with a wave
'…they're the first to dive for cover if there's any chance
of danger—and that includes the strapping ones!'

'Then you've just met the wrong men.'

She spun round to see Leo standing by the bar, arms
folded, his dark eyes amused. He had showered and

changed and was in a pair of jeans and a cream, thickly knitted jumper which did dramatic things for his colouring.

'You've come for your sandwich.' She tore her eyes away from him and quickly and efficiently began clearing the tables, getting the brunt of the work done before she had to get up at seven the following morning.

'I gathered that the crowd was beginning to disperse. The singing had stopped.' He began giving her a hand.

Clearing tables was a novel experience. When he happened to be in the country, he ate out. On the rare occasions when he chose to eat in, he ate food specially prepared for him by his housekeeper, who was also an excellent chef. She cooked for him, discreetly waited until he was finished and then cleared the table. Once a month, she cooked for both him and Harry and these meals were usually preplanned to coincide with a football game. They would eat, enjoy a couple of beers and watch the football. It was his most perfect down time.

He wondered when and how that small slice of normality, the normality of clearing a table, had vanished—but then was it so surprising? He ran multi-million-pound companies that stretched across the world. Normality, as most people understood it, was in scarce supply.

'You really don't have to help,' Brianna told him as she began to fetch the components for a sandwich. 'You're a paying guest.'

'With a curious mind. Tell me about the wannabe opera singer...'

He watched as she worked, making him a sandwich that could have fed four, tidying away the beer mugs and glasses into the industrial-sized dishwasher. He listened keenly as she chatted, awkwardly at first, but then fluently, about all the regulars—laughing at their idiosyncrasies; relating little anecdotes of angry wives showing up to drag their other halves back home when they had abused the freedom pass they had been given for a couple of hours.

'Terrific sandwich, by the way.' It had been. Surprisingly so, bearing in mind that the sandwiches he occasionally ate were usually ornate affairs with intricate fillings prepared by top chefs in expensive restaurants. He lifted the plate as she wiped clean the counter underneath. 'I'm guessing that you pretty much know everyone who lives around here…'

'You guess correctly.'

'One of the upsides of living in a small place?' He could think of nothing worse. He thoroughly enjoyed the anonymity of big-city life.

'It's nice knowing who your neighbours are. It's a small population here. 'Course, some of them have gone to live in other parts of Ireland, and a few really daring ones have moved to your part of the world, but on the whole, yes, we all know each other.'

She met his steady gaze and again felt that hectic bloom of colour invade her cheeks. 'Nearly everyone here tonight were regulars. They've been coming here since my dad owned the place.'

'And your dad is…?'

'Dead,' Brianna said shortly. 'Hence this is now my place.'

'I'm sorry. Tough work.'

'I can handle it.' She took his plate, stuck it into the sink then washed her hands.

'And, of course, you have all your friends around you for support… Siblings as well? What about your mother?'

'Why are you asking me all these questions?'

'Aren't we always curious about people we've never met and places we've never seen? As a…writer you could say that I'm more curious than most.' He stood up and began walking towards the door through which lay the stairs up to his bedroom. 'If you think I'm being too nosy then tell me.'

Brianna half-opened her mouth with a cool retort, something that would restore the balance between paying guest and landlady, but the temptation to chat to a new face, a new person, someone who didn't know her from time immemorial, was too persuasive.

A writer! How wonderful to meet someone on the same wavelength as her! What would it hurt to drop her guard for a couple of days and give him the benefit of the doubt? He might be good-looking but he wasn't Danny Fluke.

'You're not nosy.' She smiled tentatively. 'I just don't understand why you're interested. We're a pretty run-of-the-mill lot here; I can't imagine you would get anything useful for your book.' She couldn't quite make him out. He was in shadow, lounging indolently against the wall as he looked at her. She squashed the uneasy feeling that there was more to him than met the eye.

'People's stories interest me.' He pushed himself away from the wall and smiled. 'You'd be surprised what you can pick up; what you can find…useful.' There was something defiant yet vulnerable about her. It was an appealing mix and a refreshing change from the women he normally met.

'Tomorrow,' he said, 'Point me in the direction of what to do and you can relax. Tell me about the people who live here.'

'Don't be crazy. You're a guest. You're paying for your bed and board and, much as I'd love to swap the room for your labour, I just can't afford it.'

'And I wouldn't dream of asking.' He wondered how she would react if she knew that he could buy this pub a hundred times over and it would still only be loose change to him. He wondered what she would say if she knew that, in between the stories she had to tell, there would be that vital one he wanted to hear. 'No, you'd be helping me out, giving me one or two ideas. Plus you look as though you could use a day off…'

The thought of putting her feet up for a couple of hours dangled in front of her like the promise of a banquet to a starving man. 'I can work and chat at the same time,' she conceded. 'And it'll be nice to have someone lend a hand.'

# CHAPTER TWO

BRIANNA WOKE AT six the following morning to furious snowfall. Outside, it was as still as a tomb. On days like this, her enjoyment of the peace and quiet was marred by the reality that she would have next to no customers, but then she thought of the stranger lying in the room down from hers on the middle floor. Leo. He hadn't baulked at the cost of the room and, the evening before, had insisted on paying her generously for an evening meal. Some of her lost income would be recovered.

And then…the unexpected, passing companionship of a fellow artiste. She knew most of the guys her age in the village and it had to be said that there wasn't a creative streak to be found among the pack of them.

She closed her eyes and luxuriated for a few stolen minutes, just thinking about him. When she thought about the way his dark eyes had followed her as she had tidied and chatted, wiped the bar counter and straightened the stools, she could feel the heat rush all through her body until it felt as though it was on fire.

She hadn't had a boyfriend in years.

The appearance of the stranger was a stark reminder of how her emotional life had ground to a standstill after her disastrous relationship with Daniel Fluke at university. All those years ago, she had fancied herself in love.

Daniel had been the complete package: gorgeous, with chestnut-brown hair, laughing blue eyes and an abundance of pure charm that had won him a lot of admirers. But he had only had eyes for her. They had been an item for nearly two years. He had met her father; had sat at the very bar downstairs, nursing a pint with him. He had been studying law and had possessed that peculiar surety of someone who has always known what road they intended to go down. His father was a retired judge, his mother a key barrister in London. They were all originally from Dublin, one of those families with textbook, aristocratic genealogy. They still kept a fabulous apartment in Dublin, but he had lived in London since he had been a child.

Looking back, Brianna could see that there had always been the unspoken assumption that she should consider herself lucky to have nabbed him, that a guy like him could have had any pretty girl on campus. At the time, though, she had walked around with her head in the clouds. She had actually thought that their relationship was built to last. Even now, years after the event, she could still taste the bitterness in her mouth when she remembered how it had all ended.

She had been swept off her feet on a post-graduation holiday in New Zealand, all expenses paid. She shuddered now when she thought back to the ease with which she had accepted his generosity. She had returned to Ireland only to discover that her father was seriously ill and, at that point, she had made the mistake of showing her hand. She had made the fatal error of assuming that Daniel would be right there by her side, supporting her through tough times.

'Of course,' he had told her, 'There's no way I can stay there with you. I have an internship due to start in London…'

She had understood. She had hoped for weekends. Her

father would recover, she had insisted, choosing to misread the very clear messages the doctors had been giving her about his prognosis. And, when he did, she would join him in London. There would be loads of opportunities for her in the city and they would easily be able to afford a place to rent. There would be no need to rush to buy... not until they were ready really to seal their relationship. Plus, it would be a wonderful time for her finally to meet his family: the brother he spoke so much about, who did clever things in banking, and his kid sister who was at a boarding school in Gloucester. And of course his parents, who never seemed to be in one place for very long.

She had stupidly made assumptions about a future that had never been on the cards. They had been at university together and, hell, it had been a lot of fun. She was by far the fittest girl there. But a future together...?

The look of embarrassed, dawning horror on his face had said it all but still, like the young fool she had been, she had clung on and asked for explanations. The more he had been forced to explain, the cooler his voice had become. They were worlds apart; how could she seriously have thought that they would end up *married*? Wasn't it enough that she had had an all-expenses-paid farewell holiday? He was expected to marry a certain type of woman... that was just the way it was...she should just stop clinging and move on...

She'd moved on but still a part of her had remained rooted to that moment in time. Why else had she made no effort to get her love life back on track?

The stranger's unexpected arrival on the scene had opened Pandora's box in her head and, much as she wanted to slam the lid back down, she remained lying in bed for far longer than she should, just thinking.

It was after eight by the time she made it down to the

bar, belatedly remembering the strict times during which her guest could have his breakfast. As landladies went, she would definitely not be in the running for a five-star rating.

She came to a halt by the kitchen door when she discovered that Leo was already there, appearing to make himself at home. There was a cup of coffee in front of him, and his laptop, which he instantly closed the second he looked up and spied her hovering in the doorway, a bit like a guest on her own premises.

'I hope you don't mind me making myself at home,' Leo said, pushing his chair back and folding his hands behind his head to look at her. 'I'm an early riser and staying in bed wasn't a tempting thought.' He had been up since six, in fact, and had already accomplished a great deal of work, although less than he had anticipated, because for once he had found his mind wandering to the girl now dithering in front of him. Was it because he was so completely removed from his comfort zone that his brain was not functioning with the rigid discipline to which it was accustomed? Was that why he had fallen asleep thinking of those startling green eyes and had awakened less than five hours later with a painful erection?

He might be willing to exploit whatever she knew about his mother, if she knew anything at all, but he certainly wasn't interested in progressing beyond that.

'You've been working.' Brianna smiled hesitantly. His impact on all her senses seemed as powerful in the clear light of day as it had been the night before. She galvanised herself into action and began unloading the dishwasher, stacking all the glasses to be returned to the bar outside; fetching things from the fridge so that she could make him the breakfast which was included in the money he had paid her.

'I have. I find that I work best in the mornings.'

'Have you managed to get anything down? I guess it must be quite an ordeal trying to get your imagination to do what you want it to do. Can I ask you what your book is going to be about? Or would you rather keep that to yourself?'

'People and the way they interact.' Leo hastened to get away from a topic in which he had no intention of becoming mired. The last time he had written anything that required the sort of imagination she was talking about had been at secondary school. 'Do you usually get up this early?'

'Earlier.' She refilled his mug and began cracking eggs, only pausing when he told her to sit down and talk to him for a few minutes rather than rushing into making breakfast.

Brianna blushed and obeyed. Nerves threatened to overwhelm her. She sneaked a glance at him and all over again was rendered breathless by the sheer force of his good looks and peculiar magnetism. 'There's a lot to do when you run a pub.' She launched into hurried speech to fill the silence. 'And, like I said, I'm doing it all on my own, so I have no one to share the responsibility with.'

Leo, never one to indulge his curiosity when it came to women—and knowing very well that, whatever information he was interested in gathering, certainly had nothing to do with *her* so why waste time hearing her out?—was reluctantly intrigued. 'A curious life you chose for yourself,' he murmured.

'I didn't choose it. *It* chose *me*.'

'Explain.'

'Are you really interested?'

'I wouldn't ask if I wasn't,' Leo said with a shrug. He had wondered whether she was really as pretty as he had imagined her to be. Subdued lighting in a pub could do flattering things to an average woman. He was discovering that his first impressions had been spot on. In fact, they had failed to do her justice. She had an ethereal, angelic beauty about her that drew the eye and compelled him to keep on staring. His eyes drifted slightly down to her breasts, small buds causing just the tiniest indentations in her unflattering, masculine jumper, which he guessed had belonged at one point to her father.

'My dad died unexpectedly. Well, maybe there were signs before. I didn't see them. I was at university, not getting back home as often as I knew I should, and Dad was never one to make a fuss when it came to his health.' She was startled at the ease with which she confessed to the guilt that had haunted her ever since her father had died. She could feel the full brunt of Leo's attention on her and it was as flattering as it was unnerving, not at all what she was accustomed to.

'He left a lot of debts.' She cleared her throat and blinked back the urge to cry. 'I think things must have slipped as he became ill and he never told me. The bank manager was very understanding but I had to keep running the pub so that I could repay the debts. I couldn't sell it, even though I tried for a while. There's a good summer trade here. Lots of fantastic scenery. Fishing. Brilliant walks. But the trade is a little seasonal and, well, the economy isn't great. I guess you'd know. You probably have to keep a firm rein on your finances if you've packed your job in...'

Leo flushed darkly and skirted around that ingenuous observation. 'So you've been here ever since,' he murmured. 'And no partner around to share the burden?'

'No.' Brianna looked down quickly and then stood up. 'I should get going with my chores. It's snowing outside and it looks like it's going to get worse, which usually means that the pub loses business, but just in case any hardy souls show up I can't have it looking a mess.'

So, he thought, there *had* been a man and it had ended badly. He wondered who the guy was. Some losers only stuck by their women when the times were good. The second the winds of change began blowing, they ran for the hills. He felt an unexpected spurt of anger towards this mystery person who had consigned her to a life on her own of drudgery, running a pub to make ends meet and pay off bills. He reined back his unruly mind and reminded himself that his primary purpose wasn't as counsellor but as information gatherer.

'If you really meant it about helping—and I promise I won't take advantage of your kind offer— you could try and clear a path through the snow, just in case it stops; at least my customers would be able to get to the door. It doesn't look promising…' She moved to one of the windows and frowned at the strengthening blizzard. 'What do you intend to do if the weather doesn't let up?' She turned to face him.

'It'll let up. I can't afford to stay here for very long.'

'You could always incorporate a snow storm in your book.'

'It's a thought.' He moved to stand next to her and at once he breathed in the fragrant, flowery smell of her hair which was, again, tied back in a pony tail. His fingers itched to release it, just to see how long it was, how thick. He noticed how she edged away slightly from him. 'I'll go see what I can do about the snow. You'll have to show me where the equipment is.'

'The equipment consists of a shovel and some bags of sand for gritting.' She laughed, putting a little more distance between them, because just for a second there she had felt short of breath with him standing so close to her.

'You do this yourself whenever it snows?' he asked, once the shovel was in his hand and the door to the pub thrown open to the elements. He thought of his last girl-friend, a model who didn't possess a pair of wellies to her name, and would only have gone near snow if it happened to be falling on a ski slope in Val d'Isere.

'Only if it looks as though it would make a difference. There've been times when I've wasted two hours trying to clear a path, only to stand back and watch the snow cover it all up in two minutes. You can't go out in those… er…jeans; you'll be soaked through. I don't suppose you brought any, um, waterproof clothing with you?'

Leo burst out laughing. 'Believe it or not, I didn't pack for a snow storm. The jeans will have to do. If they get soaked, they'll dry in front of that open fire in the lounge area.'

He worked out. He was strong. And yet he found that battling with the elements was exercise of a completely different sort. This was not the sanitised comfort of his expensive gym, with perfectly oiled machinery that was supposed to test the body to its limits. This was raw nature and, by the time he looked at his handiwork, a meagre path already filling up with fast falling snow, an hour and a half had flown past.

He had no gloves. His hands were freezing. But hell, it was invigorating. In fact, he had completely forgotten the reason why he was in this Godforsaken village in the first place. His thoughts were purely and utterly focused on trying to outsmart and out-shovel the falling snow.

The landscape had turned completely white. The pub was set a distance from the main part of the village and was surrounded by open fields. Pausing to stand back, his arm resting heavily on the shovel which he had planted firmly in the ground, he felt that he was looking at infinity. It evoked the strangest sensation of peace and awe, quite different from the irritation he had felt the day before when he had stared moodily out of the window at the tedium of never-ending fields and cursed his decision to get there by car.

He stayed out another hour, determined not to be beaten, but in the end he admitted defeat and returned to the warmth of the pub, to find the fire blazing and the smell of food wafting from the kitchen.

'I fought the snow...' God, he felt like a caveman returning from a hard day out hunting. 'And the snow won. Don't bank on any customers today. Something smells good.'

'I don't normally do lunch for guests.'

'You'll be royally paid for your efforts.' He stifled a surge of irritation that the one thing most women would have given their eye teeth to do for him was something she clearly had done because she had had no choice. She was stuck with him. She could hardly expect him to starve because lunch wasn't included in the price of the room. 'You were going to fill me in on the people who live around here.' He reminded her coolly of the deal they had struck.

'It's not very exciting.' She looked at him and her heartbeat quickened. 'You're going to have to change. You're soaked through. If you give me your damp clothes, I can put them in front of the fire in the snug.'

'The snug?'

'My part of the house.' She leaned back against the kitchen counter, hands behind her. 'Self-contained quarters. Only small—two bedrooms, a little snug, a kitchen, bathroom and a study where Dad used to do all the accounts for the pub. It's where I grew up. I can remember loving it when the place was full and I could roam through the guest quarters bringing them cups of tea and coffee. It used to get a lot busier in the boom days.'

She certainly looked happy recounting those jolly times but, as far as Leo was concerned, it sounded like just the sort of restricted life that would have driven him crazy.

And yet, this could have been his fate—living in this tiny place where everyone knew everyone else. In fact, he wouldn't even have had the relative comforts of a village pub. He would probably have been dragged up in a hovel somewhere by the town junkie, because what other sort of loser gave away their own child? It was a sobering thought.

'I could rustle up some of Dad's old shirts for you. I kept quite a few for myself. I'll leave them outside your bedroom door and you can hand me the jeans so that I can launder them.'

She hadn't realised how lonely it was living above the pub on her own, making every single decision on her own, until she was rummaging through her wardrobe, picking out shirts and enjoying the thought of having someone to lend them to, someone sharing her space, even if it was only in the guise of a guest who had been temporarily blown off-path by inclement weather.

She warmed at the thought of him trying and failing to clear the path to the pub of snow. When she gently knocked on his bedroom door ten minutes later, she was carrying a bundle of flannel shirts and thermal long-sleeved vests. She would leave them outside the door, and indeed she was bending down to do just that when the door opened.

She looked sideways and blinked rapidly at the sight of bare ankles. Bare ankles and strong calves, with dark hair… Her eyes drifted further upwards to bare thighs… lean, muscular bare thighs. Her mouth went dry. She was still clutching the clothes to her chest, as if shielding herself from the visual invasion of his body on her senses. His *semi-clad* body.

'Are these for me?'

Brianna snapped out of her trance and stared at him wordlessly.

'The clothes?' Leo arched an amused eyebrow as he took in her bright-red face and parted lips. 'They'll come in very handy. Naturally, you can put them on the tab.'

He was wearing boxers and nothing else. Brianna's brain registered that as a belated postscript. Most of her brain was wrapped up with stunned, shocked appreciation of his body. Broad shoulders and powerful arms tapered down to a flat stomach and lean hips. He had had a quick shower, evidently, and one of the cheap, white hand towels was slung around his neck and hung over his shoulders. She felt faint.

'I thought I'd get rid of the shirt as well,' he said. 'If you wouldn't mind laundering the lot, I would be extremely grateful. I failed to make provisions for clearing snow.'

Brianna blinked, as gauche and confused as a teenager. She saw that he was dangling the laundry bag on one finger while looking at her with amusement.

Well of course he would be, she thought, bristling. Writer or not, he came from a big city and, yes, was ever so patronising about the *smallness* of their town. And here she was, playing into his hands, gaping as though she had never seen a naked man in her life before, as though he was the most interesting thing to have landed on her doorstep in a hundred years.

'Well, perhaps you should have,' she said tartly. 'Only a fool would travel to this part of the world in the depths of winter and *not* come prepared for heavy snow.' She snatched the laundry bag from him and thrust the armful of clothes at his chest in return.

'Come again?' *Had she just called him a fool?*

'I haven't got the time or the energy to launder your clothes every two seconds because you didn't anticipate bad weather. In February. Here.' Her eyes skirted nervously away from the aggressive width of his chest. 'And I suggest,' she continued tightly, 'That you cover up. If I don't have the time to launder your clothes, then I most certainly do not have the time to play nursemaid when you go down with flu!'

Leo was trying to think of the last time a woman had raised her voice in his presence. Or, come to think of it, said anything that was in any way inflammatory. It just didn't happen. He didn't know whether to be irritated, enraged or entertained.

'Message understood loud and clear.' He grinned and leaned against the doorframe. However serious the implications of this visit to the land that time forgot, he realised that he was enjoying himself. Right now, at this very moment, with this beautiful Irish girl standing in front of him, glaring and uncomfortable. 'Fortunately, I'm as healthy as a horse. Can't remember the last time I succumbed to flu. So you won't have to pull out your nurse's uniform and tend to me.' Interesting notion, though… His dark eyes drifted over her lazily. 'I'll be down shortly. And my thanks once again for the clothes.'

Brianna was still hot and flustered when, half an hour later, he sauntered down to the kitchen. One of the tables in the bar area had been neatly set for one. 'I hope you're not expecting me to have lunch on my own,' were his opening words, and she spun around from where she had been frowning into the pot of homemade soup.

Without giving her a chance to answer, he began searching for the crockery, giving a little grunt of satisfaction when he hit upon the right cupboard. 'Remember we were going to…talk? You were going to tell me all about the people who live here so that I can get some useful fodder for my book.' It seemed inconceivable that a budding author would simply up sticks and go on a rambling tour of Ireland in the hope of inspiration but, as excuses went, it had served its purpose, which was all that mattered. 'And then, I'll do whatever you want me to do. I'm a man of my word.'

'There won't be much to do,' Brianna admitted. 'The snow's not letting up. I've phoned Aidan and told him that the place will be closed until the weather improves.'

'Aidan?'

'One of my friends. He can be relied on to spread the word. Only my absolute regulars would even contemplate trudging out here in this weather.'

'So…is Aidan the old would-be opera singer?'

'Aidan is my age. We used to go to school together.' She dished him out some soup, added some bread and offered him a glass of wine, which he rejected in favour of water.

'And he's the guy who broke your heart? No. He wouldn't be. The guy who broke your heart has long since disappeared, hasn't he?'

Brianna stiffened. She reminded herself that she was not having a cosy chat with a friend over lunch. This was a guest in her pub, a stranger who was passing through, no more. Confiding details of her private life was beyond the pale, quite different from chatting about all the amusing things that happened in a village where nearly everyone knew everyone else. Her personal life was not going to be fodder for a short story on life in a quaint Irish village.

'I don't recall telling you anything about my heart being broken, and I don't think my private life is any of your business. I hope the soup is satisfactory.'

So that was a sore topic; there was no point in a follow-up. It was irrelevant to his business here. If he happened to be curious, then it was simply because he was in the unique situation of being pub-bound and snowed in with just her for company. In the absence of anyone else, it was only natural that she would spark an interest.

'Why don't you serve food? It would add a lot to the profits of a place like this. You'd be surprised how remote places can become packed if the food is good enough…' He doubted the place had seen any changes in a very long time. Again, not his concern, he thought. 'So, if you don't want to talk about yourself, then that's fair enough.'

'Why don't *you* talk about yourself? Are you married? Do you have children?'

'If I were married and had children, I wouldn't be doing what I'm doing.' Marriage? Children? He had never contemplated either. He pushed the empty soup bowl aside and sprawled on the chair, angling it so that he could stretch his legs out to one side. 'Tell me about the old guy who likes to sing.'

'What made you suddenly decide to pack in your job and write? It must have been a big deal, giving up steady work in favour of a gamble that might or might not pay off.'

Leo shrugged and told himself that, certainly in this instance, the ends would more than justify the means—and at any rate, there was no chance that she would discover his little lie. He would forever remain the enigmatic stranger who had passed through and collected a few amusing anecdotes on the way. She would be regaling her friends with this in a week's time.

'Sometimes life is all about taking chances,' he murmured softly.

Brianna hadn't taken a chance in such a long time that she had forgotten what it felt like. The last chance she had taken had been with Danny, and hadn't *that* backfired spectacularly in her face? She had settled into a groove and had firmly convinced herself that it suited her. 'Some people are braver than others when it comes to that sort of thing,' she found herself muttering under her breath.

Leading remark, Leo thought. He had vast experience of women dangling titbits of information about themselves, offering them to him in the hope of securing his interest, an attempt to reel him in through his curiosity. However, for once his cynicism was absent. This woman knew nothing about him. He did not represent a rich, eligible bachelor. He was a struggling writer with no job. He had a glimpse of what it must feel like to communicate with a woman without undercurrents of suspicion that, whatever they wanted, at least part of it had to do with his limitless bank balance. He might have been adopted into a life of extreme privilege, and that privilege might have been his spring board to the dizzying heights of his success, but with that privilege and with that success had come drawbacks—one of which was an inborn mistrust of women and their motivations.

Right now, he was just communicating with a very beautiful and undeniably sexy woman and, hell, she was clueless about him. He smiled, enjoying the rare sense of freedom.

'And you're not one of the brave ones?'

Brianna stood up to clear the table. She had no idea where this sudden urge to confide was coming from. Was she bonding with him because, underneath those disconcerting good looks, he was a fellow artist? Because, on some weird level, he *understood* her? Or was she just one of those sad women, too young to be living a life of relative solitude, willing to confide in anyone who showed an interest?

Her head was buzzing. She felt hot and bothered and, when he reached out and circled her wrist with his hand, she froze in shock. The feel of his warm fingers on her skin was electrifying. She hadn't had a response like this to a man in a very long time. It was a feeling of coming alive. She wanted to snatch her hand away from his and rub away where he had touched her… Yet she also wanted him to keep his fingers on her wrist; she wanted to prolong the warm, physical connection between them. She abruptly sat back down, because her legs felt like jelly, and he released her.

'It's hard to take chances when you have commitments,' she muttered unsteadily. She couldn't tear her eyes away from his face. She literally felt as though he held her spellbound. 'You're on your own. You probably had sufficient money saved to just take off and do your own thing. I'm only now beginning to see the light financially and, even so, I still couldn't just up and leave.' She was leaning forward in the chair, leaning towards him as though he was the source of her energy. 'I should get this place tidied up,' she said agitatedly.

'Why? I thought you said that the pub would be closed until further notice.'

'Yes, but…'

'You must get lonely here on your own.'

'Of course I'm not lonely! I have too many friends to count!'

'But I don't suppose you have a lot of time to actually go out with them…'

Hot colour invaded her cheeks. No time to go out with them; no time even to pursue her art as a hobby. She hated the picture he was painting of her life. She was being made to feel as though she had sleepwalked into an existence of living from one day to the next, with each day being exactly the same. She dragged herself back to reality, back to the fact that he was just a budding writer on the hunt for some interesting material for his book. He wasn't interested in *her*.

'Will I be the sad spinster in your book?' She laughed shakily and gathered herself together. 'I think you're better off with some of the more colourful characters who live here.' She managed to get to her feet, driven by a need to put some distance between them. How could she let this one passing stranger get to her with such breath-taking speed? Lots of guys had come on to her over the years. Some of them she had known for ever, others had been friends of friends of friends. She had laughed and joked with all of them but she had never, not once, felt like *this*. Felt as though the air was being sucked out of her lungs every time she took a peek…as though she was being injected with adrenaline every time she came too close.

She busied herself tidying, urging him to sit rather than help. Her flustered brain screeched to a halt when she imagined them standing side by side at the kitchen sink.

She launched into nervous conversation, chattering mindlessly about the last time a snow storm had hit the village, forcing herself to relax as she recounted stories of all the things that could happen to people who were snow bound for days on end, occasionally as long as a fortnight: the baby delivered by one panicked father; the rowdy rugby group who had been forced to spend two nights in the pub; the community spirit when they had all had to help each other out; the food that Seamus Riley had had to lift by rope into his bedroom because he hadn't been able to get past his front door.

Leo listened politely. He really ought to be paying a bit more attention, but he was captivated by the graceful movement of her tall, slender body as she moved from counter to counter, picking things up, putting things away, making sure not to look at him.

'In fact, we all do our bit when the weather turns really bad,' she was saying now as she turned briefly in his direction. 'I don't suppose you have much of that in London.'

'None,' Leo murmured absently. Her little breasts pointed against the jumper and he wondered whether she was wearing a bra; a sensible, white cotton bra. He never imagined the thought of a sensible, white cotton bra could be such an illicit turn-on.

He was so absorbed in the surprising disobedience of his imagination that he almost missed the name that briefly passed her lips and, when it registered, he stiffened and felt his pulses quicken.

'Sorry,' he grated, straightening. 'I missed that…particular anecdote.' He kept his voice as casual as possible but he was tense and vigilant as he waited for her to repeat what she had been saying, what he had stupidly missed because he had been too busy getting distracted, too busy missing the point of why he was stuck here in the first place.

'I was just telling you about what it's like here—we help each other out. I was telling you about my friend who lives in the village. Bridget McGuire…'

# CHAPTER THREE

So HIS MOTHER wasn't the drunk or the junkie that he had anticipated, if his landlady was to be believed...

Leo flexed his muscles and wandered restlessly through the lounge where he had been sitting in front of his computer working for the past hour and a half.

Circumstance had forced him into a routine of sorts, as his optimistic plan of clearing off within a few days had faded into impossibility.

After three days, the snow was still falling steadily. It fluctuated between virtual white-out and gentle flakes that could lull you into thinking that it was all picture-postcard perfect. Until you opened the front door and clocked that the snow you'd cleared moments previously had already been replaced by a fresh fall.

He strolled towards the window and stared out at a pitch-black vista, illuminated only by the outside lights which Brianna kept on overnight.

It was not yet seven in the morning. He had never needed much sleep and here, more than ever, he couldn't afford to lie in. Not when he had to keep communicating with his office, sending emails, reviewing reports, without her knowing exactly what was going on. At precisely seven-thirty, he would shut his computer and head outside to see what he could do about beating back some of the snow so that it didn't completely bank up against the door.

It was, he had to admit to himself, a fairly unique take on winter sport. When he had mentioned that to Brianna the day before, she had burst out laughing and told him that he could try building himself a sledge and having fun outside, getting in touch with his inner child.

He made himself a cup of coffee and reined in the temptation to let his mind meander, which was what it seemed to want to do whenever he thought of her.

His mother was in hospital recovering from a mild heart attack.

'She should have been out last week,' Brianna had confided, 'But they've decided to keep her in because the weather's so horrendous and she has no one to take care of her.'

Where was the down-and-out junkie he had been anticipating? Of course, there was every chance that she *had* been a deadbeat, a down and out. It would be a past she would have wanted to keep to herself, especially with Brianna who, from the sounds of it, saw her as something of a surrogate mother. The woman hadn't lived her whole life in the village. Who knew what sort of person she had been once upon a time?

But certainly, the stories he had heard did not tally with his expectations.

And the bottom line was that his hands were tied at the moment. He had come to see for himself what his past held. He wasn't about to abandon that quest on the say-so of a girl he'd known for five minutes. On the other hand, he was now on indefinite leave. One week, he had told his secretary, but who was to say that this enforced stay would not last longer?

The snow showed no sign of abating. When it *did* abate,

there was still the question of engineering a meeting with his mother. She was in hospital and when she came out she would presumably be fairly weak. However, without anyone to act as full-time carer, at least for a while, what was the likelihood of her being released from hospital? He was now playing a waiting game.

And throughout all this, there was still the matter of his fictitious occupation. Surely Brianna would start asking him questions about this so-called book he was busily writing? Would he have to fabricate a plot?

In retrospect, out of all the occupations he could have picked, he concluded that he had managed to hit on the single worst one of them all. God knew, he hadn't read a book in years. His reading was strictly of the utilitarian variety: legal tomes, books on the movements of financial markets, detailed backgrounds to companies he was planning to take over.

The fairly straightforward agenda he had set out for himself was turning into something far more complex.

He turned round at the sound of her footsteps on the wooden floor.

And that, he thought, frowning, was an added complication. She was beginning to occupy far too much space in his head. Familiarity was not breeding contempt. He caught himself watching her, thinking about her, fantasising about her. His appreciation of her natural beauty was growing like an unrestrained weed, stifling the disciplined part of his brain that told him that he should not go there.

Not only was she ignorant of his real identity but whatever the hell had happened to her—whoever had broken her heart, the mystery guy she could not be persuaded to discuss—had left her vulnerable. On the surface, she was capable, feisty, strong-willed and stubbornly proud. But he sensed her vulnerability underneath and the rational part of him acknowledged that a vulnerable woman was a woman best left well alone.

But his libido was refusing to listen to reason and seemed to have developed a will of its own.

'You're working too hard.' She greeted him cheerfully. Having told him that she would not be doing his laundry, she had been doing his laundry. Today he was wearing the jeans she had washed the day before and one of her father's checked flannel shirts, the sleeves of which he had rolled to the elbows. In a few seconds, she took in the dark hair just visible where the top couple of buttons of the shirt were undone; the low-slung jeans that emphasised the leanness of his hips; the strong, muscular forearms.

Leo knew what he had been working on and it hadn't been the novel she imagined: legal technicalities that had to be sorted out with one small IT company he was in the process of buying; emails to the human resources department so that they reached a mutually agreeable deal with employees of yet another company he was acquiring. He had the grace to flush.

'Believe me, I've worked harder,' he said with utmost truth. She was in some baggy grey jogging bottoms, which made her look even slimmer than she was, and a baggy grey sweatshirt. For the first time, her hair wasn't tied back, but instead fell over her shoulders and down her back in a cascade of rich auburn.

'I guess maybe in that company of yours—'

'Company of mine?' Leo asked sharply and then realised that guilt had laced the question with unnecessary asperity when she smiled and explained that she was talking about whatever big firm he had worked for before quitting.

She had noticed that he never talked about the job he had done, and Brianna had made sure to steer clear of the subject. It was a big enough deal getting away from the rat race without being reminded of what you'd left behind, because the rat race from which he had escaped was the very same rat race that was now funding his exploits into the world of writing.

'You still haven't told me much about your book,' she said tentatively. 'I know I'm being horribly nosy, and I know how hard it is to let someone have a whiff of what you're working on before it's finished, but you must be very far in. You start work so early and I know you keep it up, off and on during the day. You never seem to lack inspiration.'

Leo considered what level of inspiration was needed to review due diligence on a company: none. 'You know how it goes,' he said vaguely. 'You can write two...er... chapters and then immediately delete them, although...' He considered the massive deal he had just signed off on. 'I must admit I've been reasonably productive. To change the subject, have you any books I could borrow? I had no idea I would be in one place for so long...'

When had his life become so blinkered? he wondered. Sure, he played; he enjoyed the company of beautiful women, but they were a secondary consideration to his work. The notion of any of them becoming a permanent fixture in his life had never crossed his mind. And, yes, he relaxed at the gym but, hell, he hadn't picked up a novel in years; hadn't been to a movie in years; rarely watched television for pleasure, aside from the occasional football match; went to the theatre occasionally, usually when it was an arranged company event, but even then he was always restless, always thinking of what needed to be done with his companies or clients or mergers or buyouts.

He impatiently swept aside the downward spiral of in-

trospection and surfaced to find her telling him that there
were books in her study.

'And there's something I want to show you,' she said
hesitantly. She disappeared for a few minutes and in that
time he strolled around the lounge, distractedly looking
at the fire and wondering whether the log basket would
have to be topped up. He wondered how much money she
was losing with this enforced closure of the pub and then
debated the pros and cons of asking her if he could have
a look at her books.

'Okay...'

Leo turned around and walked slowly towards her.
'What do you have behind your back?'

Brianna took a deep breath and revealed one of the
small paintings she had done a few months back, when she
had managed to squeeze in some down-time during the
summer. It was a painting of the lake and in the foreground
an angler sat, back to the spectator, his head bent, his body
leaning forward, as if listening for the sound of fish.

'I don't like showing my work to anyone either,' she
confided as he took the picture from her and held it at a
distance in his hands. 'So I fully understand why you don't
want to talk about your book.'

'*You* painted this?'

'What do you think?'

'I think you're wasted running a pub here.' Leo was
temporarily lost for words. Of course he had masterpieces
in his house, as well as some very expensive investment
art, but this was charming and unique enough to find a
lucrative market of its own. 'Why don't you try selling
them?'

'Oh, I could never produce enough.' She sighed regret-
fully. She moved to stand next to him so that they were
both looking at the painting. When he rested it on the table,

she didn't move, and suddenly her throat constricted as their eyes tangled and, for a few seconds, she found that she was holding her breath.

Leo sifted his fingers through her hair and the door slammed shut on all his good intentions not to let his wayward libido do the thinking for him. He just knew that he wanted this woman, more than he had ever wanted any woman in his life before, and for the hell of him he had no idea why. He had stopped trying to work that one out. He was not a man who was accustomed to holding out. Desire was always accompanied by possession. In fact, as he looked down at her flushed, upturned face, he marvelled that he had managed to restrain himself for so long because hadn't he known, almost from the very start, that she was attracted to him? Hadn't he seen it there in those hot, stolen looks and her nervous, jumpy reactions when he got fractionally too close to her?

He perched on the edge of the table and drew her closer to him.

Brianna released her breath in a long shudder. She was burning up where he touched her. Never in a million years would she have imagined that she could do this, that she could *feel* this way, feel so connected to a guy that she wanted him to touch her after only a few days. Showing him that painting, had he only known it, had been a measure of how much she trusted him. She felt *easy* in his company. Gone were the feelings of suspicion which had been there when she had first laid eyes on him, when she had wondered what such a dramatic looking stranger was doing in their midst, standing there at the door of the pub and looking around him with guarded coolness.

She had let down her defences, had thawed. Being cooped up had blurred the lines between paying guest and a guy who was as amusing as he was intelligent; as witty and dry as he was focused and disciplined. He might have worked in a company and done boring stuff but you would never guess that by the breadth of his conversation. He knew a great deal about art, about world affairs, and he had travelled extensively. He had vaguely told her that it was all in connection with his job, and really not very exciting at all because he did nothing but work when he got to his destination, but he could still captivate her with descriptions of the places he had been and the things he had seen there.

In short, he was nothing at all like any of the men she had ever met in her entire life, and that included Danny Fluke.

'What are you doing?' she asked weakly.

'I'm touching you. Do you want me to stop?'

'This is crazy.'

'This is taking a chance.'

'I don't even…know you.'

No, she certainly didn't. And yet, strangely, she knew more about him than any other woman did. Not that there was any point in getting tied down with semantics. 'What does that have to do with wanting someone?' His voice was a low murmur in her ear and, as he slid his hand underneath the jumper to caress her waist, she could feel all rational thought disappearing like dew in the summer sun.

So, she thought, fighting down the temptation to moan as his fingers continued to stroke her bare skin, he wasn't going to be sticking around. He was as nomadic as she was rooted to this place. But wasn't that what taking chances was all about?

She reached up and trembled as she linked her fingers behind his neck and pulled him down towards her.

His kiss was soft, exploratory. His tongue mingled against hers and was mind-blowingly erotic. He angled his long legs open and she edged her body between them so that now she was pushed up against him and could feel the hardness of his erection against her.

'You can still tell me to stop...' And, if she did, he didn't know what he would do. Have a sub-zero shower? Even then, he wasn't sure that it would be enough to cool him down. 'Taking a chance can sometimes be a danger-ous indulgence...'

And yet there was a part of her that knew that *not* taking this chance would be a source of eternal regret. Besides, why on earth should she let one miserable experience that was now in the past determine her present?

'Maybe I want to live dangerously for once...'

His hand had crept further up her jumper and he un-hooked her bra strap with practised ease.

Brianna's breath caught in her throat and she stilled as he inched his way towards one small breast. She quivered at the feel of his thumb rubbing over it. She wanted him so badly that she was shaking with desire.

Leo marvelled that something he knew they just shouldn't be doing could feel so damned *right*. Had he been going stir crazy here without even realising it? Was that why he had been so useless at disciplining his libido? The lie that had taken him so far, that had started life as just something he had been inspired to do because he had needed an excuse for being there in the first place, hung around his neck with the deadly weight of an albatross.

He shied away from the thought that she might find out, and then laughed at the possibility of that happening.

'I won't be around for much longer.' He felt compelled to warn her off involvement even though he knew that the safest route he could take if he really didn't want to court unwanted involvement would be to walk away. 'Sure you want to take a chance with someone who's just passing through?' He spoke against her mouth and he could feel her warm breath mingling with his.

Brianna feverishly thought of the last guy she had become involved with—the guy she had thought wasn't passing through, the guy she had thought she might end up spending the rest of her life with but who, in fact, had always known that he would be moving on. This time, there would be no illusions. A fling: it was something she had never done in her life before. Danny had been her first and only relationship.

'I'm not looking for permanence,' she whispered. 'I thought I had that once and it turned out to be the biggest mistake I ever made. Stop talking.'

'Happy to oblige,' Leo growled, his conscience relieved. 'I think I wanted this within hours of meeting you.' He circled her waist with his hands and then pushed the jumper up, taking the bra with it as well.

For a split second, Brianna was overwhelmed by shyness. She closed her eyes and arched back, every nerve and pore straining towards a closeness she hadn't felt in such a long time. When she felt the wetness of his mouth surround her nipple, she groaned and half-collapsed. Her hands coiled into his thick, dark hair as he continued sucking and teasing the stiffened peaks until she wanted to faint from the pleasure of it. When he drew back, she groaned in frustration and looked at him drowsily from under her lashes, her heartbeat quickening to a frantic beat as she watched him inspecting her breasts with the same considered thoroughness with which he had earlier inspected her painting.

'I want to see you,' Leo said roughly. He was surprised at the speed with which his body was reacting, racing towards release. His erection was uncomfortable against his jeans, bulging painfully. Yet he didn't want to rush this. He had to close his eyes briefly and breathe deeply so that he wouldn't be thrown off-balance by the sight of her bare breasts, small and crested with large, pink nipples that were still glistening from where he had sucked them.

In response, Brianna traced the contours of his shoulders, broad and powerful. It was driving her crazy just thinking about touching his chest, the bronzed, muscled chest that had sent her imagination into overdrive on that first day when he had stood half-naked in front of her, waiting for the shirts she had brought for him.

'I don't want to make love to you here...' He swung her off her feet as though she weighed nothing and carried her up the stairs towards his bedroom, and then, pausing briefly, up the further flight of stairs that led to her bedroom. He didn't dare look down at her soft, small breasts or he would deposit her on the stairs and take her right there. His urgency to have her lying underneath him was shocking. Not cool; definitely not his style.

He found her bedroom, barely taking time to look around him as he placed her on the bed and ordered her to stay put.

'Where do you think I'm going to go?' She laughed with nervous excitement and levered herself onto one elbow, watching with unconcealed fascination as he began to strip off. With each discarded item of clothing, her heart rate picked up speed until she had to close her eyes and take deep breaths.

Her response was so wonderfully, naturally open and unconcealed that Leo experienced a raw, primitive thrill that magnified his burning lust a thousand-fold.

He took his time removing the jeans because he was enjoying watching her watching him. Most of all he enjoyed her gasp as he stepped out of his boxers and moved towards her, his erection thick, heavy and impressively telling of just how aroused he was.

Brianna scrabbled to sit up, pulses racing, the blood pumping in her veins hot with desire.

She couldn't believe she was doing this, behaving in a way that was so out of character. She sighed and moaned as the mattress depressed under his weight; the feel of his hands tucking into the waistband of the jogging bottoms, sliding them down, signalled the final nail in her crumbling defences

'You're beautiful.' He straddled her and kissed her with intimate, exquisite thoroughness, tracing her mouth with his tongue, then trailing his lips against her neck so that she whimpered and tilted her head to prolong the kiss.

Every small noise she made, every tiny movement, bore witness to how much she was turned on and it gave him an unbelievable kick to know that she had allowed herself to be pulled along by an irresistible force even though it went against the grain.

Her skin was supple and smooth, her breasts perfect, dainty orbs that barely fitted his large hand.

He teased the tip of her nipple with his tongue and then submerged himself in the pleasure of suckling on it, loving the way she writhed under him; the way her fingers bit into his shoulder blades; the way she arched back, eyes closed, mouth parted, her whole body trembling.

He let his hand drift over her flat stomach to circle the indentation of her belly button with one finger while he continued to plunder her breasts, moving between them, sucking, liking the way he could draw them into his mouth. He was hungry for more but determined not to take things fast. He wanted to savour every second of tasting her body.

He parted her legs gently with his hand and eased the momentary tension he could feel as she stilled against him.

'Shh,' he whispered huskily, as though she had spoken. 'Relax.'

'It's…been a long time.' Brianna gave a half- stifled, nervous laugh. He raised his head and their eyes tangled, black clashing with apple-green.

'When you say *long*…'

'I haven't slept with anyone since… Well, it's been years…' She twisted away, embarrassed by the admission. Where had the time gone? It seemed as though one minute she had been nursing heartbreak, dealing with her father's death, caught up in a jumble of financial worries, her life thrown utterly off course, and the next minute she was here, still running the pub, though with the financial worries more or less behind her. She was hardly sinking but definitely not swimming and living a life that seemed far too responsible for someone her age.

Leo tilted her face to his, kissed her on the side of her mouth and banked down his momentary discomfort at thinking that he might be taking advantage of her.

Yet she was perfectly aware of the situation, perfectly aware that he wasn't going to be hanging around. Naturally, she was not in possession of the true facts regulating his departure, but weren't those just details? Looking at the bigger picture, she knew where she stood, that this was just a fling—not even that.

'I'll be gentle.'

'I guess you…you've had a lot of girlfriends?'

'I haven't espoused a life of celibacy.' He slipped his finger into the wet groove of her femininity and felt whatever further questions she wanted to ask become stifled under her heated response. She moved against his finger and groaned.

He could have played with her body all day, all night. Right now, he couldn't get enough of her and he moved downwards. She sucked in her breath sharply and he rested the palm of his hand flat on her stomach, then he nuzzled the soft hair covering the apex between her thighs. He breathed in the musky, honeyed scent of her and dipped his tongue to taste her. How did he know that this was something she was experiencing for the first time? And why was that such a turn on?

He teased the throbbing bud of her clitoris and, when she moaned and squirmed, he flattened his hands on her thighs so that her legs were spread wide open for his delectation.

Brianna had never known anything like this before. There wasn't a single part of her body that wasn't consumed with an overpowering craving. She wanted him to continue doing what he was doing, yet she wanted him in her, deep inside. She weakly tugged at his hair but was powerless to pull him up. When she looked down and saw his dark head between her legs, and his strong, bronzed hands against the paleness of her thighs, she almost passed out.

Could years of living in icy isolation have made her so vulnerable to his touch? Had her body been so deprived of human contact that it was now overwhelmed? It felt like it.

When he rose, she was so close to tipping over the edge that she had to squeeze her eyes shut and grit her teeth together to maintain self-control.

'Enjoying yourself?' Leo raised some hair from her flushed face to whisper in her ear. He rubbed his stiff erection against her belly and felt sensation lick through his body at frightening speed.

Brianna blushed and nodded, then raised herself up so that she could kiss him on the mouth, draw him down over her so that their bodies were pressed together, fused with slick perspiration. She reached down and took him in her hand and he angled himself slightly away to accommodate her. His breathing thickened as she continued to work her movements into a deep rhythm.

He was impressively big and she shivered with heady anticipation.

'A condom... Wait; in my wallet...'

Already he was groping in the pocket of his jeans for his wallet and fumbling to fetch a condom, his eyes still pinned to her flushed, reclining body. How on earth could he be thinking of *anything* at a time like this? She just couldn't wait for him to be inside her, filling her with his bigness.

'You're well prepared.' She sighed and thought that of course he would be; he was a man of the world after all.

She groaned and felt the slippery, cool sheath guarding his arousal; her hands impatiently guided him to her, longing for the moment when he would fill her completely. She flipped onto him and arched up, her hands on his broad chest, her small breasts tipping teasingly towards him. 'I know you're moving on and I like it that way.' Did she? Yes, she did! 'I *need* this.' She leaned forward, bottom sticking up provocatively, and covered her mouth with his. 'The last thing I would take a gamble on is with a pregnancy.'

'You wouldn't want to be stuck with a loser like me?' Leo grinned, because those words had never passed his lips before. 'A travelling writer hoping to make his fortune?' He curved his hands on her rear and inserted himself into her. He drove into her and Brianna felt a surge of splintering pleasure as he moved deep inside her. Her head was flung back and he could feel the ends of her long hair on his thighs, brushing against them.

'A guy could feel insulted.'

She was on her back before she knew it and he was rear-ing up over her, big, powerful and oh, so breathtakingly beautiful, one-hundred per cent alpha male.

She came with such intensity that she had to squeeze her eyes shut on the gathering tears. She knew her fingers were digging in to the small of his back and they dug harder as she felt him swell and reach his orgasm inside her.

God, nothing had ever felt *that* good. Years of celibacy, running the pub and coping with all the day-to-day worries had obviously had the effect of making her respond like a wanton to being touched. She had never been like that before. But then, she had been so much younger when she had met Danny. Had the years and the tough times released some sort of pent-up capacity for passion that she had never known about?

'So…' Leo drawled, rolling onto his side then pulling her to face him so that their naked bodies were front to front and still touching, almost as though neither of them wanted to break the physical contact. 'You were telling me all about how you were using me to get you out of a dry patch.' He inserted his thigh between her legs and felt her wetness slippery against his skin.

'I never said that,' Brianna murmured.

'You didn't have to. The word "need" gave it away.'

'Maybe you're right. It's been a slog for the past few years. Don't get me wrong, there have been times when I've enjoyed running this place. It's just not how I expected my life to turn out.'

'What had you expected?'

'I expected to be married with a couple of kids, pursuing the art career that never took off, as it happens.'

'Ah. And the couple of kids and the wedding ring would have been courtesy of the heartbreaker?'

'He dumped me.' It had haunted her, had been responsible for all the precautions she had taken to protect herself. Yet lying here, with his thigh doing wonderful things between her legs, stirring up all the excitement that had only just faded, she could barely remember Danny's face. He had stopped being a human being and had become just a vague, disturbing recollection of a past mistake. She couldn't care less what had become of him, so how on earth had he carried on having such an influence on her behaviour?

'I wasn't good enough,' she said, anger replacing the humiliation that usually accompanied this thought. 'We went out for ages; when I thought that we really were destined to be together, he broke it to me that I had just been a good time at university. Dad was ill and I had discovered that the guy I thought I was in love with had been using me all along for a bit of fun. At least *you've* been honest and up-front.'

'Honest and up-front?'

'You're moving on. You're not here to stay. No illusions. I like that.'

'Before you start putting me on a pedestal and getting out the feather brush to dust my halo, I should tell you that you know very little about me.'

'I know enough.'

'You have little to compare me with. I'm a pretty ruthless bastard, if you want the truth.'

Brianna laughed, a clear, tinkling sound of pure amusement. She sifted her fingers through his dark hair and curled up closer to him which kick-started a whole lot of very pleasurable sensations that had him hardening in record time.

He edged her back from him and looked at her, unsmiling. 'You've been hurt once. You've spent years buried here, working beyond the call of duty to keep the wolves from the door. You've had no boyfriends, no distractions to occupy your time. Hell, you haven't even been able to wring out an hour or two to do your painting. And then along I come. I'm not your knight in shining armour.'

'I never said that you were!' Brianna pulled back, hurt and confused at a sudden glimpse of ruthlessness she wouldn't have imagined possible.

'It's been my experience that what women say is often at variance to what they think. I won't be hanging around—and even if I lived next door to you, Brianna, I don't do long-term relationships.'

'What do you mean, you *don't do long-term relationships*?'

'Just what I say, so be warned. Don't make the mistake of investing anything in me. What we have is sexual attraction, pure and simple.' He softened and gentled his voice. 'We have something that works at this precise moment in time.'

But it was more than that. What about the conversations they had had; the moments of sharing generated by close proximity? Some sixth sense stopped her from pointing that out. She was finding it difficult to recognise the cool, dark eyes of this stranger looking at her.

'And stop treating me as though I'm a stupid kid,' she bit out tightly, disentangling herself from him. 'I was one of those once.' Her voice was equally cool. 'I don't intend to repeat the same mistake twice. And, if you think that I would ever let myself get emotionally wrapped up with someone who doesn't want to spend his life in one place, then you're crazy. I value security. When I fall for someone, it will be someone who wants to settle down and isn't scared of commitment. I'm thankful that you've been honest enough to tell me as it is, but you have nothing to fear. Your precious independence isn't at risk.'

'If that's the case, why are you pulling away from me?'

'I don't like your tone of voice.'

'Just so long as it's not what I say but how I'm saying it,' he murmured softly. He tugged her back towards him and Brianna placed her hand on his shoulder but it was a pathetically weak attempt to stave off the fierce urgings of her body.

As his hand swept erotically along her thigh, she shimmied back towards him, the coolness in his eyes forgotten, the jarring hardness of his voice consigned to oblivion.

They made love slowly, touching each other everywhere, absorbing each other's pleasurable groans. She tasted him with as much hunger as he tasted her. She just couldn't get enough of him—at her breasts, between her thighs, urging her to tell him what she wanted him to do and telling her in explicit detail what he wanted her to do to him.

Eventually, just as she was falling into a light, utterly contented doze, she heard the insistent buzz of her mobile phone next to the bed where she had left it charging. She was almost too sleepy to pick up but, when she did, she instantly sat up, drawing the covers around her.

Leo watched her, his keen antennae picking up her sudden tension, although from this end of the phone he could only hear monosyllabic replies to whatever was being said.

'Remember I told you about my friend? Bridget McGuire?' Brianna ended the call thoughtfully but remained holding the mobile, caressing it absently.

Leo was immediately on red-hot alert, although he kept his expression mildly interested and utterly expressionless. 'The name rings a bell...'

'They need to release her from hospital. There's been an accident on the motorway and they need all the beds they can get. So she's leaving tomorrow. The snow is predicted to stop. She's coming here...'

# CHAPTER FOUR

'WHEN?' HE SLID out of the bed, strolled towards the window and stared down to a snowy, grey landscape. The sun had barely risen but, yes, the snow appeared to be lessening.

This was the reason he was here, pretending to be someone he wasn't. When he had first arrived, he had wondered how a meeting with his mother could possibly be engineered in a town where everyone seemed to know everyone else. Several lies down and his quarry would be delivered right to his doorstep. Didn't fate work in mysterious ways?

Brianna, sitting up, wondered what was going through his head.

'For the moment, they're going to transfer her to another ward and then, provided the snow doesn't get worse, they're going to bring her here tomorrow. You're making me nervous, standing by the window like that. What are you thinking? I have room here at the pub. It won't make any difference to you. You won't have to vacate your room—in fact, you probably won't even notice that she's here. I shall have her in the spare room next to my bedroom so that I can keep a constant eye on her, and of course I doubt she'll be able to climb up and down stairs.'

Leo smiled and pushed himself away from the window

ledge. When he tried to analyse what he felt about his birth mother, the most he could come up with was a scathing contempt which he realised he would have to attempt to conceal for what remained of his time here. Brianna might have painted a different picture, but years of preconceived notions were impossible to put to bed.

'So...' He slipped back under the covers and pulled her towards him. 'If we're going to have an unexpected visitor, then maybe you should start telling me the sort of person I can look forward to meeting and throw me a few more details...'

Brianna began plating their breakfast. Was it her imagination or was he abnormally interested in finding out about Bridget? He had returned to the bed earlier and she had thrown him a few sketchy details about her friend yet, off and on, he seemed to return to the subject. His questions were in no way pressing; in fact, he barely seemed to care about the answer.

A sudden thought occurred to her.

Was he really worried that their wonderful one-on-one time might be interrupted? He had made it perfectly clear that he was just passing through, and had given her a stern warning that she was not to make the mistake of investing in him, yet was he becoming possessive of her company without even realising it himself?

For reasons best known to himself, he was a commitment-phobe, but did he respond out of habit? Had he warned her off because distancing himself was an automatic response?

He might not want to admit it, but over the past few days they had got to know one another in a way she would never have thought possible. He worked while she busied herself with the accounts and the bookkeeping but, for a lot of the time, they had communicated. He had even looked at her ledgers, leading her to think that he might have been an accountant in a previous life. He had suggested ways to improve her finances. He had persuaded her to show him all the paintings she had ever done, which she kept in portfolios under the bed, and had urged her to design a website to showcase them. She had caught herself telling him so much more than she had ever told anyone in her life before, even her close friends. He made a very good listener.

His own life, he had confided, had been as uneventful as it came: middle class, middle of the road. Both of them were single children, both without parents. They laughed at the same things; they bickered over the remote control for the television in the little private lounge which was set aside for the guests, on those rare occasions she had some. With the pub closed, they had had lots of quality time during which to get to know one another.

So was he *scared* that the arrival of Bridget would signal the end of what they had?

With a sigh, she acknowledged that if the ambulance could make it up the lane to the pub to deliver their patient then her loyal customers could certainly make it as well. The pub would once again reopen and their time together would certainly be curtailed.

'I've been thinking,' she said slowly, handing him a plate of bacon, eggs and toast and sitting down. 'I might just keep the pub closed for a couple of weeks. Until the snow is well and truly over and the path outside the pub is completely safe.'

She told herself that this was something that made perfect sense. And why shouldn't she have a little break? The last break she had had was over summer when she had grabbed a long weekend to go to Dublin with her friends. At other times, while they'd been off having lovely warm holidays in sunny Spain or Portugal, she had always been holed up at the pub, unable to take the time off because she couldn't afford to lose the revenue.

So why shouldn't she have time off now? A couple of weeks wouldn't break the bank—at least, not completely. And she would make up for it later in the year. Leo had suggested a website to promote the pub and she would take him up on that. He had intimated that she could really take off with only minimal changes, a few things to bring the place up to date.

And, if she closed the pub for a couple of weeks, they would continue to have their quality time until he disappeared.

'It would be better for Bridget as well,' she hurried on, not wanting to analyse how much of this idea was down to her desire to keep him to herself for a little longer. 'She's going to need looking after, at least in the beginning, and it would give me the opportunity to really take care of her without having to worry about running the pub as well.'

'Makes sense, I suppose...'

'You won't be affected at all.'

'I know. You've already told me.'

'And I don't want you to think that your needs are going to be overlooked. I mean, what I'm trying to say is...'

Leo tilted his head to one side. She blushed very easily. Especially when you considered the hard life she had had and the financial worries she had faced. No one would ever be able to accuse her of not being a fighter.

'Is that you'll carry on making my breakfast for me? Fixing me sandwiches for lunch? Slaving over a recipe book for something to cook for dinner? Making sure my bed is...warm and that you're in it?'

'I'm not part of a package deal.' Brianna bristled, suddenly offended at the picture he painted of her. 'You haven't paid for me along with the breakfast, lunch and dinner.' She stood up and began clearing the dishes, only pausing when she felt his arms around her at the sink. When she looked straight ahead, she could see their dim reflection in the window pane, his head downbent, buried in her hair. He didn't like it when she tied it back so she had left it loose the past couple of days and now he wound one of the long, auburn strands around his finger.

His other hand reached underneath the sweater and she watched their hazy reflection, the movement of his hand caressing her breast, playing with her nipple, rubbing the pad of his thumb over it. Liquid pooled between her legs, dampening her underwear and making her squirm and shift in his embrace.

She could feel his hard arousal nudging her from behind and, when she half-closed her eyes, her imagination took flight, dwelling on the image of her touching him there, licking and sucking with his fingers tangled in her hair. She wanted to do the same now. She pictured him kneeling like a penitent at her feet, her body pressing against the wall in her bedroom, her legs parted as he tasted her.

He seemed to have the ability to make her stop thinking the second he laid a finger on her and he did it as easily as someone switching a tap off.

She watched, eyes smoky with desire, as he pushed the jumper up; now she could see the pale skin of her stomach and his much darker hands on her breasts, massaging them, teasing them, playing with her swollen, sensitive nipples.

She shuddered and angled her neck so that he could kiss her.

'I know you're not part of the package,' he murmured. 'And, just to set the record straight, I enjoy you a hell of a lot more than I enjoy the meals you prepare.'

'Are you implying that I'm a bad cook?' He had undone

the top button of her jeans and she wriggled as he did the same with the zip, easing the jeans down over her slim hips, exposing her pale pink briefs.

'You're a fantastic cook. One of the best.' He stood back slightly so that she could swivel to face him.

'You're a terrible liar.'

Leo flushed guiltily at this unwittingly inaccurate swipe, said in jest.

'Don't bank on that,' he murmured into her ear. 'You forget that I've already warned you that I'm a ruthless bastard.'

'If you really *were* a ruthless bastard, then you wouldn't have to warn me. I'd see all the giveaway signs.' She tiptoed and drew his head down so that she could kiss him. Her body was heating up, impatiently anticipating the moment when it could unite with his.

In the heat of passion, it was always him who thought about protection. So he was scrupulous when it came to taking no chances—that didn't mean that he wasn't becoming more attached to her, did it? The fact he didn't want an unwanted pregnancy any more than she did, didn't indicate that his nomadic lifestyle wasn't undergoing a subtle ground-change...

'Touch me,' he commanded roughly and he rested his hands on her hips and half-closed his eyes as she burrowed underneath his jumper, her hands feathering across his chest, pausing to do wonderful things to his nipples. He was breathing quickly, every sinew and muscle stretched to a point of yearning that made a nonsense of his legendary self-control.

He yanked his jumper off and heard her sigh with pleasure, a little, soft sigh that was uniquely hers. His eyes were still half-closed and he inhaled slightly to accommodate

her fumbling fingers as they travelled downwards to un-
button and unzip his jeans.

Outside a watery sun was making itself known, pushing
through the blanket of leaden grey of the past few days.
Like an unfamiliar visitor, it threaded its way tentatively
into the kitchen, picking up the rich hues of her hair and
the smooth, creamy whiteness of her skin.

He stilled as she lowered herself to begin pulling down
his jeans, taking his boxers with them until they were at
his ankles and he stepped out of them and kicked them
to one side.

He couldn't withhold his grunt of intense satisfaction
as she began delicately to lick the tip of his erection. He
was so aroused that it was painful and as he looked down
at the crown of her head, and her pink, darting tongue as
it continued to tease him, he became even more aroused.

'You're driving me crazy, woman...' His voice was un-
steady, as were his hands as he coiled his fingers into her
hair.

Brianna didn't say anything. His nakedness had her
firing on all cylinders and his vulnerability, glimpses of
which she only caught when they were making love, was
the most powerful of aphrodisiacs. She took him in her
mouth, loving the way every atom of pleasure seemed to
be transmitted from him to her via invisible, powerful
pathways. As she sucked and teased, her hands caressed,
and she was aware of his big, strong body shaking ever
so slightly. How could he make her feel so powerful and
so helpless at the same time?

She was so damp, her body so urgent for his, that she
itched to rip off her clothes. Her jumper was back in place
and it felt heavy and uncomfortable against her sensitised
skin. She gasped as he pulled her up, and she obediently
lifted her arms so that he could remove the offending

jumper. The cool air hit her heated breasts like a soothing balm.

'I can't make it to the bedroom…' He breathed heavily as she wriggled out of the jeans and then he hoisted
her onto the kitchen table, shoving aside the remnants of
their breakfast—the jar of marmalade, the little ceramic
butter dish, the striped jug with milk. Surprisingly, nothing crashed to the ground in the process.

When he stood back, he marvelled at the sight of her
naked beauty: her arms outstretched, her eyes heavy with
the same lust that was coursing through his bloodstream
like an unstoppable virus.

Her vibrant hair streamed out around her, formed a
tangle over one breast, and the glimpse of a pink nipple
peeping out was like something from an erotic X-rated
magazine. Her parted legs were an invitation he couldn't
refuse, nor was his body allowing him the luxury of fore-
play. As she raised her knees, he embedded himself into
her in one hard, forceful thrust and then he lifted her up
and drove again into her, building a furious rhythm and
somehow ending up with her pressed against the kitchen
wall, her legs wrapped around him.

Her hair trailed over her shoulder, down her back, a
silky mass of rich auburn. He felt her in every part of him
in a way that had never happened with any woman before.
He didn't get it, but he liked it. He was holding her underneath her sexy, rounded bottom and as he thrust long and
deep into her he looked down at her little breasts bounc-
ing in time to their bodies. The tips of her nipples were
stiff and swollen, the big, flattened pink discs encircling
them swollen and puffy. Every square inch of her body
was an unbelievable turn-on and, even as he felt the satiny
tightness of her sheath around him, he would have liked

to close his mouth over one of those succulent nipples so that he could feast on its honeyed sweetness.

They came as one, their bodies fused, their breathing mirroring each other.

'That was…indescribable.' He eased her down and they stood facing one another, completely naked. Sanity began restoring itself, seeping through the haze of his hot, replete satisfaction. He swore under his breath and turned away. 'The condom…it seems to have split…'

Brianna's eyes widened with shock. She went over to her bundle of clothes and began getting dressed. He looked horrified. There was a heavy, laden silence as he likewise began getting dressed.

'It's okay. It takes more than one mistake for a person to get pregnant! If you read any magazine there are always stories of women trying for months, *years,* to conceive…' Her menstrual cycle had always been erratic so it was easy to believe that.

Leo shook his head and raked his fingers through his hair. 'This is a nightmare.'

'I won't get pregnant! I'm one-hundred per cent sure about that! I know my body. You don't have to look as though…as though the sky has fallen in!'

Yes, he was a nomad. Yes, he had just jacked in his job to embark on a precarious and unpredictable career. But did he have to look so damned *appalled*? And then, hard on the heels of that thought, came wrenching dismay at the insanity of thinking that a pregnancy wouldn't be the end of the world. God, what was she *thinking*? Had she gone completely *mad*?

She snatched the various bits and pieces left on the kitchen table and began slamming them into cupboards.

'God knows, you're probably right,' he gritted, catching her by the arm and pulling her round to face him. 'But

I've had sufficient experience of the fairer sex to know that they—'

'*What* experience? What are you talking about?'

Leo paused. Money bred suspicion and he had always been suspicious enough to know that it was a mistake to trust contraception to the opposite sex.

Except, how could he say that when he was supposed to be a struggling writer existing on the remnants of his savings from whatever two-bit job he had been in? How could he confess that five years previously he had had a scare with a woman in the dying stages of their relationship. The Pill she claimed to have been on, which she then later denied… Two weeks of hell cursing himself for having been a trusting idiot and, in the end, thankfully there had been no pregnancy. There was nothing he could have done in the circumstances, but a split condom was still bad news.

But how could he concede that his vast financial reserves made him a natural target for potential gold- diggers?

'You must really think that you're such a desirable catch that women just can't help wanting to tie you down by falling pregnant!'

'So you're telling me that I'm *not* a desirable catch?' Crisis over. Deception, even as an acceptable means to an end, was proving unsavoury. He smiled a sexy half-smile, clearing his head of any shade of guilt, telling himself that a chance in a million did not constitute anything to get worked up about.

'There are better options…' The tension slowly seeped out of her although she was tempted to pry further, to find out who these determined women were—the ones he had bedded, the ones who had wanted more.

She tried to picture him in his other life, sitting in a cubicle behind a desk somewhere with a computer in front

of him. She couldn't. He seemed so at home in casual
clothes; dealing with the snow; making sure the fireplace
was well supplied with logs; doing little handyman jobs
around the place, the sort she usually ended up having
to pay someone to do for her. He now had a stubbly six
o'clock shadow on his jawline because he told her that he
saw no point in shaving twice a day. He was a man made
for the great outdoor life. And yet...

'You were going to tell me about Bridget,' Leo said
casually, moving to sit at the table and shoving his chair
out so that he could stretch his legs in front of him. 'Before you rudely decided to interrupt the conversation by
demanding sex.'

Brianna laughed. Just like that, whatever mood had
swept over her like an ugly, freak wave looming unexpectedly from calm waters dissolved and disappeared.

'As I said, you'll like her.' She began unloading the
dishwasher, her mind only half-focused on what she was
saying; she was looking ahead to the technicalities of keeping the pub shut, wondering how long she could afford
the luxury, trying to figure out whether her battered four-
wheel drive could make it to the village so that she could
stock up on food...

Leo's lips twisted with disdain. 'Funnily enough, whenever someone has said that to me in the past I'm guaranteed to dislike the person in question.' For the first time,
he thought of his birth mother in a way that wasn't exclusively abstract, wasn't merely a jigsaw piece that had to be
located and slotted in for the completed picture.

What did she look like? Tall, short, fat, thin...? And
from whom had he inherited his non-Irish looks? His
adoptive parents had both been small, neat and fair-
haired. He had towered above them, dark-haired, dark-

eyed, olive-skinned…as physically different from them as chalk from cheese.

He stamped down his surge of curiosity and reminded himself that he wasn't here to form any kind of relationship with the woman but merely finally to lay an uncertain past to rest. Anger, curiosity and confusion were unhappy life companions and the faster he dispensed with them, the better.

'You're very suspicious, Leo.' Brianna thought back to his vehement declaration that women couldn't be trusted when it came to contraception. 'Everyone loves Bridget.'

'You mentioned that she didn't have a…partner.' A passing remark on which Brianna had not elaborated. Now, Leo was determined to prise as much information out of her as he could, information that would be a useful backdrop for when he met the woman the following day. It was a given, he recognised, that some people might think him heartless to extract information from the woman he was sleeping with, but he decided to view that as a necessity—something that couldn't be helped, something to be completely disassociated from the fact that they were lovers, and extremely passionate lovers at that.

Life, generally speaking, was all about people using people. If he hadn't learned that directly from his adoptive parents, then he certainly must have had it cemented somewhere deep within his consciousness. Perhaps, and in spite of his remarkably stable background, the fact that he was adopted had allowed a seed of cynicism to run rampant over the years.

'She doesn't talk much about that.'

'No? Why not? You're her…what would you say…confidante? I would have thought that she would find it a comfort to talk to you about whatever happened. I mean, you've known each other how long? Were your parents friends with the woman?'

Brianna laughed. 'Oh, gosh, no!' She glanced round the kitchen, making sure that all her jobs were done. 'Bridget is a relative newcomer to this area.'

'Really…' Leo murmured. 'I was under the impression that she was a valued, long-standing member of the community.' He almost laughed at the thought of that. Valued member of the community? Whilst jettisoning an unwanted child like an item of disposable garbage? Only in a community of jailbirds would someone like that have been up for consideration as a valued member.

'But now you tell me that she's a newcomer. How long has she been living in the area?'

'Eight years tops.'

'And before that?'

Brianna shot him a look of mild curiosity but, when he smiled that smile at her, that crooked, sexy half-smile, she felt any niggling questions hovering on the tip of her tongue disappear.

'You're asking a lot of questions,' she murmured breathlessly. He signalled for her to come closer and she did, until he could wrap his arms around her and hold her close.

'Like I said, I have a curious mind.' He breathed in the clean floral scent of her hair and for a few seconds forgot everything. 'You shouldn't have put your jumper back on,' he remarked in a voice that thrilled her to the core. 'I like looking at your breasts. Just the perfect mouthful…'

'And I have calls to make if I'm to keep the pub shut!' She slapped away his wandering hand, even though she would have liked nothing more than to drag him up to the bedroom to lay claim to him. 'And you have a book to work on!'

'I'd rather work on you…'

'Thank goodness Bridget isn't here. She'd be horrified.'

Leo nearly burst out laughing. 'And is this because she's the soul of prurience? You still haven't told me where she came from. Maybe she was a nun in her former life?' He began strolling out of the kitchen towards the sitting room with the open fire which he had requisitioned as his working space. His computer was shut and there was a stack of novels by the side of it, books he had picked from her collection. He had already started two, abandoned them both and was reaching the conclusion that soul-searching novels with complicated themes were not for him.

'There's no need to be sarcastic.' Brianna hovered by the table as he sat down. She knew that he demanded complete privacy when he was writing, sectioning off a corner of the sitting area, his back to the window. Yet somehow it felt as though their conversation was not quite at an end, even though he wasn't asking any further questions.

'Was I?'

His cool, dark eyes rested on her and she flushed and traced an invisible pattern with her finger on the table. Was there something she was missing? Some important link she was failing to connect?

'You've known this woman for a few years...'

'Nearly seven. She came to the pub one evening on her own.'

'In other words, she has a drinking habit?'

'No! She'd moved to the area and she thought it might be a way of meeting people! We have quiz nights here once a month. She used to come for the quiz nights, and after a while we got chatting.'

'Chatting about where she had come from? Oh no; of course, you know nothing about that. And I'm guessing not many clues as to what she was doing here either? It's a small place for a woman who wants to meet people...'

'It's a community. We make outsiders feel welcome.'
She blushed at her unwitting choice of words. 'I felt sorry
for her,' Brianna continued hurriedly. 'I started an over-
forties' quiz night, ladies only, so that she could get talking to some of them.'

Leo was mentally joining the dots and was arriving at
a picture not dissimilar to the one he had always had of
the woman who had given birth to him—with a few extra
trimmings thrown in for good measure.

A new life and a new start for someone with a dubious
past to conceal. Tellingly, no one knew about this past life,
including the girl who had supposedly become her anchor
in the community.

It didn't take a genius to figure out that, where there
were secrets that required concealment, those secrets were
dirty little ones. He had received half a picture from Brianna, he was certain of it—the rosy half, the half that
didn't conform to his expectations.

'And you did all this without having a clue as to this
woman's past?'

'I don't need to know every single detail about someone's past to recognise a good person when I see one!'
She folded her arms tightly around her and glared down
at him. She should have let him carry on with his writing. Instead, she had somehow found herself embroiled
in an argument she hadn't courted and was dismayed at
how sick it made her feel. 'I don't want to argue with you
about this, Leo.'

'You're young. You're generous and trusting. You're
about to give house room to someone whose past is a mystery.' He drew an uneasy parallel with his own circumstance, here at the pub under a very dubious cloud of deceit
indeed, and dismissed any similarities. He was, after all,

as upstanding and law-abiding as they came. No shady past here.

On the very point of tipping over into anger that he was in the process of dismissing her as the sort of gullible fool who might be taken in by someone who was up to no good, another thought lodged in the back of her mind. It took up residence next to the pernicious feel-good seed that had been planted when she had considered the possibility that he might not be welcoming Bridget because he cherished their one-to-one solitude.

Was he seriously *worried* about her? And if he was… That thought joined the other links in the chain that seemed to represent the nebulous beginnings of a commitment…

She knew that she was treading on very dangerous ground even having these crazy day dreams but she couldn't push them away. With her heart beating like a jack hammer, she attempted to squash the thrilling notion that he was concerned about her welfare.

'Do you think that my friend might be a homicidal maniac in the guise of a friendly and rather lonely woman?'

Leo frowned darkly. Brianna's thoughts about Bridget were frankly none of his concern, and irrelevant to the matter in hand, but he couldn't contain a surge of sudden, disorienting protectiveness.

Brianna had had to put her dreams and ambitions on hold to take charge of her father's failing business, whilst at the same time trying to deal with the double heartbreak of her father's death and her lover's abandonment. It should have been enough to turn her into an embittered shrew. Yet there was a transparent openness and natural honesty about her that had surfaced through the challenging debris of her past. She laughed a lot, she seldom complained and she was the sort of girl who would never spare an act of kindness.

'When people remove themselves for no apparent reason to start a new beginning, it's usually because they're running away from something.'

'You mean the police?'

Leo shrugged and tugged her towards him so that she collapsed on his lap with a stifled laugh. 'What if she turns into an unwanted pub guest who overstays her welcome?' He angled her so that she was straddling him on his lap and delicately pushed up the jumper.

'Don't be silly,' Brianna contradicted him breathlessly. 'You should get down to your writing. I should continue with my stock taking…'

In response to that, Leo eased the jumper off and gazed at her small, pert breasts with rampant satisfaction. He began licking one of her nipples, a lazy, light, teasing with the tip of his tongue, a connoisseur sampling an exquisite and irresistible offering.

'She has a perfectly nice little house of her own.' There was something wonderfully decadent about doing this, sitting on his lap in the middle of the empty pub, watching him as he nuzzled her breast as if he had all the time in the world and was in no hurry to take things to the next level.

'But—' Leo broke off. 'Here…' he flicked his tongue against her other nipple '…she would have…' he suckled for a few seconds, drawing her breast into his mouth '…you…' a few kisses on the soft roundness until he could feel her shiver and shudder '…to take care of her; cook her food…'

He held one of her breasts in his hand so that it was pushed up to him, the nipple engorged and throbbing, and he delicately sucked it. 'Brianna, she might seem perfectly harmless to you.' With a sigh, he leaned back in the chair and gave her tingling breasts a momentary reprieve. 'But what do you do if she decides that a cosy room in a pub, surrounded by people and hands-on waitress service, is more appealing than an empty house and the exertion of having to cook her own food?'

At no point was he inclined to give the woman the benefit of the doubt. In his experience, people rarely deserved that luxury, and certainly not someone with her particular shady history.

Never one ever to have been possessive or protective about the women in his life, he was a little shaken by the fierce streak suddenly racing through him that was repelled by the thought of someone taking advantage of the girl sitting on his lap with the easy smile, the flushed face and tousled hair.

'You need to exercise caution,' he muttered grimly. He raked his fingers through his hair and scowled, as though she had decided to disagree with him even though she hadn't uttered a word.

'Then maybe,' Brianna teased him lightly, 'you should stick around and make sure I don't end up becoming a patsy...'

The journey here should have taken no time at all; his stay should have been over in a matter of a couple of days. There were meetings waiting for him and urgent trips abroad that could only be deferred for so long. It had never been his intention to turn this simple fact-finding exercise into a drama in three parts.

'Maybe I should,' he heard himself say softly. 'For a while...'

'And you can chase her away if she turns out to be an unscrupulous squatter who wants to take advantage of me.' She laughed as though nothing could be more ridiculous and raised her hand to caress his cheek.

Leo circled her slim wrist with his fingers in a vice-like grip. 'Oh, if she tries that,' he said in a voice that made her shiver, 'she'll discover just what a ruthless opponent I could prove to be—and just how regrettable it can be to cross my path.'

# CHAPTER FIVE

THE SNOW HAD stopped. As grey and leaden as the skies
had been for a seemingly unstoppable length of time, the
sun now emerged, turning a bleak winter landscape into
a scene from a movie: bright-blue skies and fields of purest white.

Bridget's arrival had been delayed by a day, during
which time Leo had allowed the subject of her dubious,
unknown past to be dropped. No more hassle warning
Brianna about accepting the cuckoo in the nest. No more
words of caution that the person she might have considered
a friend and surrogate mother might very well turn out to
be someone all set to take full advantage of her generous
nature and hospitality. There would be fallout from this
gesture of putting the woman up while she recuperated;
he was certain of that and he would be the man to deal
with it. So he might never have specialised in the role of
'knight in shining armour' in his life before, but he was
happy with his decision.

London would have to take a little back seat for a while.
He was managing to keep on top of things just fine via
his computer, tablet and smartphone and, if anything dramatic arose, then he could always shoot down to sort it out.

All told, the prospect of being holed up in the middle
of nowhere was not nearly as tedious as he might have

imagined. In fact, all things considered, he was in tre-
mendously high spirits.

Of course, Brianna was a hell of a long way responsible for that. He glanced up lazily from his computer to
the sofa where she was sitting amidst piles of paperwork.
Her hair was a rich tumble over her shoulders and she was
cross-legged, leaning forward and chewing her lip as she
stared at her way-past-its-sell-by-date computer which was
on the low coffee table in front of her.

In a couple of hours the ambulance would be bringing
his destiny towards him. For the moment, he intended to
enjoy his woman. He closed the report in front of him and
stood up, stretching, flexing his muscles.

From across the small, cosy room, Brianna looked up
and, as always happened, her eyes lingered, absorbing the
beautiful sight of his long, lean body; the way his jeans
rode low on his hips; the way he filled out her father's
checked flannel shirt in just the right way. He had loosely
rolled the sleeves to his elbow and his strong, brown forearms, liberally sprinkled with dark hair, sent a little shiver
of pleasurable awareness rippling through her.

'You should get a new computer.' Leo strolled towards
her and then stood so that he was looking down at the columns of numbers flickering on the screen at him. 'Something faster, more up-to-date.'

'And I should have a holiday, somewhere warm and far
away… And I'll do both just as soon as I have the money.'
Brianna sighed and sat back, keenly aware of him looking over her. 'I just want to get all this stuff out of the way
before Bridget gets here. I want to be able to devote some
quality time to her.'

Leo massaged her neck from behind. Her hair, newly
washed, was soft and silky. The baggy, faded pink jumper
was the most unrevealing garment she could have worn

but he had fast discovered that there was no need for her
to wear anything that outlined her figure. His imagination
was well supplied with all the necessary tools for providing graphic images of her body that kept him in a state of
semi-permanent arousal.

'Was the urgent trip to the local supermarket part of the
quality-service package?' He moved round to sit next to
her, shoving some of the papers out of the way and wondering how on earth she could keep track of her paperwork
when there seemed to be no discernible order to any of it.

'I know you don't agree with what I'm doing; I know
you think I should just leave her to get on with things on
her own but—'

'This conversational road is guaranteed to lead to a
dead end,' he drawled smoothly. 'Let's do ourselves a favour and not travel down it.'

'You enjoyed the supermarket experience.' Brianna
changed the subject immediately. She didn't want an argument. She didn't even want a mild disagreement, and she
knew what his feelings were on the subject of their soon-
to-be visitor, even though he had backed off from making any further disparaging remarks about her naïvety in
taking in someone whose entire life hadn't been laid out
on a plate for her perusal.

'It was…novel.' Actually, Leo couldn't recall the last
time he had set foot in a supermarket. He paid someone
to deal with the hassle of all that.

'Margaret Connelly has only just opened up that place.
Actually, it's not a supermarket as such.'

'I'd noticed.'

'More of a…a…'

'Cosy space filled to overflowing with all manner of
things, of which food is only one component? Brussels
sprouts nestling next to fishing tackle…?'

'The lay out can seem a bit eccentric but the food's all fresh and locally sourced.'

Leo grinned, swivelled her so that she had her back to him and began massaging her shoulders. 'You sound like an advertisement for a food magazine. I'm going to have to put my foot down if you're thinking of slaving over a hot stove preparing dishes on this woman's whim.'

Brianna relaxed into the massage and smiled with contentment. She felt a thrill of pleasure at the possessive edge to his voice. 'She has to be on a bland diet—doctor's orders.'

'That's irrelevant. You're not going to be running up and down those stairs because someone rings a bell and wants a cup of tea immediately.'

'*You* could always do the running for me if you think I'm too fragile to cope.'

Leo's lips curled with derision and he fought down the impulse to burst into sardonic laughter. 'Running and doing errands for people isn't something I do.'

'Especially not in this instance,' Brianna said, remembering that he *was*, after all, a paying guest despite their unusual arrangement. He had given her a shocking amount of money for his stay thus far, way too much, and had informed her that it was something to do with company expenses owed to him before he'd quit his job. She hadn't quite understood his explanation. Nor had he backed down when she refused to take the full amount.

'Take it,' he had ordered, 'Or I'll just have to find another establishment that will accommodate what I want to pay. And I shall end up having to take taxis here to see you. You wouldn't want to add that further cost to a poor, struggling writer, would you?'

'What do you mean?' Leo stilled now.

'I mean you're a customer. Running up and down stairs

isn't something I would ask you to do. That would be ridiculous. I would never take advantage of you like that.'

'But you *would* take advantage of me in other ways… because I happen to enjoy you taking advantage of me in all those other imaginative ways of yours…'

'Is *sex* all you ever think about?' she murmured, settling back against him and sighing as he slipped his hands underneath her jumper to fondle her breasts.

No. Sex most certainly had never been *all* he thought about. In fact, Leo contemplated with some bemusement, although he had always enjoyed an exceptionally varied and active sex life it had never been at the top of his priorities. Sex, and likewise women, had always taken a back seat to the more important driving force in his life, which was his work.

'You bring out the primitive in me,' he said softly into her ear. 'Is it my fault that your body drives me insane?' He relaxed into the sprawling sofa so that he had Brianna half-lying on top of him, her back pressed against his torso, her hair tangled against his chest. He removed one hand to brush some of her hair from his cheek and returned his hand to her jeans to rest it lightly on her hip. A stray sheet of paper wafted to the ground, joining a disconcerting bundle already there.

Brianna's body was responding as it always did, with galloping excitement and sweet anticipation. She might very well joke that sex was the only thing on his mind, but it certainly seemed to have taken over all her responses as well. Even the problem supplier she knew she had to deal with urgently was forgotten as she undid the button and zip of her jeans.

'Tut, tut, tut; you're going to have to do better than that, my darling. How am I expected to get my hand where it wants to be?'

Brianna giggled softly. He had no hang-ups about where they made love. His lack of inhibition was liberating and it worked in tandem with her own period of celibacy to release an explosion of passion she had never experienced in her life before. She couldn't seem to get enough of him.

She wriggled out of her jeans and he chuckled.

'For someone with a body like yours, I'm always amazed that you've stuck to the functional underwear...' He thought about seeing her in something small, lacy and sexy, lying in his super-king-sized bed in his penthouse apartment in Chelsea.

The thought was random, springing from nowhere and establishing itself with such graphic clarity that he drew in his breath sharply with shock.

Hell, where was his mind going? This was a situation that was intensely enjoyable but it only functioned within very definite parameters. Like it or not, they were operating within a box, a box of his own making, and freedom from that box in any way, shape or form was a possibility that was not to be entertained.

With that in mind, he cleared his head of any inappropriate, wandering thoughts about her being in his apartment. Crazy.

'Is that how you like your women?' Brianna asked casually. He never spoke about his love life. A sudden thought occurred to her and, although this hardly seemed the time for a deep, meaningful conversation, she had to carry on regardless. 'Is that why you're here?'

'What are you talking about?'

Brianna wriggled so that she was on her side, still nestled between his legs, and she looked up at him, breathing in that clean, tangy scent that always seemed to scramble all her thoughts. His hand was curved on her hip, fingers dipping against her stomach. Even that small, casual contact did devastating things to her already hot, aroused body. She was slippery and wet, and it was mad, because she had to get things together before Bridget arrived.

'You know, all the way from London.'

'No clue as to what you're talking about.'

'Never mind. We need to start tidying up.' She sighed. 'Bridget's going to be here soon.'

'Didn't they say that they would telephone you before they left the hospital?'

'Yes, but…'

'No phone call yet.' After the disturbing tangent his thoughts had taken only moments before when he had imagined her in his apartment, the last thing Leo wanted was a heart-to-heart. He wanted to touch her; touching her was like a magic antidote to thinking. Hell, he had worked while he had been here, but his mind had not been on the cut and thrust of business deals with its customary focus. This was as close to a holiday as he had had in years, and the last thing he had expected when he had started on this journey of discovery.

He reached under her knickers, a dull beige with not a scrap of lace in sight, and slid his finger against the wet crease, seeking out the little nub of her clitoris. This was so much better than talking and a damn sight more worthwhile than the sudden chaos of thoughts that had earlier afflicted him.

Brianna moaned softly as he continued to rub. She squirmed and sighed and half-closed her eyes, her nostrils flaring and her breathing thickening the closer she came to a point of no return.

Questions still hovered at the back of her mind like pesky insects nipping at her conscience, refusing to go away, but right now she couldn't focus on any of that. Right now, as the movement of his strong, sure hand picked up speed, she moaned and arched her body and wave upon wave of pleasure surged through her. Lying with her back to him, she couldn't see his face, only his one hand moving inside her while the other was flattened against her thigh and his legs, spread to accommodate her body between them. But she knew that he was watching her body as he brought her to orgasm and the thought of that was wantonly exciting.

She was aware of her uneven, shaky breathing as she lay back and let her heated body return to planet Earth.

For a few seconds, there was silence. Leo linked his fingers on her stomach and absently noted the way they glistened with her honeyed wetness.

'I'm going to start clearing all my paperwork away,' she said eventually. 'I don't seem to have made much progress with our snack supplier. I'm going to have a shower.' She eased herself over his legs and off the sofa, and began tidying the papers which were strewn everywhere. She didn't bother to put on her jeans, instead choosing to scoop them up and drape them over one arm.

It all came down to sex. She knew that she was being silly for objecting to that because this was a situation that was never going to last longer than two minutes. It was something she had jumped into, eyes wide open, throwing caution to the winds and accepting it for what it was, and there was no excuse now for wanting more than what had been laid on the table.

Except…had she thought that this perfect stranger would possess the sort of complex personality that she would end up finding strangely compulsive?

Could she ever have imagined that an unexpected, astounding, elemental physical attraction would turn into something that seemed to have her in its hold? That taking a walk on the wild side, breaking out of the box for just a little while, would have repercussions that struck a chord of fear into her?

She wanted more. She couldn't even begin to think of him leaving, carrying on with his travels. He had entered her life, and what had previously been bland, dull and grey was now Technicolor-bright. She alternated between reading all sorts of things behind his words and actions and then telling herself that she really shouldn't.

'You never said…' Brianna begin heading up the stairs, carrying as much with her as she could: files, her jeans and her trainers, which she didn't bother to stick on completely.

Behind her, Leo scooped up the remainder of the files and began following her.

'Never said what?'

'All those women you're so cynical about…' She paused to look at him over her shoulder. 'The ones who wear lacy underwear…'

'Did I ever say that? I don't recall.'

'You didn't have to. I can read between the lines.' She spun back round and headed towards her suite of rooms, straight to the study, where she dumped all the files she had been carrying. She stood back and watched as he deposited the remainder of them, including her computer, which was as heavy as a barrow full of bricks, and—yes, he was right—in desperate need of updating.

Brianna took in his guarded, shuttered expression and knew instinctively that she was treading on quicksand, even though he hadn't rushed in with any angry words telling her to mind her own business. She could see it on his face. Her heart was beating so fiercely that she could almost hear it in the still quiet of the room.

'I'm going to have a shower,' she mumbled, backing out of the little office. 'On my own, if you don't mind.'

Leo frowned and raked his fingers through his hair, but he didn't move a muscle.

She wanted to *talk*. Talk about what? His exes? What was the point of that? When it came to women and meaningful conversations, they invariably led down the same road: a dead end. He wasn't entirely sure where his aversion to commitment came from and he knew, if he were honest, that his parents would have wanted to see him travel down the traditional route of marriage and kids by thirty—but there it was; he hadn't. He had never felt the inclination. Perhaps a feeling of security was something that developed in a mother's womb and having been given up for adoption, by definition, had wiped that out and the security of making money, something tangible he could control, had taken its place.

At any rate, the minute any woman started showing signs of crossing the barriers he had firmly erected around himself, they were relegated to history.

He told himself that there should be no difficulty in this particular relationship following the same course because he could see, from the look in her eyes, that whatever chat she wanted to have was not going to begin and end with the choice of underwear his women were accustomed to wearing.

He told himself that in fact it would be *easier* to end this relationship because, in essence, it had never really functioned in his real life. It had functioned as something sweet and satisfying within a bubble. And within a day or two, once he had met his birth mother and put any unanswered questions to rest, he would be gone.

So there definitely was *no* point to a lengthy heart-to-,heart. He strolled into the bedroom and glanced down at the snow which was already beginning to thaw.

She emerged minutes later from the shower with a towel

wrapped round her, her long hair piled up on top of her head and held in place with a hair grip. Tendrils had escaped and framed her heart-shaped face. She looked impossibly young and vulnerable.

'What are you doing in my bedroom?'

'Okay. So I go out with women who seem to spend a lot of money on fancy underwear.' He glowered at her. 'I don't know what that has to do with anything.' He watched as she rummaged in her drawers in silence and fetched out some faded jogging bottoms and a rugby-style jumper, likewise faded.

Brianna knew that a few passing remarks had escalated into something that she found unsettling. She didn't want to pry into his life. She wanted to be the adult who took this on board, no questions asked and no strings attached. Unfortunately...

She disappeared back into the bathroom, changed and returned to find him still standing in an attitude of challenging defensiveness by the bedroom window.

'You wanted to talk...' he prompted, in defiance of common sense. 'Are you jealous that I've had lovers? That they've been the sort of women who—?'

'Don't run pubs, live on a shoestring and wear functional underwear from department stores? No, I'm not jealous. Why would I be?'

'Good. Because, personally, I don't do jealousy.' It occurred to Leo that there were a number of things he didn't do when it came to his personal relationships and yet, here he was, doing one of them right now: having a *talk*.

'Have we ended up in bed because you think I make a change?' She took a deep breath and looked him squarely in the face. He was so beautiful. He literally took her breath away. 'From all those women you went out with?' If *she* found him beautiful, if he blew *her* mind away, then why wouldn't he have had the same effect on hordes of other women?

'No! That's an absurd question.'

'Is it?' She turned on her heel and began back down the stairs to the bar area where she proceeded to do some unnecessary tidying. He lounged against the bar, hands in his pockets, and watched her as she worked. She appeared to be in no hurry to proceed with the conversation she had initiated. The longer the silence stretched between them, the more disgruntled Leo became.

Moving to stand directly in front of her, so that she was forced to stop arranging the beer mats in straight lines on the counter, he said, 'If there's any comparison to be done, then you win hands down.'

Brianna felt a stupid surge of pleasure. 'I'm guessing you *would* say that, considering we're sleeping together and you're pretty much stuck here.'

'Am I? The snow seems to be on its way out.' They weren't touching each other, but he could feel her as forcibly as if they had been lying naked on her bed.

'How long do you intend to stay?' She flushed and glanced down at her feet before taking a deep breath and looking at him without flinching. 'I'm going to keep the pub closed for another fortnight but just in case, er, bookings come in for the rooms, it would be helpful for me to know when yours might be free to, er, rent out…'

And this, Leo thought, was the perfect opportunity to put a date in the calendar. It was as obvious as the nose on his face that her reason for wanting to find out when he would be leaving had nothing to do with a possible mystery surge in bookings for the rooms. He didn't like being put in a position of feeling trapped.

'I told you I'd stick around, make sure you didn't get ripped off or taken advantage of by this so-called best

buddy of yours,' he said roughly. 'I won't be going anywhere until I'm satisfied that you're okay on that score.
Satisfied? No; you're not. What else is on your mind, Brianna? Spit it out and then I can disappear for a shower
and some work and leave you to get on with your female
bonding in peace.'

Brianna shrugged. Everything about his body language
suggested that he was in no mood to stand here, answering questions. Perhaps, she thought, answering questions
was something else he *didn't do* when it came to women.
Like jealousy. And yet he wasn't moving. 'Did you end up
here on the back of a bad relationship?' she asked bluntly.
She shot him a defiant look from under her lashes. 'I know
you don't want me to ask lots of questions...'

'Did I ever say that?'

'You don't have to.'

'Because, let me guess, you seem to have a hot line to
my thoughts!' He scowled. Far from backing away from
an interrogation he didn't want and certainly didn't need,
his feet appeared to be disobeying the express orders of his
brain. Against all odds, he wanted to wipe that defensive,
guarded expression from her face. 'And no, I did not end
up here on the back of a bad relationship.' He had ended
up here because...

Leo flushed darkly, uncomfortable with where his
thoughts were drifting.

'I'm sleeping with you, and I know it's going to end
soon, but I still want to know that you're not using me as
some sort of sticking plaster while you try to recover from
a broken heart.'

'I've never suffered from a broken heart, Brianna.' Leo
smiled crookedly at her and stroked the side of her face
with his finger.

Just then her mobile buzzed and after only a few seconds on the phone she said to him, 'Bridget's had her final check-up with the consultant and they're going to be setting off in about half an hour. They'll probably be here in about an hour and a half or so. Depends on the roads, but the main roads will all be gritted. It's only the country lanes around here that are still a little snowed up.'

*An hour and a half.* Leo's lips thinned but, despite the impending meeting with his mother, one which he had quietly anticipated for a number of years ever since he had tracked down her whereabouts, his focus remained exclusively on the girl standing in front of him.

'Everyone has suffered from a broken heart at some point.' She reverted to her original topic.

'I'm the exception to the rule.'

'You've never been in love?'

'You say that as though it's inconceivable. No. Never. And stop looking at me as though I've suddenly turned into an alien life-form. Are you telling me that, after your experience with the guy you thought you would be spending your life with, you're still glad to have *been in love*?'

He lounged against the bar and stared down at her. He had become so accustomed to wearing jeans and an assortment of her father's old plaid flannel shirts, a vast array of which she seemed to have kept, that he idly wondered what it would feel like returning to his snappy handmade suits, his Italian shoes, the silk ties, driving one of his three cars or having Harry chauffeur him. He would return to the reality of high- powered meetings, life in the fast lane, private planes and first-class travel to all four corners of the globe.

Here, he could be a million miles away, living on another planet. Was that why he now found himself inclined to have this type of conversation? The sort of touchy-feely conversation that he had always made a point of steering well clear from? Really, since when had he ever been into probing any woman about her thoughts and feelings about past loves?

'Of course I am,' Brianna exclaimed stoutly. 'It may have crashed and burned, but there were moments of real happiness.'

Leo frowned. Real happiness? What did she mean by that? Good sex? He didn't care much for a trip down happiness lane with her. If she felt inclined to reminisce over the good old days, conveniently forgetting the misery that had been dished up to her in the end, then he was not the man with the listening ear.

'How salutary that you can ignore the fact that you were taken for a ride for years… Are you still in touch with the creep?'

Brianna frowned and tried to remember what the creep looked like. 'No,' she said honestly. 'I haven't got a clue what he's up to. The last I heard from one of my friends from uni, he had gone abroad to work for some important law firm in New York. He's disappeared completely. I was heartbroken at the time, but it doesn't mean that I'm not glad I met him, and it doesn't mean that I don't hope to meet that someone special at some point in the future.'

And as she said that a very clear picture of Mr Special floated into her mind. He was approximately six-two with bronzed skin, nearly black hair and lazy, midnight-dark eyes that could send shivers racing up and down her spine. He came in a package that had carried very clear health warnings but still she had fallen for him like a stupid teenager with more hormones than common sense.

Fallen *in lust* with him, she thought with feverish panic. She hadn't had a relationship with a guy for years! And then he had come along, drop-dead gorgeous, with all the seductive anonymity of a stranger—a writer, no less. Was it any wonder that she had fallen *in lust* with him?

Was that why she could now feel herself becoming *clingy*? Not wanting him to go? Losing all sense of perspective?

'And no one special is on the scene here?' Leo drawled lazily. 'Surely the lads must be queuing up for you...'

Of course there had been nibbles, but Brianna had never been interested. She had reasoned to herself that she just didn't have the time; that her big, broken love affair had irreparably damaged something inside her; that, just as soon as the pub really began paying its way, she would jump back into the dating world.

All lies. She could have had all the time in the world, a fully paid-up functioning heart and a pub that turned over a million pounds a year in profit and she still wouldn't have been drawn to anyone—because she had been waiting for just the moment when Leo Spencer walked through the door, tall, dark and dangerous, like a gunslinger in a Western movie.

'I'm not interested in anything serious at the moment,' she said faintly. 'I have loads of time. Bridget should be arriving any minute now.'

'At least an hour left to go...' How was it possible to shove all thoughts of his so-called mother out of his head? He had almost forgotten that the woman was on her way.

'I need to go and get her room ready.'

'Haven't you already done that? The potpourri and the new throw from the jack-of-all-trades supermarket?'

She had. But suddenly she wanted nothing more than to escape his suffocating masculine presence, find a spot where she could straighten out her tangled thoughts.

'Well, I want to make sure that it's just right,' she said sharply.

Leo stepped aside. 'And I think I'll go and have a shower and do something productive with my time in my room.'

'You don't have to disappear! You're a paying guest, Leo. You can come down and do your writing in your usual place. Bridget and I won't make any noise at all. She'll probably just want to rest.'

'I'll let the two of you do your bonding in peace,' he murmured. 'I'll come down for dinner. I take it you'll be cooking for three?'

'You know I will, and please don't start on the business of me being a mug.'

Leo held up both hands in a gesture of mock-indignation that she could even contemplate such a thing.

Brianna shot him a reluctant smile. 'You wait and see. You'll end up loving her as much as I do.'

'Yes. We'll certainly wait and see,' Leo delivered with a coolness that Brianna felt rather than saw, because his expression was mildly amused. She wondered if she had perhaps imagined it.

Leo remained where he was while she disappeared upstairs to do her last check of the bedroom where Bridget would be staying, doubtless making sure that the sheets were in place with hospital precision, corners tucked in just so.

His mouth curled with derision. The thought of her being taken advantage of filled him with disgust. The thought of her putting her trust in a woman who would inevitably turn out not to be the person she thought she was made his stomach turn. He could think of no other woman whose trusting nature should be allowed to remain intact.

He slammed his clenched fist against the wall and gritted his teeth. He had come here predisposed to dislike the woman who had given birth to him and then given him away. He was even more predisposed to dislike her as the woman who, in the final analysis, would reveal her true colours to the girl who had had the kindness to take her under her wing.

The force of his feelings on this subject surprised him. It was like the powerful impact of a depth charge, rumbling down deep in the very core of him.

He didn't wait for the ambulance bearing his destiny towards him to arrive, instead pushing himself away from the wall and heading up to his bedroom. His focus on work had been alarmingly casual and now, having had a shower, he buried himself in reports, numbers, figures and all the things that usually had the ability to fully engage his attention.

Not now. His brain refused to obey the commands being issued to it. What would the woman look like? Years ago, he could have had pictures taken of her when he had set his man on her trail, but he hadn't bothered because she had been just a missing slot in his life he had wanted to fill. He hadn't given a damn what she looked like. Now, he had to fight the temptation to stroll over to the window and peer out to the courtyard which his room overlooked.

He stiffened when he eventually heard the sound of the ambulance pulling up and the muffled rise and fall of voices which carried up to his room.

Deliberately he tuned out and exerted every ounce of will power to rein in his exasperating, wandering mind.

At a little after five, he got a text from Brianna: a light early supper would be served at six. If he wanted to join them, then he was more than welcome. Sorry she couldn't come up to his room but she had barely had time to draw breath since Bridget had arrived.

She had concluded her text with a smiley face. Who

*did* that? He smiled and texted back: yes, he'd be down promptly at six.

He sat back and stared at the wall. In an hour he would meet his past. He would put that to bed and then, when that was done, he would move on, back to the life from which he had taken this brief respite.

He had an image of Brianna's face gazing at him, of her lithe, slim body, of the way she had of humming under her breath when she was occupied doing something, and the way she looked when she was curled up on the sofa trying to make sense of her accounts.

But of course, he thought grimly, that was fine. Sure, she would be on his mind. They might not have spent a long time in each other's company but it had been concentrated time. Plenty long enough for images of her to get stuck in his head.

But she was not part of his reality. He would check out the woman who had given birth to him, put his curiosity to bed and, yes, move on…

# CHAPTER SIX

LEO WASN'T QUITE sure when the snow had stopped, when the furious blizzards had turned to tamer snowfall, and when that tamer snowfall had given way to a fine, steady drizzle that wiped clean the white horizon and returned it to its original, snow-free state.

He couldn't quite believe that he was still here. Of course, he returned to London sporadically mid-week and was uncomfortably aware of his conscience every time he vaguely intimated that there were things to do with the job he had ditched: paperwork that needed sorting out; problems with his accommodation that needed seeing to; social engagements that had to be fulfilled because he should have returned to London by now.

The lie he had blithely concocted before his game plan had been derailed did not sit quite so easily now. But what the hell was he to do?

He rose to move towards the window and stared distractedly down at the open fields that backed the pub. It was nearly three. In three hours, the pub would be alive with the usual Friday evening crowd, most of whom he knew by sight if not by name.

How had something so straightforward become so tangled in grey areas?

Of course, he knew. In fact, he could track the path

as clearly as if it was signposted. His simple plan—go in, confirm all the suspicions he had harboured about his birth mother, close the book and leave—had slipped out of place the second he had been confronted with Brianna.

She was everything the women he had dated in the past were not. Was that why he had not been able to kill his ill-advised temptation to take her to bed? And had her natural, open personality, once sampled, become an addiction he found impossible to jettison? He couldn't seem to see her without wanting her. She turned him on in ways that were unimaginable. For once in his life, he experienced a complete loss of self-control when they made love; it was a drug too powerful to resist.

And then…his mother. The woman he had prejudged, had seen as no more than a distasteful curiosity that had to be boxed and filed away, had not slotted neatly into the box he had prepared.

With a sigh, he raked his fingers through his hair and glanced over his shoulder to the reports blinking at him, demanding urgent attention, yet failing to focus it.

He thought back to when he had met her, that very first impression: smaller than he'd imagined, clearly younger, although her face was worn, very frail after hospital. He had expected someone brash, someone who fitted the image of a woman willing to give away a baby. He had realised, after only an hour in her company, that his preconceived notions were simplistic. That was an eventuality he had not taken into account. He lived his life with clean lines, no room for all those grey areas that could turn stark reality into a sludgy mess. But he had heard her gentle voice and, hard as he had tried not to be swayed, he had found himself hovering on the brink of needing to know more before he made his final judgement.

Not that anything she had said had been of any importance. The three of them had sat on that first evening and had dinner while Brianna had fussed and clucked and his mother had smiled with warm sympathy and complained about her garden and the winter vegetables which would sadly be suffering from neglect.

She had asked him about himself. He had looked at her and wondered where his dark eyes and colouring came from. She was slight and blonde with green eyes. At one point, she had murmured with a faraway expression that he reminded her of someone, someone she used to know, but he had killed that tangent and moved the conversation along.

Seeing her, meeting her, had made him feel weird, confused, uncomfortable in his own skin. A thousand questions had reared their ugly heads and he had killed them all by grimly holding on to his anger. But underneath that anger he had known only too well that the foundations on which he had relied were beginning to feel shaky. He had no longer known what he should be feeling.

Since that first day, he had seen her, though, only in brief interludes and always with Brianna around. Much of the time she spent in her bedroom. She was an avid reader. He had had to reacquaint himself with literature in an attempt to keep his so-called writer occupation as credible as possible. He had caught himself wondering what books she enjoyed reading.

On his last trip to London, he had brought with him a stack of books and had been surprised to discover that, after a diet of work-related reading, the fiction and non-fiction he had begun delving into had not been the hard work he had expected. And at least he could make a halfway decent job of sounding articulate on matters non-financial.

Where this was going to lead, he had no idea.

He headed downstairs and pulled up short at the sight

of Bridget sitting in the small lounge set aside from the bar area, which Brianna had turned into her private place if she didn't want to remain in her bedroom.

Because of Bridget, the pub now had slightly restricted opening and closing hours. He assumed that that was something that could only be achieved in a small town where all the regulars knew what was going on and would not be motivated to take their trade elsewhere—something that would have been quite tedious, as 'elsewhere' was not exactly conveniently located to get to by foot or on a bike.

'Leo!'

Leo paused, suddenly indecisive at being confronted by his mother without Brianna around as an intermediary. She was sitting by the large bay window that overlooked the back garden and the fields behind the pub. Her fair hair was tied back and the thin, gaunt lines of her face were accentuated so that she resembled a wraith.

'Brianna's still out.' She patted the chair facing hers and motioned to him to join her. 'We haven't chatted very much at all. Why don't you have a cup of tea with me?'

· Leo frowned, exasperated at his inability to take control of the situation. Did he want to talk to his mother on a one-to-one basis? Why did he suddenly feel so...*vulnerable* and at odds with himself at the prospect? Wasn't this why he had descended on this back-of-nowhere town in the first place? So things had not turned out quite as he had anticipated, but wasn't it still on his agenda to find out what the woman was like?

He was struck by the unexpectedly fierce urge to find out what had possessed her to throw him to the wolves.

He thought that perhaps the facade she portrayed now was a far cry from the real person lurking underneath, and he hardened himself against the weak temptation to be swept along into thinking that she was innocent, pathetic and deserving of sympathy. Could it be that, without Brianna there to impress, her true colours would be revealed?

'I think I'll have black coffee myself. Would you like to switch to coffee?'

'No, my dear, my pot of tea will be fine, although perhaps you could refresh the hot water. I feel exhausted if I'm on my feet for too long and I've been far too active today for my own good.'

He was back with a mug of coffee and the newly refreshed pot of tea which he rested on the table by her, next to the plate of biscuits which were untouched.

'I'm so glad I've caught you on your own,' she murmured as soon as he had taken a seat next to her. 'I feel I barely know you and yet Brianna is so taken with you after such a short space of time.'

'When you say "taken with me"...' He had told Brianna that he saw it as his duty to keep an eye on her houseguest, to scope her out, because a houseguest with a mysteriously absent past was not a houseguest to be trusted. Was the houseguest doing the same with him? He almost laughed out loud at the thought. As always when he was in her company, he had to try not to stare, not to try and find similarities...

'She's, well, I suppose you know about...'

'About the guy who broke her heart when she was at university?'

'She's locked herself away for years, has expressed no interest in any kind of love life at all. I've always thought it sad for someone so young and caring and beautiful, that she wouldn't be able to share those qualities with a soul mate.'

Leo said something and nothing. He looked at the cane leaning against the chair and wondered what it must feel like to be relatively young and yet require the assistance of a walking stick.

'If you don't mind my asking, how old are you, Bridget?'

Bridget looked at him in surprise. 'Why do you ask?'

Leo shrugged and sipped his coffee.

'Not yet fifty,' Bridget said quietly. 'Although I know I look much, much older.' She glanced away to stare through the window and he could see the shine of unshed tears filming her eyes.

In his head, he was doing the maths.

'But we weren't talking about me,' she said softly.

Leo felt a surge of healthy cynicism and thought that if she figured she could disappear behind a veil of anonymity then she was in for a surprise. There were things he wanted to find out, things he *needed* to find out, and he knew himself well—what he wanted, he got, be it money, women or, in this case, answers. The unsettling hesitancy that had afflicted him off and on, the hesitancy he hated because he just wasn't a hesitant person, thankfully disappeared beneath the weight of this new resolve.

'Indulge me,' he said smoothly. 'I hate one-sided conversations. I especially hate long chats about myself… I'm a man, after all. Self-expression is a luxury I don't tend to indulge very often. So, let's talk about you for a minute. I'm curious. You're not yet fifty, you tell me? Seems very young to have abandoned the lure of city lights for a quiet place like this.' He still could not quite believe that she was as young as she said. She looked like a woman in her sixties.

'What you may call "quiet", by which I take it you mean "dull", is what I see as peace.'

'Brianna said that you've been here a while—quite a few years; you must have been even younger when you decided that you wanted "peace".' He couldn't help thinking that, although their colouring was different, he had her eyes, the shape of them. He looked away with a frown.

She blushed and for the first time he could see her relative youth peep out from behind the care-worn features.

'My life's been…complicated. Not quite the life I ever expected, matter of fact.'

Curiosity was gnawing at him but he kept his features perfectly schooled, the disinterested bystander in whom he hoped she would confide. He could feel in his bones that the questions he wanted answering were about to be answered.

'Why don't you talk about it?' he murmured, resting the cup on the table and leaning towards her, his forearms resting on his thighs. 'You probably feel constrained talking to Brianna. In such a small, close-knit community perhaps you didn't want your private life to be thrown into the public arena?' He could see her hesitate. Secrets were always burdensome. 'Not that Brianna would ever be one to reveal a confidence, but one can never be too sure, I suppose.'

'And who knows how long I have left?' Bridget said quietly. She plucked distractedly at the loose gown she was wearing and stared off through the window as though it might offer up some inspiration. 'My health isn't good: stress, built up over the years. The doctor says I could have another heart attack at any time. They can't promise that the next time round won't be fatal.' She looked at him pensively. 'And I suppose I wouldn't want to burden Brianna with my life story. She's a sweet girl but I would never want to put her in a position of having to express a sympathy she couldn't feel.'

*Or pass judgement which would certainly mean the end of your happy times with her,* Leo thought with another spurt of that healthy cynicism, cynicism he knew he had to work at.

'But I don't come from here...' he encouraged in a low voice.

'I grew up in a place not dissimilar to this,' she murmured. 'Well, bigger, but not by a lot. Everybody knew everybody else. All the girls knew the boys they would end up marrying. I was destined for Jimmy O'Connor; lived two doors away. His parents were my parents' best friends. In fact, we were practically born on the same day, but that all went up the spout when I met Robbie Cabrera. *Roberto* Cabrera.'

Leo stilled. 'He was Spanish?'

'Yes. His father had come over for a temporary job on a building site ten miles out of town. Six months. He was put into our school and all the girls went mad for him. I used to be pretty once, when I was a young girl of fifteen...you might not guess it now.' She sighed and looked at him with a girlish smile which, like that blush, brought her buried youth back up to the surface.

'And what happened?' Leo was surprised he could talk so naturally, as though he was listening to someone else's story rather than his own.

'We fell madly in love. In the way that you do when you're young and innocent.' She shot him a concerned looked and he hastened to assure her that whatever she told him would stay with him. Adrenaline was pumping through him. He hadn't experienced this edge-of-the-precipice feeling in a very long time. If ever. This was why he was here. The only reason he was here.

From nowhere, he had a vision of Brianna laughing and telling him that there was nothing more satisfying than growing your own tomatoes in summer, and teasing him that he probably wouldn't understand because he probably lived in one of those horrible apartment blocks where you wouldn't be able to grow a tomato if your life depended on it.

He thought of himself, picking her up then and hauling her off to his bedroom at a ridiculous hour after the pub had finally been closed. Thought of her curving, feline smile as she lay on his bed, half-naked, her small, perfect breasts turning him on until his erection felt painful and he couldn't get his clothes off fast enough.

'Sorry?' He leaned in closer. 'You were saying…?'

'I know. You're shocked. And I don't mean to shock you but it's a relief to talk about this; I haven't with anyone. I fell pregnant. At fifteen. My family were distraught, and of course there was no question of abortion, not that we would have got rid of it. No, Robbie and I were committed to one another.'

'Pregnant…'

'I was still a child myself. We both were. We wanted to keep it but my parents wouldn't allow it. I was shipped off to a convent to give birth.'

'You wanted to keep it?'

'I never even held it. Never knew if it was a boy or a girl. I returned to Ireland, went back to school, but from that moment on my parents were lost to me. I had three younger siblings and they never knew what had happened. Still don't. Family life was never the same again.'

'And the father of the child?'

Bridget smiled. 'We ran away. His father ended up on a two-year contract. We skipped town when we were sixteen and headed south. I kept my parents informed of my whereabouts but I couldn't see them and they never lived down the shame of what I'd done. I don't think they cared one way or the other. Robbie always kept in touch with his parents and in fact, when they moved to London, we stayed with them for several months before they returned to Spain.'

'You…ran away…' For some reason, his normally agile mind seemed to be lagging behind.

'We were very happy, Robbie and me, for over twenty years until he died in a hit-and-run accident and then I went back to Ireland. Not back to where I grew up, but to another little town, and then eventually I came here.'

'Hit and run…' The tidal rush of emotions was so intense that he stood up and paced like a wounded bear, before dropping back into the chair.

'We never had any more children. Out of respect for the one I was forced to give up for adoption.'

Suddenly the room felt too small. He felt himself break out in a fine perspiration. Restless energy poured through him, driving him back onto his feet. His cool, logical mind willed him to stay put and utter one or two platitudes to bring the conversation to a satisfactory conclusion. But the chaotic jumble of thoughts filling every corner of his brain was forcing him to pace the room, his movements uncoordinated and strangely jerky.

He was aware of Bridget saying something, murmuring, her face now turned to the window, lost in her thoughts.

There was so much to process that he wasn't sure where to start. So this was the story he had been waiting for and the ending had not been anticipated. She hadn't been the convenient stereotype he had envisaged: she wasn't the irresponsible no-hoper who had given him away without a backward glance. And, now that he knew that, what the hell happened next?

He turned to her, saw that she had nodded off and almost immediately heard the sound of Brianna returning.

'What's wrong?' About to shut the door, Brianna stood still and looked at him with a concerned frown. She had been out shopping and had had to force herself to take her time, not to hurry back, because she just wanted to *see* him, to *be* with him. 'Is…is Bridget all right?' She walked towards him and he automatically reached out to help her with the bags of shopping. Brianna stifled the warm thrill that little slice of pretend domesticity gave her.

'Bridget is fine. She appears to have fallen asleep. Have you ever…?' Leo murmured, reaching to cup the nape of her neck so that he could pull her towards him. 'Thought that you were going in one direction, only to find that the signposts had been switched somewhere along the way and the destination you were heading to turned out to be as substantial as a mirage?'

Brianna's heart skipped a beat. Was he talking about *her*? she wondered with heightened excitement. Was he trying to tell her that meeting her had derailed him? She placed her hand flat on his chest and then slipped it between two buttons to feel his roughened hair.

'What are you saying?' she whispered, wriggling her fingers and undoing the buttons so that she could now see the hard chest against which her fingers were splayed.

'I'm saying I want to have sex with you.' And right at that moment it really was exactly what he wanted. He wanted to drown the clamour of discordant voices in his head and just make love to her. With the bags of shopping in just one hand, he nudged her towards the kitchen.

'We can't!' But her hands were scrabbling over him, hurrying to undo the buttons of his shirt, and her breasts were aching in anticipation of being touched by him. 'Bridget…'

'Asleep.' He shut down the associated thoughts that came with mention of her name.

'I've got to start getting ready to open up.'

'But not for another half-hour. I assure you…' They

were in the kitchen now and he kicked the door shut behind him and pushed her towards the wall until she was backed up against it. 'A lot can be accomplished in half an hour.'

The low drawl of intent sent delicious shivers racing up and down her spine and she groaned as he unzipped her jeans and pushed his hand underneath her panties. Frustrated because his big hand couldn't do what it wanted to do thanks to the tightness of her jeans, he yanked them down, and Brianna quickly stepped out of them.

Bridget, she thought wildly, would have another heart attack if she decided to pop into the kitchen for something. But fortunately her energy levels were still very low and if she was asleep then she would remain asleep at least for another hour or so.

Her fingers dug into his shoulders and she uttered a low, wrenching groan as he pulled the crotch of her panties to one side and began rubbing her throbbing clitoris with his finger.

Her panties were damp with her arousal. She gave a broken sigh and her eyelids fluttered. She could feel him clumsily undoing his trousers and then his thick hardness pushing against her jumper.

This was fast and furious sex.

Where was his cool? Leo was catapulted right back to his days of being a horny teenager lacking in finesse, except he couldn't remember, even as a horny teenager, being as wildly out of control as he was now. He didn't even bother with taking off her jumper, far less his. He hooked his finger under her knickers and she completed the job of disposing of them. He could barely get it together to don protection. His hand was shaking and he swore in frustration as he ripped open the packet.

Then he took her. He hoisted her onto him and thrust into her with a grunt of pleasurable release. Hands under her buttocks, he pushed hard and heard her little cry of pleasure with intense satisfaction.

They came together, their bodies utterly united, both of them oblivious to their surroundings.

He dropped her to the ground, his breathing heavy and uncontrolled. 'Not usually my style.' But, as he watched her wriggle back into her underwear and jeans, he figured it could well become part of his repertoire without a great deal of trouble.

'You look a little hot and flustered.' He gently smoothed some tendrils of hair away from her face and Brianna added that tender gesture to the stockpile she was mentally constructing. She felt another zing of excitement when she thought back to what he had said about his plans not going quite as he had anticipated. She would have loved nothing more than to quiz him further on the subject, but she would let it rest for the moment. One thing she had learnt about him was that he was not a man who could be prodded into saying anything or doing anything unless he wanted to.

'Right—the bar. I need to get going. I need to check on Bridget.'

Plus a million and one other things that needed doing, including sticking away the stuff she had bought. All that was running through her head as a byline to the pleasurable thought of the big guy behind her admitting to wanting more than a passing fling. A nomad would one day find a place to stay put, wouldn't he? That was how it worked. And, if he didn't want to stay put *here*, then she would be prepared to follow him. She knew she would.

Her mind was a thousand miles away, so it took her a few minutes to realise that something was wrong when she entered the little lounge to check on Bridget.

She should have been in the chair by the window. It was where she always sat, looking out or reading her book. But she wasn't there. Her mind moved sluggishly as she quickly scanned the room and she saw the limp body huddled behind the chair about the same time as Leo did.

It felt like hours but in fact it could only have been a matter of seconds, and Leo was on it before her brain had really had time to crank into gear. She was aware of him gently inspecting Bridget while barking orders to her at the same time: make sure the pub was shut; fetch some water; get a blanket; bring him the telephone because his mobile phone was in his bedroom, then amending that for her to fetch his mobile phone after all.

'I'll call an ambulance!'

'Leave that to me.'

Such was his unspoken strength that it didn't occur to her to do anything but as he said. She shut the pub. Then it was upstairs to fetch his mobile phone, along with one of the spare guest blankets which she kept in the airing cupboard, only stopping en route to grab a glass of water from the kitchen.

'She's breathing,' was the first thing he said when she returned. 'So don't look so panicked.' He gestured to his phone, scrolled down and began dialling a number. She couldn't quite catch what he was saying because he had walked over to the window and was talking in a low, urgent voice, his back to her. Not that she was paying any attention. She was loosely holding Bridget, talking to her in soft murmurs while trying to assess what the damage was. It looked as though she had fallen, banged her head against the table and passed out. But, in her condition, what could be the ramifications of that?

'Right.' Leo turned to her and slipped the mobile phone into his jeans pocket. 'It's taken care of.'

'Sorry?'

'It's under control. The main thing is to keep her still. We don't know what she's broken with that fall.'

'I'm glad you said that it was a fall. That's what I thought. Surely that must be less serious than another heart attack. Is the ambulance on its way? I've made sure the "closed" sign's on the front door. When I get a chance, I'll ring round a couple of the regulars and explain the situation.'

Leo hesitated. 'No ambulance.'

Brianna looked at him, startled. 'But she's got to go to hospital!'

'Trust me when I tell you that I have things under control.' He squatted alongside them both. The time of reckoning had come and how on earth had he ever played with the thought that it wouldn't? How had he imagined that he would be able to walk away without a backward glance when the time came?

Of course, he certainly hadn't reckoned on the time coming in this fashion. He certainly hadn't thought that he would be the one rescuing his mother because it now seemed that there was more conversation left between them.

'You have things under control?' Brianna looked at him dubiously. 'And yet there's no ambulance on the way?'

'I've arranged to have her air-lifted to the Cromwell Hospital in London,' Leo said bluntly.

'I beg your pardon?'

'It should be here any minute soon. In terms of timing, it will probably get here faster than an ambulance would, even an ambulance with its sirens going.'

In the midst of trying to process what sounded like complete gibberish to her, Brianna heard the distant sound of an overhead aircraft. Landing would be no problem. In fact, there couldn't have been a better spot for an air ambulance to land. The noise grew louder and louder until it felt as though it would take the roof off the pub, and then there was a flurry of activity while she stood back, confused.

She became a mystified bystander as the professionals took over, their movements hurried and urgent, ferrying Bridget to the aircraft.

Then Leo turned to her. 'You should come.'

Brianna looked at him in complete silence. 'Leo… what's going on?' How had he managed to do *that*? Who on earth could arrange for someone to be airlifted to a hospital hundreds of, miles away? She had thought that maybe he had been in computers, but had he been in the medical field? Surely not. She was uneasily aware that there were great, big gaps in her knowledge about him but there was little time to think as she nodded and was hurried along to the waiting aircraft.

'I don't have any clothes.'

'It's not a problem.'

'What do you mean, it's *not a problem*?'

'We haven't got time to debate this. Let's go.'

Brianna's head was full of so many questions, yet something in her resisted asking any of them. Instead she said weakly, as they were lifted noisily into the air and the aircraft swung sharply away, leaving the pub behind, 'Do you think she'll be all right?' And then, with a tremulous laugh, because the detachment on his dark face filled her with a dreadful apprehension, 'I guess this would make a fantastic scene in your book…'

Leo looked at her. She was huddled against him and her open, trusting face was shadowed with anxiety.

This was a relationship that was never going to last. They had both been aware of that from the very start. He had made the position perfectly clear. So, in terms of conscience, he was surely justified in thinking that his was completely clear? But it still took a great deal of effort to grit his teeth and not succumb to a wave of unedited, pure regret for what he knew now lay on the horizon. But this wasn't the time to talk about any of this so he chose to ignore her quip about the book that was as fictitious as the Easter Bunny.

'I think she'll be fine but why take chances?'

'Leo...'

'We'll be at the hospital very shortly, Brianna.' He sighed deeply, pressed his thumbs against his eyes and then rested his head against the upright, uncomfortable seat. 'We'll talk once Bridget's settled in hospital.'

Brianna shivered as he looked away to stare out of the window but she remained silent; then there wasn't much time to do any thinking at all as everything seemed to happen at once and with impressive speed.

Once again she stood helplessly on the sidelines and watched as the machinery of the medical world took over. She had never seen anything like it and she was even more impressed at Leo's handling of the situation, the way he just seemed to take charge, the way he knew exactly what to do and the way people appeared to listen to him in a way she instinctively knew they wouldn't have to anyone else.

Like a spare part, she followed him into the hospital, which was more like a hotel than anything else, a hotel filled with doctors and nurses, somewhere designed to inspire confidence. The smallness of her life crowded her as she watched, nervously torn between wanting to get nearer to Bridget, who had now been established in a room of her own, and wanting to stay out of the way just in case she got mown down by the crisp efficiency of everyone bustling around their new patient.

It felt like ages until Bridget was examined, wheeled off for tests and examined again. Leo was in the thick of it. She, on the other hand, kept her distance and at one point was firmly ushered to a plush waiting room, gently encouraged to sit, handed a cappuccino and informed that she would help matters enormously if she just relaxed, that everything was going to be perfectly fine.

How on earth was she supposed to relax? she wondered. Not only was she worried sick, but alongside all her concerns about her friend other, more unsettling ideas were jostling in her head like pernicious, stinging insects trying to get a hold.

She was dead on her feet by the time Leo finally made an appearance and he, too, looked haggard. Brianna half-rose and he waved her back down, pulled one the chairs across and sat opposite her, legs apart, his arms resting loosely on his thighs.

More than anything else, she wanted to reach out and smooth away the tired lines around his eyes and she sat on her hands to avoid giving in to the temptation which here, and now, seemed horribly inappropriate.

'Leo, what's going on?'

'The main thing is that Bridget is going to be okay. It seems she stood up and fell as she was reaching for her cane. She banged her head against the edge of the table and knocked herself out. They've done tests to make sure that she suffered no brain damage and to ascertain that the shock didn't affect her heart.' He looked at her upturned face and flushed darkly.

'I'm amazed you rushed into action like that when she could have just gone to the local hospital.' She reached out tentatively to touch his arm and he vaulted upright and prowled through the shiny, expensive waiting room of which they were the only occupants.

'Brianna…' He paused to stare down at her and all of a sudden there was no justification whatsoever for any of the lies he had told. It didn't matter whether they had been told in good faith, whether the consequences had been unforeseen. Nor did the rights and wrongs of sleeping with the girl, now staring up at him, come into play.

'It's late. You need to get some rest. But more importantly we have to talk...'

'Yes.' Why was she so reluctant to hear what he had to say? Where was that gut reaction coming from?

'I'm going to take you back to my place.'

'I beg your pardon? You still have a place in London? What place? I thought you might have sold that—you know?—to do your travelling.'

Leo shook his head and raked his fingers through his dishevelled hair. 'I think when we get there,' he said on a heavy sigh, 'some of the questions you're asking yourself might begin to fall into place.

# CHAPTER SEVEN

BRIANNA'S FIRST SHOCK was when they emerged from the hospital and Leo immediately made a call on his mobile which resulted, five minutes later, in the appearance of a top-of-the range black Range Rover. It paused and he opened the back door for her and stood aside to allow her to slide into the luxurious leather seat.

Suddenly she was seeing him in a whole new light. He was still wearing the jeans in which he had travelled, a long-sleeved jumper and one of the old coats which he had found in a cupboard at the back of the pub and which he had adopted because it was well lined. But even with this casual clothing he now seemed a different person. He was no longer the outdoor guy with that slow, sexy smile that dragged on her senses. There was a harshness to his face that she was picking up for the first time and it sent a shiver of apprehension racing up and down her spine.

The silence stretched on and on as the car slowly pulled away from the kerb and began heading into central London.

When she looked over to him, it was to quail inwardly at the sight of the forbidding cast of his features, so she pretended to be absorbed in the monotonous, crowded London landscape of pavements and buildings.

It was very late but, whereas in Ireland the night sky

would be dense and black at this hour and the countryside barely visible, here the streetlights illuminated everything. And there were people around: little groups shivering on the pavements, the odd business man in a suit and, the further towards the centre of London the car went, the busier the streets were.

Where one earth were they going? So he had a house in London. Why had he never mentioned that? Her mind scrabbled frantically to come up with some logical reason why he might have kept it a secret. Perhaps he was in the process of selling it. Everyone knew that it could take for ever to sell a property and, if he *was* selling it, then maybe he thought that there was no point mentioning it at all. But when she glanced surreptitiously at his forbidding profile, all the excuses she tried to formulate in her head withered and died.

'Where are we going? I know you said your house, but where exactly is that?'

Leo shifted and angled his body so that he was facing her. Hell, this was a total mess; he could only lay one-hundred per cent of the blame for that at his own door. He had behaved like a stupid fool and now he was about to be stuck handling the fallout.

Brianna was a simple country girl. He had known that the second he had seen her. She might have had the grit and courage to single-handedly run a pub, but emotionally she was a baby, despite her heartbreak. She was just the sort of woman he should have steered clear from, yet had he? No. He had found that curious blend of street-wise savvy and trusting naivety irresistible. He had wanted her and so he had taken her. Of course, she had jumped in to the relationship eyes wide open, yet he couldn't help but feel that the blame still lay entirely on his shoulders. He had been arrogant and selfish and those qualities, neither of which had caused him a moment's concern in the past, now disgusted him.

He harked back to his conversation with Bridget. Before it had turned to the illuminating matter of her past, she had wanted to talk to him about Brianna, had opened the subject by letting on that Brianna hadn't been involved with anyone since her loser boyfriend from university had dumped her. Leo now followed the path of that conversation which had never got off the starting blocks as it turned out.

Had she been on the brink of confiding just how deeply Brianna was involved with him?

Of course she had been! Why kid himself? He might have laid down his ground rules and told her that he was not in the market for involvement, but then he had proceeded to demonstrate quite the opposite in a hundred and one ways. He couldn't quite figure out how this had happened, but it had, and the time had come to set the matter straight.

'Knightsbridge,' he told her, already disliking himself for the explanation he would be forced to give. Less than twenty-four hours ago they had been making love, fast, furious love, her legs wrapped around him, as primitive and driven as two wild animals in heat. The memory of it threatened to sideswipe him and, totally inexplicably, he felt himself harden, felt his erection push painfully against his zip so that he had to shift a little to alleviate the ache.

'Knightsbridge. Knightsbridge as in *Harrods,* Knightsbridge?' The last time Brianna had been to London had been three years ago, and before that when she had been going out with Daniel. She would have had to be living on another planet not to know that Knightsbridge was one of the most expensive parts of London, if not the most expensive.

'That's right.' On cue, the gleaming glass building in which his duplex apartment was located rose upwards, arrogantly demanding notice, not that anyone could fail to pay attention and salute its magnificence.

He nodded towards it, a slight inclination of his head, and Brianna, following his eyes, gasped in shock.

'My apartment's there,' he told her and he watched as the colour drained away from her face and her eyes widened to huge, green saucers.

Before she could think of anything to say, the chauffeur-driven Range Rover was pulling smoothly up in front of the building and she was being ushered out of the car, as limp as a rag doll.

She barely noticed the whoosh of the lift as it carried them upwards. Nor did she take in any of her surroundings until she was finally standing in his apartment, a massive, sprawling testimony to the very best money could buy.

With her back pressed to the door, she watched as he switched on lights with a remote control and dropped blinds with another remote before turning to her with his thumbs hooked into the pockets of his jeans.

They stared at each other in silence and he finally said, the first to turn away, 'So this is where I live. There are five bedrooms. It's late; you can hit the sack now in one of them, or we can talk'

'You actually *own* this place?' Her gaze roamed from the slate flooring in the expansive hall to the white walls, the dark wood that replaced the slate and the edge of a massive canvas she could glimpse in what she assumed would be another grand space—maybe his living room.

'I own it.' He strolled through into the living area, which had been signposted by that glimpse of wall art. Following behind him, Brianna saw that it was a massive piece of abstract art and that there were several others on the walls. They provided the only glimpse of colour against a palette that was uniformly white: white walls, white rug against the dark wooden floor, white leather furniture.

'I thought you were broke.' Brianna dubiously eyed the chair to which she was being directed. She yawned and he instantly told her that she should get some rest.

'I'd prefer to find out what's going on.'

'In which case, you might need a drink.' He strolled towards a cabinet and she looked around her, only to refocus as he thrust a glass with some amber liquid into her hand.

He sat down next to her and leaned forward, cradling his drink while he took in her flushed face. He noticed that she couldn't meet his eyes and he had to steel himself against a wave of sickening emotion.

'We should never have slept together,' he delivered abruptly and Brianna's eyes shot to his.

'What do you mean?'

'I mean…' He swirled his drink round and then swallowed a long mouthful. Never had he needed a swig of alcohol more. 'When I arrived in Ballybay, it was not my intention to get involved with anyone. It was something that just seemed to happen, but it could have and should have been prevented. I blame myself entirely for that, Brianna.'

Hurt lanced through Brianna. Was this the same guy about whom she had been nurturing silly, girlish daydreams involving an improbable future? One where he stuck his hat on the door and decided to stay put, so that they could explore what they had? She felt her colour rise as mortification kicked in with a vengeance.

'And why is that?'

'Because I knew you for what you were, despite what you said. You told me that you were tough, that you weren't looking for anything committed, that you wanted nothing more from me than sex, pure and simple. I chose to believe you because I was attracted to you. I chose to ignore the voice of reason telling me that you weren't half as tough as you claimed to be.' Even now—and he could see her stiffening as she absorbed what he was saying—there was still a softness to her mouth that belied anything hard.

He found that he just couldn't remain sitting next to her. He couldn't feel the warmth she was radiating without all his thoughts going into a tailspin.

'I'm pretty tough, Leo. I've been on my own for a long time and I've managed fine.'

Leo prowled through the room, barely taking in the exquisite, breathtakingly expensive minimalist décor, and not paying a scrap of attention to the Serpentine glittering hundreds of metres in the distance, a black, broad stripe beyond the bank of trees.

'You've taken over your father's pub,' he said heavily, finishing the rest of his drink in one long gulp and dumping the glass on the low, squat table between the sofa and the chairs. It was of beaten metal and had cost the earth. 'You know how to handle hard work, but that's not what I'm talking about and we both know that. I told you from the start that I was just passing through and that hasn't changed. Not for me. I'm…I'm sorry.'

'I understood the rules, Leo.' Her cheeks were stinging and her hands didn't want to keep still. She had to grip the glass tightly to stop them from shaking. 'I just don't get…' she waved her hand to encompass the room in which they were sitting, with its floor-to-ceiling glass windows, its expensive abstract art and weirdly soulless, uncomfortable furniture '…all of this. What sort of job did you have before?'

Leo sighed and rubbed his eyes. It was late to begin this conversation. It didn't feel like the right time, but then

what *would* be the right time? In the morning? The following afternoon? A not-so-distant point in the future? There
*was* no right time.

'No past tense, Brianna.'

'Sorry?'

'There's no past tense. I never gave my job up.' He
laughed mirthlessly at the notion of any such thing ever
happening. He was defined by his work, always had been.
Apart from the past few weeks, when he had played tru-
ant for the first time in his life.

'You never gave your job up…but…?'

'I run a very large and very complex network of companies, Brianna. I'm the boss. I own them. My employees
report to me. That's why I can afford all of this, as well as
a house in the Caribbean, an apartment in New York and
another in Hong Kong. Have another sip of that drink. It'll
steady your nerves. It's a lot to take in, and I'm sorry about
that, but like I said I never anticipated getting in so deep…
I never thought that I would have to sit here and have this
conversation with you, or anyone else, for that matter.'

Brianna took a swig of the brandy he had poured for
her and felt it burn her throat. She had a thousand angry
questions running through her head but they were all silenced by the one, very big realisation—he had lied to her.
She didn't know why, and she wasn't even sure that it mattered, because nothing could change the simple truth that
he had lied. She felt numb just thinking about it.

'So you're not a writer.'

'Brianna, I'm sorry. No. The last time I did any kind
of creative writing was when I was in school, and even
then it had never been one of my stronger subjects.' She
wasn't crying and somehow that made it all the harder. He
had fired a lot of people in his time, had told aspiring em-

ployees that their aspirations were misplaced, but nothing had prepared him for what he was feeling now.

'Right.'

Unable to keep still, he sprang to his feet and began pacing the room. His thoughts veered irrationally, comparing the cold, elegant beauty of his sitting room and the warm, untidy cosiness of the tiny lounge at the back of her pub, and he was instantly angry with himself for allowing that small loss of self-control.

He had had numerous girlfriends in the past. He had always told them that commitment wasn't an option and, although quite a few had made the mistake of getting it into their heads that he might have been lying, he had never felt a moment's regret in telling the deluded ones goodbye.

'So what were you doing in Ballybay?' she asked. 'Did you just decide on the spur of the moment that you needed a break from…from the big apartment with the fancy paintings and all those companies you own? Did you think that you needed to get up close and personal with how the other half lives?'

She laughed bitterly. 'Poor Leo. What a blow to have ended up stuck in my pub with no mod cons, having to clear snow and help with the washing up. How you must have missed your flash car and designer clothes! I bet you didn't bank on having to stick around for as long as you did.'

'Sarcasm doesn't suit you.'

But he had flushed darkly and was finding it difficult to meet her fierce, accusatory green-eyed stare. 'I'm sorry,' Brianna apologised with saccharine insincerity. 'I find it really hard to be sweet and smiling when I've just discovered that the guy I've been sleeping with is a liar.'

'Which never made our passion any less incendiary.'

Her eyes tangled with his and she felt the hot, slow burn

of an unwitting arousal that made her ball her hands into angry fists. Unbelievable: her body responding to some primitive vibe that was still running between them like a live current that couldn't be switched off.

'Why did you bother to make up some stupid story about being a writer?' she flung at him. 'Why didn't you say that you were just another rich businessman who wanted to spend a few days slumming it and winding down? Why the fairy story? Was that all part of the *let's adopt a different persona*?' She kept her eyes firmly focused on his face but she was still taking in the perfection of the whole, the amazing body, the strong arms, the length of his legs. Knowing exactly what he looked like underneath the clothes didn't help. 'Well?' she persisted in the face of his silence.

'The story is a little more complex than a bid to take time out from my life here...'

'What do you mean?' She was overwhelmed by a wave of giddiness. She couldn't tear her eyes away from his face and she found that she was sitting ramrod erect, as rigid as a plank of wood, her hands positioned squarely on her knees.

'There was a reason I came to Ballybay.' Always in control of all situations, Leo scowled at the unpleasant and uncustomary sensation of finding himself on the back foot. Suddenly the clinical, expensive sophistication of his surroundings irritated the hell out of him. It was an unsuitable environment in which to be having this sort of highly personal conversation. But would 'warm and cosy' have made any difference? He had to do what he had to do. That was just the way life was. She would be hurt, but she was young and she would get over it. It wasn't as though he had made her promises he had had no intention of keeping!

He unrealistically told himself that she might even *ben-*

*efit* from the experience. She had not had a lover for years. He had crashed through that icy barrier and reintroduced her to normal, physical interaction between two people; had opened the door for her to move forward and get back out there in the real world, find herself a guy to settle down with…

That thought seemed spectacularly unappealing and he jettisoned it immediately. No point losing track of the moment and getting wrapped up in useless speculation and hypotheses.

'A reason?'

'I was looking for someone.' He sat heavily on the chair facing hers and, as her posture was tense and upright, so his was the exact opposite as he leaned towards her, legs wide apart, his strong forearms resting on his thighs. He could feel her hurt withdrawal from him and it did weird things to his state of mind.

'Who?'

'It might help if I told you a little bit about myself, Brianna.'

'You mean aside from the lies you've already told me?'

'The lies were necessary, or at least it seemed so at the time.'

'Lies are never necessary.'

'And that's a point we can possibly debate at a later date. For now, let me start by telling you that I was adopted at birth. It's nothing that is a state secret, but the reason I came to Ballybay is because I traced my birth mother a few years ago and I concluded that finding her was something I had to do. Not while my adoptive parents were still alive. I loved them very much; I would never have wanted to hurt them in any way.'

Brianna stared at him open-mouthed. It felt as though the connections in her brain were all backfiring so that nothing made sense any more. What on earth was he going on about? And how could he just *sit there* as though this was the most normal conversation in the world?

'You're adopted?' was all she could say weakly, because she just couldn't seem to join the dots in the conversation.

'I grew up in leafy, affluent suburbia, the only child of a couple who couldn't have children of their own. I knew from the beginning that I was adopted, and it has to be said that they gave me the sort of upbringing that most kids could only dream about.'

'But you didn't want to find your real mother until now?'

'*Real* mother is not a term I would use. And finding her would not have been appropriate had my adoptive parents still been alive. Like I said, I owe everything to them, and they would have been hurt had I announced that I was off on a journey of discovery.'

'But they're no longer alive. And so you decided to trace your…your…'

'I've had the information on the woman for years, Brianna. I simply bided my time.'

Brianna stared at him. He'd simply *bided his time*? There was something so deliberate and so controlled about that simple statement that her head reeled.

'And…and…you came to Ballybay and pretended to be someone you weren't because…?'

'Because it was smaller than I imagined,' he confessed truthfully. 'And I wanted to find out about the woman before I passed judgement.'

'You mean if you had announced yourself and told everyone why you were there…what? Your mother—sorry, your *birth* mother—would have tried to…to what?' She looked around her at the staggering, shameless testimony to his well-heeled life and then settled her eyes back on him. 'Did you think that you needed to keep your real identity a secret because if she knew how rich you were she would have tried to latch on to your money?'

Leo made an awkward, dismissive gesture with his hand. 'I don't allow people to latch on to my money,' he said flatly. 'No, I kept my identity a secret, as indeed my purpose in being there in the first place, because I wasn't sure what I would do with the information I gathered.'

'How can you talk about this with such a lack of emotion? I feel as though I'm seeing a stranger.'

Leo sat back and raked his fingers through his hair. He was being honest. In fact, he was sparing no detail when it came to telling the truth, yet he still felt like the guy wrecking Christmas by taking a gun to Santa Claus.

'A stranger you've made love to countless times,' he couldn't help but murmur in a driven undertone that belied his cool exterior. He took a deep breath and tried to fight the intrusive memory of his hands over her smooth, slender body, tracing the light sprinkling of freckles on her collarbone, the circular discs of her nipples and the soft, downy hair between her legs. She was the most naturally, openly responsive lover he had ever had. When he parted her legs to cup the moisture between them, he felt her responding one-hundred per cent to his touch. She didn't play games. She hadn't hidden how he had made her feel.

'And I wish I hadn't.' Brianna was momentarily distracted from the direction of their conversation.

'You don't mean that. Whatever you think of me now, your body was always on fire for mine!'

Again she felt that treacherous lick of desire speed along her nerve endings like an unwanted intruder bypassing all her fortifications. This was not a road she wanted to travel down, not at all. Not when everything was collapsing around her ears.

'And did you find her?' she asked tightly.

'I did,' he answered after only the briefest of hesitations.

'Who is she?'

'At the moment, she's lying in the Cromwell Hospital.'

Brianna half-stood and then fell back onto the chair as though the air had been knocked out of her lungs.

His mother was Bridget. Bridget McGuire. And all of a sudden everything began falling into place with sickening impact. Perhaps not immediately, but very quickly, he had ascertained that she knew Bridget, that she considered Bridget one of her closest friends. Try as she might, Brianna couldn't reference the time scale of this conversation. Had it happened *before* he'd decided to prolong his stay? Surely it would have?

That realisation was like a physical blow because with it came the inevitable conclusion that he had used her. He had wanted to find out about his mother and she had been an umbilical cord to information he felt he might have needed; to soften her up and raise no suspicions, he had assumed the spurious identity of a writer. When he had been sitting in front of his computer, she'd assumed that he had been working on his book. Now, as head of whatever vast empire he ran, she realised he would have been working, communicating with the outside world from the dreary isolation of a small town in Ireland he would never have deigned to visit had he not needed to.

How could she have been so stupid, so naive? She had swooned like a foolish sixteen-year-old the second she had clapped eyes on him and had had no qualms about justifying her decision to leap into bed with him.

She had been his satisfying bonus for being stuck in the boondocks.

'I didn't even know that Bridget had ever had children...

Does she know?' Her voice was flat and devoid of any expression.

That, without the tears, told him all he needed to know about her state of mind. He had brought this on himself and he wasn't going to flinch from this difficult conversation. He told himself that there had never been any notion of a long-lasting relationship with her, yet the repetition of that mantra failed to do its job, failed to make him feel any better.

'No. She doesn't.'

'And when will you tell her?'

'When I feel the time is right.'

'If you wanted to find your mother and announce yourself—if you weren't suspicious that she would try and con money out of you—then why the secrecy? Why didn't you just do us all a favour: show up in your fancy car and present yourself as the long-lost prodigal son?'

'Because I didn't know what I was going to find, but I suspected that what I found would—how shall I put this?— not be to my liking.'

'Hence all your warnings about her when I told you that she was going to be coming to the pub to stay after her bout in hospital…' Brianna said slowly, feeling the thrust of yet another dagger deep down inside her. 'You knew she was hiding a past and you assumed she was a lowlife who would end up taking advantage of me, stealing from me, even. What changed?'

Leo shrugged and Brianna rose to her feet and managed to put distance between them. For a few seconds she stared down at the eerily lit landscape below her, devoid of people, just patches of light interspersed with darkness. Then she returned to the chair and this time she forced herself to try and relax, to give him no opportunity to see just how badly she was affected by what he had said to her.

'So you were using me all along,' she said matter-of-factly. 'You came to Ballybay with a purpose, found out that it wasn't going to be as straightforward as you anticipated—because it's the kind of small place where everybody knows everybody else, so you wouldn't be able to pass unnoticed, without comment—you adopted an identity and the second you found out that I knew your mother…sorry, your *birth mother*…you decided that it would be an idea to get to know me better.'

Leo's jaw hardened. Her inexorable conclusions left a bitter taste in his mouth but he wasn't going to rail against them. What was needed here was a clean break. If she had become too involved, then what was the point in encouraging further involvement by entering into a debate on what he had meant or not meant to do?

His failure to deny or confirm her statement was almost more than Brianna could bear but she kept her voice cool and level and willed herself just to try and detach from the situation. At least here, now; later, she would release the emotion that was building inside her, piling up like water constrained by paper-thin walls, ready to burst its banks and destroy everything in its path.

She could read nothing from his expression. Where was the guy she had laughed with? Made love to? Teased? Who was this implacable stranger sitting in front of her?

How, even more fatally, could she have made such a colossal mistake again? Misjudged someone so utterly that their withdrawal came as complete shock? Except this time it was all so much worse. She had known him for a fraction of the time she had known Daniel. Yet she knew, without a shadow of a doubt, that the impact Daniel had made on her all those years ago was nothing in comparison to what she would feel when she walked away from this. How was that possible? And yet she knew that what Leo had generated inside her had reached deeper and faster and was more profound in a million ways.

'I guess you decided that sleeping with me would be a good way to get background information on Bridget. Or maybe it was just something that was given to you on a silver platter.' Bitterness crept into her voice because she knew very well that what she said was the absolute truth. He hadn't had to energise himself into trying to get her into bed. She had leapt in before he had even finished asking the question.

'We enjoyed one another, Brianna. God, never have I apologised so much and so sincerely.'

'Except I wasn't using you.' She chose to ignore his apology because, in the big picture, it was just stupid and meaningless.

'I...' *Wasn't using you?* How much of that statement could he truthfully deny? 'That doesn't detract from the fact that what we had was real.'

'Don't you mean that the *sex* we had was real? Because beyond that we didn't have anything. You were supposed to be a writer travelling through, getting inspiration.' The conversation seemed to be going round and round in circles and she couldn't see a way of leading it towards anything that could resemble a conclusion. It felt like being in a labyrinth and she began walking on wooden legs towards her coat which she had earlier dumped on one of the chairs.

'Where are you going?'

'Where do you think, Leo? I'm leaving.'

'To go where? For God's sake, Brianna, there are guest rooms galore in this apartment. Pick whichever one you want to use! This is all a shock, I get that, but you can't just run out of here with nowhere to go!' Frustration laced his words with a savage urgency that made him darken and he sprang up, took a couple of steps towards her and then stopped.

They stood staring at one another. Her open transparency, which was so much part and parcel of her personality, had been replaced by a frozen aloofness that was doing all sorts of crazy, unexpected things to his head. He was overcome with an uncontrollable desire to smash things. He turned sharply away. His head was telling him that if she wanted to go, then he should let her go, but his body was already missing the feel of hers and he was enraged with himself for being sidestepped by an emotion over which he appeared to have no control.

Brianna could sense the shift of his body away from her, even though she was trying hard not to actually look at him, and that was just a further strike of the hammer. He couldn't even look at her. She was now disposable, however much he had wanted her. He had found his mother, had had whatever conversation with her that had changed his mind about her, and now he had no further use for the woman he had taken and used.

'Well?' he demanded roughly. 'Where are you going to go at this hour? Brianna, please...'

She wanted to tell him that the last thing she could do was sleep in one of his guest bedrooms. Just the thought of him being under the same roof would have kept her up all night.

She backed towards the door. 'I'm going to go to the hospital.'

'And do *what* there, Brianna? Visiting hours are well and truly over and I don't think they'll allow overnight guests in the common area.' He felt as though he was being ripped apart. 'You have my word that I won't come near you,' he said, attempting to soften his tone. 'I'll leave the apartment, if you want. Go stay in a hotel.'

Did he think that she was scared that he might try and break down her bedroom door so that he could ravish her? Did he honestly imagine that she was foolish enough to fear any such thing after what he had said?

'You can leave or you can stay, Leo.' She gave a jerky shake of her shoulder. 'I don't honestly care. I'm going to the hospital and, no, I won't be trying to cadge a night's sleep on the sofa in the common area. I'm going to leave a letter for one of the nurses to hand to Bridget in the morning, explaining that I've had to get back to the pub.'

'And the reason for that being…?' There were shadows under her eyes. He didn't feel proud to acknowledge the fact that he had put them there. His guilty conscience refused to be reined in. 'What reason could you have for needing to rush back to the pub? Or do you intend to tell Bridget the truth about who I am?'

'I would never do that, Leo, and the fact that you would think that I might just shows how little you know me. As little, as it turns out, I know you. We were just a couple of strangers having fun for a few weeks.' Her heart constricted painfully when she said that. 'I know you think that I'm all wrapped up in you, but I'm not. I'm upset because I didn't take you for a liar and, now that I know what you are, I'm glad this is all over. Next to you, Daniel was a walk in the park!'

For several reasons, none of which she intended to divulge, this was closer to the truth than he could ever imagine and she could see from his dark flush that she had hit home. He had been fond of referring to her distant ex as one of life's great losers.

She stuck her chin up and looked him squarely in the eyes without flinching. 'After I've been to the hospital, I shall find somewhere cheap to stay until I can catch the first train out of London.'

'This isn't Ballybay! London isn't safe at night to be wandering around in search of cheap hotels!'

'I'll take my chances!' Of course he would see no problem with her sleeping in his apartment, she thought with punishing reality. She meant nothing to him, so why on earth would he be affected by her presence? And, if that were the case, then wouldn't it be the same for her? 'And when I leave here I never, ever want to see you again.'

# CHAPTER EIGHT

'DIDN'T THIS OCCUR to you at all, Miss Sullivan?'

Her doctor looked at her with the sort of expression that implied this was a conversation he had had many times before. Possibly, however, not with someone who was unmarried. Unmarried and pregnant in these parts was a rare occurrence.

Her head was swimming. It had been over a month since she had walked out of Leo's life for ever and in the interim she had heard not a word from him, although she had heard *about* him, thanks to Bridget, who emailed her regularly with updates on the joys of finding her long-lost son.

Bridget had remained in London in his apartment, where she had all the benefits of round-the-clock care and help courtesy of a man who had limitless funds. She hadn't even needed to fetch any of her clothes, as she was now the fortunate recipient of a brand-new wardrobe.

On all fronts, he was the golden child she thought she had lost for ever.

In between these golden tributes, Brianna never managed to get any answers to the questions she *really* wanted to ask, such as did he ever talk about her? Was he missing her? Was there someone else in his life?

And now *this*.

'No, not really.' Brianna found that she could barely

enunciate the words. Pregnant. They had been so careful. Aside from that one time… She resisted the temptation to put her hand on her still flat stomach. 'I…I didn't even notice that I'd skipped a period…' Because she had been so wrapped up thinking about him, missing him, wishing he was still around. So busy functioning on autopilot that she had missed the really big, life-altering thing happening.

'And what will you do now, Brianna?

Brianna looked at the kindly old man who had delivered her and pretty much everyone her age in Ballybay and beyond.

'I'm going to have this baby, Dr Fallow, and I shall be a very proud, single mother.' She stuck her chin up defiantly and he smiled at her.

'I would have expected nothing less from Annie Sullivan's daughter. And the father?'

*And the father…?*

The question plagued her over the next few days. He deserved to know. Or did he? He had used her and then dispatched her once her usefulness was at an end. Did a man like that deserve to know that she was having his baby? He had been ultra-careful with precautions. How ironic that despite the best laid plans—because of a split condom, a one-in-a-million chance—here she was, the exception to the rule. And a cruel exception, because having a baby was not on his agenda, least of all with a woman he had used. So what would be his reaction should she show up on his doorstep with the happy news that he was going to be a daddy? She shuddered when she thought of it: horror, rage, shock. And, although there was no way he could blame her, he would still be upset and enraged that fate had dealt him a blow he couldn't deal with.

Yet, how could she *not* tell him? Especially given the circumstances of his adoption? Would he appreciate being left in the dark about his own flesh and blood? Perhaps finding out at some much later date down the road, and being destined forever to imagine that his son or daughter had grown up thinking of him as someone who had not taken enough interest to make contact? Being left in the awful position of wondering whether his own life story had been repeated, except without him even being aware of it?

The pros and cons ran through her head like a constant refrain, although beneath that refrain the one consolation was that she was in no doubt that she was happy about the pregnancy, however much it would disrupt her way of life. In fact, she was ecstatic. She had not thought about babies, having had no guy in her life with whom to have them. And, although she couldn't have chosen a less suitable candidate for the role of father, she was filled with a sense of joyous wonder at the life slowly growing inside her.

A life which would soon become apparent; pregnancy was not a condition that could be kept secret. Within a month or two, she would be the talk of the town, and of course Bridget would know. How could she fail to?

Which pretty much concluded her agonising. Leo would find out and she would have to be the one to tell him before he heard it second-hand.

It seemed the sort of conversation to be held in the evening and, before the bustle of the pub could begin, sweeping her off her feet, she got on the phone and dialled his mobile.

Around her, the pub lacked its usual shine and polish. She would have to start thinking about getting someone in to cover for her on a fairly permanent basis. There was no way she and Shannon could cope but there was also no way she could afford to close the pub, far less find a buyer for it.

Money, she foresaw, was going to be a headache and she

gritted her teeth together because she knew what Leo's solution would be: fling money at the problem. Which would
leave her continually indebted to him and that was not a
situation that filled her with joy.

But then, she would never, ever be able to break contact
with him from here on in, would she?

Even if he just paid the occasional visit in between running those companies of his, he would still be a permanent
cloud on her horizon. She would have to look forward to
seeing him moving on, finding other women, other women
to whom he hadn't fabricated a convoluted story about
himself. Eventually, she would have to witness his happiness as he found his soul mate, married her, had children
with her. It didn't bear thinking about.

His disembodied voice, deep, dark and lazy, jolted her
out of her daydreaming and fired up every nerve in her
body. All at once, she could picture him in every vivid,
unsettling detail: the way he used to look at her, half-
brooding, full of sexy promise; the way he used to laugh
whenever she teased him; the way the muscles of his amazing body rippled and flexed when he moved…

'It's me,' she said a little breathlessly, before clearing
her throat and telling herself to get a grip.

'I know who it is, Brianna,' Leo drawled. He rose to shut
his office door. She had caught him as he had been about
to leave. Ever since his mother had arrived on the scene
and was recuperating happily at his apartment, he had been
leaving work earlier than normal. It was a change of pattern he could not have foreseen in a million years, but he
was strangely energised by getting to know his mother a
little better. She could never replace the couple who had
adopted him, but she was a person in her own right, and
one he found he wanted to get to know. It seemed that a

genetic link was far more powerful a bond than he could ever have conceived possible.

He thought back to that moment when he had sat next to her at her hospital bed and taken her hand in his. An awkward moment and one he had never envisaged but as she had lain there, frail and bewildered at her expensive private room, it had seemed right.

And he had told her—haltingly at first, trying to find the words to span over thirty years. He had watched her eyes fill up and had felt the way her hand had trembled. He had never expected his journey to take him there and he had been shocked at how much it had changed his way of thinking, had made him see the shades of grey between the black and white. No one could ever replace the wonderful parents he had had, but a new road had opened up—not better, but different—and he had felt a soaring sense of fulfilment at what lay ahead. He had known that they both did.

For a man who had always known the way ahead, he had discovered the wonder of finding himself on a path with no signposts, just his feelings to guide him, and as he had opened up to his mother, asked her questions, replied to the hundreds she had asked him in return, he had turned a corner. The unknown had become something to be embraced.

'How's Bridget?'

'I thought you spoke and emailed daily?' He sat back down at his desk and swivelled his chair so that it was facing the broad floor-to-ceiling glass panes that overlooked the city.

'Why are you calling?' It had been more of a struggle putting her behind him than he could ever have believed possible. Was it because Bridget was staying with him? Because her presence kept alive memories he wanted to bury? He didn't know. Whilst his head did all the right things and told him that she no longer had a place in his life—that what they'd had had been good but it had never been destined to last—some irrational part of him insisted on singing a different tune.

He had found his concentration inexplicably flagging in the middle of meetings. On more than one occasion, he had awoken from a dream-filled sleep to find himself with an erection. Cold showers were becoming the rule rather than the exception. All told, he felt as though he was in unchartered territory. He was taking new steps with his mother and discovering that old ways of dealing with exes did not apply to Brianna.

He knew that she and Bridget were in touch by phone daily and it took every ounce of willpower not to indulge his rampant curiosity and try to prise information out of his house guest. What was she up to? Had she found a replacement for him in her bed? There was no denying that she was hot; what man wouldn't want to try his luck? And she was no longer cocooned within those glacial walls of celibacy. She had stepped out from behind them and released all the unbelievable passion he knew her to be capable of. There was no way that she could ever return to living life like a nun. And, however much she had or hadn't been wrapped up in him, she was ripe for a rebound relationship.

Was that what she was doing right now—engaging in wild sex with some loser from the town or another passing stranger?

He had never considered himself someone who was prone to flights of fancy, but he was making up for lost time now.

All of this introduced a level of coolness to his voice as he stared out of the window and waited for her to come up with an answer.

She damn well wasn't phoning for an update on Bridget, so why was she?

Brianna picked up the unwelcoming indifference in his voice and it stung. Had he *completely* detached from her? How was that possible? And how was he going to greet what she had to tell him, were that the case?

'I…I…need to talk to you.'

'I'm listening. But make it quick. I was on my way out.'

'I need to see you…to discuss what I have to say.'

'Why?'

'Can't you be just a little more polite, Leo? I know you have no further use for me, but the least you can do is not treat me as though I'm something the cat dragged in.'

'Is it money?' His anger at himself for continuing to let her infiltrate his head and ambush his thoughts transferred into a healthy anger towards her and, although he knew he was being unfair, there was no way he was going to allow himself to be dragged down the apology route.

'I beg your pardon?'

'You know how rich I am now. You must know the lifestyle Bridget's enjoying—I'm sure she's told you so. Have you decided that you'd like me to throw some money in your direction for old times' sake?' God, was this *him*? He barely recognised the person behind the words.

Brianna clutched the phone so tightly that she thought she might break it in two. Did he know how insulting he was being right now? Did he care? How could she have misread someone so utterly? Was there some crazy missing connection in her head that allowed her to give everyone the benefit of the doubt, including people who were just bad for her health?

'You mentioned more than once that the place needed updating: new bar stools, new paint job on the outside, less tatty sofas in front of the fire…' The sofas had been damn near perfect, he seemed to recall. The sort of sofas a person could sink into and remain sunk in for hours, remain sunk in for a lifetime. 'Consider it done. On me. Call it thanks for, well, everything'

'How generous of you, Leo.' She reined in her explosive rage and kept her voice as neutral as she possibly could. 'And I suppose this might eventually have something to do with money. But I really need to see you face to face to talk about it.'

Perversely, Leo was disappointed that he had hit the nail on the head. Other women played the money angle. Other women assessed his wealth and expected a good time at his expense. It had never bothered him because, after all, fair's fair. But Brianna… She wasn't like other women. Apparently, however, she was.

'Name the figure,' he said curtly.

'I'd rather not. If you could just make an appointment to see me. I could come to London and take the opportunity to look in on Bridget as well…'

'I have no free time during the day. I could see you tomorrow some time after six thirty, and I'm doing you a favour because that would involve cancelling a conference call.'

'Er…' Money she knew she didn't have disappeared through the window at the prospect of finding somewhere to stay, because there was no way she would be staying at his apartment, especially after she had dropped her bombshell.

'Take it or leave it.' He cut into her indecisive silence. 'I can meet you at seven at a bistro near my office.' He named it and then, from nowhere, pictured her sitting there at one of the tables, waiting for him. He pictured her face, her startling prettiness; he pictured her body, which would doubtless be concealed underneath something truly unappealing—that waterproof coat of hers of indeterminate green which she seemed to wear everywhere.

On cue, his body jerked into life, sourly reminding him of the way just thinking of her could manage to turn him on.

Tomorrow, he resolved, he would rifle through his address book and see whether there wasn't someone he could date, if only as a distraction. Bridget, oddly, had not referred back to that aborted conversation she had had with him at the pub, had made no mention of Brianna at all. She would think there was nothing amiss were he to start dating. In fact, she would think something was amiss if he *didn't*.

'Well?' he said impatiently. 'Will you be there? This is a going, going, gone situation.'

'I'll be there. See you tomorrow.'

Brianna barely slept through the night. She was having a baby! Unplanned, unexpected, but certainly not unwanted.

She was on edge as she finally landed on English soil. The weather had taken a turn for the better but, to be on the safe side, she had still decided to wear her faithful old coat just in case. The deeper into the city she got, the more ridiculously out of place she felt in her clothing. Even at nearly seven in the evening, the streets were packed. Everyone appeared to be dressed in suits, carrying briefcases and in a massive rush.

She had given the address of the bistro to the taxi driver but, when she was dropped off, she remained outside on the pavement, her battered pull-along in one hand, her other hand shoved into the capacious pocket of her coat. Nerves threatened to overwhelm her. In fact, she wanted nothing more than to hop into the nearest taxi and ask it to deliver her right back to the airport.

There were people coming and going from the bistro. She stood to one side, shaking like a leaf, aware of the pathetic figure she cut, and then she took a deep breath and entered with all the trepidation of someone entering a lion's den.

The noise was deafening, exaggerated by the starkness of the surroundings and the wooden floor. It was teeming with people, all young, all beautiful. A young woman clacking along in her high heels, with a leather case clutched to her side, tripped over her pull-along and swore profusely before giving her the once-over with contempt.

'Oh God, darling, are you lost? In case you haven't noticed, this isn't the bus station. If you and your luggage take a left out of the door and keep walking, you both should hit the nearest bus stop and they can deliver you wherever you're going.'

Brianna backed away, speechless, and looked around desperately for Leo. Right now, he felt like the only safe port in a storm and she spotted him tucked away towards the back of the room, sitting at a table and nursing a drink. A wave of relief washed over her as she began threading her way towards him, her pull-along bumping into ankles and calves and incurring a trail of oaths on the way.

Leo watched her zig-zag approach with brooding intensity. Amongst the city folk, snappily dressed and all braying in loud voices that competed to be heard, she was as natural and as beautiful as a wild flower. He couldn't fail to notice the sidelong looks she garnered from some of the men and he quickly knocked back the remainder of his whisky in one gulp.

So she had come here on her begging mission. He would have to do a bit better than stare at her and make favourable comparisons between her and the rest of the overpaid, over-confident, over-arrogant crowd on show. He

signalled to a waiter to bring him another drink. It was a
perk of this bar that he was the only one to receive waiter
service, but then again, had it not been for his injection
of cash years previously, the place would have been run
into the ground. Now he owned a stake in it and, as soon
as he clicked his fingers, the staff jumped to attention. It
certainly saved the tedium of queuing at the bar trying to
vie for attention. It also secured him the best table in the
house, marginally away from the crowds.

'I'm sorry I'm a little late.' Brianna found that she could
barely look at him without her entire nervous system gathering pace and going into overdrive. How had she managed
to forget the impact he had on her senses? The way those
dark, dark eyes could make her head swim and scramble
her thoughts until she could barely speak?

'Sit.' He motioned to the chair facing him with a curt
nod and she sank onto it and pulled her little bag alongside her. 'So…' He leant back and folded his arms. She
was pink and her hair, which had obviously started the
trip as a single braid down her back, was in the process
of unravelling.

'I hadn't expected so much noise.' Her eyes skittered
away from his face but then returned to look at him with
resolve. She had to forget about being out of her depth. She
had come here for one reason and one reason only and she
wasn't going to let an attack of nerves stand in her way.
How much more could he hurt her?

Leo cast a cursory glance around him and asked her
what she wanted to drink: a glass of water. He would have
expected something a little more stiff to get her through
her 'begging bowl' speech, but to each their own. He ordered some mineral water and another stiff drink for himself then settled back with an air of palpable boredom.

Something in him railed against believing the worst of

her, knowing her to be the person that she was, yet he refused to give house room to that voice. He felt he needed to be black and white or else forever be lost. Let it not be forgotten that she had refused to listen to him when he had attempted to explain the reason for his fabrications. She had turned her back and stalked off and for the past month he had seen and heard nothing from her.

She had taken off her coat, the gruesome coat which he was annoyed to discover made inroads into his indifference, because he could remember teasing her that she needed something a little less worn, that waterproof coats like that were never fashion statements.

'What's it like?' Brianna opened the conversation with something as far removed from what she actually needed to say as she could get, and Leo shot her a perplexed glance.

'What's what like? What are you talking about?'

'Having your… Having Bridget in your life. It must be very satisfying for you.'

Leo flushed. No one knew about Bridget, aside from Harry. He had never been the sort of man who spilled his guts to all and sundry and there had been absolutely no temptation to tell anyone about his mother living with him. He had not been dating, so there had been no women coming to his apartment, asking questions. Even if there had been, it was debatable whether he would have confided in any of them or not. He looked at her open, upturned face and found it hard to resurrect his cynicism.

'It's working for me,' he said gruffly. Working for them both. The years had dropped off his mother. She had been to the hairdresser, had her hair styled, had her nails done… She bore little resemblance to the fragile creature he had first set eyes on.

Drinks were brought and he sat back to allow the waiter to fuss as he put them on the table, along with a plate of appetisers which had not been ordered. 'But you didn't come here to talk about my relationship with Bridget.'

'No, I didn't, but I'm interested.' She just couldn't launch into her real reason for coming to London without some sort of preamble.

And, an inner voice whispered, didn't she just want to prolong being in his company, like a thief stealing time that didn't belong to them? Didn't she just want to breathe him in, that clean, masculine scent, and slide her eyes over a body she knew so well even when, as now, it was sheathed in the finest tailored suit money could buy?

'Just tell me why you're here, Brianna. You said something about money. How much are you looking for?'

'It's a bit more complicated than that.'

'What's more complicated than asking for a hand-out?'

Brianna looked down and fiddled with the bottle of water before pouring a little more into her glass. She envied him his stiff drink. She felt that under different circumstances, without this baby inside her, she could have done with a little Dutch courage.

'Leo…' She looked him directly in the eye and felt that this was the last time that she would be seeing him like this: a free man who could do whatever he wanted to do. She could even appreciate that, however dismissive he was of her now, it was an emotion that would soon be overtaken by far more overwhelming ones. Perhaps, thinking about it, it was just as well that they were having this conversation somewhere noisy and crowded.

'I'm pregnant.'

For a few seconds, Leo thought that he might have misheard her, but even as his mind was absorbing her body language—taking in the way she now couldn't meet his eyes, the hectic flush on her cheeks, the way her hand was trembling on the glass—he still couldn't put two and two together.

'Come again?' He leaned forward, straining to catch her every word. There was a buzzing in his ears that was growing louder by the second.

'I'm having a baby, Leo. Your baby. I'm sorry. I do realise that this is probably the last thing in the world you expected to hear, and the last thing you *wanted* to hear, but I felt you ought to know. I did think about keeping it to myself but that would have been impossible. Well, you know how small the place is, and sooner or later Bridget would have found out. In fact, there's no way that I would have wanted to keep it from her.'

Why wasn't he saying anything? She had expected more of an immediate and explosive reaction, but then he was probably still in a state of shock.

'You're telling me that you're having my baby.' The words felt odd as they passed his lips. The thought had taken root now with blinding clarity and he looked down at her stomach. She was as slender as she had always been. He heard himself asking questions: how pregnant was she? Was she absolutely certain? Had it been verified by a doctor? He knew home tests existed but any test that could be done at home would always be open to error…

'I'm not expecting anything from you,' Brianna ended. 'I just thought that you ought to know.'

'You thought that *I ought to know*?' Leo shot her a look of utter incredulity. The impersonal bistro he had chosen now seemed inappropriate. Restless energy was pouring through his body and, as fast as he tried to decipher a pattern to what he was thinking, his thoughts came unstuck, leaving him with just the explosive realisation that in a matter of months he was going to be a father.

'I realise that you might want to have some input…'

'You have got to be kidding me, Brianna. You come here, drop this bombshell on me, and the only two things you can find to say are that you felt I *ought to know* and you realise that I *might want some input*? We have to get out of here.'

'And go where?' she cried.

'Somewhere a little less *full of chattering morons.*'

'I'm not going to your apartment,' she said, refusing to budge and clutching the sides of her chair as though fearful that at any moment he might just get it into his head to bodily pick her up and haul her over his shoulder to the front door, caveman style.

'I haven't said anything to Bridget yet and I'd rather not just at the moment. I…I need time to absorb it all myself so, if you don't mind, I'd quite like to stay here. Not that there's much more for me to bring to the table.'

'And another classic line from you. God, I just don't believe this.'

Brianna watched as he dropped his head to his hands. 'I'm so sorry to be the bearer of unexpected tidings. Like I said, though…'

'Spare me whatever pearls of wisdom are going to emerge from your mouth, Brianna.' He raised his head to stare at her. 'It is as it is, and now we're going to have to decide how we deal with this situation.' He rubbed his eyes and continued holding her gaze with his.

'Perhaps you should go away and think about this. It's a lot to take on board. We could fix a time to meet again.'

'I don't think so.' He straightened and sat back. 'Waiting for another day isn't going to alter this problem.'

Brianna stiffened. 'This isn't your problem, it's mine, and I don't see it as a *problem*. I'm going to be the one having the baby and I shall be the one looking after it. I recognise that you'll want to contribute in some way, but let me assure you that I expect nothing from you.'

'Do you honestly believe that you can dump this on me and I'm going to walk away from it?'

'I don't know. A few weeks ago I would have said that the guy at the pub who helped clear snow wouldn't, but then you weren't that guy at all, were you? So, honestly? I have no idea.' She sat on her hands and leaned towards him. 'If you want to contribute financially, then that would be fine and much appreciated. I don't expect you to give anything to me, but helping to meet the needs of the baby would be okay. They may be small, but they can be very expensive, and you know all too well what the finances at the pub are like. Especially with all the closures of late.'

'I know what you think of me, Brianna, but I'm not a man to run away from my responsibilities—and in this instance my responsibilities don't stop at sending you a monthly cheque to cover baby food.'

'They don't?' Brianna queried uneasily. She wondered what else he had in mind. 'Naturally you would be free to see your child whenever you wanted, but it might be difficult, considering you live in London…' She quailed inwardly at the prospect of him turning up at the front door. She wondered whether the onslaught of times remembered, before she had discovered who he really was, would be just too much for her. Not that she would have any choice. It would be his right to visit his child, whether it made her uncomfortable or not.

'Visiting rights? No, I don't think so.'

'I won't let you take custody of my baby.'

'*Our* baby,' he corrected.

Brianna blanched as her worst imaginings went into free fall. She hadn't even thought that he might want to take the baby away from her, yet, why hadn't that occurred to her? He was adopted. He would have very strong feelings about being on hand as a father because his own real father had not been on hand. And, whatever concoctions he had come up with to disguise his true identity, she knew instinctively that he possessed a core of inner integrity.

And those concoctions, she was reluctantly forced to conclude, had not been fabricated for the sheer hell of it. They had been done for a reason and, once he had embarked on that road, it would have been difficult to get off it.

Would that core of integrity propel him to try and fight her for custody of the baby? He was rolling in money whilst she was borderline broke and, when it came to getting results, the guy who was rolling in money was always going to win hands down over the woman who was borderline broke. You didn't need a degree in quantum physics to work that one out.

'You can stop looking as though you're about to pass out, Brianna. I have no intention of indulging in a protracted battle with you to take custody of our baby.' He was slightly surprised at how naturally the words 'our baby' rolled off his tongue. The shock appeared to have worn off far more quickly than might have been expected, but then he prided himself as being the sort of guy who could roll with the punches and come up with solutions in the tightest of spots.

Brianna breathed a sigh of relief. 'So what are you proposing?'

'We get married. Obvious solution.'

'You have got to be joking.'

'Do I look like someone about to burst into laughter?'

'That's a crazy idea.'

'Explain why.'

'Because it's not a solution, Leo. Two people don't just

*get married* because, accidentally, there's a baby on the way. Two people who *broke up.* Two people who wouldn't have laid eyes on one another again were it not for the fact that the girl in question happens to find herself pregnant.'

'Brianna, I'm not prepared to take a backseat in the upbringing of my child. I'm not prepared for any child of mine to ever think that they got less of me than they might have wanted.'

'I'm not asking you to take a back seat in anything.'

'Nor,' Leo continued, overriding her interruption as though it hadn't registered, 'am I willing to watch on the sidelines as you find yourself another man who decides to take over the upbringing of my child.'

'That's not likely to happen! I think I've had enough of men to last a lifetime.'

'Of course, you'll have to move to London, but in all events that won't depend on the sale of the pub. In fact, you can hand it over to someone else to run on your behalf.'

'Are you listening to a *word* I'm saying?'

'Are you listening to what *I'm* saying?' he said softly. 'I hope so, because the proposal I've put on the table is the only solution at hand.'

'This isn't a maths problem that needs a solution. This is something completely different.'

'I'm failing to see your objections, aside from a selfish need to put yourself ahead of our child.'

'I could never live in London. And I could never marry someone for the wrong reasons. We would end up resenting one another and that would be the worst possible atmosphere in which to raise a child. Don't you see that?'

'Before you knew who I was,' Leo said tautly, his dark eyes fixed intently on her face, 'did you hope that our relationship would go further?'

He sat forward and all of a sudden her space was invaded and she could barely breathe. 'I knew that you weren't intending on hanging around,' she said and she could hear the choked breathlessness in her voice. 'You said so. You made that perfectly clear.'

'Which doesn't answer my question. Were you hoping for more?'

'I didn't think it would end the way it did,' she threw back at him with bristling defiance.

'But it did, and you may not have liked the way it ended, but what we had…' He watched the slow colour creep up her cheeks and a rush of satisfaction poured through him, because behind those lowered eyes he could *smell* the impact he still had on her.

'This wouldn't be a marriage in name only for the sake of a child. This would be a marriage in every sense of the word because—let's not kid each other—what we had was good.' Her naked, pale body flashed through his mind, as did the memory of all those little whimpering noises she made when he touched her, the way her nostrils flared and her eyelids quivered as her body gathered pace and hurtled towards orgasm. He already felt himself harden at the thought and this time he didn't try to kill it at source because it was inappropriate given she was no longer part of his life. She was a part of his life now, once again, and the freedom to think of her without restraint was a powerful kick to his system.

'What we had was…was…'

'Was good and you know it. Shall I remind you how good it was?' He didn't give her time to move or time even to think about what was coming. He leant across the small table, cupped his hand on the nape of her neck and pulled her towards him.

Brianna's body responded with the knee-jerk response of immediate reaction, as though responding with learned behaviour. Her mouth parted and the feel his tongue thrusting against her was as heady as the most powerful drug. Her mind emptied and she kissed him back, and she felt as though she never wanted the kiss to end. The coolness of his withdrawal, leaving her with her mouth still slightly parted and her eyes half-closed, was a horrifying return to reality.

'Point proven,' he murmured softly. 'So, when I tell you that you need to look outside the box and start seeing the upsides to my proposal, you know what I'm talking about. This won't be a union without one or two definite bonuses.'

'I'll never move to London and I'll never marry you.' Her breathing was only now returning to normal and the mortification of what she had done, of how her treacherous body had *betrayed* her, felt like acid running through her veins. 'I'm going now but I'll give you a call in a couple of days. When you're ready to accept what I've said, then we'll talk again.' She stood up on wobbly legs and turned her back. The urge to run away as fast as she could was overpowering, and she did. Out to the pavement, where she hailed the nearest taxi and instructed him to drive her to a hotel—something cheap, something close to the airport.

She wouldn't marry him. He didn't love her and there was no way that she would ever accept sacrificing both their lives for the wrong reason, whatever he said about the bonus of good sex. Good sex would die and then where would they be?

But she had to get away because she knew that there was something craven and weak in the very deepest part of her that might *just* play with the idea.

And there was no way she was going to give that weak, craven part of her a voice.

# CHAPTER NINE

LEO LOOKED AT the sprawling house facing him and immediately wondered whether he had gone for the wrong thing. Too big, maybe? Too ostentatious? Too much land?

He shook his head with frustration and fired a couple of questions at the estate agent without bothering to glance in her direction.

In the space of six weeks, this was the eighth property he had personally seen out in the rolling Berkshire countryside, sufficiently far away from London to promote the idea of clean air, whilst being within easy commuting distance from the city.

Brianna had no idea that he was even hunting down a house. As far as she was concerned, he was the guy she'd refused to commit to who seemed intent on pursuing her even though she had already given him her answer—again and again and again, in varying formats, but all conveying the same message.

*No thank you, I won't be getting married to you.*

On the upside, he had managed to persuade her temporarily to move to London, although that in itself had been a task of no small order. She had refused to budge, had informed him that he was wasting his time, that they weren't living in the Victorian ages. She had folded her arms, given him a gimlet stare of pure stubbornness. He had been reduced to deviating from his intention to get what he wanted—what was *needed*, at all costs—in favour of thinking creatively.

For starters, he had had to pursue her to Ireland because she'd refused to continue her conversation with him in London. And then, he had had to travel to the pub to see her, because she didn't want him staying under her roof, not given the circumstances. He had refrained from pointing out the saying about horses bolting and stable doors. He had initiated his process of getting what he wanted by pointing out that it made sense.

He had done that over the finest meal to be had in a really very good restaurant not a million miles away from the pub. He had used every argument in the book and had got precisely nowhere. Then he had returned, this time to try and persuade her to see his point of view during a bracing walk by one of the lakes with the wind whipping his hair into disarray and his mega-expensive coat proving no match for the cold. He had tried to remind her of the sexual chemistry that was still there between them, but had cut short that line of argument when she'd threatened to walk back to the pub without him.

He had informed her that there wasn't a single woman alive who wouldn't have chewed off his arm to accept an offer of marriage from him, which had been another tactical error.

He had dropped all talk of anything and concentrated on just making her feel comfortable in his presence, whilst marvelling that she could carry on keeping him at arm's length, considering how close they had been. But by this point he had been clued up enough to make sure that he didn't hark back to the past. Nothing to remind her about how much she clearly loathed him, having found out about his lies.

Never in his life had Leo put this much effort into one woman.

And never in his life had he had so many cold showers. From having given no thought whatsoever to settling down, far less having a child, he now seemed fixated by the baby growing inside her and, the more fixated he became, the more determined he was that she would marry him. He was turned on by everything about her. Turned on by the way she moved, the way she looked at him, by all her little gestures that seemed ingrained inside his head so that, even when she wasn't around, he was thinking about her constantly.

Was it a case of the inaccessible becoming more and more desirable? Was it because she was now carrying his baby that his body seemed to be on fire for her all the time? Or was it just that he hadn't stopped wanting her because it had been a highly physical relationship that had not been given the opportunity of dying a natural death?

He didn't know and he didn't bother analysing it. He just knew that he still wanted her more than he could remember wanting anyone. He wanted her to be his. The thought of some other man stepping into his shoes, doing clever things behind the bar of the pub and having a say in his child's welfare, made him grit his teeth together in impotent rage.

The estate agent, a simpering woman in her thirties, was saying something about the number of bedrooms and Leo scowled.

'How many?'

'Eight! Perfect for having the family over!'

'Too many. And I can look at it from here and see straight away that it would be far too big for the person I have in mind.'

'Perhaps the lucky lady would like to pop along and have a look for herself? It's really rather grand inside...'

Leo flinched at the word 'grand'. He pictured Brianna wiping the bar with a cloth, standing back in her old jeans and sloppy jumper to survey her handiwork, before retiring to the comfy sofa in the lounge which had been with her practically since she'd been a kid. She wouldn't have a clue what to do with 'grand' and he had a gut feeling that if he settled on anything like this she would end up blaming him.

How, he thought as house number nine bit the dust, had he managed to end up with the one woman in the world to whom a marriage proposal was an insult and who was determined to fight him every inch of the way? Even though the air sizzled between them with a raw, elemental electricity that neither of them could deny.

But at least he had managed to get her to London. It was a comforting thought as his Ferrari ate up the miles back to the city centre and his penthouse apartment.

He had appealed to her sense of fairness. He wanted to be there while she was pregnant and what better way than for her to move to London? No need to live in his apartment. He would find somewhere else for her, somewhere less central. It would be great for Bridget as well. Indeed, it would be a blessing in disguise, for Bridget was tiring of the concrete jungle of inner London. She was back on her feet, albeit in a restricted way, and the constant crowds terrified her. They could share something small but cosy in West London. He would personally see to it that a manager was located for the pub...

She had acquiesced. That had been ten days ago and, although he had made sure to visit them both every evening after work, he had ostensibly dropped all mention of marriage.

That aggressive need to conquer had been forced into retreat and he was now playing a waiting game. He wasn't sure what would happen if that waiting game didn't work and he preferred not to dwell on that. Instead, he phoned his secretary and found out what other gems were available on the property market in picturesque Berkshire.

'Too impressive,' he told her about his last failed viewing. It was added to all the other too 'something or other' that had characterised the last eight viewings, all of which had come to nothing. He laughed when she suggested that he send someone in his place to at least narrow the possibilities.

He couldn't imagine anyone he knew having the slightest idea as to what to look for when it came to Brianna. They were people who only knew a London crowd, socialites for whom there could be nothing that could ever be too grand.

'Find me some more properties.' He concluded his conversation with his long-suffering PA. 'And forget about the marble bathrooms and indoor swimming pools. Go smaller.'

He hung up. It wasn't yet two-thirty in the afternoon. He had never taken this much time off work in his life before. Except for when he had voluntarily marooned himself at Brianna's pub. And yet, he was driven to continue his search. Work, meetings and deals would just have to take a back seat.

His secretary called him on his mobile just as he was leaving the M25, heading into London.

'It's a small village near, er, Sunningdale. Er, shall I read you the details? It's just on the market. Today, in fact. Thank goodness for estate agents who remember we exist…'

Leo thought that most estate agents would remember

any client for whom money was no object. 'I'll check that out now.' He was already halfway back to London but he manoeuvred his car off the motorway and back out. 'Cancel my five o'clock meeting.'

'You've already cancelled Sir Hawkes twice.'

'In that case, let Reynolds cover. He's paid enough; a little delegation in his direction will do him the world of good.'

He made it to the small village in good time and, the very second he saw the picture-postcard cottage with the sprawling garden in the back and the white picket fence at the front, he knew he had hit the jackpot.

He didn't bother with an offer. He would pay the full asking price and came with cash in hand. The estate agent couldn't believe his luck. Leo waved aside the man's ingratiating and frankly irritating bowing and scraping and elicited all the pertinent details he needed for an immediate purchase.

'And if the occupants need time to find somewhere else, you can tell them that they'll be generously compensated over and beyond what they want for the house to leave immediately.' He named a figure and the estate agent practically swooned. 'Here's my card. Call me in an hour and we'll get the ball rolling. Oh, and I'll be bringing someone round tomorrow, if not sooner, to look at it. Make sure it's available.' He was at his car and the rotund estate agent was dithering behind him, clutching the business card as though it were a gold ingot.

'What if...?' He cleared his throat anxiously as he was forced to contemplate a possible hitch in clinching his commission. 'What if the sellers want to wait and see if a better offer comes along?'

About to slide into the driving seat, Leo paused and

looked at the much shorter man with a wry expression. 'Oh, trust me, that won't be happening.'

'Sir...'

'Call me——and I'll be expecting a conversation that I want to hear.' He left the man staring at him red-faced, perspiring and doubtless contemplating the sickening prospect of sellers who might prove too greedy to accept the quick sale.

Leo knew better. They simply wouldn't be able to believe their luck.

He could easily have made it back to the office to catch the tail end of the meeting he had cancelled at the last minute. Instead, he headed directly to Brianna's house, which was an effortless drive off the motorway and into London suburbia.

Brianna heard the low growl of the Ferrari as it pulled up outside the house. It seemed her ears were attuned to the sound. She immediately schooled her expression into one of polite aloofness. In the kitchen Bridget was making them both a cup of tea, fussing as she always seemed to do now, clucking around her like a mother hen because she was pregnant, even though Brianna constantly told her that pregnancy wasn't an illness and that Bridget was the one in need of looking after.

'He's early this evening!' Bridget exclaimed with pleasure. 'I wonder why? I think I'll give you two a little time together and have a nice, long bath. The doctor says that I should take it easy. You know that.'

Brianna raised her eyebrows wryly and stood up. 'I don't think chatting counts as not taking it easy,' she pointed out. 'Besides, you know Leo enjoys seeing you when he gets here.' Every time she saw them together, she felt a lump of emotion gather at the back of her throat. However cut-throat and ruthless he might be, and however much of a lying bastard he had been, he was always gentle with Bridget. He didn't call her 'Mum' but he treated her with the respect and consideration any mother would expect from her child. And they spoke of all the inconsequential things that happened on a daily basis. Perhaps they had explored the past already and neither wanted to revisit it.

At any rate, Bridget was a changed person. She looked healthier, more *vibrant*. The sort of woman who was actually only middle-aged, who could easily get out there and find herself another guy but who seemed perfectly content to age gracefully by herself.

She quelled the urge to insist to Bridget that she stay put as the older woman began heading to her bedroom on the ground floor—a timely coincidence because the owners of the house from whom they were renting had had to cater for an ageing relative of their own.

Her stomach clenched as she heard the key being inserted into the front door.

She still wondered how he had managed to talk her into moving to London, a city she hated because it was too fast, too crowded and too noisy for her tastes.

But move to London she had, admittedly to a quieter part of the city, and now that she was here she was in danger of becoming just a little too accustomed to having Leo around. Okay, so he didn't show up *every* evening, and he never stayed the night, but his presence was becoming an addiction she knew she ought to fight.

He had dropped all talk of marriage and yet she still felt on red alert the second he walked through the door. Her eyes still feasted surreptitiously on him and, even though she knew that she should be thanking her lucky stars that he was no longer pursuing the whole marriage thing—because he had 'come to his senses' and 'seen the foolishness of hitching his wagon to a woman he didn't love'—she was oddly deflated by the ease with which he had jettisoned the subject.

As always, her first sight of him as he strode into the small hallway, with its charming flagstone floor and tiny stained-glass window to one side, was one of intense *awareness*. She literally felt her mouth go dry.

'You're here earlier than…um…normal.' She watched as he dealt her a slashing smile, one that made her legs go to jelly, one that made her want to hurl herself at him and wrap her arms around his neck. Every time she felt like this, she recalled what he had said about any marriage between them having upsides, having the distinct bonus of very good sex…

Leo's eyes swept over her in an appraisal that was almost unconscious. He took in the loose trousers, because there was just a hint of a stomach beginning to show; the baggy clothes that would have rendered any woman drab and unappealing but which seemed unbelievably sexy when she was wearing them.

'Is Bridget around?' He had to drag his eyes away from her. Hell, she had told him in no uncertain terms that mutual sexual attraction just wasn't enough on which to base a marriage, so how was it that she still turned him on? Even more so, now that she was carrying his baby.

'She's upstairs resting.'

'There's something I want to show you.' He had no doubt that he would be able to view the property at this hour. He was, after all, in the driving seat. 'So…why don't you get your coat on? It's a drive away.'

'What do you want to show me?'

'It's a surprise.'

'You know I hate surprises.' She blushed when he raised one eyebrow, amused at that titbit of shared confidence between them.

'This won't be the sort of surprise you got two years ago when you returned from a weekend away to find the pub flooded.'

'I'm not dressed for a meal out.' Nor was she equipped for him to resume his erosion of her defences and produce more arguments for having his way...although she killed the little thrill at the prospect of having him try and convince her to marry him.

'You look absolutely fine.' He looked her over with a thoroughness that brought hectic colour to her cheeks. And, while he disappeared to have a few quick words with Bridget, Brianna took the opportunity—cursing herself, because why on earth did it matter, really?—to dab on a little bit of make-up and do something with her hair. She also took off the sloppy clothes and, although her jeans were no longer a perfect fit, she extracted the roomiest of them from the wardrobe and twinned them with a brightly coloured thick jumper that at least did flattering things for her complexion.

'So, where are we going?' They had cleared some of the traffic and were heading out towards the motorway. 'Why are we leaving London?'

Leo thought of the perfect cottage nestled in the perfect grounds with all those perfect features and his face relaxed into a smile. 'And you're smiling.' For some reason that crooked half-smile disarmed her. Here in the car, as they swept out of London on a remarkably fine afternoon, she felt infected with a holiday spirit, a reaction to the stress she had been under for the past few weeks. 'A man's allowed to smile, isn't he?' He flashed her a sideways glance that warmed her face. 'We're having a baby, Brianna. Being cold towards one another is not an option.'

Except, she thought, *he* hadn't been cold towards *her*. He had done his damnedest to engage her in conversation and, thus far, he had remained undeterred by her lack of enthusiasm for engagement. She chatted because Bridget was usually there with them and he, annoyingly, ignored her cagey responses and acted as though everything was perfectly fine between them. He cheerfully indulged his mother's obvious delight in the situation and, although neither of them had mentioned the marriage proposal, they both knew that Bridget was contemplating that outcome with barely contained glee.

'I hadn't realised that I was being cold,' she said stiffly. Her eyes drifted to his strong forearms on the steering wheel. He had tossed his jacket in the back seat and rolled up the sleeves of his shirt to his elbows. She couldn't look even at that slither of bare skin, the sprinkling of dark hair on his arms, without her mind racing backwards in time to when they were lovers and those hands were exploring every inch of her body.

'No, sometimes you're not,' he murmured in a low voice and Brianna looked at him narrowly.

'Meaning?'

'Meaning that there are many times when your voice is cool but the glances you give me are anything but...' He switched the radio on to soft classical music, leaving her to ponder that remark in silence. Did he expect her to say something in answer to that? And what could she say? She *knew* that he had an effect on her; she *knew* that she just couldn't stop herself from sliding those sidelong glances at him, absorbing the way he moved, the curve of his mouth, the lazy dark eyes. Of course he would have noticed! What *didn't* he notice?

She was so wrapped up in her thoughts that she only noticed that they had completely left London behind when fields, scattered villages and towns replaced the hard strip of the motorway, and then she turned to him with confusion.

'We're in the countryside.' She frowned and then her breath caught in her throat as he glanced across to her with amusement.

'Well spotted.'

'It's a bit far to go for a meal out.' Perhaps he wanted to talk to her about something big, something important. Maybe he was going to tell her that he had listened to everything she had said and had come to the conclusion that he could survive with her returning to Ireland whilst he popped up occasionally to see his offspring. Perhaps he thought that a destination far away would be suitable for that kind of conversation, because it would allow her time to absorb it on the return trip back into London.

Had having her at close quarters reminded him of how little he wanted any kind of committed relationship? Had familiarity bred the proverbial contempt? For maybe the first time in his life, he had been tied to a routine of having to curtail his work life to accommodate both her and Bridget. Had he seen that as a dire warning of what might be expected should he pursue his intention of marrying her, and had it put him off?

The more she thought about it, the more convinced she was that whatever he had to say over a charming pub dinner in the middle of nowhere would be...

*Something she wouldn't want to hear.*

Yet she knew that that was the wrong reaction. She needed to be strong and determined in the road she wanted to follow. She didn't want a half-baked marriage with a guy who felt himself trapped, for whom the only option looming was to saddle himself with her for the rest of his life. No way!

But her heart was beating fast and there was a ball of misery unfurling inside her with each passing signpost.

When the car turned off the deserted road, heading up a charming avenue bordered by trees not yet in leaf, she lay back and half-closed her eyes.

She opened them as they drew up outside one of the prettiest houses she had ever seen.

'Where are we?'

'This is what I wanted to show you.' Leo could barely contain the satisfaction in his voice. He had been sold on first sight. On second sight, he was pleased to find that there was no let-down. It practically had her name written all over it.

'You wanted to show me a *house*?'

'Come on.' He swung out of the car and circled round to hold her door open for her, resisting the urge to help her out, because she had already told him that she hadn't suddenly morphed into a piece of delicate china simply because she was pregnant.

Brianna dawdled behind him as he strode towards the front door and stooped to recover a key which had been placed underneath one of the flower pots at the side of the front step. What the hell was going on? She took a deep breath and realised that, although they were only a matter of forty-five minutes out of West London, the air smelled different. Cleaner.

'This isn't just any house.' He turned to look at her and was pleased at the expression on her face, which was one of rapt appreciation. 'Bar the technicalities, I've bought this house.'

'You've *bought* this house?'

'Come in and tell me what you think.'

'But...'

'Shh...' He placed a finger gently over her parted lips

and the feel of his warm skin against hers made her tremble. 'You can ask all the questions you want after you've had a look around.'

Despite the fact that he had only looked around the place once, Leo had no hesitation on acting as tour guide for the house, particularly pointing out all the quaint features he was certain she would find delightful. There was a real fire in both the sitting room and the snug, an Aga in the kitchen, bottle-green bedrooms that overlooked an orchard, which he hadn't actually noticed on first viewing, but which he now felt qualified to show her with some pride. He watched as she dawdled in the rooms, staring out of the windows, touching the curtains and trailing her finger along the polished oak banister as they returned downstairs, ending up in the kitchen, which had a splendid view of the extensive back gardens.

The owners had clearly been as bowled over by his over-the-top, generous offer as he had anticipated. There was a bottle of champagne on the central island and two champagne glasses.

'Well? What do you think?'

'It's wonderful,' Brianna murmured. 'I'd never have thought that you could find somewhere like this so close to London. Is it going to be a second home for you?'

'It's going to be a first home for us.'

Brianna felt as though the breath had temporarily been knocked out of her. Elation zipped through her at the thought of this—a house, the perfect house, shared with the man she loved and their child. In the space of a few seconds, she projected into the future where she saw their son or daughter enjoying the open space, running through the garden with a dog trailing behind, while she watched from the kitchen window with Leo right there behind her, sitting by the big pine table, chatting about his day.

The illusion disappeared almost as fast as it had surfaced because that was never going to be reality. The reality would be her, stuck out here on her own, while Leo carried on working all hours in the city, eventually bored by the woman he was stuck with. He would do his duty for his child but the image of cosy domesticity was an illusion and she had to face that.

'It's not going to work,' she said abruptly, turning away and blinking back stupid tears. 'Nothing's changed, Leo, and you can't bribe me into marrying you with a nice house and a nice garden.'

For a few seconds, Leo wasn't sure that he had heard her correctly. He had been so confident of winning her over with the house that he was lost for words as what she had said gradually sank in.

'I didn't realise that I was trying to bribe you,' he muttered in a driven undertone. He raked his fingers through his hair and grappled with an inability to get his thoughts in order. 'You liked the house; you said so.'

'I do, but a house isn't enough, just like sex isn't enough. That glue would never keep us together.' The words felt as though they had been ripped out of her and she had to turn away because she just couldn't bear to see his face.

'Right.' And still he couldn't quite get it through his head that she had turned him down, that any notion of marriage was over. He hesitated and stared at the stubborn angle of her profile then he strode towards the door. He was filled with a surge of restlessness, a keen desire to be outside, as if the open air might clear his head and point him towards a suitably logical way forward.

It was a mild evening and he circled the house, barely taking in the glorious scenery he had earlier made a great show of pointing out to her.

Inside, Brianna heard the slam of the front door and

spun around, shaking like a leaf. The void he had left behind felt like a physical, tangible weight in the room, filling it up until she thought she would suffocate.

Where had he gone? Surely he wouldn't just drive off and leave her alone here in the middle of nowhere? She contemplated the awkward drive back into London and wondered whether it wouldn't be better to be stuck out here. But, when she dashed out of the front door, it was to find his car parked exactly where it had been when they had first arrived. And he was nowhere to be seen.

He was a grown man, fully capable of taking care of himself, and yet as she dashed down the drive to the main road and peered up and down, failing to spot him, she couldn't stop a surge of panic rising inside her.

What if he had been run over by a car? It was very quiet here, she sternly told herself; what called itself the main road was hardly a thoroughfare. . In fact, no more than a tractor or two and the occasional passing car, so there was no need to get into a flap. But, like a runaway train, she saw in her mind's eyes his crumpled body lying at the kerbside, and she felt giddy and nauseous at the thought of it.

She circled the house at a trot, circled it again and then…she saw him sitting on the ground under one of the trees, his back towards the house. Sitting on the *muddy* ground in his hand-tailored Italian suit.

'What are you doing?' She approached him cautiously because for the life of her she had never seen him like this—silent, his head lowered, his body language so redolent of vulnerability that she felt her breath catch painfully in her throat.

He looked up at her and her mouth went dry. 'You have no intention of ever forgiving me for the lie I told you, have you?' he asked so quietly that she had to bend a little to hear what he was saying. 'Even though you know that I had no intention of engineering a lie when I first arrived. Even though you know, or you *should* know, that what appeared harmless to me at the time was simply a means towards an end. I was thinking on my feet. I never expected to end up painting myself into the box of pathological liar.'

'I know you're not that,' Brianna said tentatively. She settled on the ground next to him. 'Your suit's going to be ruined.'

'So will your jeans.'

'My jeans cost considerably less than your suit.' She ventured a small smile and met with nothing in response, just those dark, dark eyes boring into her. More than anything else she wanted to bridge the small gap between them and reach for his hand, hold it in hers, but she knew that that was just love, her love for him, and it wouldn't change anything. She had to stand firm, however tough it was. She had to project ahead and not listen to the little voice in her head telling her that his gesture, his magnificent gesture of buying this perfect house for her, was a sign of something more significant.

'You were right,' he admitted in the same sort of careful voice that was so disconcerting.

'Right about what?'

'I was trying to bribe you with this house. The garden. Anything that would induce you to give us a chance. But nothing will ever be enough for you to do that because you can't forgive me for my deception, even though it was a deception that was never intended to hurt you.'

'I felt like I didn't know who you were, Leo,' Brianna said quietly. 'One minute you were the man helping out at the pub, mucking in, presumably writing your book when you were closeted away in the corner of the bar…and then the next minute you're some high-flying millionaire with a penthouse apartment and a bunch of companies, and the book you were writing was never a book at all. It was just loads of work and emails so that you could keep your businesses ticking over while you stayed at the pub and used me to get information about Bridget.'

'God, Brianna it wasn't like that...' But she had spelt out the basic facts and strung them together in a way that made sense, yet made no sense whatsoever. He felt like a man with one foot off the edge of a precipice he hadn't even known existed. All his years of control, of always being able to manage whatever situation was thrown at him, evaporated, replaced by a confusing surge of emotions that rushed through him like a tsunami.

He pressed his thumbs against his eyes and fought off the craven urge to cry. Hell, he hadn't cried since his father had died!

'But it was,' she said gently. 'And even if I did forgive you...' *and she had* '...the ingredients for a good marriage just aren't there.'

'For you, maybe' He raised his head to stare solemnly at her. 'But for me, the ingredients are all there.'

# CHAPTER TEN

HE LOOKED AT her solemnly and then looked away, not because he couldn't hold her stare, but because he was afraid of what he might see there, a decision made, a mind closed off to what he had to say.

'When I came to search out my mother, I had already presumed to know what sort of person she was: irresponsible, a lowlife, someone without any kind of moral code... In retrospect, it was a facile assumption, but still it was the assumption I had already made.'

'Then why on earth did you bother coming?'

'Curiosity,' Leo said heavily. Rarely given to long explanations for his behaviour, he knew that he had to take his time now and, funnily enough, talking to her was easy. But then, he had talked to her, really talked to her, a lot more than he had ever talked to any other woman in his life before. That should have been a clue to the direction his heart was taking, but it had been a clue he had failed to pick up on.

Now he had a painful, desperate feeling that everything he should have said had been left too late. In his whole life, he had never taken his eye off the ball, had never missed connections. He had got where he had not simply because he was incredibly smart and incredibly proactive but because he could read situations with the same ease with which he could read people. He always knew when to strike and when to hold back.

That talent seemed to have deserted him now. He felt that if he said one wrong word she would take flight, and then where would he be?

'I had a wonderful upbringing, exemplary, but there was always something at the back of my mind, something that needed to fill in the missing blanks.'

'I can get that.'

'I always assumed that…' He inhaled deeply and then sat back with his eyes closed. This was definitely not the best spot to be having this conversation but somehow it felt right, being outside with her. She was such an incredibly outdoors person.

'That?'

'That there must be something in me that ruled my emotions. My adoptive parents were very much in love. I had the best example anyone could have had of two people who actually made the institution of marriage work for them. And yet, commitment was something I had always instinctively rejected. At the back of my mind, I wondered whether this had something to do with the fact that I was adopted; maybe being given away as a baby had left a lasting legacy of impermanence, or maybe it was just some rogue gene that had found its way into my bloodstream; some crazy connection to the woman who gave birth to me, something that couldn't be eradicated.'

Brianna let the conversation wander. She wanted to reassure him that no such rogue gene existed in anyone, that whatever reasons he might have had in the past for not committing it was entirely within his power to alter that.

Except, she didn't want him to leap to the conclusion that any altering should be done on her behalf. She was still clinging to a thread of common sense that was telling her not to drop all her defences because he seemed so vulnerable. He might be one-hundred per cent sincere in wanting her to marry him, but without the right emotions she would have to stick fast to her decision. But it was difficult when her heart wanted to reach out to him and just assure him that she would do whatever it took to smooth that agonised expression from his face.

'As you know, I've been biding my time until I made this trip to find her. I had always promised myself that hunting down my past would be something I would do when my parents were no longer around.'

'I'm surprised you could have held out so long,' Brianna murmured. 'I would have wanted to find out straight away.'

'But then that's only one big difference between us, isn't it?' He gave her a half-smile that made her toes curl and threatened to permanently dislodge that fragile thread of common sense to which she was clinging for dear life. 'And I didn't appreciate just how *good* those differences between us were.'

'Really?' Brianna asked breathlessly. The fragile thread of common sense took a serious knocking at that remark.

'Really.' Another of those smiles did all sorts of things to her nervous system. 'I think it was what drew me to you in the first place. I saw you, Brianna, and I did a double take. It never occurred to me that I would find myself entering a situation over which I had no control. Yes, I lied about who I was, but there was no intention to hurt you. I would never have done that…*would* never do that.'

'You wouldn't?'

'Never,' he said with urgent sincerity. 'I was just passing through then we slept together and I ended up staying on.'

'To find out as much as you could about Bridget.'

'To be with you.'

Hope fluttered into life and Brianna found that she was holding her breath.

'I didn't even realise that I was sinking deeper and deeper. I was so accustomed to not committing when it came to relationships that I didn't recognise the signs. I told myself that I was just having time out, that you were a novelty I was temporarily enjoying but that, yes, I'd still be moving on.'

'And then you met her.'

'I met her and all my easy black-and-white notions flew through the window. This wasn't the lowlife who had jettisoned a baby without any conscience. This was a living, breathing human being with complexities I had never banked on, who overturned all the boxes I had been prepared to stick her in. I wanted to get to know her more. At the back of my mind—no, scratch that, at the forefront of my mind—I knew that I had dug a hole for myself with that innocuous lie I had told in the very beginning—and you know something? I couldn't have chosen a more inappropriate occupation for myself. Reading fiction is not my thing, never mind writing it. I didn't like myself for what I was doing, but I squashed that guilty, sickening feeling. It wasn't easy.'

'And then Bridget had that fall and...'

'And my cover was blown. It's strange, but most women would have been delighted to have discovered that the guy they thought was broke actually was a billionaire; they would happily have overlooked the "starving writer" facade and climbed aboard the "rich businessman" bandwagon. I'm sorry I lied to you, and I'm sorry I wasn't smart enough to come clean when I had the chance. I guess I knew that, if there was one woman on the planet who would rather the struggling writer than the rich businessman, it was you...'

Brianna shrugged.

'And, God, I'm sorry that I continued to stick to my facade long after it had become redundant... I seem to be apologising a heck of a lot.' His beautiful mouth curved into a rueful, self-deprecatory smile.

'And you don't do apologies.'

'Bingo.'

'What do you mean about sticking to your facade after it had become redundant?'

'I mean you laid into me like an avenging angel when you found out the truth about my identity and what did I do? I decided that nothing was going to change; that you might be upset, and we might have had a good thing going, but it didn't change the fact that I wasn't going to get wrapped up in justifying myself. Old habits die hard.'

He sighed and said, half to himself, 'When you walked out of my life, I let you go and it was the biggest mistake I ever made but pride wouldn't allow me to change my mind.'

'Biggest mistake?' Brianna said encouragingly.

'You're enjoying this, aren't you?' He slanted a glance at her that held lingering amusement.

'Err...'

'I can't say I blame you. We should go inside.'

'We can't sit on anything, Leo. We're both filthy. I don't think the owners would like it if we destroyed their lovely furniture with our muddy clothes.'

'My car, then. I assure you that that particular owner won't mind if the seats get dirty.' He stood up, flexed his muscles and then held out his hand for her to take.

She took it and felt that powerful current pass between them, fast, strong and invisible, uniting them. He pulled her up as though she weighed nothing and together they walked towards his car, making sure that the house was firmly locked before they left and the key returned to its original hiding place.

'No one living in London would ever dare to be so trusting,' he said, still holding her hand. She hadn't pulled away and he was weak enough to read that as a good sign.

'And no one where I live would ever be suspicious.'

He wanted to tell her that that was good, that if she chose to marry him, to share her life with him, she would be living somewhere safe, a place where neighbours trusted one another. If he could have disassociated himself from his extravagantly expensive penthouse apartment, he would have.

She insisted that they put something on the seats and he obliged by fetching a rug from the trunk, one of the many things which Harry had insisted would come in handy some day but for which he had never before had any use. Then he opened the back door of the car so that he wasn't annoyed by a gear box separating them.

Brianna stepped in and said something frivolous about back seats of cars, which she instantly regretted, because didn't everyone know what the back seats of cars were used for?

'But you liked the house; you said so.' Had he mentioned that before? Was he dredging up an old, tired argument which she had already rejected? 'It's more than just the house, Brianna, and it's more than just marriage because it makes sense. It's even bigger than my past, bigger than me wanting to do right by this child because of what happened to me when I was a baby.' He rested back and sought out her hand without looking at her.

Brianna squeezed his fingers tentatively and was reassured when he returned the gesture.

'If you hadn't shown up, if you hadn't sought me out to tell me about the pregnancy, I would have eventually come for you because you were more than just a passing relationship. I may have wanted to keep you in that box, but you climbed out of it and I couldn't stuff you back in and, hell, I tried.' He laughed ruefully. 'Like I said, old habits die hard.'

'It means a lot for you to say that you would have come for me,' Brianna said huskily. They weren't looking at one another but the connection was still thrumming between their clasped fingers.

'I wouldn't have had a choice, Brianna. Because I need you, and I love you, and I can't imagine any kind of life without you in it. I think I've known that for a long time, but I just didn't admit it to myself. I've never been in love with any one before, so what were my points of comparison? Without a shred of vanity, I will admit that life's been good to me. Everything I touched turned to gold, but I finally realised that none of the gold was worth a damn when the only woman I've ever loved turned her back on me.'

Brianna had soared from ground level to cloud nine in the space of a heartbeat.

'You *love* me?'

'Which is why marriage may not make sense to you, but it makes sense to me. Which is why all the ingredients are there…for me.'

'Why didn't you say?' She twisted to face him and flung her arms around his neck, which was an awkward position, because they were sitting alongside one another. But as she adjusted her body, so did he, until they were face to face, chest to chest, body pressed tightly against body. Now she was sure that she could feel his heart beating, matching hers.

'I love you so much,' she whispered shakily. 'When you proposed, all I could think was that you were doing it because it was the sensible option, and I didn't want us to be married because it was a sensible option. If I hadn't loved you so much, Leo, maybe I would have jumped at the chance—but I knew that if you didn't love me back that road would only end up leading to heartbreak.'

His mouth found hers and they kissed urgently and passionately, holding on to one another as if their lives depended on it.

'I've never felt anything like this before...' The feel of her against him was like a minor miracle. He wanted just to keep holding her for ever. 'And I didn't have the vocabulary to tell you how I felt. The only thing I could do was hope that my actions spoke on my behalf and, when they didn't, when I thought that I was going to lose everything...'

'You came out there...' She reached up and sighed with pleasure as their mouths met yet again, this time with lingering tenderness. She smoothed her fingers over his face and then through his hair, enjoying the familiarity of the sensation.

'So...' he said gravely. Even though he was ninety-nine per cent certain of the answer she would give him, he still feared that one per cent response he might hear. This, he thought, was what love felt like. It made you open and vulnerable to another person. It turned wanting into needing and self-control into a roller-coaster ride. He could think of nowhere he would rather have been.

'Yes. Yes, yes, yes! I'll marry you.'

'When?' Leo demanded and Brianna laughed with pleasure.

'When do you think? A girl needs time to plan these things, you know...'

'Would two weeks be time enough?'

She laughed again and looked at him tenderly. 'More than enough time!'

\* \* \*

But in the end, it was six long weeks before they tied the knot in the little local church not a million miles away from her pub. The entire community turned out for the bash and, with typical Irish exuberance, the extremely happily wedded couple were not allowed to leave until for their honeymoon until the following morning.

They left a very proud Bridget behind to oversee the running of the pub because Ireland was her home in the end and she had been reluctant to leave it behind for good.

'But expect a very frequent visitor,' she had said to Brianna.

Brianna didn't doubt it. The older woman had rediscovered a joy for living ever since Leo had appeared on the scene, ever since she had rediscovered the baby, now a man, whom she had been compelled to give away at such a young age. She had spent her life existing under a dark cloud from which there had been no escape, she had confided to Brianna,. The cloud had now gone. Being asked to do the job of overseeing the pub, which had been signed over to her, was the icing on the cake.

Now, nearly two days after their wedding, Brianna sat on the veranda of their exquisite beach villa, a glass of orange juice in her hand and her baby bump a little bigger than when she had first headed down to London with a madly beating heart to break the news of her pregnancy to the man who she could hear padding out to join her.

The past few weeks had been the happiest of her life. By the time they returned to England, the house which she had loved on sight would be theirs and what lay ahead glittered like a pathway paved in precious jewels: a life with the man she adored; a man who never tired of telling her how much he loved her; a baby which would be the perfect celebration of their love. And not forgetting Bridget, a true member of their family.

'What are you thinking?'

Brianna smiled and looked up at him. The sun had already set and the sea was a dark, still mass lapping against the sand. It was warm and the sound of myriad insects was harmonious background music: the Caribbean at its most perfect.

'I'm thinking that this must be what paradise is like.'

'Sun, sand and sea but without the alcoholic cocktails?' Leo teased, swinging round so that he could sit next to her and place his hand on her swollen stomach. He marvelled that he never seemed to tire of feeling the baby move. He was awestruck that he was so besotted with her, that he hated her being out of sight, that work, which had hitherto been his driving force, had taken a back seat.

'That's exactly right.' Brianna laughed and then her eyes flared as he slipped his hand under the loose cotton dress so that now it rested directly on her stomach, dipping below the swell to cup her between her legs.

'Have I told you how sexy I find your pregnant body?' he murmured into her ear.

'You may have once or twice, or more!' She lay back, as languorous as a cat, and smiled when he gave a low grunt of pleasure.

'And now…' he kissed the lobe of her ear and felt her smile broaden '…I think there are more pressing things for us to do than watch the sea, don't you?'

He could have added that he too now knew what paradise felt like.

\* \* \* \* \*

# MILLS & BOON

## THE HEART OF ROMANCE

---

## A ROMANCE FOR EVERY READER

---

### MODERN

Prepare to be swept off your feet by sophisticated, sexy and seductive heroes, in some of the world's most glamourous and romantic locations, where power and passion collide.

### HISTORICAL

Escape with historical heroes from time gone by. Whether your passion i for wicked Regency Rakes, muscled Vikings or rugged Highlanders, awa the romance of the past.

### MEDICAL

Set your pulse racing with dedicated, delectable doctors in the high-pres sure world of medicine, where emotions run high and passion, comfort love are the best medicine.

### True Love

Celebrate true love with tender stories of heartfelt romance, from the rush of falling in love to the joy a new baby can bring, and a focus on t emotional heart of a relationship.

### Desire

Indulge in secrets and scandal, intense drama and plenty of sizzling ho action with powerful and passionate heroes who have it all: wealth, stat good looks…everything but the right woman.

### HEROES

Experience all the excitement of a gripping thriller, with an intense ro mance at its heart. Resourceful, true-to-life women and strong, fearless face danger and desire - a killer combination!

To see which titles are coming soon, please visit

**millsandboon.co.uk/nextmonth**

# LET'S TALK
## Romance

For exclusive extracts, competitions
and special offers, find us online:

- [facebook] facebook.com/millsandboon
- [twitter] @MillsandBoon
- [instagram] @MillsandBoonUK

### Get in touch on 01413 063232

For all the latest titles coming soon, visit
**millsandboon.co.uk/nextmonth**

# JOIN US ON SOCIAL MEDIA!

Stay up to date with our latest releases, author news and gossip, special offers and discounts, and all the behind-the-scenes action from Mills & Boon...

 @millsandboon

 @millsandboonuk

 facebook.com/millsandboon

 @millsandboonuk

*It might just be true love...*

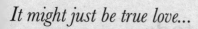

# GET YOUR ROMANCE FIX!

Get the latest romance news, exclusive author interviews, story extracts and much more!